SAVING
Tess

I0587862

J. Lynn Bailey

Visit my website at www.jlynnbaileybooks.com
Cover Designer: Hang Le, By Hang Le, www.byhangle.com
Editor and Interior Designer: Jovana Shirley,
Unforeseen Editing, www.unforeseenediting.com
Proofreader: Julie Deaton

ISBN-13: 978-1-7341395-3-2

For my great grandmother, Eledice Douglas.
Thank you for always being with me.

Prologue

August 2021
Present Day

Dear Reader,
There are some decisions that stick to your heart, lay against your conscience like rotting soil. It clings; it burrows itself into your skin, pushing you to feel every inch of its pain.

Some decisions that feel rightfully just simply aren't because of the way it sits with you for the years that come afterward.

I'd take back that night if I could. The guilt simply isn't worth the heartache of what we caused each other and others.

"Tess and Casey? Please, follow me."

I remember how our names slipped past her lips. Concern sat at the forefront of her tone while judgment sat in the back seat, waiting for the right time to announce itself—probably when Corrine went home after her day. I bet she had a hard time sleeping at night just because of what she must do in her line of work.

The pain began to sear through me like electric shock, and I remember that I dropped to my knees, both from heartache and from the physical pain that pushed against my body.

That night, I didn't make it any further. I stopped right there, in the hallway, unable to move, unable to cry, unable to right the wrong or wrong the right that was just about to happen.

I knew we'd made a decision that night that would cost us our future together and change the course of our lives forever.

In the end, when you've finished this book, I hope you'll understand, and I hope you'll continue to root for Casey and me.

All my love,
Tess

I

Tess
End of August 2020

There's one thing about Sarah Beth you must know. She never cries. Once, I saw her take a punch to the face on accident. Her nose exploded into a mess of red ooze. Her eyes stayed bruised for what seemed like months. She wore it quietly and proudly because when it was all said and done and Tommy Renner apologized profusely because the punch had been meant for Luke DeLoach, not a single tear fell.

Sarah Beth is our principal at Dillon Creek Elementary and a friend of mine.

But I suppose this story isn't about Sarah Beth or the fact that she's on the verge of tears at this very moment. It's about why I've been summoned to the superintendent's office, Eric Town—who we also grew up with, though he was more Tripp, my brother's, age.

Fear can start as a tiny pin drop that lives in one's stomach and then quickly metastasize to a gigantic ball of raging fire in just a matter of seconds. But just as quickly, fear can shrink back down to its tiny pin-drop size again because the brain has convinced the fear that this isn't a big deal.

This is where I'm at right now when I take notice of the people in Eric's office.

Yolanda, the representative from Human Resources.

Sarah Beth, my supervisor.

And Eric.

"What's this about, Eric?" I say as I keep my hands clasped tightly in my lap, trying to hide the slight tremble that's started.

I can see by the dark circles under his eyes that he's lost sleep. Holds his stress on his shoulders like boulders, a nuisance, an unwanted family member at Christmastime.

In our district meetings, which include the elementary school and the high school, we've discussed our steady decline in enrollment in the past few years.

My hands begin to sweat.

On the other hand, I think to myself, not allowing the fear to metastasize to my brain quite yet, we've also discussed the need for more teachers for more subjects at the high school.

The office grows smaller with each second that Eric doesn't speak.

This is maybe a promotion, my head says. Maybe they've decided to change the grade I teach. First grade is my favorite; however, I'd be willing to learn a different curriculum if it meant I got to be with the kids.

The fear seems to shrink only momentarily until Eric says, "Our enrollment numbers are declining. They have been for the past three years." He runs his hands through his short brown hair, and then he folds them together and places them on his desk. "Because of our declining enrollment and because you have the least seniority at the elementary school, I have to …" He pauses.

And all of a sudden, I connect the dots.

Yolanda, our Human Resources person.

Sarah Beth, my direct supervisor.

The white piece of paper sitting in front of me, which I've just now noticed.

"We have to let you go, Tess." I think Eric whispers.

Sarah Beth sucks in a long breath, and I turn to look at her for a long moment, unable to comprehend what Eric just said.

All I can do is stare at Sarah Beth's eyes and how she stares back at me. She takes my hand into hers, and now, I'm looking at our joined hands.

Eric's muffled voice sounds.

A loud hum begins in my ears.

I need to breathe, and I can't because it's caught somewhere between my lungs and my throat.

My chest grows heavy.

The hum gets louder.

Yolanda says something, touches the white piece of paper in front of me.

I ache to breathe while the office grows smaller and Yolanda, Sarah Beth, and Eric grow bigger.

Am I losing my mind?

Breathe. I need to breathe.

The hum gets louder in my ears and turns into a drumming noise—a consistent, loud, dramatic drumming.

"Excuse me," I say as I stand, trying to hold myself up.

I fumble into the hallway. I hear arguing, loud voices behind me in the office. I don't know if they're calling for me. I just need to breathe, and somehow, the school corridor has become a small cave of entrapment—dark, lonely, and stifling.

My legs seem to carry me to the outside. My lungs on fire, my body trembling, my stomach in a fit of knots, I try to collect the information I was just given, but everything is so blurry, so out of focus.

The coastal air slithers down my throat and into my lungs, and I absorb it, crave it, and swallow another mouthful, attempting to gain clarity of what just happened.

The fog is rolling in, which means it's just past three o'clock. I was working in my classroom—

And then tendrils of reality start to seep in.

The classroom. It's no longer mine.

My new students.

The new students I've been preparing for all summer. The students whose parents I've grown up with.

What am I going to do?

Purse. You need to go back inside and get your purse and your phone.

The fog moves in like waves of unwelcome houseguests, and with the fog comes the anger.

I march back into Eric's office and slam the door behind me.

"You're firing me? After three years of hard work, volunteering for every committee, helping my students after work hours, working summers to tutor my students for free, you're firing me?"

Eric sits back in his leather chair. I wonder how much that chair cost the district, and this makes me fume.

"You goddamn know as well as I do that I am the best first grade teacher you have. I love my kids!" Emotion seeps into my words. I push it down, so it won't surface again, so I don't let Eric and this situation get the best of me.

"I know," Eric whispers.

"I know why I'm the person the district needs to let go. I understand. But it also isn't fair."

"My goal is to bring you back next year, Tess. We just need to be patient."

Now that Yolanda from Human Resources is gone, I say it. "Diane needs to retire, and you know that."

Diane is the other first grade teacher, and she's been teaching since I was a student at Dillon Creek Elementary. Which is saying a long time since I'm twenty-seven.

"I know. You don't think I tried every avenue to keep you before I delivered this news to you, Tess? Come on. You know me better than that."

"This is bullshit, Eric, and you know it." I turn to leave his office for the second time, but before I do, I say, "I'll leave my lessons in my classroom, Eric, but know this—it's not for you. It's not for Diane. It's for the kids in hopes that she might use them."

"Thank you."

I storm out of the superintendent's office, leaving a trail of three years of hard work in my wake.

Before I shut off the light in my classroom for the last time, I look at the small desks and remember the tiny little bodies that fill them.

The squeals of happiness on the first day of school.

The tears.

The chatter.

The questions about why I'm a Miss and not a Mrs.

Why don't you have a husband, Miss Morgan?

You're real pretty, Miss Morgan, and nobody wants to marry you?

Who takes out your trash?

Who puts up your Christmas tree?

I shut off the light in room two and leave behind the memories.

As I walk to my car, my phone rings in my purse, and I dig it out. It's Anna. My eyes fill with tears. She knows. I'm sure the entire world knows by now that I've lost my job—because it's been eight minutes and it's Dillon Creek.

"Hey," I say in my best attempt at finding normal in my tone.

"Meet me at The Whiskey Barrel in ten minutes. I love you."

I whisper, " 'Kay," as I choke back a sob.

"And, Tess?"

"Yeah?" I reach up and wipe the tear descending down my cheek.

"This is just the beginning of your story. You're meant for more."

" 'Kay." I can't manage any more words than that, for fear I'll lose it in the school parking lot.

I hold on to Anna's words and tuck them into my heart.

Dave's tending bar. Sunday nights are slow.

I sit down at the long mahogany bar, attempting to put this afternoon behind me but I know better. I know I wear my mood like a shawl with holes the size of Texas.

Dave walks over, drying a glass, and sets it in front of me. "On the house tonight, Tess."

I bite my lower lip, willing the tears to leave my eyes before I speak, "You heard."

He turns to the bottles of hard liquor, grabs the Elijah Craig Single Barrel, and fills the small glass.

I nod in acknowledgment of the gesture.

"Hey." I hear Anna say and feel her hand slide across my back.

She kisses the side of my head.

"Pick your poison, Anna," Dave says.

"I'll have what she's having, Dave, thank you." Anna sets her purse around the back of the chair and then puts an arm around me. "It's their loss, Tess."

I nod as I put the glass to my lips and take a sip, allow the feel-good to wander into my mouth and slide down my throat. Dave sets a glass down in front of Anna.

She takes a sip. "Smooth."

Dave walks down the bar and gives us our space.

"What am I going to do, Anna?" I breathe, putting the glass to my lips again.

"You're going to show up for life. Have you ever thought that maybe you're not supposed to teach? Maybe the Big Guy has bigger and better plans for you. A detour? A lesson to be learned?"

"I thought ... I thought I had my life figured out. I-I feel like I've been punched in the gut. I feel ... lost ... numb, I guess." The elixir reaches my head; my shoulders come down, and my head feels lighter.

"Sometimes, we just have to sit with things. See how they feel against our hearts, our heads. Move through the feelings." Anna takes another sip of the bourbon. Leans into my ear. "It's really not that smooth."

She tries to stifle a cough, and I feel the corners of my mouth turn up into a smile.

"It's not that smooth," I say as I take another sip. "But it feels pretty good."

"What's Colt up to?" I try to change the subject.

"Game film via Zoom with the team."

"Ah." I set my glass down. "The famous Colt Atwood watches game film in the off-season with his team."

"It's really just an excuse to see each other during the off-season. I think Pitts, one of Colt's teammates, is in Paris right now, and a few of the other guys are on the East Coast. I think they just miss each other," she sighs and proceeds with caution. "Have you talked to Casey?"

I give her *the* look. "Is he still in town?"

"You're an awful liar."

I set my glass down. "No, I haven't."

Anna looks down at her glass. "I believe my best friend gave me some sound advice last year when she said I was just scared with Colt."

"She's a shitty best friend. You should find a new one."

What Anna doesn't know is the secret that Casey and I share. The reason we weren't there the night Tripp and Conroy were killed—because we were driving back from Oregon, trying to fix the big, gaping hole between us.

"I don't know why you both always kept things so casual when it was clear to all of us that you two felt something so much more."

I swallow the guilt that starts to reach my heart. "People grow apart."

Anna shakes her head. "No, you both grieved. You both lost brothers that day, and I think all that shit pushed you both apart."

When Anna says *brothers*, I feel the pain, the heaviness of the weighty word. I went from living most of my life as a sister to losing some of my identity when Tripp died.

Tripp and I had been closer than most siblings. And I wasn't there to help him. I wasn't there to save him. Tell him not to get in the Jeep. Tell him to stop being stupid.

But I try not to live there, so I take down the last of my drink, the last ounces of guilt closer to my toes, farther away from heart so I won't feel it so much.

"Hey, Tess. Sorry to hear about the job," Pixie Puckett says as she and her husband, Tony, leave The Whiskey Barrel.

"Thank you." I put my pride and ego aside, try my best to be gracious like Grandma Morgan would have told me to be.

I look at Anna. "Wonderful. The whole town knows, and now, everyone can acknowledge it."

"They care, Tess—that's all." Anna finishes her drink. "Come on. Let's grab a table for dinner."

It's a quarter to seven when I return home. My brother's ashes sit in my linen closet in the same plastic white box that they were sent home in from the mortuary eight years ago, existing between the hand towels and the washrags.

"Lost my job today," I say as I grab a towel to wash the day's events from my face. "But I'm sure you already know, just like the whole damn town."

I shut the door and then open it again. "You were my person, Tripp. And now, there are so many things I can't share with you." I shut the door again, only to open it. "I don't know what the hell I'm going to do."

The house phone rings.

"You make me crazy." I shut the door and walk into the kitchen. I look at the caller ID. Roll my eyes. "Hey, Mom."

"Oh, hooooney. We just heard. We're beside ourselves. Don't worry. Dad will talk to the school board."

I can tell the way she drags out the word *honey* that she's been into the wine tonight. Maybe a bottle. This isn't unusual.

I never call Mom past six in the evening, knowing full well that she'll drawl out her words, condemn the Atwoods again, blame the whole world for why her son isn't here anymore. As if she were the only person who lost someone that day. As if Dad and I hadn't lived through it. As if the Atwoods hadn't lost a son. As if our whole town hadn't died that day too.

"Mom, no. You can't fix this. It's not your job."

"Tess, are you *lisssteninnng?*"

"What, Mom?"

"Your fatherrrr and I will talk to Eric on Monday."

"No."

"Hooooney."

I push my index finger and thumb over my brow line, the aftereffects of the alcohol lingering just enough to protect my mother from the words I want to say at her.

"Mom, I need to go."

She's talking and not listening.

"Mom."

Now, she's talking to my dad, who's most likely across the room from her.

"Mom!"

She stops abruptly because she's been interrupted. "Whaaaat?"

"Just stop. I'll deal with it, okay? Just stop. Just stop trying to fix other people. Stop trying to fix me." And with that, I hang up, slamming the receiver over and over and over into its rightful spot. Then, I take it off the hook and let it fall to the floor.

My eyes burn as I slide down the wall and allow the tears to come.

Something is ringing, and it pulls me from my slumber. Sleep—the protection and preservation of the mind.

My house phone.

The phone abruptly stops ringing, and I sit up. This means only one thing.

I sigh, throw my feet over the side of my bed, take a sip of water. Hold my head in my hands for a moment.

It's my mother. She let herself in. Put my phone back on the hook. She's probably done my dishes. Cleaned my entire house because it didn't pass her white-glove test—I'm sure of it.

"Hey, honey." Her head peeks in the door to my bedroom.

"Who was that on the phone?" I stand.

"I handled it."

"Mom, who was it?"

I set the glass down and look at my cell phone to check the time. I notice several missed calls and texts. Some from Sarah Beth and Anna. When I see the last name, butterflies ignite in my stomach, and my heart picks up pace. *Casey.* I fight the butterflies and try to force them out.

"It was Sarah Beth, checking on you."

I sit back down on the bed, staring at my phone. I open the text from Casey.

Casey: Hey, Morgan. Just checking on you.

Casey used to call me Morgan when he whispered secrets in my ear as we made love, but our relationship goes much deeper than that. He sent me a pity text. Part of me wants to protect our hearts, mine and his. The history we had was pleasant for a time, but now, what's left of us are only embers and ashes.

"Tess? Are you listening to me?" my mom asks.

"What?" I look up at my mom, who's folding a dish towel.

"When's the last time you dusted?"

"I haven't had time, Mo—" And the realization of the time I have now hits me like a belt across my backside. My face drops back to my phone as I realize that I'm no longer a teacher.

"Don't worry; Dad went to talk to Eric."

My eyelid begins to twitch in anger. "Why can't you and Dad just let me be? Stop interfering in my life! I'm twenty-seven years old, Mom."

"You think I don't know that? We're just trying to do what's right for you, Tess."

"No, you're trying to protect me because you couldn't protect Tripp, and now, you and Dad meddle in my life because you're both crazy or bored—I haven't quite figured out which yet."

Mom's bottom lip stiffens, and I know what it means. It means she's countering her argument, preparing for war. She's the master of manipulation.

"Mom." I hold out my hand.

"No, no." She toys with the dishrag, pulling at the loose thread, and sets the towel on my dresser. "I'm sorry I care, Tess. I'll call your father."

"I didn't mean it."

"Yes, you did."

She's right; I did. But it came out all wrong.

Mavis Morgan is a woman of integrity and high standards with a limited amount of tears that she'll give the world. The only times I've seen her cry in my life was the day I graduated from college and the day Tripp died.

"It came out wrong."

My mom's heels click across the hardwood floor—also part of her master-manipulation process—across the kitchen and to the front door. She spins back around, only to face in my direction momentarily. "You are my only child left, Tess. I was just trying to help." My mother lets herself out.

I drop my head in defeat and roll back into bed.

My cell phone rings. I look down at the screen, and it's The Whiskey Barrel.

"Hello?" I try not to sound meek, tired, or desperate.

"Hiya, Tess. It's Dave."

"Yeah. What's up, Dave?"

"I was wondering if you could work my shift tonight. I've got to tend to something."

"Did my mother put you up to this?"

"Uh, what? No. Why would she do that?"

"Because I lost my job yesterday. Because I no longer have an income. Because she's terrified I'll fall into a deep, dark depression and never find my way out, and then she'll never have grandchildren because of it."

Dave covers the phone, and all I hear are muffled voices.

He comes back on. "No, no. I have a date actually. Headed into Eureka tonight."

"Whatever, Dave. I'll cover your shift." I could use the money.

My parents have been the long-standing owners of The Whiskey Barrel and the Dillon Creek Movie House.

It's past four in the afternoon when I pull myself from bed and into the bathroom. I shower, throw on some eye shadow and mascara, and take one final look in the mirror before I leave for my shift at The Whiskey Barrel.

You could put some lipstick on, I hear my mother's voice say in my head. *A woman always dresses for success even if it's just lunch with the ladies.*

I pull my hair back into a ponytail and throw some lip gloss on—not lipstick, in spite of my mom. I turn and open the door to the linen closet, pretending not to have an ulterior motive to blame my dead brother for the faults of our mother but I can't hold my tongue.

"It's all your fault, you know. If you hadn't died, Mom wouldn't be meddling in my business. Acting like a crazy person." I grab some deodorant and roll it on. "Thanks a lot for leaving me to pick up the pieces," I whisper, shut the door, and leave.

Becky is on days. "Hey, kid." She's putting clean glasses away when I come behind the bar and set my purse in the cubby.

"Hey. Slow today?"

"Oh, the regulars, you know, but not too slow," she drawls. She finishes with the glasses and wipes her hands down with a rag. Looks at me.

"What?"

"Nothin'. Just wondering how something so beautiful can look so tired."

I laugh and begin to cut lemons. "You mean, you haven't heard?"

Becky tosses the rag over her shoulder and leans on the counter. "Heard what?"

"Lost my job at Dillon Creek Elementary yesterday."

"What?"

"Anyhow, I need the money, so if you have some extra shifts, I'll take them."

"You're shittin' me?"

"Nope."

"Eric?"

"That's the one."

"I'll tell you what. He hasn't got the sense God gave geese, that boy," Becky says and pulls me in for a side hug. "Sorry, kid."

Becky hails from Mississippi, but she's been in Dillon Creek and worked for my parents since I was a kid. *Kid, darlin', dollface, sugar, baby* are nicknames she's given me and every other woman my age over the years.

"They won't find another teacher who is just as good or cares about those kids more than you do. Chaps my ass." Becky grabs her purse and walks around to the other side of the bar so that I'm facing her.

"Give me a double shot of Grey Goose, would you, sugar?"

I smile. "You going somewhere tonight?"

"Got me a date." She doesn't sit but throws a ten-dollar bill down on the bar.

"Yeah?"

She takes the shot. Nods. Takes a small sip of water from her water bottle.

"Local?" I ask.

"Eureka. Gonna pick me up at my place at five." Becky glances down at her watch. "Oh shit. I gotta go. Bye, baby." She blows me a kiss, and before she turns to go, she says, "I never thought I'd be tendin' bar at my age, dollface, but it's the happiest I've ever been. And that's sayin' a lot." Becky winks and leaves.

Funny. Dave has a date tonight in Eureka too.

They've been at each other's throats for years though. I highly doubt they're going on a date.

I cut lemons. Wash glasses. Pour drinks. Earn tips. Listen to patrons.

After last call, I turn the sign from *Open* to *Closed* and walk back behind the counter to clean up. It's only Toby Lemon left, and he's slumped over in the corner, passed out cold, waiting for his ride. It's a nightly thing with Toby. Part of our closing shift duties is to call Denton down at the Police Department to come pick him up, take him to the PD, and help him sober up before taking him home.

Putting away the hard alcohol, I hear the door chime, and I look up, expecting to see Denton, but instead, it's Casey.

Instantly, I freeze. He's been home for some time. Came home for Don Brockmeyer's funeral, and we sat on opposite sides of the church, like three states sat between us. I was even able to escape him during Anna and Colt's wedding.

I certainly didn't expect him to show up here. But there's nowhere to run now.

When our brothers were killed, there was an imaginary line drawn right down the middle of Dillon Creek. Residents were either with the Morgan family or with the Atwood family. I think it's all bullshit. But the last time an Atwood set foot in The Whiskey Barrel, it wasn't good.

My breathing becomes quicker, shallower, and my heartbeat accelerates.

Like all of the Atwood men, Casey is taller than most men. Dark stormy-blue eyes. Long legs with a lean body.

He removes his cowboy hat, and I catch a whiff of his scent.

"Morgan, I was worried about you." He sits down at the bar, as if I'd invited him. As if he were here to make small talk.

I try to collect my thoughts and form a sentence or string a few words together. But both the anger from that night and the residual aftereffects come to the surface of my thoughts.

"We're closed," I whisper, bending at my waist, putting the bottles of hard alcohol in a cupboard below the bar.

"Told Denton I'd get Toby tonight."

I stop. Push back a strand of hair that fell into my face. "Why?"

"Because you didn't answer my text and I heard you were working here tonight."

"You didn't ask me to respond."

Casey leans in. "I was checking on you to see if you were okay."

"I'm alive. As you can see. You can go about your business now, Casey. Thank you for your concern."

Stay the course, Tess.

I grab the last of the bottles and put them below, locking them up. I stand, and he's still here, at the bar, staring at me.

"When are we going to talk, Tess?"

I shrug and try not to breathe in his scent. "Talk about what?"

Casey cocks his head to the right. His eyes narrow. There's a long pause between us. I wipe down the counter that I've wiped down a million times already tonight.

I shrug. "Anyway, you said it yourself that night we came back from Oregon—after this, you're done. Clearly, you're not holding up your end of the bargain, Casey."

He deepens his tone when he says, "You and I both know that's not what I meant."

"Oh, it's not? Because you were gone the next day. Off to your next bull-riding event, leaving me to pick up the mess."

Toby Lemon shoots up from his slumber, yelling about a fire, making my heart explode from my chest, but his head falls to the bar again with a smack.

We both wince.

Casey's eyes meet mine. "I told you that I wanted to marry you, and you said you had other plans. What was I supposed to do? You broke my heart, Tess."

My fingers grow restless, and my eyes become pained. "You were supposed to stay, Casey."

With that, he stands and backs away from the bar, and I see the tension in his shoulders, his arms.

After one long stare, he pulls his eyes from me and says, "Come on, Toby. Let's get you home."

2

The Ladybugs

"Erla Brockmeyer is just fine, ladies." Never in the history of the world has Erla ever referred to herself in third person, and she often wonders why people do it. *Pompous*, she says to herself, *egocentric*, and now, here Erla is, referring to herself in the same manner.

Erla once read in *Redbag Magazine*, that even if you don't feel it, if you tell yourself you're okay, well then, the heart and mind will always follow suit. Erla is beginning to think that *Redbag Magazine* is all a crock of crap based loosely on wives who have nothing better to do but decorate, cook, and talk about decorating and cooking.

She's spent the last month trying to tell herself and her friends that she's all right, but deep down, her heart is broken to a million little pieces, and all she wants is the glue so that she can reconstruct the muscle. She's on the verge of tears most days, waiting for Don to wander back inside from tending to his flowers. After fifty-four years of marriage, she'd just as soon die too. That's how she feels anyway.

"I'm just fine, ladies. I wish you'd stop making such a stink over me."

Lies—or rather, misguided advice—follow her each day, like now. But instead of telling her friends what they clearly see, she bites her bottom lip, takes her napkin, and sets it in her lap.

Pearl and Delveen exchange glances.

Erla grabs the menu and attempts to read it. *When on earth did Dillon Creek Pizza change their menu?* Erla can't read a lick of it. It could be her eyesight—she should give Dr. Kennedy a call to make an appointment.

Erla feels Clyda's hand gently touch her arm. She takes the menu and turns it right side up.

"The words are too small anyway. It's really hard to see which way is up." Erla tries to convince herself that this heartbreak won't continue forever. That there has got to be a time and place when she says, *Enough is enough.* That seemed to have been last week—or so she thought.

Erla remembers when Don started to get forgetful.

It's easy to brush forgetfulness under the rug when you're old, Erla tells herself.

She tries not to think about going home to a big, empty house and how her heart will sink when she goes into the bedroom they shared and stares at his pillow, which still sits in the same spot it did the day he died.

Once she's home and in their bedroom, she will try to convince herself where he took his last breath, that she did the right thing by following Don's wishes and asking for the end to come sooner than she was ready for, sooner than his body was ready. But alas, it wasn't about her then, and it's not about her now.

She's got to order something to eat before her friends start to think she's losing her marbles. "I think I'll have the salad bar." Erla sets down her menu, stands, and attempts to walk toward the spread of vegetables.

"Erla, are you forgetting something?" Delveen calls and stands.

Erla turns, walks back, and reaches across the table for the plate. "Oh, yes. That's right. Thank you."

Delveen follows Erla to the salad bar.

The Lunch Guys are playing dice at their table. Bo Richards, Lance Belotti, Rue Samuels, and Ben Taft. Archie Tander is the hospital.

"Rumor has it," Delveen starts, "that Archie had a heart attack because he took too much Viagra."

It irritates Erla to no end—Delveen's constant gossip of others.

"Delveen, Archie Tander is almost eighty years old. Who gives a rat's behind what he takes? It doesn't change the fact that he's still in the hospital."

Delveen rolls her right shoulder, ignoring Erla's words. "I wonder why on earth he was taking it."

Erla rolls her eyes, goes to make her salad, and walks back to the table.

"It's beyond me why it takes half a day for Tony to have my car." Pearl shakes her head. "I've got errands to do."

Clyda asks, "Pearl, you live a block north of Main Street. You can't just walk?"

Pearl shrugs. "Suppose I could. But for a woman of my advanced age …" she starts.

All four Ladybugs sigh at the same time.

Pearl has been using that line a lot lately. *Woman of my advanced age.*

Pearl, Delveen, Mabe, Clyda, and Erla are all around the same age, so it offends the group as a whole when Pearl strings the entire sentence behind her without true validity.

"I swear on my dead husband's life, Pearl, you say—" Clyda pauses mid-sentence as she feels her friend's body tense up with the two words Erla's been having a hard time with.

Dead.

Husband.

"I'm sorry, Erla. I didn't mean that," Clyda says.

Erla wants to throw up and run and cry and scream, all at the same time. Most days, she wishes it had been him left on

21

God's green earth and not her to pick up the pieces of their lives together and somehow negotiate a do-over.

Instead, she smiles. Chokes down a bite of her salad with Italian dressing. Swallows.

"Oh my word! Did you all hear that Tess Morgan lost her job at Dillon Creek?" Pearl asks the group, the rumor—or truth—coming in hot off the presses.

"That's it." Erla stands and throws down her napkin. "I can't handle this anymore." She grabs her purse, throws a twenty-dollar bill down, and marches out of The Ladybugs' August meeting and right out of Dillon Creek Pizza.

In all of Erla's years of being part of The Ladybugs, she's never been so fed up as to walk out of an official meeting, although she's wanted to.

Don is gone, and all Pearl wants to talk about is how inconvenient her life is or spreading rumors about others' hardships.

I'll show you, Pearl Harvey. I quit The Ladybugs.

It's later in the afternoon when Mabe stops by Erla's house with a container of ice cream as Erla drafts her letter of resignation to The Ladybugs.

"You know they have computers for that?" Mabe asks, leaning against the counter.

"I don't know how to use one. Not going to start now."

Mabe nods. "Want to talk about it?"

"No."

It's quiet for a moment as Erla underlines the words *unprofessional manner* in the letter.

Mabe says, "I've always been told that I should sleep on a big decision before I make it."

"I won't have the gumption in the morning, Mabe—you know that."

"Then, maybe it's not a decision you need to make. Maybe it's your grieving heart telling you to stop smiling because it's okay to be sad. Isn't that what you told me when I lost John and then Francine?"

Tears start to well in Erla's eyes.

Erla has gone mad.

Crazy.

Maybe she'd die a crazy, old coot with no one left.

A brokenhearted, crazy, old lady.

Maybe she'd dye her hair purple and call herself Lucy and have a million cats.

Erla lays down the pen as her eyes start to overflow.

"Come on, old friend. I brought ice cream. Let's go sit in the living room, eat ice cream, and cry."

Erla nods as Mabe takes her hand, two spoons, and the carton of vanilla.

3

Casey

I look Tess straight in the eye.
Is that what she remembers? That I just walked away?

She'd been emotionally unavailable for weeks before that. Sure, I knew her heart was breaking. But mine was too. She forgets there were two of us who lost more than our hearts that night.

Two of us who traveled the long road home from Oregon that night, in silence, waiting for a sign to convince us we'd made the right decision.

But nothing came of any of it, except broken hearts.

I had been at the beginning of my career with the Professional Bull Riders at that time. Eighteen and stupid as hell. Sometimes, I made decisions based on my ego. Truth was, if she'd asked me to stay, I would have. I'd still have ridden bulls, lived in and out of airports, my truck, done interviews like the PBR asked me to. I would have stayed. But she wasn't ready. Tell you the truth, maybe I wasn't either.

I take Toby by the arm and pull him up so that I'm using my body weight to carry his.

Before I get him in the truck, I look back in The Whiskey Barrel, and Tess is holding her head in her hands, just like she did the night in my truck when we pulled up to her house. I knew she did the same thing every time I got on a bull.

Bull riding is my blood. After my first big win and when I finally saw I could make a living on the PBR circuit, I knew I wasn't supposed to do anything else. Sure, in the beginning, I did side jobs in the off-season to make ends meet, but I made a promise to myself that I'd make damn sure it wasn't for too long.

I knew it broke Tess a little more every time I got on a bull. At that time, at thirteen, we were friends. Good friends. But I think deep down, she had feelings for me, just like I did for her. I'd be lying if I said I didn't see the fear in her eyes every time I walked away for a mere eight seconds. After, I'd thank God I hadn't died, and at the same time, it allowed my ego just eight more seconds. One step closer to becoming a world champion.

When Conroy died, it was easier to leave, and when Tess asked me to stay, I didn't—maybe a real man would have. I did exactly what she'd asked. The loss of our brothers was hard. But even harder was what we'd just walked through twelve hours earlier.

All this town is to me is one big tragedy after another.

We had no idea what we were coming home to until the next morning when the air seemed somehow thinner and sad, and my reasons to breathe became minimal.

I drop Toby off at Dillon Creek PD, so he can sleep it off. Denton is there to help me get Toby inside.

"Wish he'd get sober," Denton says after he shuts the jail cell.

"He won't. Not when we do things to take care of him. It's too easy to stay drunk and not have to face your life."

He nods. "Take care of yourself, Atwood. That last ride in Texas blew me away."

Denton is referring to my ride on Traitor.

"Thanks, man."

He smiles, leans against the cell for a minute. "Sure you get all the buckle bunnies everywhere, huh?"

I'd be lying if I said I didn't from time to time. Sometimes, they made it easier to forget a shitty ride. Made me forget about my broken bones, my pains, my ailments. Made me forget about the loss of a brother or the poor decisions I'd made.

But instead of telling him what I think he knows to be true, I say, "Not worth it."

Denton laughs. "Well, if they're looking for a badge, send one my way, would ya?"

"Roger that." But I won't.

They're just in search for the next million bucks, the biggest belt buckle. Denton deserves a better gal.

I suppose the cowboys who invest the time in them might be trying to fix their souls and have a piece of ass at the same time.

Rounding my truck, I start to think about what I have left in life. I'm a twenty-seven-year-old bull rider who's made a living putting my life on the line. I know I can't stay on top forever, but I've had some real good rides this year. I'm still making a good living. I was world champion twice. Partly endorsements for boots, belts, jeans, and hats. But nobody's going to want a washed-up cowboy in their ads ten years from now. Nobody's going to want to see a cowboy try to fight for a way to come back even though his body says no.

We ride bulls with broken arms.

Broken jaws.

Broken ankles.

Broken legs.

Torn ligaments.

Torn tendons.

Dislocated shoulders.

That's just a small list of my injuries.

It's just a matter of time before my card is pulled, when I'm hit with another major injury. Doctors put us back together just so we can go back to the arena and do it all over again.

Not Billy Thornton though. Billy was at the top of his game from eighteen to twenty-seven until he took a hit so hard that he had no choice but to retire. Brain injuries aren't fixable or flexible.

There went the endorsement deals.

His bull-riding career.

His money.

His wife.

He lost it all.

Saw him in an IcyHot commercial not too long ago. I guess there are some companies that are willing to put you in front of their ads, even when you've lost the only thing the world agreed you were good at.

Is that what my life will amount to once everything else is gone?

An IcyHot commercial, a broken body, and a whole lot of belt buckles in a big, empty house full of memories?

I'll be at my parents' place until the next event. It's familiar. It's the life I know. I've never lived in Dillon Creek and not lived at home.

I run a hand over my face.

Tess used to run her hand over my face when she didn't want me to see her laugh. She said it was because she didn't like her smile, and when she laughed, it only got bigger. The left side of her face didn't smile. In fact, it stayed the same. Never changing. But the other side of her smile and her eyes overcompensated for all of it. Like I could always see who she truly was when she smiled.

Her smile was one thing I loved most about her, and I haven't seen it in years. I know why. A lot of little things, two big things, and an unforgivable world can wear on a heart. Especially one like Tess's. I think about how she just lost her job and she's not willing to talk about.

Suppose I'd feel the same way if the PBR fired me. But I also suppose I make them too much money for them to kick me out. You'd have to do or say something really shitty for them to ask a cowboy to leave and not come back.

I pull into my parents' driveway and park my truck. My phone chimes as I make my way inside. A mild pain spreads to my chest, and I'm not sure if it's from my past heartache or if it's just what she does to me, but the text is from Tess.

Tess: Sometimes, it's easier to blame the scapegoat.

I smile and start to type.

Me: I get it.

I delete it.

Me: Makes sense.

I delete it.

Sometimes, words just don't fill a moment the way you'd like them to. I guess it's true—sometimes, silence is the only answer. So, instead of doing what I want to do, which is make her feel better, I slip my phone back in my pocket.

Dad is sitting at the table by the window, watching *M*A*S*H*.

"Where'd you run off to?" he asks as I get a glass of water.

Every so often, I get the inclination to lie to my dad. Not because of what he'll think of me, but because sometimes, I think it's easier for him. Truth is, I don't want to tell him I was at The Whiskey Barrel because that would make him think of the Morgans, which would make him think of Tripp, which would make him think of Conroy and the day he lost one of his sons. Nobody should outlive a child. I don't want him to think about Conroy. I'm afraid he won't be able to fall asleep tonight because this is what he does. He doesn't sleep but maybe four hours a night. It makes my mom worry, especially if he's got a long day ahead of him on the ranch.

"Ran to Eureka to get a few things."

Dad glances at the clock. "Little late for that?"

29

"Shouldn't you be sleeping, Dad?"

He gives a half-smile. The other half he saves for Conroy. "Yeah, I should."

Dad turns off the small television at the table, stands, touches my shoulder, and kisses the top of my head. "Night, son."

"Night."

Dad was never affectionate before Conroy. He was tough on us boys. After all, he had to make cowboys of us all. Dad always told me as long as my legs weren't broken, I'd better be able to walk out of the arena.

Calder comes through the door.

"It's late, cowboy," I kid.

"What do you care?" Calder grabs a couple of beers and hands me one.

I open it. "I don't."

"Where's the next ride?"

"Idaho." I take a long swig of my beer.

Calder is almost finished with his, and he peels at the label. "When you leavin'?"

I smirk. "Are you trying to get rid of me?"

"Nah. But you've been home for a month. I'm wondering what's keeping you here. Couldn't be a certain teacher, could it?"

"No. There hasn't been an event."

"Never kept you home before."

"Stuff then."

"Stuff. Like what?"

I think twice before I answer Calder. Of all my brothers, he and I are most alike. We're slow to speak up; I guess it's because we sometimes overthink things. But maybe I'm stalling because I really don't know what the hell I'm feeling.

"You … you ever feel like life is passing you by? Like, people we went to high school are having kids and getting married and finding their careers and shit." I take another swig of my beer as Calder grabs another one. "The bull riding won't sustain me forever," I say.

Calder sits down and stares at the red-checkered tablecloth. "You thinking about retiring?"

No. "A cowboy never quits. Besides, I don't think I could. I love it too much."

"What will be the straw that breaks the camel's back? Another major injury? Haven't you won enough money? Collected enough belt buckles?"

Calder's questions hit me square in the eyes.

"It's not about the money or the belt buckles. It's just about being better than you were the year before. Maybe the adrenaline."

"Ego."

Leave it to my brother to call me out.

I smile. "Yeah, that too."

"What about Tess?"

I cock my head. "What about Tess?"

He rolls his eyes. "Come on, man. I think that's why you've stayed here this time. I think you've realized that she's it. She's the one."

I shake my head. "You're wrong."

"Am I? Saw you leaving The Whiskey Barrel with Toby Lemon awfully late tonight."

"Can't I help out a friend?"

"Who's that? Tess or Denton?"

I let out a long mouthful of air. Rub my face with my hand. "I don't know, man."

"Bullshit. You're just scared to say it out loud."

His words get under my skin.

"And how's it going with Camilla? Made a move yet?"

Calder holds my stare. "That's different."

"Oh, yeah? How? Come on. You've had the hots for her since she moved here to marry Joe Crane—rest his soul."

"It's different because I don't think she's ready for me."

"How do you know that? You barely say hi to her in public. You barely—"

"I fix her fence. I take care of the shit around there when she needs my help. I'm there when she needs me." He takes another swig of his beer.

"Oh, so you're her handyman?"

"Yeah."

We both start to laugh.

When our laughter dies down, Calder says, "All I'm saying is, if it's Tess, you'd better hang on. I'm not sure our families can live through all that shit again if there's no happy ending this time."

I know.

Calder, Colt, Dad, and I are moving cattle on horseback this morning when something spooks the cattle in the tall grass, and they divide. The dogs move them up the pasture and gather them again.

"What is it?" Dad calls to Colt, who jumps off his horse to take a look.

"It's a baby fox." Colt kneels down next to it.

I jump off my horse and walk over to Colt. "He's a little bastard." I look around for its mom.

Calder and Dad keep an eye out on the cattle and an eye for Mom. They can be mean as hell when you stand between them and their babies.

Foxes are bad for the cattle business.

"We can relocate him to the Barbett Ranch," Calder says, and we laugh.

Barbetts have a big cattle ranch that butts up to ours. Dad and Rudy Barbett have gone rounds for years over a slice of land that sits just beyond the joined property line. They both want to buy it. But some guy from Seattle owns it, and he's not willing to sell.

Barbett has accused Dad of some shady shit, but Dad's not that way. And Barbett is also crazier than a rabid raccoon.

"Dad, hand me the gun," Colt says. "We've got to take care of this problem."

Dad always packs a pistol in his saddle sack. Usually though, it isn't for tiny animals; it's to protect the cattle and ourselves from bigger problems like bears, mountain lions, and other larger predators.

Colt loads the gun. Stares down the barrel. Clicks off the safety.

Five seconds go by.

Ten seconds go by.

"Twinkle toes, what the hell are you waiting for?" Calder calls out.

Another five seconds go by.

Colt drops the gun. "I can't do it."

Colt hands the gun to me, and I take aim, putting the little bastard in my sights. My finger toys with the trigger, and my hand begins to shake. Curled up in a tiny ball, as if trying to protect itself by making itself the smallest it can from predators—or four guys on horses. It picks up its small head and tries to cry out.

My heart sinks, and I slowly lower the gun. "I can't ... I can't shoot it either."

Calder rolls his eyes and jumps off his horse, muttering something about pussies under his breath.

Calder takes the gun from me. Takes aim at the baby fox.

Five seconds go by.

Ten seconds go by.

"You can't do it either," I say.

"Shut up." As the fox struggles to get up on all fours, Calder lowers the gun.

"You've gone soft, boys." Dad dismounts his horse. Takes the gun from Calder, walks it back to his saddle sack, unloads it. "Leave it. It'll die from natural causes out here."

But Colt is already on the phone with Anna. "Yeah, okay." He walks to his saddlebag, grabs his gloves, puts them on, and walks back over to the fox, who is too little to fight Colt's grip when he picks it up. He shoves it in his jacket. "If it survives the day, I'll take it to Anna."

Dad sighs. "You new-age cowboys are something else."

He smiles, and we start to move the herd to the lower pasture and spread out. Dad's point rider. Calder is the swing rider. Colt is flank rider, and I'm drag.

Borges Atwood, Dad's dad, was tough. Old school when it came to the ranch life. Dad's old school, too, but he's got a soft spot for animals. Always has. Because Dad didn't shoot the baby fox either.

We finish out the ride, and cleaning up the horses. Sure as shit, the fox is still alive, so I jump in with Colt to take the little guy to town to Anna's clinic.

Tess's car is parked outside the clinic when we get there, but there's a commotion on Main Street in front of the *Dillon Creek Echo*, the town newspaper. Michael—Ike, the publisher's, son—along with Delveen and Pearl are standing outside.

"What's going on?" I say to my brother as we get out of the truck and watch.

Colt grabs the box with the fox. "Who the hell knows?"

He goes inside, and I follow with a pounding heart. Part of me needs to see Tess, see how she's doing, and part of me doesn't.

Kimber is at the front desk. "Did you guys hear?"

"No. What's going on?" Colt asks.

"Ike Isner died last night. Found him at the *Echo* office, dead as a doornail."

"No shit?" Colt says.

Anna and Tess walk out from her office. Tess looks as though she's been crying as she walks past. I want to reach out and touch her, ask if she's okay, but I don't. Instead, I take in her scent and catch her eye.

I follow her out because I can't help it.

"Hey." I touch her arm. "Are you all right?"

And she stops. Sighs. Allows my hand to stay where it is, which is at her elbow. "Fine, Casey."

"No, you're not. You're lying through your teeth."

But sadness hits me the second I realize today's date. A cowboy is a freak of nature. We can hold in a lot of pain. We never complain because that's not the way Dad raised us. We allow the pain to stew and stay inside us for a long time, fester and spread like a cancer to the most vulnerable spots in our bodies, like the heart. But we have a gift, a special talent. The heart is also a muscle, and if used correctly, it can lock up a whole lot of shit.

"September 1." My words are barely audible.

Tess turns to me, buries her eyes into mine, searches for answers that might make her heart unfeel what's going through her head right now. Answers that I don't have because I haven't been able to find my own. Her bottom lip quivers, but she doesn't say anything.

I want to tell Tess this is exactly what I was scared of—her heart breaking into a million pieces, full of regret, and longing, and what-ifs.

I give her the only answer I have. The one I want to believe. The one I think about every single day. "He's fine, Tess."

She nods and bites her bottom lip and stares at me, as if willing herself to believe what I said is truth.

Sometimes, people make decisions for the moment. Sometimes, they make decisions where the outcome will be okay for just now.

"Do you have regrets?" she asks.

I squeeze her elbow, hoping she won't feel my heart shatter when I nod.

Tess's eyes fill with tears again. Slowly, she steps away, and my hand unwillingly lets go of her elbow.

What I didn't say eight years ago are words I wish I had said. I gave her the answers I thought she wanted to hear, and I've held that in for a long time. Managed to bury it deep. Like a dark, hidden secret that nobody knows, you carry it around with you like a cross you bear. Shame. Your conscience gnaws at your soul while you sleep and while you're awake.

I watch her make her way to her car. I want to make this better, but I know I can't. I can only imagine what the Morgans would think of me after they found out what we did that night. They hate our family now—just wait until this secret is out of the bag.

Waiting outside the truck, I open up the text message that Tess sent me.

Tess: Sometimes, it's easier to blame the scapegoat.

I respond.

Me: I'll be the scapegoat for as long as you need.

I hit Send.

Colt comes outside with an empty box.

"What happened?" I ask as I shove my phone in my front pocket.

"Anna's going to keep the fox for observation and then call the wildlife refuge from up north."

We hop in the truck and head back to the ranch.

"Did Tess say anything? She okay?" Colt asks as he stares out the windshield.

"Yeah, she's fine," I lie because nobody knows what happened that night, and I'm not sure Tess wants anyone to know.

4

Tess

"Hey, Tess. It's Twila. Per Ike Isner's estate, there's a certified letter that I need to give you. I can drop by today if that works for your schedule."

Ike? Why?

"Why would Ike have written a letter to me?"

"We can discuss this when I drop off the letter."

"I can come by the office if that's easier for you." Turns out, I don't have a lot going these days. I wallow in self-pity only momentarily.

"That will be great. When's a good time for you?"

"Now?"

"Sure, now works."

Turning the car around, I drive back to Main Street and park in front of her office. The bell jingles as I walk in.

"Hey, Tess," Twila says in her twill pencil skirt from the door of her office.

Twila has a job. One that pays well. She has a purpose in her life.

Get over it already, Tess, I tell myself.

"Come on in." She motions me to her office and sits behind her big, lawyerly mahogany desk as I grow smaller by the second, my ego being stepped on by her cute red heels.

From across the desk, she hands me a manila envelope, and in black cursive, it says, *Tess Morgan.*

I'm hesitant to reach for the letter. Once I touch it, it's mine, and whatever is in that letter, I'll have knowledge of, and I'll never be able to play ignorance or unsee what I've read.

"I'm sorry, Twila. I'm sure you understand my confusion. I mean, I knew Ike. Great man. But why would he have written me a letter?" Reluctantly, I take the manila envelope.

Something bulky is in with the letter too.

What about Michael? I want to ask about Ike's son. *Shouldn't he know something about this letter, be here, just in case, as I'm sure he's the executor of Ike's will?*

"Call me once you've opened the letter, and we'll make arrangements."

"Arrangements?"

Twila laughs. "Take a breath, Tess. While I don't know what exactly he wrote in the letter, I am well aware of his assets. What's in the envelope isn't bad. Okay?"

Anna and I sit at the table. Colt is at the counter.

The manila envelope rests in the middle of their dining room table.

Bones and Tupac are sprawled out on the kitchen floor, unaware of the tabby cat sitting outside the kitchen window, staring down at them.

Bones and Tupac were a big help when Gypsy, my dog, passed away. Just being in their presence gave my heart solace.

"It can't be bad, right?" Anna asks. "I mean, it could be. But it's probably not."

"I'm not sure what could go more wrong right now, honestly."

My supportive friend gives me a nudge. "You'll get back up, Tess. You always do."

"Maybe it's the key to his Shelby Mustang he has in his garage," Colt says.

"Why would he give her his Shelby? Why not give that to his son?" Anna looks back at Colt.

Colt nods, crossing his arms. "Good point."

I hold the manila envelope up to the natural light of the room for another inspection. "I should just open it." I look to Anna and Colt for reassurance.

"Open it." Anna puts her hand on mine. "Whatever it is, it will be fine."

I take in a deep breath, push my hair behind my ears, and begin to tear at the opening. I pull out a single piece of white paper with cursive writing in black ink and a set of keys. I put them on the table and begin reading the letter.

Dear Tess,

I was raised in a community where forgiveness is the cornerstone to happiness.

Here are the keys to our place in Ketchikan, Alaska. Twila will give you the details once you've accepted the house.

It's yours.

It might need some fixing up, but if you can do the work and sell it, then the money is yours.

Sometimes, you've got to find the healing in order to mend the bridges.

Best,

Ike

I look up from the letter as shock registers on my face.

Colt drops his head. "You're killing us, Tess. What does the letter say?"

I can't speak because I'm not sure what to say.

Handing the letter to Anna to read, I take the keys in my hand and ask, "Why?"

Anna reads the letter aloud.

I listen to the words just so I can be sure I read it correctly. That's what I used to tell my students. Read it once quietly to yourself and then read it out aloud.

Anna finishes, and her eyes move from me to Colt and back to me. "Looks like you're going to Ketchikan." She hands the letter back to me.

I laugh but when I realize she's serious, I say, "Anna, I can't go to Ketchikan. I have a life here."

Her hand falls on top of mine. "Look, I'm going to be brutally honest here, and I'm doing this purely out of love." She's still for a moment. "You lost your job. You've left Dillon Creek for small snippets of life, but, Tess, this … this is the perfect time to go."

With an impatient huff, I read the letter again. *Fixing up? What does that even mean?*

"I can't do this. I mean, winter. Winter is coming." I drop the letter. "Winter in Alaska? Are you out of your mind?" Uncertainty sits in my stomach.

Anna tightens her grip on my hand. "Have faith."

I laugh. Really, it starts out as a giggle and then turns into a full-blown belly laugh.

Colt and Anna smile but only because I'm laughing hysterically out of fear.

I stop abruptly. "So, I'm supposed to go to Alaska. Fix a place up. And sell it."

Anna looks at the letter once more. Meets my gaze again. "Yeah, that's what the letter says." She doesn't mention the part in the letter that says *once I accept the house.*

Shaking my head, I pick up the letter again. "I can't do this. This isn't a good time."

"Why?" Colt asks.

I turn back to Colt. "Now, you too? Remind me to start cheering for a different NBA team."

Colt chuckles.

"I can't just up and leave my responsibilities in Dillon Creek."

Anna and Colt exchange glances.

"What responsibilities?" Anna asks.

"My house."

"We will make sure it's taken care of," Colt says.

"Traitor. What about my job at the bar?"

This time, Anna laughs. "You're filling in, Tess. I'm sure The Whiskey Barrel can manage without you. They have for years."

I bite the inside of my cheek. "But why did Ike pick me?"

"Stop asking why but rather ask yourself, *Why not me?* You know, most people would have flipped the hell out. Have you seen Ketchikan, Alaska, T?" Colt asks as he types on his phone. "See?" He shows me a picture.

"They're going to show you all the pretty parts of the place online, Colt. They won't show you the ugly parts." My tone is sharp. "I just can't. I'm going to go to Twila and decline the offer."

"Sleep on it, would you? Sleep on it first and decide tomorrow," Anna pleads.

Pulling the covers over my head, I allow my mind to drift to the proposition that I've been offered.

What about bears?

What about the winter?

What about it being dark all winter long?

But what about the northern lights?

What about someplace different for once?

What about a break from Mom and Dad?
What about leaving Tripp's memory here?
What about me?

I grab my phone from the nightstand and Google *Ketchikan, Alaska.* I hit the button called images.

It's right on the water.

That's pretty, but there are places like this all over, where winter isn't so bad.

Rich, native culture.

Definitely a plus.

I watch a video of humpback whales migrating through Ketchikan.

I don't see that every day.

Average snowfall is ninety inches a year.

Oh, that's not as bad as I thought it was going to be.

Rain to locals in Ketchikan is known as liquid sunshine.

That's cute. Dillon Creek averages about one hundred inches of rain per year.

I scroll through pictures of Ketchikan, watching an occasional video or two, read a few travel blogs, follow destinations on Instagram, and like Facebook pages based in Ketchikan. A small fishing resort called Salmon Falls looks like it has great burgers. I make a mental note—I mean, just in case.

It's one o'clock in the morning before I put my phone on my nightstand and push the covers from my body because all of a sudden, I'm on fire with anxiousness.

What do I have going in Dillon Creek? I quietly ask myself in the stillness of night.

The clock in the living room ticks the seconds away.

What if this is a good move?
If I don't like it, it's only temporary after all.
It would give me some extra money if I can sell the place.
I don't know the first thing about fixing up a house or selling a house.
But I could learn.
What if this is all about the process?
What if I am supposed to go to Ketchikan?

I'm on my way uptown to Twila's office this morning to give her back the keys and turn down Ike's proposal. I don't know what I was thinking, trying to convince myself that moving to Ketchikan—even if temporarily—might be a good idea. I can't just uproot my life from Dillon Creek. I'll apply for teaching jobs in Eureka, Fortuna, or Hydesville. I'll get my feet back under me.

It's far more realistic than moving to Alaska. I laugh at myself for even considering the thought.

"Come on in, Tess," Twila says.

I follow her into her office, sit down on the chair in front of her desk, and push the envelope toward her. "I can't accept Ike's offer."

"I was afraid of this."

"I'm sorry?"

Twila sighs. "Leigh, bring in the contract," she calls.

Leigh comes in with a small stack of papers and hands them to Twila. "Hey, Tess."

"Hey, Leigh."

"In Ike's will, he stated to sell the property to the highest bidder if you and the other party did not accept his gift."

"Other party? Who's the other party?"

"I'm sorry. I cannot disclose that information to you."

Questions begin to spin in my mind. "Did the other party decline as well?"

"That I cannot disclose either," she sighs. "Are ... are you sure you'd like to decline the offer, Tess?"

"Do you have a bidder yet?"

Twila shrugs. "We have feelers out."

"Who?"

"I can't say."

"Are you guys allowed to talk about anything?"

"Not really."

Twila leans forward and is methodical with her words. "Let's just say, if it goes to who we think it will, they'll most likely tear down the house and build condominiums."

"Oh."

This is for the best, I try to convince myself.

I don't know the first thing about Alaska. I don't know the first thing about fixing up a house. *I mean, will the changes be cosmetic? Do we have to tear down and rebuild? It's September, for God's sake.* We're going into fall and then winter. And with all the rain Ketchikan gets, there's no way we can do this before winter. *And what money do I have to do all this work if it's needed? I can't blow my life savings. This is an awful idea.*

But is it worth the look?

No.

Is it worth the time?

Probably not.

It's not my problem if it goes to a corporation. I don't owe the people of Ketchikan anything. I haven't met a single soul in my life who has lived there but Ike.

Twila takes the envelope from her desk and puts it in a drawer. "I'm really sorry things didn't work out, Tess." She prints out another piece of paper and slides it across the desk. "I just need you to sign this, declining the gift, so we can move forward."

I stare down at the piece of paper in front of me.

Twila's phone starts to ring. "Can you hold on?"

"Sure."

Twila starts to talk to the person on the other end of the line.

What do you have to lose, Tess? You can always come home if it doesn't work out.

But what if it doesn't work out? I'll have failed.

My heart starts to slam against my chest. If I sign this piece of paper, there's no going back. Things will be final.

Will I spend my life in regret? Wondering what could have happened with the house in Ketchikan? Is Ike trying to tell me something? And if he is, I'll never know because I'm too stuck in fear to take the leap of faith.

It's safer, Tess. It's the safer decision to stay home and go about your life.

"I want the house," slips through my lips before I have the next thought.

"Can you hold on just a moment, Rick?" Twila covers the phone. "What did you say?"

"I want the house." A pit of fear starts in my stomach.

A grin spreads across Twila's face. "I'm sorry, Rick. There's been a change in plans."

Twila hangs up the phone, her eyes full of excitement. "Let's get the paperwork started."

"I won't even have a car there, Anna," I say into my phone. "Oh my goodness, I need a paper bag to breathe into." I pace outside Twila's office. It would have been easier to decline all this. "Shit."

Anna's voice is calm. "You did the right thing, Tess. Leave Dillon Creek even if it's just for a bit. Clear your head. I see this as an opportunity of a lifetime. I mean, think about it. What person is gifted a house in one of the most beautiful places in the world?"

Anna's words make me start to feel a little excited inside. She could be right.

"When are you leaving?"

"I ... I don't know. I suppose sooner than later. Winter is coming."

"I'm so jealous."

I fidget with a hangnail. "I guess I should book a plane ticket."

"Why don't you take the jet?" Anna says. "It's at Rohnerville Airport."

"No, I couldn't ask that of you guys. I'll fly commercial."

Anna sighs into the phone. "Would you stop? Besides, Colt and I feel semi-responsible for helping you with this decision."

"And if it all goes south, I'm blaming you two!"

We both laugh, and then the line grows silent.

I whisper, "Anna, am I making the right choice?"

"Without a doubt, Tess."

I nod into the phone and look down Main Street, my home for the past twenty-seven years.

But maybe Anna's right. Maybe I need something different, and maybe, just maybe, this is my opportunity.

5

Casey

"Heard Tess left for Ketchikan, Alaska, this morning," Colt says as we eat at The Rusty Nail.

"I heard." Ice runs through my veins, and my jaw tightens.

Was it that easy for her to just leave? Pick up her life here in Dillon Creek and leave?

I try to act like I don't care. Take another bite of my eggs. It was Calder who told me last night.

I can't chase her. If she wants to leave, that's her choice.

Colt laughs. "Why are you still here, man?"

I put my fork down because I haven't had an appetite since last night. Take a drink of my coffee. Stare down my brother. "Why would I chase her? It's not my fucking business what she does."

Colt wipes his mouth, finishes chewing, takes a long drink of water, and says, "Do whatever the hell you want, Case. But if you're not happy in five years because Tess has gone off and married some dude and has two little rug rats and a great fucking life, remember this conversation."

Twila stops by our table. "Hello, Casey, Colt." She looks to me. "Casey, could you stop by my office later? I have something for you."

"Am I being summoned?" I say, only half-kidding, and wipe my mouth with my napkin.

Twila laughs. "No, nothing like that. I'll see you this afternoon?"

"Yeah. All right."

Delveen walks up to our table next. "Colt, a minute of your time?"

"Yes, Mrs. Constance. What can I do for you?"

"Well, The Ladybugs are having their annual Christmas auction, and we were wondering if you'd be so kind as to donate a signed jersey from the MBA?"

Colt smiles. "The NBA?"

"Oh, did I get it wrong again? Your grandmother has to correct me all the time. In fact, she was supposed to ask you, but, well, I saw you and Casey here and thought I'd take my chances."

"Of course, Mrs. Constance. I'll give the jersey to my grandmother."

"That'd be great, Colt. Bless your heart. Thank you." Delveen touches his shoulder as she makes her way to the door.

Colt looks down at his watch. "I gotta run. Anna and I are meeting at home in ten minutes."

We stand and throw some cash down.

Merry approaches the table. "How was it, boys?"

"Excellent. Thanks, Merry," Colt says.

Merry looks down at my plate. "Did you not like your omelet, Casey? I can get you a new one or a box."

"No. It was great, as usual. I just … don't have an appetite."

Colt leans toward Merry. "He's lovesick."

Merry nods. "We heard." She reaches up and touches my shoulder. "Tess left for Ketchikan."

I roll my eyes. "I'm not lovesick." I eye my brother across the table. Smile at Merry. "Thanks again, and a box would be great."

"I told him he needs to follow her, Merry."

"True love only comes around once in a lifetime, Casey Atwood. I mean, just think if you missed your opportunity and she marries a guy from Alaska and has two kids—or worse, what if she brings her family back here and you have to see them every day? All because your ego wouldn't let you fall for love." Merry shakes her head. "A damn shame, for sure. And besides, maybe you two are the missing link, just what the town needs to reunify ..." She pauses, knowing what she's digging herself into. "Anyway, Lord knows our town needs some healing."

I stare down my brother, smirk, shake my head.

"Anyway, I'll go get you a box, Casey," Merry says.

As we leave, I ask Colt what he and Anna are doing.

"Making a baby."

"No shit?"

"No shit. Yeah, she's got about a half hour between patients today." Colt is about to head across the street to the clinic.

I pause. "You're going to do it ... in there?"

"No, dumbass. We're going home together real quick."

"Real quick, my ass."

"Don't forget Twila's office."

I give a nod. My phone chimes with a text message. It's from Garrison, another bull rider and friend.

Garrison: You driving or flying to Idaho?

Adrenaline sets fire to my bones.

Maybe the drive will help me clear my head. Help me figure all this shit out.

Me: Drive.

Garrison: Meet you there.

If I leave now, I can get there by late tonight.

Instead of going to Twila's office, I go home instead, pack my bag, and leave for Idaho.

I ease onto Chiseled, who's fifteen hundred pounds of muscle. He's angry, and I can feel it with every jerk in the chute. He twists against the gate.

My heart slams against my chest as I push my right hand underneath the rope—the only thing that keeps this beast from tossing me into the air with one single jump. He's a ranked bull in the PBR right now. Fucking lucky as hell I got him in the draw. Some bull riders might not see it that way. If I can ride this guy for eight seconds, I have a chance at taking the purse, and that would push me closer to the World Finals.

Adrenaline shoots through my body like nails.

There's a moment between life and death. I ask myself a question every damn time I get on a bull, hoping like hell it won't be my last ride. The question is, *Would you do it all differently, Casey?*

And every time my answer is, *No.*

I'm familiar with a bull. I'm comfortable. It's what I know, and it's what I've known most of my life. Hell, even before I was allowed to ride bulls, I was riding bulls. I can't imagine doing anything else. This all comes to me the second my hand is secure.

Maybe I should want something else. Something stabler. Non-life-threatening. Less dangerous and easier on the body. But bull riding is like a cheap drug that goes straight to your veins, gets in your head, and never lets go.

I've grown addicted to the adrenaline rush.

I've grown addicted to the nerves.

I've grown addicted to my own ego, I suppose.

And I've grown addicted to the need to be a world champion just one more time.

I want the hard bulls.

I want each and every one of them.

The clock will start ticking the minute the bull breaks the plain—hell, maybe that's true in life too.

The clock's ticking, and I'm just begging for another day.

"You ready, cowboy?" Randy, the gate guy, yells.

I nod the single nod that puts my life on the line every time. I know by doing that, I'm just living on a chance.

The chute opens, and the entire arena goes silent and moves in slow motion.

Spin.

Buck

Twist.

Spin.

Spin.

Twist.

Jerk.

Spin.

Jerk.

My eyes are focused on the rope and my hand under it. Bulls are a hell of a lot smarter than we think they are. If I stay ahead of the bull, then he doesn't get power over me. It's like a dancing partner—they move, and you follow. Jump for jump.

Eight seconds seems a lot longer than it actually is when I'm on a beast that wants to kill me.

The machine of an animal and its massiveness can't be described; it can only be felt, as I'm doing as its muscles contract underneath me. When the buzzer sounds, I pray I land on my feet because only on a good day can I reach the fence faster than the bull can.

I land on my feet and run for the fence but not without listening to the crowd explode.

I'd do this without a crowd. But it sure feels good to hear them scream.

The announcer says, "Well, I'll be doggone! What a ride from Casey Atwood, ladies and gentlemen! What. A. Ride! Let's wait for the judges' scores."

Breathing hard, my ass safe up on the fence, the crowd still screaming, and with the bull safely behind a fence, I jump down. My heart pounding with excitement, I throw my hat in the air. Eight seconds isn't an accomplishment; it's a necessity. But riding Chiseled for eight seconds and having a great score are like winning the conference league in sports; it's not quite the Super Bowl, but I know I matched him jump for jump. We danced in the arena as if we were old lovers. While it clung to freedom, I clung to my guts.

Garrison runs to me, picks me up, and screams in my face.

Several cowboys, fellow riders, the bullfighters slap me on the back.

Everyone knows it was a damn good ride.

I feel it in my chest. In my head.

The bright lights from the arena make everything more surreal.

I wonder if my dad is watching at home, I think to myself. *My brothers? Tess?*

"We have a score, folks! Ninety-two points for this cowboy and his bull! Ninety-two! Stan, I haven't seen a ride like that in quite some time! Hell, maybe Atwood can pull off a third title!"

Ninety-two.

Garrison slaps my back again. "Fuck yeah!"

The crowd is wild.

The adrenaline rush I have right now makes all of this worth it.

The pain in my legs from surgeries.

Pain in my wrists, my neck, my shoulders.

All fucking worth it right now.

"Ninety-two," I say to myself, bending over and resting my hands on my knees. "Ninety-fucking-two!" I might be sick.

Making my way out of the arena, my head full of nothing and everything, I try to wrap my mind around the last minute and a half of what just transpired.

Pence, Ratcliff, and Bridges, fellow bull riders, high-five me as I toss my rope over my shoulder, just trying to live in this moment for just a few more seconds.

A news reporter shoves a camera in my face. "Casey Atwood, what a ride. Can you tell me what you were thinking when you climbed on that bull tonight?"

I laugh out of truth. "Surviving."

She laughs like it's a joke, but it's not.

"Yes, I'm sure. But when you got on Chiseled, were you working through what you needed to do to win?"

"Not really. Oftentimes, when we think too much, we're too stuck in our heads, and we're unable to run on instinct."

"How many more of these great rides do you think you have in you, Casey?"

"I'm not sure, but this one felt real good."

"You're ranked seventh right now in the standings, and most likely, after this ride, you will move up. What'd you do to regroup, knowing that you are riding well and also knowing you just haven't had a good pick of bulls in the past?"

"I got Chiseled. Enough said."

"You finally finished the way you wanted to?"

"Yeah, I did on this one."

"Thank you for your time, Casey, and good luck."

"Thank you."

I walk into the extra room at the arena, take off my gloves, shove them in my riggin bag along with my rope. I sit down on the bench and put my head in my hands, trying to collect myself.

My cell phone sounds from my bag.

It's a text from Cash, my bull-fighter brother.

> Cash: *What a ride, asshole. Keep it up, and you'll be back on top.*

Other texts roll in, but I only pay attention to the one from my brother, who I haven't heard a goddamn thing from for some time. I got hung up on a bull about six months ago and broke my wrist. I heard nothing from him.

And I'd never let him fight bulls for me. I'd stick a feather in my hat on that one. Swear my life on it. He's reckless, irresponsible. Makes split decisions. And yet, here he is, the top bullfighter in the world right now. How the hell that happened, I have no idea.

Me: What fucking rock have you been living under?

I see the bubbles when he starts to type.

They disappear.

They start again.

I throw my phone back in my riggin bag. He won't text back.

Garrison struts in, grinning from ear to ear. "Hell of a ride, man. Let's go to Teddy's, the bar across the street from the hotel, after this?"

"Who's going?"

"Bunch of us."

Garrison is a buckle-bunny whore. He'd take them all to bed if he could. All at the same time.

"I'll think about it. I'm going to go back to my hotel room and shower. I'll let you know."

"Dude, you just had a fantastic ride. What's to think about? You need to celebrate."

I throw my bag over my shoulder. "I still have to sign autographs on the way out. You done yours yet?"

"Yeah. Got that shit out of the way."

Every bull rider has to spend at least seven and a half minutes with the fans before he vacates the arena. It's part of the bull-rider contract with the PBR.

The roar of the crowd is still in my chest. The high I just sat on feels unbelievable. I just need to ride like that two more nights to win the whole damn thing. Celebrating shouldn't be on my list of things to do. It should be to stay focused. I need a good night's rest.

I exit a hallway that leads to the outside to a path that's blocked off for the riders to leave, and the fans are assembled on the right side.

When I walk out, the crowd erupts into cheers when they see me.

I fix my cowboy hat, and I can't help but smile.

It's been a while since I had a ride that good.

I sign autographs.

"I'm your biggest fan, Casey."

"You're a legend, Casey."

"Can you sign my boobs, Casey?"

"What's it like to be on top, Casey?"

"Will you go home with me tonight?"

I come across a little boy, and my heart seizes. I invited them here. He's got a photo of me on Blaze, a bull I rode a few years back.

I set my riggin bag on the ground and bend down. "What's your name, kid, and where are you from?" I know his name, but I just want to hear him say it.

"Austin, Mr. Atwood, and Idaho."

His eyes are wide, and I'm not real sure if it's from fear or something else. But it takes everything in me not to pull him into my arms.

"My father is Mr. Atwood. You can call me Casey."

"My mama says it's respectful to address adults like that." I hear the Southern drawl.

"It doesn't sound like you're from Idaho, Mr. Austin." I wink.

"Nah, I'm from Texas. Moved to Idaho a while ago with my mama and daddy."

I nod and take the photo from him.

"I just never met a hero before."

God, don't fall apart, Casey. Don't lose your shit.

In all my years of doing this, I've never been called a hero. I've also never felt like one, especially for this eight-year-old little boy, and this causes a lump in my throat and takes the air from my lungs. I try to maneuver around his words. Try to allow them to settle inside me, but they won't. They feel uncomfortable. Because I don't feel like a hero. I feel like a guy who's let a little boy down. I feel like a bull rider who's had a pretty damn good career, doing what he loves. I don't rescue people from burning buildings. I don't protect my country. And I certainly don't risk my life for another's life.

"I'll let you in on a little secret, Mr. Austin. You want to be a hero?" But I stop there.

A boy his age needs to have someone believe in his dreams, like my dad did in mine. I always wanted to be a bull rider and nothing else. I wasn't the type of kid who was a natural on a bull. I didn't have the God-given talent, but I sure as hell had a hard-work ethic that never slept.

So, instead of telling him to go be the type of hero I thought he needed to be, I tell him, "Balance on basketballs every minute you can. Study the bulls. You know about YouTube?"

Austin smiles and looks confused at the same time. As if to say, *Doesn't everybody know what YouTube is?*

Instead, he says, "Yes, sir."

"Watch all the bull rides you can. Get your balance right. You ride horses?"

"Yes, sir."

"Ride those too. All the time. And I guarantee, you'll make it to this level, Mr. Austin."

I stand and put my hand out. He puts his right hand out and takes mine firmly.

"Man"—I shake my head—"a great handshake is a good start. It was nice to meet you, Mr. Austin." The lump in my throat grows as I feel his little hand in mine. My dry, callous, experienced hand to his soft, gentle hand.

He nods. "Mr. Atwood—I mean, Casey, can I ask one more question?"

"Shoot." I pick up my riggin bag and throw it over my shoulder, trying to act casual.

"You ever feel like you're at the right place at the right time?"

My eyes meet his. For a moment, I see myself, and all I want is to hold him more than I've ever wanted to hold anything in my life.

"Yes, Mr. Austin."

"Me too, Casey."

Back at the hotel room, I shower and try to get Mr. Austin out of my head, cleaning my body from the bulls, the dirt, the smell of the arena. With the adrenaline slowly leaving my body, I feel the aches and pains of the ride. My left hip is sore, along with my knees, which will probably cause a bit of a limp later. I think about Tess as I wash my body, remembering her hands and what she used to do to me. I wonder what she's doing in Ketchikan, Alaska.

There's a knock on my door, so I jump out of the shower, dry off, throw a towel around my waist, and walk to the door. I look through the peephole and see it's Garrison.

I didn't plan on going to the bar. But I know he'll make me go for a beer.

When I open the door, he shoves his phone in my face. "And now, you're breaking women's hearts all across the country. Fucking A, man. You've become this overnight sensation." Garrison walks past me.

"It was a great ride. That's it. Not everybody and their mother watch bull riding, Gar."

He throws himself on the bed. He looks up at me. "What? No, I'm talking about the little boy."

"What?" I take his phone from him and watch the short clip of me with Austin.

Shit. That's not what I meant to do.

"This shit has gone viral. Look at the bottom. Look how many times it's been viewed."

I look down at the number. "Two point five million?"

57

"And you know half that number are hot moms who are just creaming all over you. And the ones without kids too. Dude, you're so getting laid tonight. Fuck you, man."

I throw his phone back on the bed. Walk to the bathroom and get changed into shorts and a T-shirt and think of Austin's hand in mine.

I walk out, and Garrison says, "Fuck no. Come on, man. One beer. Then, you can walk back to your room and be alone."

I grab the volleyball I'd packed, throw it down on the floor, and begin to balance on top of it.

Garrison drops his head forward. "Ugh, come on. Just one."

"Why do you want me to go so bad?" I push through the pain that's now settled in my ankles with the balance on the ball.

"Because women—buckle bunnies—will flock to you tonight. They have seen the ride and now the video that has somehow exploded over the internet. I can be your sideshow and get some ass."

We've been riding bulls on the circuit since we were eighteen. Both young and dumb and thinking with the wrong head.

"Fine, just one beer." I step off the ball and go change into a long-sleeved plaid button-up shirt, Wranglers, the belt buckle my dad gave me when I won my first bull-riding event at eighteen and my black cowboy hat. "Let's go."

6

The Ladybugs

It's early when Erla wakes and walks to the kitchen, makes her coffee, and prays that it won't be too quiet in the house today. Prays that the city might have road work that includes a jackhammer close to her house or maybe rain or thunder, just so things aren't so quiet.

She sees the letter she wrote on the counter.

Her resignation letter to The Ladybugs.

Erla wonders if her memory and her irritability are a direct result of grief or if it's the fact that she's done with dealing with people's crap. Life is short—she knows this to be true.

She pours a cup of coffee, sits down in her chair, and waits for the sun to rise.

Life was supposed to be simpler when she got older. Don wasn't supposed to die before her. They'd agreed one night when they got lost in each other's arms that he was supposed to outlive her because they both knew Erla simply wasn't strong enough to withstand the grief.

Don was such a wonderful father to Devon. A father he didn't have to be and when Devon was born, Toby, her biological father, never asked any questions. He knew he couldn't be the father that Devon deserved. Erla also knew that she'd never have to ask Toby to sign over parental rights because he was a good man; he was just brokenhearted. He has the kind of broken heart that can never be fixed. Some things one can never unsee. She knows that Toby thought highly of Don and knew he'd be a great dad to Devon.

If only Devon could see these things. Sure, Erla can understand why Devon is angry that she and Don didn't tell her who her biological father is, but it was all for good reason.

Erla takes a sip of coffee as Millie jumps down from Don's chair and into her chair. Wedges herself between the arm of the chair and Erla's hip—something she used to do with Don.

Erla still hasn't talked to Devon since she left Dillon Creek for yet another country to photograph another piece of the world.

And besides, it isn't Devon or Scarlet, Erla's granddaughter, who is going to fix Erla's grief. Sure, it was nice to have them here even if Devon was a million miles away in her thoughts. Devon and Scarlet had their own grief to figure out. Erla does hope that one day, Devon will understand that Erla and Don did what they did to protect Devon and to give her a good life. It isn't Devon's fault that Toby can't stay sober, and why have a little girl carry that guilt?

Oh, no. Did I pay the water bill for August?

Craig, down at the water company, was so good about calling her to remind her last month.

It simply slipped her mind.

But the peculiar thing is, her memory has gotten much worse lately. In fact, just last week, she forgot to deposit Don's retirement check, and boy, did that cause a mess at the bank.

The checks she'd written for their car insurance, their homeowners insurance, and the gas bill bounced.

Her debit card had been declined at The Flowerpot when she purchased seeds and potting soil.

It wasn't until she marched into the bank that she found out it had been her mistake.

Scarlet mentioned some direct deposit ordeal, but Erla liked knowing when money was coming in and going out. It seemed like a bit of a hassle to set up the direct deposit with the online stuff anyway, and she'd just rather not deal with it.

What happened to the old-fashioned way of doing things? Erla thinks to herself.

Next to her chair, on the small table that sits between her and Don's chair, she takes a pad of paper and makes a note to remind herself later this morning to call Craig down at the water company.

The small, slight pain returns to her chest. It's the one she's been having for a few weeks now, and she's filed the pain away as anxiety. Erla was never one to get anxiety, but since Don died, she feels every minute of it.

She hasn't told anybody about it either because worry won't do anyone any good.

At Don's funeral, Dr. Cain offered her medication to help with her nerves, but Erla wasn't about to start taking another pill for another ailment if she could help it. Besides, pills for mood make her head feel like it is in left field. And she isn't going to end up like Percy Kettenpom, who dropped dead in the nude in his living room because he had taken one too many mood enhancers. Granted, he was ninety-seven years old, but why he was naked, God only knows.

Dying isn't what Erla is scared of. In fact, if she had a choice, she'd choose death. It's the naked part that frightens her the most—and not being in control of her mind.

Erla misses the old days when doctors didn't prescribe medication just for simple chest pains and whatnot.

When people read the actual newspaper in print and not on a computer screen.

When Sunday was a day for family and church and small-town potlucks.

When *Neighbor Dorothy* came across the radio waves and families gathered around it.

Erla swears the invention of the television was when society began its slow and steady decline.

What happened to books and printed publications, for God's sakes? Now, there are Kindles, and i-things, and smartphones!

The pain in her chest slowly starts to subside when she walks to the kitchen and drinks a small glass of water.

Maybe Erla just doesn't fit into the modern times.

She glances at the resignation letter on the counter again.

Sure, Delveen and Pearl could be small-minded and trivial. But does that mean that Erla has to walk away from something that has meant so much to her? No, it does not. She convinces herself to leave it there for the day before making a final decision on her future with The Ladybugs.

Mabe is worried about Erla, and the worry follows her into the late morning while she prunes her roses. Grief can be wild. One minute, you think you will live, and the other minute, you want to die.

Guilt can also be wild, she thinks to herself as she snips an old stem from her rose bush.

Could she come clean about what she saw the night Tripp and Conroy were killed? Or would it just drudge up more wounds, more broken hearts, and unneeded sadness?

Mabe Muldoon was the first person on the scene the night of the accident, and she just left. Just drove away.

What would make the difference anyway?

She has felt it on her conscience since the night it happened, and if it doesn't matter, then why does she feel it so deeply?

Which leads to her next thought. *If it does matter, why can't I bring myself to say anything?*

Fear.

Betty Lewindowski is her sponsor from the Alcoholics Anonymous meetings that Mabe secretly attends. Betty told her that a clear conscience makes for a soft pillow. After attending AA meetings regularly—a soft comfort, part of a less lonely road on Monday nights at seven thirty p.m. at the Catholic church—Mabe has come to the conclusion that she is an alcoholic. But just for good measure and as an added precaution, in times like these—the summertime, when it is light out until late into the evening—Mabe wears a scarf and sunglasses as a disguise into the meetings.

But everybody knows Betty started AA in Dillon Creek, and she never flaunts it. She's always at the church to start the coffee every Monday night. Mabe isn't sure what the fuss is all about with her and AA meetings, but maybe that fuss just existed between her own two ears, and really, nobody else gives a lick about what she does or doesn't do.

Mabe doesn't have a clear conscience. She doesn't sleep well at night.

It seems that my worries are better served toward helping Erla, she thinks to herself, *or it's just an excuse to not deal with my own guilt.*

What if she comes clean?

Who would she come clean to?

The Atwoods?

The Morgans?

Chief McBride?

Betty?

Mabe stands back to look at the progress of the rose bush and realizes she's stripped it bare.

Perhaps this is what she's supposed to do—strip herself bare (metaphorically speaking because nobody wants to see a seventy-something woman naked)—so that she can grow.

Who the hell knows, but Mabe isn't excited about metaphorically growing today—or tomorrow for that matter.

She stands back and admires the chop job she just did on her rose bush.

Mabe's phone begins to ring from her front porch steps. She removes her garden gloves. "Hello?"

"Mabe, this is Betty Lewindowski."

Mabe isn't sure why Betty has to announce her full name when she calls her. There is only one Betty Lewindowski in Dillon Creek.

"Yes, hello, Betty."

"Listen, there's a new gal from Fortuna who needs your help. A housewife and kind of like you."

"What do you mean, kind of like me?" Mabe eases down onto the steps with a grunt.

"The hat-and-scarf type, you know. She's not quite sure she's an alcoholic, but everybody knows she is. Anyway, here's her number."

She didn't waste any time in giving Mabe the woman's number.

Betty had a knack for setting her up with newcomers—the crazy ones too.

Patty C. was the escaped mental patient from Simpervirens Mental Health Facility in Eureka. She happened upon our meetings one night, and Betty thought they'd be a great fit until she was arrested for grand theft. Mabe had brought that woman to her house, and she could have robbed her blind! To this day, they're still not sure if Patty C.—short for Cupcakes, as she introduced herself—was her real last name.

Mabe had a hunch it wasn't.

And let's not forget about Sharon B. The one-eyed widow from Petrolia. Come to find out, in a fit of rage, she had two good-working eyes and one heck of a temper. Mabe wasn't so sure Sharon needed AA. But she needed some sort of twelve-step program. Ended up killing her husband for cheating on her.

"Anyway, here nor there, wait for her to call you. If she doesn't want it bad enough, she won't call," Betty reminds Mabe and hangs up.

Betty has no phone etiquette, and it drives Mabe mad.

At least you could say good-bye, she thinks to herself and hangs up.

Oh shoot. Mabe didn't get the woman's name. *Oh well.* She's sure she'll know when and if the woman calls.

Mabe's phone begins to ring again.

"Hello?" Mabe answers.

"He-hello?" A soft voice is on the other end.

"Oh, hello. Is that you?"

"Yes, it's me. Is that you?"

"Yes, it's me. From AA. The name's Mabe. What's yours, sweetheart?"

"Patty."

Oh Lord. Not another Patty. This is going to be a long day.

Mabe wipes the sweat from her brow. "You, by chance, didn't do a stint in prison for grand theft, did you? Or murder your husband? Either way, I'd be fine with it as long as you're honest."

"Prison?" she whispers softly. "The only four walls I've been confined to is my house."

Thank the heavens, Mabe thinks to herself.

If Mabe has learned anything in AA, it's to feel people out before she invites them to her home.

"What's your story, Patty?"

There's a silence that falls on the other end of the phone line. "I-I'm not sure if I qualify for AA," she starts.

"There are no qualifiers, dear. The only requirement is that you want to stop drinking."

"I do."

Mabe hears the brokenness in her tone. The loneliness. After all, she, too, has experienced both.

"I drink after my children and husband go to bed. It's just wine. Listen, I need to go. My husband just came home. I'll call you later." Patty hangs up.

Tess

It's cold when the plane lands. My phone says the temperature is forty-two degrees, and the sun is slowly beginning its descent.

Forty-two degrees at home is warmer than forty-two degrees in Alaska, I'll admit. Maybe it's the humidity that hangs in the air at home while the temperature in Alaska comes straight from the towers of mountains neighboring Ketchikan.

I brought just a sweatshirt for the flight, and I slide it over my head as I disembark the airplane.

The airport ferry leaves on the half hour, and it's no more than a ten-minute ride, according to Ketchikan visitors website, so it allows me just enough time to grab my suitcase and board the ferry.

When I called ahead of time to rent a car, the man on the other end of the line laughed.

When he was finished, he said, "Ma'am, there are only four ways to get to Ketchikan, Alaska: bush plane, ferry, a cruise ship, or your own boat." He followed up with, "I suppose you don't have your own boat?"

I think he enjoyed my naivety more than I did.

Stepping off the plane at dusk, I barely make out the silhouette of green that surrounds me. The trees sit neatly against the tall mountains, enclosed almost exclusively by water. The streaks of clouds that lie across the sun-setting sky like race tracks beckon me deeper into the unfamiliar state.

I feel the ruggedness upon me and push down the fear that starts to creep into my throat, strangling me from behind.

The beauty should call to me, but it doesn't.

The smell of salt and the fresh mountain air and the sound of seagulls make me feel both at home and far away at the same time.

Making my way inside the terminal, I hold open the door for an elderly couple with their son, who's in dress blues—I believe, the Marines—but the soldier refuses to allow me to hold open the door.

"You first, ma'am," he says and takes the door.

I nod. "And thank you for your service."

"It's my pleasure."

Ma'am—like I'm some old lady holding on to old politics, carrying a newspaper and complaining about the state of the nation, like my mother. My mother is a ma'am.

I'm a miss.

But this man is maybe eighteen. Probably returning home from boot camp or basic training.

To him though, I am a ma'am, and this makes me feel old as I make my way to baggage claim.

His parents seem older, too old to have to have a son at eighteen. Maybe they're grandparents. Maybe they started having children later in life, but my curiosity has been piqued.

Their quiet reunion moves me.

They're speaking a different language among themselves that sounds intoxicating and beautiful.

The elderly woman is beaming at the young man as the elderly man has his hands shoved in his pockets, speaking to the soldier, smiling. As if they have missed time and are soaking up all of the small moments life gives them together. Content in this moment, grateful for what they have together, the soldier lifts his green bag from the belt, and they exit baggage claim.

I can't help but notice the elderly woman has taken several glances back at me, perhaps because since I landed, I haven't been able to take my focus from the three of them.

For some reason, I have a hunch they're going to the same place I am, so I follow them outside.

A waiting boat is out front, and there's a woman tending to a rope.

"Is this the ferry to Ketchikan?" I ask.

"It is. First time to our neck of the woods?" she asks.

"It is."

"Business or pleasure?"

"Maybe a little of both." I try to smile and swallow any uncertainty.

"You know what they say about Ketchikan," she says.

"No, what's that?"

"Once you get ketched, you never go back." She laughs. "So, whether you're here for either or both, you might just fall in love with our slice of heaven and never leave."

"I'll take that into consideration. Thank you"—I glance at her name tag—"Willow."

Wheeling my bag onto the ferry, I take in the views once more.

In many ways, Ketchikan reminds me of home.

The mountains of trees.

The rugged terrain.

The unforgivable ocean.

And the body of water that sits between the coasts.

Willow takes the microphone and begins. "Welcome to Ketchikan, Alaska! My name is Willow, and I will be your two-to-five-minute tour guide based on which way the wind blows. The body of water you're on right now is the Tongass Narrows, which serves as Southeast Alaska's Inside Passage.

This being the quickest boat ride you'll probably ever take, you might see pods of whales—typically humpbacks or killer whales—bald eagles, and the occasional dolphins. Or Finn, the town drunk. Not in the water, hopefully, but on the boat, as he tends to wander. I wouldn't recommend taking a dip in these waters unless you have a wet suit."

I chuckle to myself as my mind drifts to Toby Lemon. I suppose every town has one. But I also wonder if Finn is well taken care of by its town like Toby is in Dillon Creek.

"And that concludes our trip."

The travelers laugh as Willow continues to talk about the history of Ketchikan and of Alaska for a few more minutes.

It's getting darker and harder to see our surroundings, but Ketchikan is brightly lit from where we are.

Before I depart the ferry, I wait for all seven passengers to exit and walk to Willow. "What language are they speaking?" I motion to the elderly couple and the young soldier.

Willow smiles. "Tlingit. A native tribal language that has somehow vanished into the American culture. That is Martin and Esther Walters and their grandson, Jacob."

"Where are his parents?"

"His mother?"

"Yes."

"Oh, that is a story for another day."

I take Willow's suggestion. "Thank you for the entirely too-short boat ride."

Willow smiles proudly and pulls her chin up just a smidgen. "You're welcome. Enjoy your stay, Tess."

"I don't remember telling you my name."

Willow points down toward my suitcase. "Unless you borrowed an overnight bag, it's on your luggage tag." She shrugs. "It's my job to know these things."

"Oh." I laugh.

Willow and I exchange good-byes, and I exit the ferry, watching as Jacob helps his grandmother into the car while Martin walks to the driver's door. I'm drawn to them, their story, and I'm not sure why.

I pull out the address from my purse, my luggage in tow, and realize how cold it's getting as the sun has finally made its descent behind the mountains.

Instead of retrieving my phone, I think better of it. Walk back to the boat. "Willow!" I call.

She looks down at me from the top of the boat.

"Can you tell me where 93 Baker Street is?"

She pauses. "You're in the old Isner house?" Her look is both peculiar and questioning.

Some sort of whistle sounds from Willow's boat just as I say, "He ... he passed away."

"What?" she calls down.

"He died!" I yell back.

"What?"

"He's dead!" I yell again.

"What?"

The whistle stops.

"Ike Isner is dead!"

"He's dead?" Willow asks.

I'm careful with my words now, uncertain of how she knows Ike, uncertain of their relationship. So, I tread lightly. "Yes. I'm sorry if you're just hearing the news now."

"Oh, the Isners were big in our community. Not in my time, but my grandfather's time." Willow is probably eighteen, maybe nineteen. She's quiet for a moment, almost lost in thought. "Anyhow, 93 Baker Street is that house right there on the hill with all the windows. Take Bunker to Baker. It's about a two-minute walk." She smiles. "But it's uphill."

I take the keys that Twila gave me from my purse and breathlessly set my bag down against the house. It's cold in Ketchikan, Alaska. But not as cold as I thought it would be. Then again, it's only September, and things aren't always what they seem. My hands are like ice as I slide the key into the lock, and the door opens with a long, smooth creak.

The scent of age and time and old memories fill my nose. A familiar scent. A scent I can't quite put my finger on.

It's dark inside, and I reach for a light switch against the wall as I step into the old house.

The living room illuminates. Twila said in an e-mail she'd get the power and water turned on, something I didn't even think about, as I was too caught up with *should I stay or should I go.*

To the right, the living room is big and open, and tucked behind it is a wall of windows, but it's too dark to see the view tonight.

I pull my suitcase in behind me and shut the door.

There's a knock at the door, which nearly makes me jump out of my skin. I turn back to the door, and my heart begins to race.

"Who-who is it?"

"Jacob."

My eyebrows draw together. *Jacob? He's safe, Tess. He's military. Calm yourself down.*

I open the door.

Jacob is holding a casserole dish with pot holders. "My grandmother wanted me to bring you this."

"Oh, that … that's very kind of you, your grandparents." *How did they know I was at this address?* I take the dish from Jacob.

"My grandmother says you can keep the pot holders. She makes them."

"This … this is very thoughtful. I'm sorry. I just don't know what to say."

"My grandmother says if you bring back the dish, she'll fill it for you again."

I smile. "Where can I return it?"

"The Tlingit Visitor Center. She's a Tlingit elder and a volunteer there."

"I'll do that—bring back the dish."

"Anyhow, welcome to Ketchikan." Jacob turns to leave.

"Jacob? How did you know I was here, in this house?"

He stops, turns back to face me, rubs the back of his neck, and shrugs. "My grandmother knew. She says, 'Welcome home.'"

My eyebrows furrow. *Welcome home?* She probably has me confused with someone else.

"Enjoy." He smiles.

"Thank you, Jacob. And tell your grandmother I said thank you."

"Sure will." And he leaves.

I quietly shut the door behind me and find the kitchen to the left. I turn on the light. It's a big, open kitchen, though it dates back to the early '90s. It's dusty. I set the dish down on the counter and take off the lid. It's salmon, and the scent of the dish smells of garlic and butter. My mouth begins to water. Next to the salmon is some sort of small potatoes.

I put the lid back on to keep it warm while I unpack.

It was awfully kind of Esther. The thoughts of what Jacob meant by *welcome home* prickles at the back of my brain as I wander through the house. The furniture is covered in sooty white sheets. Two sofas face the wall of windows along with two big recliner chairs and a coffee table. I carefully pull the sheets from the furniture.

The sofas' pattern is roses with green stems while the recliners are brown leather.

A fireplace sits in the middle of the windows, and the rock-lined wall goes clear up to the middle of the vaulted ceiling.

The hardwood floor creaks under my feet from years of weight and it makes me wonder what the walls have seen and called to those who've lived between them.

I walk back to the front door and get my bag, wheel it down the hallway past the kitchen, and find two bedrooms. The beds are down to bare bones. A headboard and a naked mattress, a window with drawn curtains.

I take the bedroom in the back. I'm not sure why. Maybe if a wild animal made its way inside, I suppose I could buy myself a few more minutes to think of a plan to save myself.

This makes me think of *The Great Outdoors*, a favorite movie of my dad's. This thought leads me to my parents. I should probably let my mom know I made it safely.

Sitting on the edge of the bed, I text my mom. Then, I shoot an e-mail to Twila and thank her for turning on the power and water. Then, I start a to-do list.

Fear starts to creep in. I flew over a thousand miles to a place I've never been, to live in house, in a community I've never been to, to fix and sell a house. I've officially lost it.

But instead of going into panic mode, I add *Take a homemade dish to Esther* to my to-do list.

I also add *Grocery store* to my to-do list. Then, I start a grocery list.

The fear gets louder in my head as I think of the creaks in the floor, the repairs that will need to be made, the money that I don't have.

A soft pour of rain starts. It's gentle, as if the weather gods were asking the house for forgiveness beforehand.

The downpour starts.

The wind begins to howl. At first, it's quiet, but once the wind and the rain starts to dance, the house begins its song, both somber and merciful, all at the same time. As I listen, I make a note to call a contractor to see what needs to be done structurally to the house in order to sell this place.

My phone begins to ring, and his name slides across the screen.

It's Casey.

8

Casey

One beer led to three and the shot that Tuff Hedeman bought me. We talked bulls and riding and all the shit. We talked about Disaster—his spins, kicks, and twists.

When Tuff leaves, I'm alone at the table.

A brunette who reminds of Tess sits down across the table from me and doesn't say a word. She sits and stares at me.

After a long minute, I say, "Can I help you?"

She eyes me. "Yes, you can actually. I've been sitting across the bar, watching the women fall all over you this evening, and never once did you pay them any mind." She pauses. "Who are you in love with?"

"What makes you think I'm in love?"

God, she reminds me so much of Tess. This could be a problem.

I push my beer out of the way. *No more,* I tell myself.

"Well"—she shrugs—"if you had even stopped to notice how beautiful these women were and you didn't have a pure heart, then I'd say you would have taken one or more home by now."

I lean back, cross my arms against my chest, and stare back at her. The jukebox plays a Chris Stapleton tune, something about drinking and losing things. I'm curious about the woman who sits in front of me.

"What's your name?" she asks.

"Casey. And you?"

"Ava."

The waitress sets a shot down in front of me.

"I didn't order—"

"I did," Ava interrupts as the waitress also sets one down in front of her.

"Congrats on a great ride." She holds her shot glass up.

I hold up my shot glass, and we take them.

"I thought you didn't know my name," I say.

Ava smiles. Sets her shot glass down. "Just wanted to confirm it was you."

I settle into my own skin. Get comfortable with the fact that I just rode a hell of a ride, and all of a sudden, I'm at ease with the attention.

It is always the last shot that makes everything feel all right, makes me content in my own skin.

I scan the room for Garrison, who's making out with some buckle bunny in the corner of the bar.

"What's her name?" Ava asks. "The woman you're in love with."

I don't know this woman from Eve. How do I know she's not some trashy magazine reporter, looking for untrue stories?

"You remind me of someone." I change the subject.

"Who's that?"

"Someone I used to love."

She smiles. "Ah, so it is a lost love."

"Something like that." The shot finally explodes in my stomach. I stare into her eyes, and all I see is Tess. Against my better judgment, I say, "You want to get out of here?"

"Thought you'd never ask."

I put my hand on the small of her back as we exit the bar. When we're outside, I grab her by her hips and back her up against the wall outside the bar. I'm barely an inch away from her lips.

"Are you okay with this?" I whisper.

"Yes," she says breathlessly.

I cover her mouth with mine and use my tongue to explore her.

I feel her breasts against my chest.

Her body against mine.

I kiss her hard and fast, and all I can picture is Tess.

I try to chase her out of my mind.

Pushing Ava's head to the side, I caress her neck, trailing kisses down the side. Pull her tank top strap back and kiss her collarbone. The one place that was Tess's weakness. Part of me prays she'll enjoy it and let me know. Because maybe I can have a Tess without our past. Maybe I can fall in love with someone who isn't Tess.

I harden against her, and I know she feels me.

"Do you have somewhere we can go?" she asks. "If you don't, I can arrange something."

"Come on." I pull her by the hand, as if I owned her, and lead her across the street and upstairs to my hotel room.

After I fumble with the key, we make it inside the room. Grabbing both of her legs, I wrap them around my waist and walk to the bed, set her down, and crawl on top of her.

Kiss her until my lips hurt.

Kiss her like she's my Tess.

Something I've wanted to do for a long time.

I slide in next to her. Set my cowboy hat up on the bedpost.

"Is this okay?" I ask again, more urgent and with more hunger.

"Yes."

She grabs her breasts in her hands, her legs spread, and I run my hand up her thigh and underneath her skirt. I push her panties to the side, trace around her folds, and push lightly.

She whimpers beneath my touch, and I look at her.

In this light and by the face she's making, she isn't Tess at all.

She's just a gorgeous woman who's almost naked, in my room, in my bed.

She doesn't have Tess's dimple or her giggle when I did things to her like this in the front seat of my pickup truck when we were seventeen. Or the night we went all the way and made love.

I took her virginity that night. She took mine.

In this light, I see a woman who isn't Tess at all, but a figment of what I want her to be.

Ava is a beautiful woman, but she isn't Tess.

I drop my head. Pull my hand from her panties. "I ... I'm sorry. I can't ... I can't do this."

Ava smiles, breathing hard, staring up at the ceiling. "It's the woman you're in love with, isn't it?"

"Something like that." I stop and look at Ava. "I'm sorry."

She sits up and pushes herself to the end of the bed. Stands. Pulls down her skirt. Puts herself back together.

No, she isn't Tess at all, but God sure made her beautiful.

"Seeing as you're not wearing a wedding ring, is she your girlfriend?"

"Was. Long time ago." I sit up. "I'm really sorry, Ava." I drop my head.

"No, it's fine. I knew what I was getting myself into when I sat down at your table. Thought I might be able to change your mind."

"You're a stunning woman."

She puts her long, dark hair into a ponytail. "It's fine, Casey. But let me know if things don't work out."

I stand to walk her out.

"Will you stop with all your gentlemanly ways? You don't need to walk me to the door."

"I'm not. I'm walking you to your car at the bar."

Ava laughs. "Why?"

"Because that's how I was raised. I'm not letting you walk back without me. And I don't take no for answer."

Ava rolls her eyes, but she wants this. She wants this in a man, and I'm not the one to give it to her.

"I have a driver."

"Great. I'll get to meet him."

We walk back downstairs.

There's a man who's bigger than the state of Alaska with a panicked look on his face. His neck is thicker than my thighs. He's outside the hotel. "Holy shit, Miss Ava. God. Where the hell did you go?"

"Needed a break. That's all." She winks at me.

"Who is this guy?" I whisper.

"My security," she whispers back.

"Is this cowboy giving you a hard time, Miss Ava?"

Shit, this guy could crush me with one punch. Knock me into Tuesday.

"No, not at all. Come on, Gavin. Take me to the car."

"Good night, Casey. Thank you," Ava says with a wink.

"Hey, what do you do for a living?" I ask.

She turns back, and Gavin laughs.

"Does it matter?" she asks.

I guess it doesn't. "Just making sure you're not some news reporter, looking for a story." I smile.

"See you around, Casey. And I really hope that woman is worth your heart."

Night two. Round two.

"And now, Downey Records' double-platinum recording artist and Grammy winner Ava will perform 'If I Were You.' "

The crowd erupts.

I drop my head and smile.

Ava takes the stage and finds me standing with the other bull riders in the middle of the arena.

"This performance is dedicated to the good guys, one in particular. Right, Casey?" She winks at me.

I look back at her, shaking my head, and smile back. *Definitely not a reporter.*

As I listen to Ava's performance. Once she's done, I try to get my head in the game, I go over Tuff's advice in my head. Visualize my ride. And then wipe my mind clean.

Just me and Disaster.

Dancing partners.

Old lovers.

It's late when I pull into Dillon Creek. I ended up winning the event and taking home the whole pot of money.

Suppose I got lucky this time.

Got some good rides.

Got some good bulls.

Didn't die.

I drive down Main Street.

As much as I try to run from this town, I always come back. There is a sense of calmness, a sense of knowing. This will always be home. It hurt to be home after Conroy died. Everything reminded me of him. Being at the ranch hurt too.

I pull over at Wilson's Grocery to grab a few things.

"Casey!" Twila yells.

Shit. Just what I don't need right now.

"Hey, Twila. Sorry I didn't stop by."

"That's okay because I have what I need to give you here." She reaches into her slim briefcase and hands me a manila envelope with my name on it. "Call me after you've read it, and we can go over the details."

Whatever it is, I probably won't want it, but I don't tell her this. "Will do."

"Oh," she says as she continues on her way. "That was a cute video with you and that little boy."

After I'm home, I toss my riggin bag and my overnight bag on the counter. I throw the manila envelope down on the counter too.

"Hello?" I call out.

But nobody seems to be inside.

Mom and Dad's truck are here.

"Hey, son." My dad walks into the house behind me. "Great rides." He grabs my shoulders and then points to the manila envelope on the counter. "What's that?"

I shrug, almost annoyed. "I don't know. Some letter from Twila."

Dad cocks his head. "Have you opened it?"

"Nah. Probably some political thing or something. I don't know."

"Well, I'd say if an attorney hands you a letter, it's in your best interest to open it."

"I will. I'm going to shower first."

"All right. I'm headed back outside to do some work in the barn."

"Need any help?"

"Sure, I could use your help."

"I'll meet you out there."

Dad walks back outside, and I grab my stuff from the counter and head to my room. I put the ten-thousand-dollar check in the top drawer of my dresser and take a shower.

When I get out, for whatever reason, there's more urgency to open the letter, especially after Dad's comment.

I throw on some work clothes, grab the letter, and sit down on the edge of my bed.

I open the envelope.

Dear Casey,

I was raised in a community where forgiveness is the cornerstone to happiness.

Here are the keys to our place in Ketchikan, Alaska. Twila will give you the details once you've accepted the house.

It's yours.

It might need some fixing up, but if you can do the work and sell it, then the money is yours.

Sometimes, you've got to find the healing in order to mend the bridges.

Best,

Ike

What in the fucking hell?
I read the letter again.
There's got to be some mistake.
I dial Twila's number.
"I assume you opened the letter?" Twila says without a hello.
"What the hell is going on?" I say.
"Come down to the office, and I'll explain."

"We cannot disclose the other party who has received the letter, so I can't tell you that information. But you can choose to accept the house as a gift or decline."

"Do I have time to think about it?" I run my hand through my still-wet hair. I can't just show up in Ketchikan and impose on Tess—if she is the other party. She left for a reason.

"I can give you twenty-four hours," Twila says. "The other party has the option to have sole proprietorship of the property should you choose to decline."

"And you can't tell me if it's Tess or not? Come on, Twila. We've known each other since we were kids. I'm not going to say anything. I just ... I just need to know."

Twila thinks on it. "I will say this: Ike had a way of knowing things."

"Thank you. Thank you for that insight." Sarcasm leaks from my tone.

I take the letter and leave the office.

"Twenty-four hours!" she calls behind me.

9

Tess

I ignored his call last night.

Too scared my emotions would allow my heart to feel something I'm just not ready to feel.

Maybe he just needed to talk.

Maybe he needed to be heard.

And when the images of him and Ava surfaced, I'm not going to lie, it ripped me open. Exposed my heart in ways I hadn't felt in a long time. Their bodies pressed together—dug nails deep into my heart.

But what killed me the most was the video with the little boy and Casey.

I watch the video once more, only for the tenth time. Viewers can't hear what's being said, but it's the way Casey gets down on his knee and looks at the little boy and how the little boy looks up at him with hope and admiration and maybe some envy. He's always been great with children.

How do you know when it's all over?

How do you know when it's time to throw in the towel forever?

When there's too much between two people that it starts to form a wall and it rises between them like an angry leader who is calling the shots, calling the kettle black, calling everyone names, pointing fingers at the wrong and the right, and it's all really messy.

But it's always been Casey's heart that won me over first.

It's always been about his heart.

But there comes a time when two people need to just walk away because some things are too heavy to carry into the future.

I also can't say my heart didn't seize when I saw his long, lean body pressed against another woman's. That, too, should be expected, right? He's not taken. He's free to date whomever he wants to date.

Don't scan through the photos again, Tess. Don't do that to yourself.

My phone rings.

It's Anna.

"Hey."

"Hey yourself, beautiful. How's Alaska?" Excitement gathers in her voice.

I try to reciprocate. "I don't know yet. I haven't ventured outside because I've been here not even twenty-four hours."

"You know what I mean."

"Well, the house is old. Someone brought me dinner last night. And it rains a lot here."

"Oh, so you're saying it's home."

I smile against the phone. Feel a little rush of warmth against my heart. "Yeah, I guess so." I didn't think of it like that.

"What are you going to do today?"

My eyes wander around the living room. "I need to get groceries. Call a contractor to come take a look at the place. See what work needs to be done, I guess."

The rain sounds.

"Do you hear that?"

"No, what is it?"

"The rain. It rains a lot harder here than it does at home."

It's now that I hear a quiet drip that begins by the front door.

Anna begins to talk, and I stand and follow the incessant drip.

Now, with the natural light from the outside, I see the large stain on the hardwood floor and look up just in time for a water drop to hit me in the face. Then another. Then another.

I step out of the rapid fire as Anna continues to talk.

"Shit," I whisper.

"What?" she says.

"The roof is leaking." I step on the dark spot and notice that the hardwood is spongy, which means it's been here for quite some time. There could be a rotting subfloor.

Shit.

"Did you call someone to fix it?"

"No, I just noticed it."

"Add it to the contractor's list," Anna says.

The rain begins to hit down on the roof like a beat that has unforgivable, angry song lyrics.

The wind twists and turns against the walls of the house.

The drip turns to a slow, steady trickle of water.

"Shit," I say again.

"What?"

"There's a waterfall in the living room." I look from the roof to the floor. "I need to get a bucket. Listen, I'll call you back when I get the waterfall fixed."

"Okay. But call me back."

"I will."

"Hey, Tess?"

"Yeah?" I stare up at the ceiling.

"You've got this."

I sigh. "That's what you keep saying."

"I love you."

"Love you too. Call you back later." I hit End, push my phone into my back pocket, and remember the basement.

Off the kitchen, there's a door that leads to the basement. There ought to be a bucket down there. I open the door, and cold air meets my face. I pull the long string, and the dark hallway illuminates only momentarily, as the lightbulb sputters, blinks, and then dies into complete darkness.

"Add lightbulbs to the list," I sigh. I pull my phone out of my back pocket again and flick on the Flashlight app.

Taking steps down toward the darkness, I'm reminded of when Casey and I were just kids. Somehow, a rabid raccoon had made its way into one of their old barns on the ranch. Daryl sent Casey and me to take care of it. We were ten years old or so at the time. Casey had just passed his hunters safety course and knew how to pack a gun.

But that's life on the ranch. Kids learn how to survive.

That's when the Atwoods, Morgans, and Cains did holidays together. Before anyone died. Before the travesty sat between the families like a big black cobra, waiting to spread its poison like it did. Like it has over the past eight years.

Casey told me to stay behind him, and I reluctantly agreed. If this thing was going to come at us, I wanted to be there to protect him as much as he would me. And the only reason I agreed to stay behind him was that he had the rifle. So, when we stepped inside the damp, old barn, the raccoon came screaming at us like some sort of crazy, mean loon, literally flying at us, Casey quickly pushed me backward with his one free hand, flicked the safety off, aimed, and fired. The flying raccoon fell from the air like a sack of potatoes.

Casey turned to me. "Are you all right, Morgan?" he whispered.

"Yeah."

He turned back to the raccoon and started to laugh, and so did I.

"Have you ever seen a raccoon fly?" Casey asked.

"I have now."

But in that moment, I looked at Casey differently for the first time, not like a like friend, not like a brother. He ignited something deep within my chest that burned. A burning I'd never felt before, that made my chest ache and my knees weak, and that ten-year-old girl knew then that she was standing next to the boy that God had made just for her.

I can't explain what he specifically did that day to win over my heart, but like my mother says, "You just know the day you fall in love."

It isn't tracked by landmarks or buildups or monumental growth; it's a feeling that seemingly arises out of nowhere. At least, that's been my experience.

I allow the memory to linger in my thoughts for far too long because when I come back to the present moment, I'm still standing in the middle of the staircase, and the same ache I felt at ten years old is back.

The flashlight on my phone only lights a path two feet in front of me, so I carefully proceed down the staircase, and as I go deeper into the basement, it gets colder and darker.

"Just a bucket," I tell myself.

When I make it to the bottom of the staircase, I realize that it's not a basement at all. It's a whole other floor of living space. Pine walls, just like upstairs. There are stacks of newspapers on a pool table and another hallway behind the staircase that leads somewhere. I search the walls for a light switch.

"Bingo." When I flip it, the room illuminates, exposing the bottom layer of the Isner house.

A kitchen. Curtains line one wall of the downstairs. I push them open. The windows overlook the Tongass Narrows, and the view takes my breath away.

The ocean water sits quietly, waiting for the visitors.

A cruise ship waits in the harbor.

Bush planes are lined up on the right side of the harbor.

Charter boats.

And people.

The colors of the trees and the houses that line the bank are just like a postcard.

Looking at the wild, vast Alaska that just beyond the Tongass Narrows with its thick, lush green trees that fill every inch up the side of the mountain, I'm taken aback.

The rain is a slow sprinkle now, and this takes me to why I'm down here in the first place. A bucket.

If peace had a color, a shape, a picture, it would be this one. I tuck this view into my heart, so I can pull it out when I need it.

I walk to the sink in the kitchen, and it's smaller than the one upstairs. I pull open the doors underneath the sink and find a bucket. I walk down the hallway and see three other bedrooms that are almost exactly the same as the upstairs—bare bones. A headboard, a dresser, a nightstand.

In the hallway, I notice a black-and-white photograph hanging on the wall, which catches my eye. It's the only picture displayed in the whole house. It's a picture of a family, and it's evident that they're happy—most of them anyway. But when I move closer, I see Ike in the photo, who stands all the way to the left, maybe in his early fifties. Another man and woman I'm unfamiliar with stand next to Ike.

Martin and Esther are in the photograph, too, though much younger. Next to Esther is a young woman who looks just like Esther. Though the quality of the photograph is minimal, I can see the young woman's sadness through the storm set in her eyes, the wind she tries desperately to hide from. In a world surrounded by smiles and *how do you do*s, she almost stands alone, in a different world, hiding from herself. In her arms sits a little girl, no older than maybe three, clinging to her mother. Same dark hair but a smile that brings light to the world.

I've never felt so mesmerized by a photograph. A memory captured so long ago, taken of people I hardly know, and yet I feel like it has buried itself into my skin, pushed itself upon me, imprinted itself within me.

It is the wind that calls to me, bringing me back to the present moment. The rain is so loud; it pounds against the roof upstairs. I remember the bucket. Quickly, I turn off the light, flip on the flashlight of my phone, and try to leave the feelings, the thoughts of the photograph downstairs, but they follow me up the stairs, whirl around me just like the wind. It's when I close the door to the downstairs that the feeling fades.

The water from the roof runs like a piece of fishing wire; it's not always visible, but it's consistent. I place the bucket under the small waterfall and look back up at the roof.

I need a handyman, I think to myself.

Hiring a handyman would probably be a lot quicker job than a general contractor. But maybe there's someone in town who could give a recommendation of a reputable person and not some serial killer I'd invite into the house, who would only kill me and leave my remains under the house, where I'd become a cold case before my body was only found twenty years later when the old house was being demolished to erect condominiums. And just my luck, the killer would have died five years prior in a car accident with bodies in the trunk.

You're overreacting, Tess.

I grab my shopping list, my purse, and find a big raincoat hanging behind the front door.

Pull your shit together, Tess.

In the wind and rain, I make my way down the hill, pulling the coat tighter around my body, burying my chin deep against my chest.

When I make it to the bottom of the hill, a smidgen to the right is Creek Street, and between Sockeye Sal's—a bar, I assume—and Adventure's Edge is a small place called Olive's.

Under the awning of Olive's, I pull off my hood and walk inside.

To my surprise it, too, is a bar, but on the other side is a small convenience store that doubles as a gift shop. Guess the owner knew what they were doing when they opened this place. Three birds. One stone.

Stop for milk and get a beer. I laugh to myself.

"Welcome to Olive's," a woman says. Her beautiful light-brown skin, long eyelashes, and long black hair are stunning in a natural, unapologetic way.

She greets me with a smile that feels warm. For a moment, I feel less alone.

"Are you passing through?" Her voice is smooth, and it floats in the air like music notes.

"Something like that." Perhaps it's the lonely piece of me that wants to wallow in self-pity, and yet a piece of me could use a friend.

"Let me know if I can help you," she sings.

I grab some instant coffee and a mug that says *Welcome to Ketchikan*, cereal, soy milk—which I'm really surprised she has—a postcard, two sweatshirts, a few frozen dinners, and several bottles of water. I set all of it down on the counter.

She smiles at the instant coffee. "Just so you know, I make good coffee here if you ever feel so inclined to stop in."

"I might need to take you up on that." I grab my debit card.

"Oh, we don't take cards here."

"Oh, you don't?"

"No, there's an ATM three blocks up. But I can set you up with a tab, if you'd like?"

Tabs. This makes me think of home. I smile. "But … but you don't know me."

She eyes me cautiously. "Have you robbed a bank?"

"No."

"Have you been arrested?"

"No."

"Have you ever been to prison?"

"Uh, no."

"Do you have a drinking problem?"

"No."

"A drug problem?"

"No."

She winks. "Then, you're okay in my book. Seems to me you'll make good on your tab."

"I will walk down to the ATM and get you the cash immediately. Thank you, um …"

"Olive."

"Oh. Olive." I thought the store name was in reference to a martini, but I don't say that to Olive. "Thank you, Olive."

She bags my purchases, and I take them from the counter and turn to leave, but I stop and turn back.

"You wouldn't know of someone I could call to repair a roof, would you?"

"Call Stanley. He fixes a little of everything around the house." Olive writes down his name and number.

"Thank you." I nod. Take the number from her.

"You're welcome ..."

"Tess."

"Tess."

I stop before I hit the door. Turn back to Olive. "What about a general contractor?"

"Emmitt." She takes the slip of paper back from me and writes down his number. "He's also my granddad. But trust me, he does great work. Don't let his age fool you."

This time, I shove the piece of paper into my pocket. "Thanks again."

"It's no problem, Tess. I hope to see you around. Oh, and a forewarning: Stan is single, and he'll let you know as much. He's harmless though. Just lonely."

"Well, you want the good news or the bad news first, Ms. Morgan?" Stanley doesn't look like a man who matches his name. He looks much younger, much skinnier. Maybe thirty. He wears dark blue jeans that hang from his hips, smokes a pipe, and wears suspenders.

"Bad news first, Stanley."

"Please, call me Stan." He awkwardly runs his hand through his light-brown hair. Takes his non-lit pipe from his lips. "You definitely have water damage, and we won't know the extent until we tear up the floors." He puts his pipe back between his mouth.

All I see are dollar signs. I have a life savings, but that's for my future. On the other hand, if I can turn around and sell this place for far more and make my money back and then some, it might be worth it. That's my best attempt to stay positive.

"What's the good news, Stanley?" I keep it professional by calling him by his full name, not wanting him to get any ideas.

"Emmitt Crane can fix this. And I can patch this hole, but you might need a new roof. That's a question for Emmitt though."

I'm impressed by how well he can speak with a pipe between his lips.

"If you can patch the hole, Stanley, that would be wonderful."

"Yep, yep," he says real slow as he eases down the ladder like a man twice his age. "Just let me go get a few things from my truck right quick."

When Stanley is done, I try to write him a check because I still don't have cash.

"No, your money is no good to me. It took me a whole twenty minutes, Ms. Morgan."

"But you have to take the money. I'd feel guilty if you didn't."

"Nah. You know what? Buy me a bottle of Pendleton, and we can call it even."

Quickly, I jot down the name and nod. "Okay, I can do that."

Stanley dusts his hands off, hikes his pants up, and pulls a pencil from behind his ear. He grabs a notepad from his chest pocket and begins to write something down.

His hand shakes as he writes.

"This is Emmitt's number."

"Thank you." I take the piece of paper from him even though I already have Emmitt's number.

"That's all right, Ms. Morgan." He hands me his card.

I walk him to the door before he can say anything else, and we exchange good-byes.

Shutting the door behind him, I fall against it.

What if I run out of money, fixing this old place?

The question game begins again.

I wonder if the other party has agreed to accepting the house. Maybe they could help me split the cost of the repairs, which also means they'd split the sale price of the house. But with these views and the square footage, this house could likely sell for quite a bit of money. I look around the space that could make or break me and the bank.

But these words come to me, and they're not mine. *You can, and you will.*

"I hope you're right," I say out loud to the house.

I sigh, and then I make a call to Emmitt next and leave a message.

It's about six in the evening, and I just finished the frozen meal I'd bought at Olive's when my cell phone rings.

"Hello?"

"Hello. This is Emmitt Crane. Is this ... Tess Morgan?" he asks.

"Yes. Hi, Emmitt." I explain the situation and ask if he can come over for an estimate of all that needs to be done to the house. "I don't know if you have the time, but you came highly recommended by Stanley and Olive."

There's a long silence over the line.

"Emmitt? Hello?"

"Yes ... yes. I'm sorry. Yes. I can come by tomorrow, if that works best for you?"

"That would be great. I'll give you the address."

"No, no. I have it. I know the address."

"Oh."

How would Emmitt know the address? How would he make the connection between me and this house and the address? But small towns and all. Being from one, I understand one.

"Well then, Emmitt, I will see you tomorrow."

Yet again, my words are met with silence.

"Emmitt?"

"Oh, yes, that sounds good. See you tomorrow, Ms. Morgan."

"See you tomorrow."

Later, Anna calls. The wind has stopped irritating the old house. I settle in for the evening.

"Well, I had a man named Stanley fix a hole in the roof, and I have a contractor coming by tomorrow to look at the house. See what needs to be done." I bite my lip. "I met a woman named Olive who owns a bar-slash-grocery store in town, and I know she owns it because the store's name is also called Olive's. She sells instant coffee and liquor and soy milk, just in case I decide to become a raging alcoholic or a vegan—because I'm scared to death, Anna."

"Tess Morgan, you hired someone to fix the roof. You've called a contractor. You met Olive. I'd say, you're on a roll."

"I had a solid teaching job. I liked my life. And now … and now, everything is so uncertain."

A big gust of wind returns, and the house creaks, as if to give me a nudge in the other direction.

"You were settling," Anna says.

"Settling?"

"Settling." Anna pauses. "You know as well as I do, Tess, that God had bigger plans for you."

"That's why he decided to uproot me from our small, safe, comfortable, little town and drop me in the middle of the Alaskan wilderness?"

"You're not in the Alaskan wilderness. You're in Ketchikan, silly. Do you see a bathroom?"

"Do I what?"

"See a bathroom?"

"I-I guess. Yes, I see a bathroom."

"Then, you're not in the wilderness."

"I'm not going to argue that point because I'm tired." I massage my forehead with my free hand. "I can't believe I let you and Colt talk me into this."

"It's a matter of choice, Tess. Are you going to take this project on or not? You can decide to move home. You can sell the house outright."

"No, there's another party that Ike also gave the house to."

"You still don't know who it is?"

"No, and Twila hasn't called me back yet."

"Tess," Anna whispers, "just trust this path you're on. You might not know the reason right now, but you'll know it when you're supposed to. Don't spend this time living in what you know is comfortable. Start living in the present and the uncomfortable."

Anna's words fall over me. *Start living in the present and the uncomfortable.* I toy with them and allow them to resonate in my mind.

I draw a deep breath in and let it out.

"Listen, I'll call you tomorrow to make sure you're surviving the rugged wilderness and all."

"Funny."

We hang up after we exchange good-byes.

The wind returns, blowing every which direction, and I hear the quiet creak in the house's wood, her bones. The house is talking. She's trying to tell her story. Maybe she's trying to convince me to stay. There are no other words to describe the feeling I have in my gut—the one that says, *Stay.*

I hold my breath and smile. "I can't believe I'm going to say this out loud to a house, but here goes." I sit up straight on the edge of the couch. "You've got to help me," I say to the big house on the hill that overlooks the Tongass Narrows. "I don't know what the hell I'm doing."

The wind screams. The house shrills with excitement, shudders, as if to say, *I accept.*

My eyes fall upon the fireplace that's dark and cold. I decide to follow Anna's advice—to start living.

I pull on my new Ketchikan sweatshirt, feeling more Alaskan by the minute. I brave the rain and wind and grab four logs from the wood box on the porch, trying my best not to get eaten by spiders.

Once inside, I set the logs down, dry my face with my sleeve, and go into the kitchen in search of matches and some old newspapers.

There's a stack of old newspapers in the corner of the kitchen. I find matches in the drawer next to the stove and walk to the fireplace, put the old newspaper at the bottom, place the logs on top of it, and light the match.

While the fire begins its slow start, I move the couch closer. *I will not freeze tonight, Satan.*

The heater doesn't work. I tried it last night. It blew black smoke everywhere, which was probably not a good sign about the central heat.

I need to prepare a list of questions for the contractor, I suppose. At least I can get some rough numbers from a contractor. I'm not out any money. Besides, maybe I can get a few contractors to come out, and then I can take the cheapest bid.

The fire starts to take off and crackles, bringing me out of my thoughts.

The wind howls its long cries, and the rain begins to thunder against the roof once again.

I get underneath a pile of blankets and watch the fire that begins to twist and turn and dance. "I made that," I say to the house, who still occasionally calls out from her dark corners.

Tonight, I don't pull out my phone because I don't want to be reminded of a man I used to love. Last night, I watched his bull rides in Idaho. Watched his face when the camera closed in on it.

Excitement.

Exhilaration.

Hard work.

Determination.

He'd worked hard for those rides.

And who could take that away from him?

Stop living in the past, Tess.

And with those words tucked in tight, I close my eyes and try to get a good night's rest.

But not before a loud bang makes me spring from the couch.

A fire ball ignites in the fireplace and pushes out into the living room.

I scream.

"Thank you, Chief Spalding," I say.

"And remember, get this chimney cleaned at least once a year."

Embarrassed, I say, "I will."

I shut the door behind him. Rest my back against the door and look at the mess of black soot that has plagued the beautiful rock fireplace. I mentally add a to-do list item, *Get chimney cleaned.*

Thankfully, the Ketchikan Fire Department arrived so quickly that there wasn't any more damage to the chimney or the house.

"Listen," I say to the old house, "thanks for not burning to the ground, but please, next time, give me a sign beforehand."

And just as I hear the chief's car tires pull out of the driveway, I hear a knock at the door.

Probably Chief Spalding with some added advice, or maybe he forgot something.

I pull open the door, but it isn't the fire chief. It isn't one of his men.

My heart begins to slam against my chest as I try to find my words. "Casey?"

Casey Atwood steps into the light of the dim porch.

His broad chest.

His long, lean jaw.

His black cowboy hat. My favorite one.

His legs that go on for days.

And he makes my body feel every sensation I'd rather not feel right now.

"What … what are you doing here?" I try not to allow our close proximity to affect my tone.

10

Casey

"I got a letter from Ike," I say. "Can I come in?"

Hesitantly, she pulls open the door, allowing room for me to pass.

I'd be lying if I said I didn't want to take her in my arms and hold her heart against me. Tess's whole body against mine. Her dark hair is pulled back, but strands have fallen into her face, framing it perfectly.

I breathe her in, and I'm reminded of our time when things were so much simpler. Easier.

I see the shock registering on her face.

I've had at least the last fifteen hours to process all of this.

I set my bag down next to the doorway and look around.

It's not in bad shape.

I notice the black soot that sits above the fireplace. "Chimney fire?" I ask.

Tess nods. She's behind me, her mind probably blown, just like mine was. Her arms are across her chest.

"You didn't get the chimney cleaned before you lit a fire?" I give her shit.

She rolls her eyes. "In my defense—never mind." Tess walks to the couch, grabs a blanket. Sits down and stares at the black space of where a fire once was.

I turn and grab a few logs from the wood box outside. Walk them back to the fireplace. Stare up through the chimney and see that it's now clear. I start a fire and don't say much. Once I'm done, I take my bag from the front door and walk down the hallway. I see Tess has taken the room all the way at the end.

"Hey, Morgan?"

"Yes?" she sighs.

"You're at the end of the hall?"

"Yes."

"I'll take the room next to yours then."

She doesn't answer, and I set my bag down in the other room.

House looks stable. I take in the pine walls and walk back into the living room. Sit on the other side of the couch.

There's a long silence that sits between us like an old, well-worn suit—one you're sure you shouldn't wear but you can't help but love what it's made from.

"I assume you took Ike's offer?" she asks.

"I did."

She looks at me from across the couch. "I called a contractor, who's coming by tomorrow."

I nod. "House looks pretty solid, Morgan."

"Please, don't call me that anymore."

"Why?"

A few seconds beat through us like hours.

"It hurts too much."

My heart sinks when she says this. I rest my arm over the back of the sofa.

The fire cracks, and the flames twist and move to the rain that has begun.

"Rains here a lot," she says. "And"—she looks back toward the front door—"there's a leak in the roof. But Stanley, the handyman, fixed it."

I see the bucket but no stream of water. "Well, that's not good. Guess it depends on how old the roof is."

Tess looks back at me. "How long are you going to be here for, Case?"

Case.

She hasn't called me that in years.

"As long as you'll have me."

She tries not to smile.

I miss her smile and everything that goes along with it.

Her dimple.

Her sigh.

The way she overthinks things. The inner dialogue that runs through her head that only those close enough to her get to hear.

I miss her body and the way she used to give it to me only when I needed it most.

Her scent.

The way she allowed me in, trusted me with information she never shared with anyone.

The fire pops.

"Just so we're clear, Casey, I don't need you here. If you want, you can buy me out, or I can buy you out. But I don't think we can do this together."

I'm here for all the wrong reasons.

I'm here to be with Tess.

I'm not here to make money.

I'm here to make amends.

"I'd like to propose an offer." I get more comfortable on the sofa. It isn't half-bad in terms of comfort even if it is circa 1980.

"An offer?"

"We restore this thing together." I look around the living room. "I get one week with you. Just me and you. No work.

No phones. No nothing. Just us in this house for a week. Seven days. Not five. So we're clear."

Tess mulls this around in her head. Her eyes move from mine to the fire and back to me again. "And if we don't restore this place together? I mean, if you leave? Because that seems to be your motto, right?"

Ouch. I shake it off. I don't argue with her. "If I leave, then you get sole ownership, and you keep the profit once we sell it. Simple."

"What makes you think I want to restore this house with you?"

"The profit we'll make. You need the money, right?"

She shakes her head, sits forward, and places her elbows on her knees. Ponders my wager. I can tell because she's biting the inside of her cheek.

Through gritted teeth, she says, "Fine."

I laugh. "You know an Atwood never agrees to a business deal without a handshake."

The warmth of the fire feels good on my old bones. My body took a beating this past week, and I'm not sure how well it'll hold up against Alaska's winter cold, but I'm willing to try.

Tess stares at me. She sticks her right hand out, and I follow her lead.

Our hands touch, and I feel the same connectedness since we were kids. Sparks. Her skin against mine.

The night we made love. The times we had sex just to feel each other, to feel close to one another.

We were younger then. Our hormones were those of teenagers touching her in places only boys dreamed about.

This makes her feel uncomfortable, and she tries to pull her hand away, but I hang on tight. She looks up at me with her big green eyes.

"What do you want from me?" she whispers.

"Seven nights."

"I'd rather have the money," she spits back.

The rain starts in again as she leaves me there with the fire and walks to her bedroom.

"Besides"—she stops before she closes the door—"I'm not so sure Ava would agree with your little agreement. Would she?" And with that, she quietly shuts the door behind her.

I was waiting for that. Part of me hoped she hadn't seen it. In reality, I'm certain America saw the pictures—hell, the world. And not because of who I am, but because of who Ava is. Tess doesn't know the truth of what all went down that night. I don't need to explain it to her. I just need to spend my time here, helping us get better.

The truth is, I saved a lot of ten-thousand-dollar checks and kept them in my dresser drawer at home. I kept so many that the PBR calls me and asks why I haven't cashed them yet. Truth be told, I don't need all the money. I could live simple and survive. But I'm beginning to think that I can't live without Tess.

The next morning, Tess is at the counter, coffee in hand, looking down at a piece of paper.

Another cup sits on the counter, steam pouring out from it.

I take the towel and throw it over my shoulder.

"Shower isn't half-bad. It didn't cave in with the water pressure. Suppose that's a plus," I say.

I look around for a coffeepot.

"The cup of coffee is for you," she says, alluding to the other mug on the counter. Maybe a peace offering. "It's instant. But it gets the job done." She looks down at my bare chest, and I see her face grow pink, but it drains when she sees the bruise on my side. The jeans and belt buckle protect my lower half. "What happened?"

"Landed on my side after a ride. Thank you." I pick up the coffee mug. "You remembered I like my coffee black."

"I remember a lot of things, Case. I just choose to keep those memories behind me." She takes a sip of her own coffee. "Look, I didn't mean the comment I made last night before I went to bed. You have every right to be with another woman. I guess …" She pauses. "I guess it's just never been in my face like that."

I listen. Take another sip of the bitter coffee. "What's on the list today?" I motion with my eyes to the piece of paper on the counter.

"Well, since you're here now, I suppose I need to buy some real food. Soy milk is still not one of your favorites, I guess?" She looks up at me.

I grin. "Still not my thing."

I remember her words when I used her old nickname. *It hurts too much.* The last damn thing I want to do is hurt her.

"Emmitt, the contractor, will be by today to give us an estimate of the work that needs to be done on the house. I was also thinking we might need Wi-Fi, so we don't use all of our data on our phones. So, how about you meet with Emmitt, and I'll go to the store and work on Wi-Fi?"

"Sounds like a plan."

There's a stillness between us, and it's interrupted by the house, which makes a long-drawn-out sound deep within the walls.

"What's that?" I ask.

"She's been doing that a lot lately."

"She?"

Tess shrugs. Looks around the house. "Yes."

But I catch her eyes as they move from my torso.

Her cheeks turn pink again when she grabs her coffee mug from the counter, turns to the sink, washes the mug.

I smile as I watch her backside.

Her hourglass shape. The hips I've taken between my hands before. I remember every square inch of her body. Men don't forget bodies like Tess Morgan's.

"Tess," slips from my mouth before I have time to catch it.

"Yeah?" she says, scrubbing the cup for what seems like a long time.

"It's all right if you look at my body."

She feels the tension between us. I can tell from the way she carries it in her shoulders. I feel it too.

A knock at the door makes her jump. Quickly, she dries her hands.

"I got it," I say.

"A shirt, Casey. You need a shirt."

"Right." I walk back to my bedroom and grab a T-shirt from my bag.

I hear Tess at the door.

I walk up behind her and see a man who looks to be about in his mid-seventies. Surely, this can't be the contractor. He seems too delicate to be doing contractor work. If he fell off a ladder, he'd break every bone in his body.

But his handshake is firm when he reaches for mine.

Emmitt stares at Tess for too long. I'm not sure what to make of it. It's not like it makes me feel uncomfortable, but it's not normal either.

"Well, it's very nice to meet you, Emmitt. My business partner will take it from here."

Business partner. One thing I never thought Tess and I would be.

The rain has stopped for the moment.

She grabs a jacket from behind the door and her purse and leaves. "Call me if you need anything," she says.

Emmitt stands in the middle of the living room and takes it all in, like he's been here before, just collecting memories.

II

The Ladybugs

Was it yesterday that I paid the insurance or the day before? Did I pay it at all?

She looks back at her bank register and can't find the entry, so she drives down to the water department to pay her bill.

"To what do I owe this pleasure, Mrs. Brockmeyer?" Craig says from behind the counter.

"Hello, Craig. I'm here to pay my water bill," Erla says as she retrieves her checkbook from her purse.

Craig cocks his head just a tinge. "Already taken care of."

"What?" Erla stops digging through her purse and looks at Craig.

He pulls up her account on the computer and moves the monitor so that she can see it. "See, paid in full."

She drops her head. "I could have sworn all I did was call you to see if I paid it."

Erla now is too scared to ask if she walked the check in or mailed it in, for panic that if she asks the question out loud, it will make her fears become a reality.

Erla says, "Well, Craig, it was nice visiting with you. Tell your mother I said hello."

"Certainly will, Mrs. Brockmeyer."

As Erla leaves the water company, the pain in her chest returns, and it almost stops her in her tracks.

But through her pain, Erla keeps on walking.

Keeps on breathing.

And keeps on going.

It's a wonder she doesn't drop dead on the spot. She gets into her Cadillac and drives home.

Her resignation letter for The Ladybugs is still on the counter.

That, she remembers.

She remembers Mabe coming over and the two of them eating a gallon of ice cream. She just remembers.

But she doesn't remember paying the water bill.

Strange.

If she calls Dr. Cain and he requests to see her, the whole town will know that Erla Brockmeyer is losing her marbles. She need not cause worry.

It's heartache, she tells herself, as she walks inside her house.

The house phone rings, drawing her attention elsewhere.

"Hello?"

"Hello, Erla. It's Clyda. Please, just hear me out before you say anything. Now, I'm sorry I haven't called. I was trying to allow you some space before breathing down your neck, but, we—no, I—I could really use your help with planning The Ladybug holiday fundraiser. There's so much to be done, and I'm afraid that Delveen and Pearl work slower than two snails in a rat race."

Erla has to giggle to herself. Clyda doesn't put up with nonsense, and she is a workhorse, so Erla could only imagine her patience with Delveen and Pearl.

Erla glances over at her resignation letter on the counter. *Does she really feel that way anymore? Was it the heat of the moment, the aggression, her grief maybe that caused such hostile words? Unprofessional? She sees the word underlined. Really, how could five women in their mid-seventies be unprofessional?* They all work for free and do good for the community, and they all meet at the pizza place once a month. *Unprofessional* might have been a strong word.

"That'll be fine, Clyda," Erla says, but Clyda doesn't hear her because she's rattling off the consequences of high blood pressure and the rate of death, directly related to stress, among seventy-plus-year-old women.

"Clyda," Erla says again.

"What?"

"I'll do it. I'll help."

"Oh! This will be great, Erla. We have a planning meeting tomorrow at Dillon Creek Pizza at noon sharp."

Erla writes this down. She doesn't want to forget, and she thinks, only for a moment, about mentioning her chest pain to Clyda but decides not to. Clyda has enough stress as it is.

"See you tomorrow, Clyda."

"See you tomorrow, Erla. And, Erla?"

"Yes?"

"Thank you."

"You're welcome."

Erla can tell Clyda is relieved when she hangs up the phone. She reaches for the resignation letter on the counter, reads it one last time, and thinks Mabe was right. Sleeping on it, even if it was longer than she planned, really does take the power of these awful words because, now, Erla doesn't feel this way.

Today, she is willing to deal with the bullcrap of Delveen and Pearl.

She's about to throw the letter in the trash when the phone rings again. It's Scarlet. She tosses the piece of paper on the counter before she picks up the phone.

Down on Main Street, Mabe is going to meet Patty at The Rusty Nail. Mabe chose the place in Dillon Creek so that they both could be less conspicuous. Besides, there is no way in hell that Mabe is going to bring Patty back to her house without a thorough and proper interview first, just to make sure this Patty isn't two bricks shy of a load.

Before Mabe approaches, she sees a woman in the window with a hat, scarf, and sunglasses and knows immediately that it's Patty.

Mabe looks down at her own attire and wonders if Betty L. might be on to something. Mabe meets Patty at the window table. Mabe removes her own sunglasses, hat, and scarf.

"You must be Patty?" She sits across the table. She notices the slight tremor in Patty's hands.

Patty looks nice enough. A slim figure in her late twenties, early thirties maybe, perfectly well put together. A soccer mom, maybe a PTO mom. She doesn't look like Patty C. or Sharon B. No, this Patty looks sad, maybe a little lost, and lonely.

Patty removes her sunglasses and her hat. "You must be Mabe? Betty said you'd look just like me."

Mabe can't help but chuckle to herself.

Merry approaches their table. "Mabe, good afternoon. Can I get you two something to eat?"

"Just iced tea for now, Merry, thank you."

Patty shakes her head. "I'm fine, Merry, thank you."

When Merry leaves, Patty looks out the window, and Mabe sees the shame in her eyes, so she reaches across the table and touches Patty's hand. Patty isn't quite sure she's an alcoholic or not, but what Mabe recognizes in the woman who sits across from her are the same feelings she feels inside her heart. Mabe feels Patty's hand shaking in hers.

Tears fill Patty's eyes. "I drink at night until I don't remember."

Mabe drank her beer to subside her feelings—her deep, dark feelings that lived inside her. She tried to bury her grief, her fear, her sadness, her loneliness and mask it with late-night shopping, television dinners, and her beer.

"Do you work?" Mabe asks.

"Not outside the home. I'm a stay-at-home mom. My kids are at school."

"How old are your children?"

"Eight and nine."

Mabe is transported to a simpler time when Francine was that age and John was still alive. Back then, she drank but not like after they both passed on. Nothing was lonelier than that.

"How much do you drink?"

Patty shrugs, too afraid to make eye contact with Mabe. "Box of wine at night."

"Where do you hide all the boxes?" pops out from her mouth because this was Mabe's routine too.

Patty brings her eyes from the window to Mabe, and Patty knows that Mabe absolutely understands.

"After my husband and children go to bed and before I start to drink, I set my alarm to three in the morning. I wake up, take the box out into the garage, stomp it down flat, and put it in the bottom of the recycle bin, and then I go back to bed and sleep until six in the morning when I get up, choke down a cup of coffee because that's what good mothers drink in the morning, and start my day."

Mabe starts to say something, but Patty speaks instead, "And sometimes, when the wine isn't enough, I tap into my husband's vodka that he keeps in the freezer."

And Mabe sees it—Patty almost smiles.

"Turns out, however, that when you try to replace the missing vodka with water in hopes to hide what you've consumed, hard alcohol does not freeze, and water does. My husband was quite surprised when he went to pour his vodka and the top was frozen solid."

Mabe lets out a big laugh.

Patty does too.

"What about you?" Patty asks.

Mabe would rather not tell her story because it's awfully sad, but like she learned in the meetings, in order to keep what she has in her sobriety, she has to give it away. Mabe knows that most people don't react the same way that she and Patty do in the world when it relates to booze.

"My drinking really took off when I lost my husband and my daughter."

"Did you find them?"

Mabe's eyebrow rises. She begins to wonder if Patty might not be as quick on the uptake. "No."

"They left?"

Mabe shakes her head. "They both died."

Patty freezes and stares at her new friend from across the table. "Oh … I'm so sorry."

Mabe sees the tinge of shame that lingers on her face for too long, as if Patty shouldn't drink because she hasn't lost anything yet.

"Honey, in my short time in AA, I've seen people wander in and out, searching for answers to life's troubles. What they don't see is that they have a drinking problem, which has contributed to their difficulties and that alcoholics drink because they like the effects that alcohol produces—no matter life's problems."

A moment of quiet passes between the two women.

While others carry on at their tables, laughing and telling stories and sharing love, Patty says, "Last week, I put whiskey in my coffee." Her lower lip starts to shake. "I told my husband that I wasn't feeling well and couldn't drive the children to school, so he did." Patty's eyes meet Mabe's. "I … I'm afraid, Mabe. I'm afraid that if I continue on this path, I'll make a decision so reckless and stupid that my children will have to pay the price. And I think like this when I'm sober. But the second I put alcohol in my body, I don't care about anything. How … how does that happen so quickly, Mabe? All the regret, the humiliation, the remorse go out the window. I … I'm afraid that when I put alcohol in my body, I can't control what I'll do or what I'll say."

Mabe reaches into her purse and gives Patty a tissue to dab the tears that are beginning to fall.

Mabe is taken back to that night when Tripp and Conroy were killed.

She was the first on the scene.

When the two boys in the field cried out for help, Mabe simply left.

Truth be told, she isn't so sure she drank over the loss of her husband and daughter or if it was more so to mask the fault of what she hadn't done that night.

Maybe it's all of it.

To her core, Mabe identifies with the embarrassment, the penitence, the guilt that Patty talked about.

Mabe gives Patty the truth about herself that she hasn't given in a long time. "Me too."

"What did you do about it?"

"Well, there's a meeting on Mondays at seven thirty in the evening at the Catholic church here in Dillon Creek. Would you like to go with me?"

Patty shrugs. "I suppose it wouldn't hurt."

12

Tess

The cold rushes into my lungs as I make the brisk walk down to Creek Street.

My heart is thumping against my chest, and I can't tell if it's from the walk or Casey Atwood.

Anna is working today, and I don't want to interrupt her.

Things have drastically changed in the past twenty-four hours.

How could you, Ike? I think to myself.

I think about all the things I'd tell Ike right now if I could. Forgiveness?

Hope?

It's all a crock of shit, Ike. All of it.

I stop at the ATM Olive pointed out and get cash. Then, I head back down to Olive's. Inside, it smells like freshly brewed coffee, and instead of immediately shopping, I take a seat at the bar with Olive.

"Coffee?" she asks.

"It smells divine. Please."

She smiles. I can see how she's related to Emmitt. They have the same eyes. They twinkle when they smile.

She pours me a cup. "Did my granddad make it by?"

"He did. He's there now."

She sets the mug of steaming hot coffee down in front of me. Hands me creamer in a small silver tin and packets of sugar.

"Is someone at the house with him?"

"Yes, my ..." I pause, thinking about how I used the term earlier. "Business partner." It sounds much clearer, less convoluted than *childhood boyfriend who really wasn't my boyfriend.*

"Oh." She wipes down the counter, waiting for an explanation but also not wanting to pry.

"It's a long story. What kind of time do you have on your hands?" I smile.

"A lot."

"Well ..." I take a sip of coffee and revel in its thick, rich goodness. "Now, this is a cup of coffee."

"You've got to make it strong here in Alaska, or most people might not survive winter."

I set my mug down. "Casey Atwood is his name, my business partner and"—I'm not quite sure how to describe our past—"longtime friend. And, well, Ike left us his house in his will."

Olive places her hand on her hip, thinks on it. "Casey Atwood—that name sounds so familiar."

Could be his bull riding. Could be Ava, which makes my stomach grow queasy as I remember the photos of them, or it could be the video with him and the little boy. But I don't say any of this.

"Anyway, we're here, trying to fix up the house so we can sell it."

"Sell it? Why would you want to do that?"

I'm taken aback by her question. *Why wouldn't we want to sell it?*

"Would you keep it?" I ask, curious.

"Oh, if the walls could talk in that house, they'd have stories to tell."

Curious, I ask, "What kind of stories?"

"It's housed presidents. Famous movie stars. Writers. Great tribal leaders. And some secrets."

"Really?"

"The Isner Inn was the premier place to stay in Ketchikan back in the late 1930s, '40s, and '50s—when Ike's parents ran it."

I make a mental note to Google the Isner Inn.

"I'm almost certain that the Isners were going to turn the house into a historical landmark before Ike's father fell ill. So much history of our town exists in the Isner residence. Ike's great-grandparents, when they had the house, took in natives who didn't want to conform to the American way back in the 1800s. I know the state of Alaska has wanted to purchase the house for quite some time, but the Isners weren't willing to sell."

"What?"

Olive nods. Leans on the counter. Takes a sip of her coffee. "You know, Esther could give you more information on this."

"She works down at the Tlingit Visitor Center, right?"

"That's right."

I finish my coffee and pull out a hundred-dollar bill. "For groceries yesterday and today and coffee this morning."

Olive takes the hundred-dollar bill, and I go and shop for food.

Once I'm done, I place everything on the counter.

"I think the hardware store sells coffeepots," Olive says as she rings me up.

"Oh," I say, "do you have any Pendleton Whiskey?"

"I do." She reaches beneath the counter. "For Stan?" she asks.

"He wouldn't take my money yesterday, so he said a bottle of this whiskey would do."

"Sounds about right. Do you need a ride up the hill?"

My shoulders drop. "I didn't think of that."

Olive looks outside, grabs a notepad, and sticks a piece of tape to it. She scribbles, *Be back in five.*

Olive sticks the piece of paper to the door. "Come on."

"Oh, Olive. This isn't necessary."

"It's what we do for friends." She holds open the door.

Friends, I say to myself and see how the word feels.

At twenty-seven, I just expected to have the same friends I'd had for years. The friends I've had in Dillon Creek. The ones I grew up with. It's now that I realize how true Anna's words are. Maybe I'm meant for more. Maybe all of these moments in my life are preparing me for something bigger. Like meeting people in my life I'm supposed to walk this journey with.

We arrive at the Isner house, and Olive peers through the windshield. "Hasn't changed a bit." She looks at me. "No offense. I mean, you did just move in."

"None taken." I grab the groceries in the back.

Olive gets out to help. "Looks like Granddad is still here."

I eye Olive. "Do you think that's a good thing or a bad thing?"

"Depends on how you look at it. He's very thorough, and he will make sure the house is in tip-top shape by the time he's done with it."

I can't help but see dollar signs.

We walk inside, and I set the bags on the kitchen counter.

"I can't thank you enough, Olive, for all your help."

"Got me out of the store for a minute." She bumps my shoulder with hers as she goes to leave.

Olive feels familiar. Comfortable. As if our conversations were like favorite old sweaters—broken in, warm, and expected. They're unrehearsed, and I settle into them as if we'd had them for years.

I decide I really like Olive.

Maybe I'll ask her to do dinner sometime.

It's late afternoon when I establish that we can get internet connection at the house. It'll be seventy dollars a month. But do we really need internet? Maybe I will be less tempted to use my phone to do mindless scrolling if I know I'm paying an arm and a leg for it.

Casey comes through the front door, soaked, as I sit by the fire he made this morning.

"Thanks for the fire," I say as he takes off his coat, boots, and cowboy hat.

"You're welcome."

He takes his spot on the sofa. A good four feet from me.

"What did Emmitt say?"

"Roof is good. Just a few repairs. The house is well built though. The central heating needs a whole new system. That won't be cheap. New floor on this level. The subfloor is toasted. All new windows if we want to hold the heat. That, he said, needs to be done sooner than later with winter coming."

"Did he give you a quote?"

"No, not yet. Said he'd get back to me tomorrow."

Casey settles into the sofa. I watch his shoulders come down just a few inches, as if he's tense, as if he's carrying something with him and he's not sure how to proceed.

"Are you all right?"

"Yeah." But he bites his tongue.

We've been … whatever we've been for a long time. More than half our lives. I know when he's holding back. I don't feel it's my place to push even though I want to.

"Are you all right?" he asks as the fire crackles.

"A question for the ages," I whisper. "Listen, I checked into internet, and it's going to be seventy dollars a month. I'm okay with working off data instead of the expense. Are you?"

And then I realize who I'm asking. Casey Atwood only carries a phone because his mother makes him.

The look on his face makes me laugh out loud. It's half-goofy and half-*what the hell did you just ask me.*

His expression changes when he sees me laugh, and I try my best to look away, but for the first time in a long time, I can't.

Casey drops his head.

When we were younger, I'd drape my hand over his face because I didn't want him to see me laugh. Only half of my smile works, and the other half never has.

But I'm also not the same insecure girl I was as a child. I know I've changed, but maybe I don't drape my hand over his face because I'm terrified of what it will do to my heart once I touch him.

"I've been thinking," I say. "We should probably figure out our finances and what we'd like to put into the house. Keep it fair and equitable. What we put in is what we get out."

Casey doesn't say anything. He just rests his head on his hand and stares at me. "Whatever you want, Tess."

Under his stare, I feel as though he sees every last inch of me, like a mosaic strung together by wire and all the little pieces left behind fall in a trail behind me. He pieces those together too—the pieces I'd rather forget.

His gaze makes me feel exposed, and unwillingly, I feel the need to speak. "I have about seventeen thousand in my savings. And"—this hurts me to say—"I've filed for unemployment. I will receive about twelve hundred a month until I find a new job."

"Will you be okay if you're not teaching?" he asks.

I'm not sure. I've always felt like it was my calling to be a teacher. Like God set forth my goal at an early age.

Instead of saying this, I shrug. "I'll have to be."

Casey doesn't say anything for a few seconds. "I have about seventy thousand in uncashed checks in the top drawer of my dresser at home."

"Excuse me, what?"

Casey laughs, and I watch as his Adam's apple slides up and down his throat. A place I've kissed too many times to count.

A rush of heat pushes through me, and I try not to show Casey, so I turn my gaze back to the fire.

The wind kicks up and casts its anger against the house. She screams. Her tough, old bones move and bend against the resistance.

"Have a little over five in savings."

I turn my head to face him. "Five thousand?"

Slowly, he shakes his head. "Hundred thousand."

"Casey Atwood, what the hell do you spend your money on?"

He laughs again. "I don't need much."

"So, you're telling me, you have over half a million just … sitting." I gawk.

"I have investments too."

We're quiet for a moment, and then I say, "What does the PBR think about your uncashed checks?"

"They're hollering at me to cash them."

"Why the hell don't you?"

"Been busy, I guess."

"You've been too busy to cash seventy thousand dollars in winnings?" I sigh. Fall back against the couch. "You're unbelievable."

The rain begins softly again, but I know this is just a warning for the evil intent the weather has on its agenda for later this afternoon and early evening. I've learned this about Alaska.

"Tess, I'll do whatever you want me to do."

I drop my head. "Don't say that. Don't say that to me. Clearly, you don't need the money, Case, and if you aren't here for the money, then why are you here?"

13

Casey

Because I wasn't there when you needed me most, is what I should say. But she's not ready for the honest answer, so I feed her a line. "Investment opportunity."

"And what if you lose the wager?" she asks.

Her eyes burn into mine.

I have flashes of us as kids—when life was simple, not as hard, when our biggest worry was what assignments were due at school or eating something we didn't like for dinner. Not our brothers dying and all the ramifications that went along with that. Broken hearts. Broken families. And all the memories we'd just as soon not remember. I'm reminded of Tess's strength, her tenaciousness, and her unwillingness to give up.

She said she wanted to ride a steer. We were fifteen or so. I put Bulldog in the chute because he was just that—a bulldog. Docile. Slow. And didn't give a shit what you had him do as long as he got his grain. Got Tess on him. She didn't want to wear the helmet, but I made her anyway.

I explained to her the basics.

One hand.

Dancing partner.

Balance.

It was a fifteen-minute crash course on bull riding.

But it was her first time on a steer, so honestly, I wasn't expecting much from either of them, but Tess was convinced she needed to ride a steer.

"When you're ready," I told her, "give Cash the nod, and he'll open the chute."

Conroy came out from the house just as Tess gave Cash the nod.

"You know she's liable to kill herself, right?" Conroy knew Tess. Knew she wouldn't give up, come what may.

In one second flat, she was down on the ground.

"Again," she said as she pulled herself up from the ground. She went back to the chute, climbed the fence, and got back on the steer.

"Come on, Morgan," Conroy called.

"Remember, balance," I said to her.

She flipped me off.

Conroy, Cash, and I all laughed.

Tess did this seventeen times.

On the seventeenth ride, filthy from sixteen falls before with a bruised ego and a cut above her eye, she rode Bulldog as if her life had depended on it. She made it to ten seconds.

I fell in love with her that day. I thought, no matter what, she'd fight for us because that was who she was.

But there are some things that happen between two people that only God can forgive, I suppose. I thought I was doing the right thing at the right time. My biggest regret in life is getting in my truck and driving us to Oregon that night. I should have fought for us. But I was a baby, just fresh out of high school with dreams the size of Texas.

I give her an honest answer this time. "I'm in it for the long haul, and I won't lose, Tess Morgan."

The fire cracks, and the wind starts again.

"Does the rain ever stop?" I ask.

As I stare out the wall of windows, watching the world wash away, it makes me think about the picture I saw downstairs of Ike and a few others. What I don't tell Tess is that the woman in the picture, holding the toddler, she looks just like her.

She's probably seen it, right?

If she's not concerned, I shouldn't be. I don't tell her that when I saw it, it made my stomach clench. I recognized Ike and now Emmitt. But it's who I didn't recognize that makes me feel uneasy.

"Do you want some wine, Case?" she asks.

I'm not really a wine guy—I'm more of a Coors guy—but I don't tell her this because it's like a peace offering.

"Yes."

Tess stands and walks into the kitchen behind us.

I hear the cork pop.

She walks back into the living room with two red Solo cups.

"They were out of wineglasses at Olive's." She smiles down at me. "Do you even like wine?" she asks. "I mean, legally, I don't think we've ever drunk together." She sits down on her side of the sofa.

"It's all right."

She nods as she puts the Solo cup to her mouth.

"You miss the kids? At school, I mean." I push myself against the corner of the sofa and rest my arm on the back. Open my body to her, an attempt to let her know that I'm not going anywhere.

There's a smug smile that appears. "Yes."

I trace her neckline with my eyes and remember, only for a second, what her skin felt like beneath my fingers. Her tender skin felt like silk against my rough, callous hands.

She's hesitant—I can see it in her eyes. Her lips part only for a moment and then quickly come together again. She takes a sip of wine and sets the cup down by her feet.

Tess begins to speak again, "There are injustices that surround everyone every day. I just felt like I was supposed to be a teacher. I never thought I'd lose my job. And especially to a woman who has one foot in the grave." Tess smiles against her sadness. But she looks to me, through me. "That video—" She stops.

I know what she's going to say, and it makes my heart seize.

"Did you ever—"

"Every day since ..." I whisper. I take a big swig of the wine and nearly finish the cup.

Tess nods. Bites her cheek. Her eyes search the fire in front of us—maybe for answers, maybe for solace.

I try to console her heart. Fix it. Make it whole again. "I almost told him not to be a bull rider."

Tess's head moves to me in one quick motion. "Why?"

I laugh—not because it's funny, but because I'm trying to buy my heart some time. "He said I was his hero." I shake my head and stare down at my hands. "I don't feel like a hero, Tess. I feel like a guy who hides behind a bull in order to run from whatever he needs to."

My eyes meet hers. Her body perfectly still, she stares back and bites her cheek again. What I want to do is reach out to her, hold her. Take back every-fucking-thing that happened between us and ask for a do-over. But I can't.

"We're all imperfect, Case. No matter if we run into burning buildings, fight crime, fight for our country. We're all imperfect humans, fulfilling a hole deep inside us. When I work with kids, it helps fill my hole, and I think when you ride bulls, you help little boys reach for their dreams."

Cowboys don't cry. I didn't cry when my brother died. The last time I cried was when I was ten and I was grazed by a horn of a steer. My brother had dared me to ride the meanest steer we had. It was actually a bet. I won a hundred bucks that day. I'd ridden the eight seconds, and I had an open wound to prove it. It also hurt like a son of a bitch. Ten stitches from Dr. Cain and an earful from my mom.

"Well, I'll start dinner." Tess stands, pushing our sadness to the floor, the holes we're trying to fill.

I stand, too, and tower over her. Take a step toward her, and I'm not sure why I do this, but I can't help myself. We're inches apart.

"What are you doing, Casey?" she whispers. Her lips barely parted, she looks up at me with her soft, protective green eyes.

I push the piece of hair that's fallen to her face behind her ear. "I kissed Ava that night because she reminded me so much of you."

"And?" Tess barely whispers. "Did she kiss like me?"

A response I was not expecting.

I reach up and run my fingers along her jawline, my body fully aware of hers. "Not even close."

Her phone starts to ring, and it breaks us apart.

"I should get that." She motions to the kitchen.

Tess grabs her Solo cup and leaves me standing here.

She answers her phone as I walk outside to the wood box and get some more wood for the fire.

By the time I come back in, she's off the phone and cutting up chicken.

"Can I help?" I ask, leaning in the doorway of the kitchen.

"No, I'm fine."

Tess has shut down again. My body still feels the aftereffects of us.

A text message sounds from my phone.

It's from Garrison.

> Garrison: *You made the finals. Did you see? You fucker.*

I knew I was a contender, but I didn't think it would happen. I check the PBR website and see my name—second name from the top after last weekend.

"Everything okay?" Tess asks.

I look up at her. "Yeah, fine."

I run my fingers over my lips. Giddiness building inside me.

What does this mean? This means, every weekend from now until November, I'll have to leave to ride to keep my spot in the World Finals, which means, one, I'm going back on my commitment to Tess and, two, I'll lose the bet, and I won't get the seven days with her.

I never cared about the money in the first place.

The date for the PBR World Finals is the first weekend in November.

I run my hand along my chin. My heart starts to jackhammer against my chest.

"Yeah, fine doesn't reflect the face you're making now," Tess says, rinsing the chicken.

I also know Tess. The bull riding has always scared her. But I also know she's scared because of love.

Shoving my phone back in my pocket, I take our Solo cups and fill them with wine. There's a small area between the island she's cutting chicken on and the counter. Taking my time, I squeeze between the small space and am careful not to touch her backside, but if this gives me another few seconds of her scent, her body, I'll take it.

What are you doing, Casey? If you're going to leave, you'd better make damn sure you don't break her heart again.

Quickly, I remove myself from the space, go to the other side of the island, and set her Solo cup out in front of her.

"I noticed there are no televisions here," is my best attempt at conversation.

"No, I haven't seen any."

Her phone sounds, and she peeks over at the screen. "You made the finals?"

My head drops to the side. "You get PBR updates?"

"That's not the point of the question, Casey." She blushes and tries to hide her fluster. She takes another sip of wine.

"Say something, Tess."

"Looks like I win the bet." A plastic smile spreads across her face as she moves the chicken, potatoes, garlic, and green onions to a baking dish.

I don't say whether I'm going or not, and I also don't counter her statement.

After dinner is ready, we sit down on the couch to eat in front of the fire.

I ask her again, "Since when do you get PBR updates?"

She chews. It's longer than expected, so I think she's buying time to drum up an answer.

"There's a lot you don't know about me, Casey."

"Would you just admit it?"

"Admit what?"

I smile. "You get PBR updates, so you can see what I'm up to."

"Don't flatter yourself." She takes another bite and then a sip of wine to wash it down.

"Admit it."

She shakes her head. "I have a boyfriend in the PBR, okay?"

Maybe it's the wine, or maybe it's her in the fire's light, but I move my plate to the coffee table and slowly scoot to her.

Don't do this, Casey. If you leave for the finals, you will fuck her up.

She allows this, so our bodies are barely an inch apart. She leans back, and I'm almost over the top of her, our mouths and our bodies in close proximity.

I stare down into her eyes and see the broken little girl I saw in the picture downstairs.

It takes everything in me not to kiss her, so instead, I lean into her ear and whisper, "I don't think your boyfriend would approve of this position we're in, Miss Morgan."

My chest moves closer to hers, and I'm not sure if it's my heart that's pounding, her heart, or ours together.

When I reluctantly move, she grabs my shirt and pulls my mouth to hers, and I fall into her.

I lose myself in her scent, her mouth, and the way her tongue feels against mine, like old memories and fire. A fire I

131

only feel for Tess. A fire that's burned for so many years now that I can't keep track.

The taste of red wine.

More of her I want, which only deepens the kiss.

I need to stop this.

But I can't.

It's when I feel her hands on my chest and I start to harden against her that I pull away, breathless and almost unable to control myself. My body is pulsating.

"I'm sorry, Tess," is all I say before taking my plate and walking to the kitchen.

14

The Ladybugs

Nobody says anything about Erla's incident at the last meeting. But Mabe, Clyda, Delveen, and Pearl are gathered around the table in the back of Dillon Creek Pizza, preparing for the holiday fundraiser. Erla sits too.

Thank goodness for The Lunch Guys playing dice in front of the window, breaking up the silence between the five women.

Finally, Erla says, "I was thinking of having a Santa's village theme, ladies. Where children can sit on Santa's lap for free and receive a gift. We can sell pies and candles, hot chocolate and hot cider, and Christmas wreathes. Have a silent auction."

The whole group collectively sighs once Erla speaks, and they begin to laugh, joke, and get to work.

The tension that hovered above them disappears.

Erla isn't leaving The Ladybugs after all.

She had a moment. An awful moment, and maybe Erla was right to some degree. Perhaps it was a wake-up call for Delveen and Pearl because after an hour of planning, neither Delveen nor Pearl make any mention of cheating, divorcing, Viagra, or small-town scandal.

All five women leave Dillon Creek Pizza with to-do lists and things to gather for their planning meeting next week.

Planning parties is Erla's sweet spot, and she enjoys it from start to finish.

Whether The Ladybugs are holding a community event or collecting money to help kids, it doesn't matter.

As The Ladybugs disperse and go their separate ways, Mabe puts on her hat, sunglasses, and scarf.

Erla leans over and whispers, "Mabe, I thought the AA meetings were in the evenings on Monday?"

Mabe turns to her old friend and cousin with surprise. Does everyone in the world know that she attends AA meetings in this attire? Mabe thinks about it for a moment. Not many women in their seventies, wearing a hat, scarf, and sunglasses, walk in Dillon Creek without being noticed. What a dumb idea it was in the first place—the disguise, not the meetings.

"If you must know, Erla"—Mabe sighs, slightly annoyed—"I'm headed to Fortuna to speak with someone. Official AA stuff."

Now, Erla knows if Mabe adds the word *official* to anything, it really means *mind your own business*, but Erla doesn't care. Someone she has left in this world, who she loves with all her heart, is finally doing something good for herself.

"Good on you, Mabe."

The truth is, Mabe finally has someone to help. Sure, Mabe helps Erla. The Ladybugs help the community. But this is different. This help with Patty, that Betty threw in her lap, finally gives her purpose.

Erla looks around for her car.

Panic begins to fill her insides.

Oh dear, she thinks. *Where in the world did I park my car?*

Confusion begins to set in, followed by fear. She doesn't remember driving it here.

The pain in her chest starts again, but it isn't as severe as it is sometimes.

Mabe is driving by and stops. "What'd you lose?"

"I ... I can't find my car."

"Honey"—Mabe's face grows an off shade of white—"you didn't drive here, remember? You decided to walk."

Oh. That's right. Erla plays it off well.

One thing about Erla is, she is a chameleon. She can fit in anywhere, blend in anywhere. She can tell you anything, and you'll believe it. Some might call the last one manipulation. But Erla only uses that special skill set when it is absolutely necessary—for instance, like now.

"Get in. I'll drive you home."

"No, no. Go to Fortuna on your business, and I'll walk home. Truly, I'm fine, Mabe." Erla laughs it off. "I'll call you when I get home, so you don't worry."

Mabe is hesitant, but it is Dillon Creek after all. If she gets lost from here to there, someone will help her. Besides, she does have the cell phone she never uses, and if she does wander off, Mabe can track her down with the Find My app. Sometimes, Mabe is grateful that technology has always been in her wheelhouse.

"All right, honey."

On her way to Fortuna, Mabe allows her fear to take her places she'd rather not go. She plays *Dillon Creek Echo* headlines in her head.

ELDERLY WOMAN DIES IN THE ELEMENTS

LOST ELDERLY WOMAN SUCCUMBS TO INJURIES

ERLA BROCKMEYER DIES OF GRIEF

And perhaps this is just Mabe's subconscious mind, reactivated by the wrongdoing of leaving two severely injured boys in the field to die that night. Mabe swallows the guilt one more time and drives to Fortuna to meet Patty.

It's just a left and a right, Erla. Goodness' sake, how can you be so stupid?

Erla looks around at the houses that surround her. None of them look familiar.

How did you get so turned around?

Don't call anyone, she tells herself. *That will just cause unnecessary worry.*

But the pain in her chest continues.

"Erla?" Betty Lewindowski comes out from her house. "Honey, did you lose something?"

Bingo! Betty lives two houses down from Erla.

And there, at the end of the street, is Erla's house.

"Have you seen Millie?" Erla lies. *Please, God, forgive me.*

"No, I haven't. Would you like me to help you look?"

"Oh, heavens no. I'll check at home one more time. Thanks, Betty."

Betty waves from her steps.

The pain in Erla's chest subsides, and she makes her way back home. And for the first time in a long time, Erla is scared she might be losing all of her marbles.

Mabe calls Erla as she's walking through the front door.

"Hello?"

"You didn't call."

"I just walked in the door, Mabe."

"I pegged you as dead, and all the headlines that played through my head—sweet Jesus!"

"What?"

"Never mind."

Mabe sighs. "What took you so long?"

Erla lies again, but in her defense, there is also some truth, "I was talking to Betty."

"Betty? What'd she say?"

Everyone knows that Betty Lewindowski is Mabe's AA sponsor, but nobody talks about it. And Mabe thinks it's one big old secret.

"Nothing, Mabe. Everything is fine. I'm home safe." Erla can feel Mabe's tension on the line. "Come on, Mabe. It's just grief. Don't worry about me. I'll probably outlive you." Erla laughs.

"Let's hope so." Mabe finally comes around. "Lord knows, I'd be a mess without you, Erla," she whispers.

Erla's heart curls into a ball as she tries to fight off the guilt of not telling Mabe that she in fact did get lost—sort of—and that she has shortness of breath, all to keep Mabe Muldoon from worry.

But sometimes, it's just easier to lie. "I'm fine, Mabe."

Later that day, Scarlet calls, and Erla tells her granddaughter all about the Christmas fundraiser meeting and what happened at church last Sunday. She skips the part about chest pains, getting lost, her lack of memory. After all, there isn't much Scarlet can do, being this far away, and she needn't cause worry to her granddaughter.

"I'm coming home for Christmas this year, Grandma. I'll let you know when I firm up dates."

"Oh, Scarlet. That will be wonderful," Erla says as tears form in her eyes.

Erla does remember a certain boy that Scarlet has always had a thing for. Now that she's divorced, maybe there's an opportunity for a new start.

"What about that Cash Atwood? He was always such a pleasant young man."

Erla isn't senile yet. She knows Cash has been known to be reckless and might drink a little too much at times, but he's got great parents, and Erla has always believed that second chances are important.

"Oh, Grandma. I was just a girl. Besides, I'm sure he's moved on, just as I have."

"Don't be so sure, honey."

"Anyway, I love you, Grandma. I'll call you tomorrow."

"Love you too, sugar."

It's later into the evening when Erla gets a knock at the door. Quickly, she opens the door, and her stomach falls to her knees.

"Chief McBride? What brings you here so late in the evening?"

15

Tess

What are you thinking, Tess?
It's the wine.

Once, I read a story about a bottle of wine that was laced with cocaine, and the woman who purchased the wine, after she ingested it, had to be rushed to the hospital.

I pull myself from the floor, grab my plate and Solo cup, and follow Casey into the kitchen.

I try not to picture Casey with his shirt off, and this only makes things between us more awkward as we move like robots throughout the kitchen, trying to clean up.

"You know, Case. I've got this. I'll clean up the kitchen," I say.

"Are you sure?" His voice is deeper than it normally is.

"Yeah, good change of pace."

He jumps on the opportunity and walks back to the living room. He takes his spot on the sofa, and knowing Casey, it isn't that he doesn't want to be helpful; he's just trying to make things easier on me.

A loud crack of thunder makes me jump, and the noise filters through my bones.

The wind blows, hollering around the perfect edges of the old house.

But she fights back with her groans and creaks. Her ability to adapt to change.

I finish the dishes just as the house goes dark.

"Tess, are you all right?" I hear Casey's voice.

"Yeah." I grab a glass of water from the tap as the fire's light guides me back into the living room to the roaring fire, where Casey is adding a few more logs.

Darkness surrounds us, and the orange flickers give us light.

Casey makes his way to the window just as the sky ignites with an unnatural bright light.

I, too, move to the window and stand a safe distance from him, looking down below to Ketchikan and the Tongass Narrows, waiting for the lightning to return.

Watching the town, the body of water, the unassuming world below us, I'm moved by the powers of the world and my inability to control my surroundings.

No matter what, I can't control any of this. Not the lightning. Not the rain. Not the wind. And certainly not Casey Atwood.

A loud crack of thunder vibrates the floor below my feet, and it rolls on longer than I'd like to believe.

"It's beautiful," Casey says.

But when I look at him, he's not looking down at the town; he's looking right at me.

In the dark, he whispers, "Just so we're clear, Tess, I didn't pull away from you because of you. I pulled away because of me."

Isn't that always the way of things? I nod and don't say this to him.

"Good night, Casey." I tear myself away from the only man I've ever loved, knowing he'll leave to make the finals because that's what cowboys do.

I wake up, feeling refreshed after the best night of sleep I've had in months. Pushing the covers back, I look at my phone to see what time it is. It's still so early as I pull myself from the heaven of warmth and walk down to the kitchen.

Whether he's here or he's gone, Tess, you can't control that as much as you can control the lightning.

But when I round the corner just out of my bedroom, Casey is standing there, reading a newspaper, standing at the counter.

He looks up at me as I enter the kitchen, and I see his eyes rake over my body. Thankfully, this time, he has a shirt on.

"Good morning," he says. "I hope you take your coffee the same. Two sugars and that hippie shit."

"Soy milk?" I purse my lips and walk to the island, standing opposite of where he's standing. "Thank you," I say as I put the mug to my lips.

"Yeah, hippie shit."

"So, I was thinking, once we get the estimate from Emmitt, we can discuss the priorities of what needs to be done first," I say, cutting to the chase.

"Yeah, sounds good."

"All right." I look down at my coffee and shrug. "Even if it's instant coffee, it's not that bad. I meant to go by the hardware store and buy a coffeepot yesterday."

Casey reaches into his wallet and throws a stack of cash down on the island counter.

"What's that for?"

He shrugs. "Food. Coffeepots. Whatever we need it for."

"You carry that much cash on you?"

"No, but the walk to the bank in town was steeper than I'd thought."

"When did you walk down?"

"Last night. Needed to clear my head."

"In the thunderstorm?"

"No, I waited for it to slow down."

I look down at the wad of one-hundred-dollar bills.

Casey pulls out his phone and touches his screen several times. "Emmitt e-mailed me the estimate. Just forwarded it to you. He's going to start renovations today."

"Today?"

Casey looks at me. "I hope that's okay?"

"But I thought we were going to talk about it? Prioritize."

I grab my phone and pull up my e-mail. My eyes grow just as big as the zeros that I see in the estimate. Panic fills my chest. I can't afford this. I can't even afford half.

"Casey"—my voice fails me—"I can't afford this."

"I can," he says like it's no big deal. Like he's agreed to go to the store and grab some milk and cheese.

"No."

"What do you mean, no?"

"This isn't what I agreed to."

"Tess, we agreed to do the renovations."

"But that was before I saw the estimate." I count the zeros in my head, just to be sure I have it right.

Emmitt's broken it down into each job.

"Would you just let me do this?" he asks, his eyes pleading.

I shake my head. "No. No way. If I'm a partner in this, I pay half." *Or somehow get the price lower*, I think to myself.

"Why do you have to be so stubborn about things, Tess? Why can't you just accept help?"

My mouth falls open. "Says the bull rider ..."

He ignores my comment. "Besides, it's too late. I've already sent in the payment."

"You did what? I can't believe you'd do this without talking to me first."

"Says the woman who rides a steer without prior knowledge."

"You're impossible!" I huff and walk back to my bedroom and slam the door.

Shit!

I roll my eyes, walk back out to the kitchen, grab my coffee from the counter, and say, "I like the hippie shit!" And I storm back to my bedroom.

I pace. I'm so mad.

I look at the estimate again. Even if I help with labor and put ten grand into this, it's still not going to cover half. But once we sell the house, if we ask for twenty thousand more than the cost of the renovations, I can give that back to Casey.

Hastily, I pull my checkbook out, write a check for ten thousand, and open my door again. I walk out to the kitchen.

My heart thumps against my chest with anger. "Here's the deal." I push the check across the counter to him. "You take this. I will help with the labor, and then, when we sell the place, we're going to ask twenty thousand more than the renovations. That will pay you back for the portion I can't come up with up front. If you can't agree to that, then there's no deal." I cross my arms over my chest and bite down on the inside of my cheek as I wait for his answer.

A smile begins to form on his face as he watches me.

This pisses me off even more. "I always pay my own way, Casey—you know that."

"Can I have time to think about it?" he asks.

"Fuck you, Casey."

I stomp back to my bedroom to grab my shower stuff, storm back out of my room and to the bathroom we share, and slam the door behind me for good measure.

Who in the hell does he think he is? Mr. Moneybags?

I slide my T-shirt over my head and shimmy out of my panties.

There's a knock at the bathroom door.

"*What?*" I say.

"Your mom is calling on your phone."

I press the T-shirt to my body, covering up my essentials, open the door, grab my phone from Casey, and then shut the door.

"Tess"—he sighs against the door—"I'm sorry for not talking to you first."

"It's a little late for that, Casey Atwood." I hit Ignore and turn on the shower to drown out his voice.

"But," he yells through the door, "this is a business deal! In order to move forward, we need to invest."

I turn off the water. Cover my body back up with my T-shirt. "What happened to *I'm not in it for the money?*" I make a snide face as I give his words back to him. I sigh. "Casey, all I'm asking is that you talk to me before you agree to do anything that includes my livelihood. Give me a chance to say my piece first."

"You're right. I'm sorry."

"Look, if you're trying to right our past with this little business venture, you can't just throw money at it and make it better."

"You're right."

And with that, I turn the water back on, and I'm a little less angry than I was five minutes ago. I drown out my inability to stay mad at Casey Atwood.

It's late afternoon when the supplies start arriving for the renovations. As we agreed, Casey asks the delivery guys to put them downstairs, so they don't get wet.

Emmitt will start the work tomorrow, as winter is fast approaching. We agree to have Sundays off, but he and his crew will work Monday through Saturday.

"If you'd like Saturday off, too, to be with your family, Emmitt, please feel free to take it off."

He chuckles into the phone. "Alaska in the winter, don't you rem—" Emmitt cuts himself off.

There's a long pause.

"Remember, is what you were about to say. Why?" I ask, confused.

"What I meant was, you won't forget it." There's an unease to his voice. Something has shifted, and I can't quite put my finger on it.

"Oh."

I don't know Emmitt well enough to understand his communication style. What side he stands on politically—not that it matters. Where he goes for Thanksgiving, Christmas. What he does when he goes home at night. I don't know Emmitt at all, so I take his words at surface level.

"You'll have to excuse my age, Tess. Sometimes, it has a mind of its own." There's a short pause. "Anyhow, we will get the work done. Don't you worry about me."

"All right then, it's settled. Also, one other thing."

I hear a sharp suck of air on the other end of the line.

"Would you be willing to cut off some of the labor costs if I'm willing to help with the labor of the renovations? It's part of my agreement with Casey."

It's silent for a moment.

"Emmitt?"

"Uh … yes, of course. Quite honestly, Tess, I wasn't going to charge for the labor."

"But why?"

Again, a long pause. I'm starting to believe he's either holding many secrets or many lies, or maybe he's hard of hearing.

"Ike was an old friend. This house has been in Ketchikan since before I was a boy. We consider the Isner house to be a historical landmark—even if it's not. It's important to us, our people, that we keep it in good working condition."

"It was in the quote. Emmitt, we can't *not* pay you for your time." I sigh.

"It's a programmed thing when she runs the billing. The system automatically includes the labor based on the job. Anyhow, Tess, I'll see you tomorrow."

"Emmitt?" I ask before he hangs up. "Thank you for agreeing to take this on."

"Wouldn't have it any other way."

"Good-bye."
"Good-bye."

16

Casey

Four more rides. Four more weekends until the PBR World Finals.

That's four weekends that I'm riding and then back to Ketchikan on Sundays to help Tess through the week.

And if I win the finals, shit, that's a one-million-dollar purse. Not that I care about the money, but a million dollars wouldn't be a bad thing. Not to mention, endorsement deals. Then, could I be done with bulls?

Could I walk away from a career that I've been doing for what seems like all my life?

The smell of the arena.

The adrenaline rush.

The feeling of euphoria coming off a good ride.

The fans.

The roar of the crowd.

But the travel.

In and out of airports every weekend.

Stranded on puddle jumpers, just trying to make my way to the next event.

"Hey." I hear Tess say from behind me, and I turn to her.

I'm in my bedroom. I just got out of the shower, a towel around my hips. I know where her eyes go. To the scar on my shoulder from tearing my rotator cuff—twice. The long scar just below my rib cage on the right side where a nighthawk grazed me five years ago.

But I'll retire at an early age; my body though will be of an aging man.

"Noticed you've been limping today." Her eyes avoid mine.

"Sore."

"Emmitt says he's not charging labor because the house means too much to the community."

I nod. "Seems like a good guy."

Tess bites the inside of her cheek as I move past her to the closet and pull a T-shirt off the hanger.

"Can I help you with something, Tess?" I know she's got something on her mind.

She whispers, "Thank you. Thank you for helping financially. And"—she sighs—"I'm sorry for freaking out earlier."

It's as if she'd just admitted defeat.

I smile down at her and slide the T-shirt over my head.

I swear I see a tiny glimpse of disappointment cross her face the moment my body is covered.

"I don't take help well, Case." Her eyes search the floor and then the walls before finally meeting my gaze.

I want to reach out and touch her, but I don't. Instead, I motion her out of the bedroom because I'm afraid I'll do something that I'll regret later.

We walk back out to the kitchen. The kitchen is a neutral spot. Neutral ground. A neutral place where people naturally gather. There's no bed, no immoral thoughts—well, maybe some.

"In order to keep my spot in the World Finals, I need to ride four more rides. That's four more weekends. So"—I clear my throat with a simple cough—"I will be here during the week to help out. I'll catch a plane on Fridays to wherever the PBR is holding an event, and then fly back here on Sundays. No matter what."

"Whatever you need to do, Casey," is all she says.

The purse from the World Finals, if I win, would help set us up right. Give us a possibility at life together. It isn't about money, but it's a chance for us to be more comfortable—if she would ever consider taking me back. Maybe a start at something, but that sounds fucked up, too, because we've loved each other for a long time.

So, this is me, fixing our love. One thing's for sure—I know Tess Morgan has never stopped loving me. Also, I know it was too hard to love me and be with me at the same time.

I won't announce this until the finals are over, but this will be my last tour. Sometimes, us cowboys just know when to walk away. Throw in the towel. When our bodies are too badly scarred and we know our time is limited. One day, I'm going to wake up and realize I'm all I have. This body, this vessel, is the only thing tying me to this earth. And when my body is gone, beaten to shreds, or maybe I've been too lax on a bull, too comfortable, all that will be left is a pile of ashes of a tough, old cowboy who fought like hell for his ego.

Just four more rides.

"Casey?" I hear Tess's voice.

I jerk my head up to look at her.

"Is it this Friday?" she asks.

"Yeah, this Friday."

Tess nods, collecting her thoughts and whatever she's feeling, stuffing them into a bag much too small for the price we'll both pay if something does happen. "I'll get the wine."

I smile at her.

She sighs. "Please don't do that."

"What?" I laugh.

"You know it's that smile that's gotten you into trouble for years, Casey Atwood."

"This?" I point to it.

I do this just to try to get her to laugh, and when she does, I see her almost attempt to reach for my face, to cover my eyes, so I can't see her laugh. But at the last minute, she doesn't. Instead, she turns to the cabinet behind her and grabs a bottle of wine.

My heart slides out of my chest. I don't know that she'll ever come back to me.

The house moans as the wind begins to kick up again. Tess took my weekend plans better than I'd thought.

I turn to the refrigerator and grab a Coors Light and set it on the counter behind me. Grab the steaks I bought from Olive's when I was downtown today.

"I'm barbecuing tonight," I say.

Tess Morgan could never turn down a medium-rare steak. Her eyebrows rise.

I also pull out a few potatoes and a premade bag of salad.

"Bag salad?" Tess cringes.

"What?"

Tess walks to the refrigerator where I'm standing. I take in her scent and try like hell not to touch her. With her shoulder to my chest, she bends at her waist and pulls out romaine lettuce, tomatoes, carrots, and cucumbers, and then she stands. Our faces are inches apart, and I don't dare move.

"I can do something with this." And then she walks away to a safe distance and stands on the other side of the island. She grabs a knife and a cutting board, and she begins to chop.

"Better get started on those steaks, Atwood. Bag salad." I hear her say under her breath with a slight smile.

Later, after dinner, when the dishes are done and put away, we sit on the sofa, staring at the fire.

"You seem more relaxed," I say.

And for a long moment, we just sit, sipping our drinks.

Tess finally says while looking at the fire's flames, "Remember when we were kids and Ethan Handler dared me to jump off the rock and into Mad River?"

I cringe. "Yeah, that was a long drop."

"Remember when you whispered in my ear, 'Live in the moment, Morgan, and don't worry about tomorrow. And if you die, I'll make sure they don't bury you because I know how claustrophobic you are. I'll make sure they cremate you.' " She turns to look at me and laughs. And at the same time she does that, she doesn't reach over and cover my face; she doesn't turn away. She stares at me. And my heart doesn't leave my chest this time because I see in her eyes that this is an act of love. She wants me to see her for her. "I'm trying real hard to live in the present moment, Casey. Trying not to live in the past because my heart is no good there."

"Can we talk about—"

"I know you need to, Casey. But ... I just can't. I'm not ready, and I'm sorry." Her voice is soft, light.

I understand. Because it's easier to push that shit under the rug. It's easier to move forward. But are we really moving forward?

"I'm glad you didn't die after taking Ethan up on his dare. Truth be told, I think he was hoping you'd lose your bikini top when you jumped. I think all the guys were."

"And you?"

"I was thirteen, Tess. Of course I wanted to see your boobs. But it was only your boobs I wanted to see."

She takes her eyes away from the fire. Sets her wine down on the coffee table. Pulls her knees up to her chest. "I need to not drink wine or any alcohol for that matter when I'm around you."

The wind begins to pick up its pace again, a nightly, even daily, ritual.

"Why?"

Her eyes burrow into mine, into my chest, as if she sees only me for who I am and nothing else.

"Because left to my lack of inhibitions, I can't trust myself, my heart."

Badly, I want to take her in my arms, make love to her, or fuck her right here on the sofa. Whatever she needs from me, I'll give her.

"What do you need from me, Tess?"

She puts up her invisible force field, but I see right through it. I know how she wants to answer, and I understand she feels it's not the right answer but the feel-better answer. The easy answer. But I see she wears the regret like shame. I, too, know I'm not the regret, but the act of sex is. Masking feelings is the easy way out.

I remember her breasts were perfectly round and fit in my mouth as if they had been made for me. The way I slowly pushed into her for the first time. We were both young, and I didn't know what the hell I was doing. I lasted maybe a minute. I've grown more in stamina, learned a lot of tricks along the way. But with Tess, things are just different with us.

"I just want to feel tonight. I don't want to feel the weight of our decisions, the awfulness that lies in front of us like a rug full of snakes. I want it to be easy. I want you inside me but for all the wrong reasons, Casey. Because in the morning, I'll regret it. Not you, not what we did, but why we did it."

I set my beer down, scoop her up in my arms, and carry her to bed.

In her bedroom, I gently lay her down on her bed. Slowly, she begins to unbutton the front of her shirt, and I sit back on my feet and watch. She pushes off her top, so I can see the way her breasts rest in her bra.

"I brought you in here to go to sleep, Tess," I whisper.

But I don't know that I can stop myself now. I feel the bulge in my jeans harden.

She's lying here on the bed, a thin piece of satin protecting her from my hands, my mouth.

"There are a million reasons why we shouldn't do this, Tess."

"I know." She reaches back and unclasps her bra, so her breasts are released, pulling her bra out from underneath her so she's lying there in only her jeans.

You can't do this, Case.

But she's asking me to.

It's not the right time.

It's all fucked up.

I slowly shake my head, unable to look away from her.

"Please, Casey. Just touch me." A single tear slips from her eye and runs down the side of her face, falling to the bedspread.

My heart begs for mercy while my head spins, but it's when I see her tear that it all becomes unraveled.

Slowly, I reach down and take her breasts in my hands, running my callous palms over her hard nipples.

She lets a whimper out.

The bulge in my pants begins to ache.

And I can't stop fighting what I'm feeling.

I fucking can't anymore.

Leaning down, I take her breast in my mouth, and then the other one.

Pull her jeans from her body.

Slide my hands down her thighs and stick my fingers into her panties. And I slide my finger into her folds.

She cries out, "More."

In one swift motion, I drag her panties from her body and put my mouth where my fingers were. I look up at her. Tess's eyes are locked on mine, and all I see is a mix of emotion in her eyes.

Passion.

Love.

Sadness.

Regret.

I drop my head to her stomach, panting in the darkness as the wind swirls around the house.

"Please," she begs me.

"Tess." My voice is hoarse with need, with love. I want to give her what she wants, and this feeling is all too familiar. The last time we made a decision like this, we lived with the decision for years. "I want this more than you do, but we can't."

She pulls my mouth to hers.

Breathing her in, I allow my tongue to explore her again. Finding pace and rhythm does no good for what's in my pants.

She pushes her hands through my hair, and I settle between her thighs. With each probe and push of our tongues, our bodies move together like they haven't missed eight years.

"Tess, please," I pant and pull away, not allowing my dick to win this match.

I sit back on my feet, staring down into her eyes, trying to catch my breath. Her body is fully exposed to me, available for my touch.

As I rub my hand across my face, she stares up at me. I know she sees the conflict in my eyes through the darkness, so instead of asking me to do something, she pulls me to her, and I rest my head on her chest.

"Go to sleep, Casey," she says. "But first, take your clothes off. It's only fair."

I stand and slip my pants off, followed by my T-shirt, and she moves the covers, so I can climb in next to her.

The wind blows around us.

The rain starts.

And there's no place in the world I'd rather be.

I know Tess Morgan will own my heart forever—if we're together or not.

The Ladybugs

Some things are just better left unsaid, Erla thinks to herself when she remembers the chief coming to the door.

Her mind spun out of control.

Was the chief here because he'd heard that Don's body wasn't quite ready to go to heaven to be with the Lord?

Was the chief here because Betty had told him she was worried about Erla? That she'd looked lost that day?

Was the chief here on a different matter altogether?

These thoughts put her mind into a tailspin until the chief finally said, "I hate to ask you this, Erla, but, well, we received an anonymous tip yesterday, and I'm questioning many, many of our folks here in Dillon Creek. Anyway, it was brought to my attention that when Tripp and Conroy were killed, there might have been a witness. A woman about seventy or so. There's no car identification or license plate, as it was dark, but ..." Chief ran his fingers along the folds of his hat. "Anyway, just thought I'd pursue the tip."

Erla took a big breath in.

She hadn't been there.

She hadn't seen anything. She had been in bed next to Don.

But she did remember the morning after. It was an awful nightmare.

The whole town mourned for the Atwoods and the Morgans.

But Erla Brockmeyer would have definitely never left two boys to die in a field.

What kind of evil person would do that?

Erla said to the chief, "I'm sorry, Chief, but any person who leaves two boys to die in a field deserves what's coming."

Chief McBride nodded. "Well, sorry to disturb your evening, Erla. And again, if there's anything you need from Sandy and me, you know who to call."

But a lingering thought has stayed with her since Chief McBride paid her a visit. *If it had been so dark, how did the tipster know the woman was about seventy or so?*

A ringing telephone brings Erla to the present moment.

"Hello?"

"Hello, Mrs. Brockmeyer. This is Bevie down at Dr. Cain's office, reminding you of your doctor's appointment tomorrow."

"Tomorrow." Erla tries to recollect making a doctor's appointment.

"Yes, tomorrow at nine a.m."

Erla doesn't dare ask what the appointment is for so as not to create a stir of unwanted rumors. "I will be there. Thanks, Bevie. And tell your grandmother hello for me, would you, dear?"

"I sure will, Mrs. Brockmeyer."

When she hangs up the phone, the pain starts in her chest again.

Possibly, she thinks, *it's a gentle reminder from God that I'd better get my chest examined.*

But she knows she won't make a peep about it because if the good Lord is ready to bring her home, well then, Erla

Brockmeyer has her heavenly bags packed, which reminds her to start the letter for Scarlet and Devon. *The good-bye letter.*

And a tiny thought in her head stirs—the thought of her smooth exit to heaven, so no one has to find her if these chest pains continue or are something more serious.

Erla knows Mabe wouldn't be able to handle it. Most likely, Mabe would start boozing again. Erla isn't so sure Mabe's heart could handle her losing her last living relative.

Erla is certain most of her friends would have a hard time.

Clyda though, she'd be okay. The woman used to slaughter her own cows, help run a ranch, mend fences, and raise boys. Clyda's heart could handle it. But that doesn't mean Clyda is supposed to.

If she drove out to Eel River, tied her feet to cement bricks, and made her way out to the deep spot, nobody would think to look for an old woman's body in Eel River. Oh shoot, but they'd see her unattended car. Chief McBride was a softy, but he wasn't a dunce!

Erla looks down at her wedding ring. How she wishes she could feel Don's comforting arms around her once more. Smell the scent of his aftershave, his minty breath.

And when Bevie called her Mrs. Brockmeyer, it made her think, just for a moment, that Don was still alive. That she was still a Mrs. and not a widow. But she highly doubts the town of Dillon Creek would ever refer to her as Widow Brockmeyer. But still, it feels lonely when she's referred to as a name she's worn for longer than she hasn't.

Erla glances down at the pad of paper where she wrote the appointment down on. "Oh shoot." She didn't get the time.

Erla swallows her pride and calls Dr. Cain's office.

"Dr. Cain's Family Medical Practice. This is Bevie. How can I help you?"

Two things Erla loves about Dr. Cain's office is that Erla can speak to a live person immediately, and she doesn't have to hit several buttons to get to who she needs.

"Hey, Bevie. This is Erla. I just need to confirm my appointment time tomorrow."

"Yes, Mrs. Brockmeyer. It's at nine a.m."

Erla writes the time down on her calendar. "That's what I thought. Thank you, dear. And tell your grandmother hello for me."

There's a pause on the other end of the line. "Yes … yes, Mrs. Brockmeyer, I will do that."

"Wonderful. Good-bye, dear."

The next day at fifteen minutes to nine, Erla is in the waiting room, purse in her lap. She remembers the last time she was in here. It was with Don—when everything started. His memory. His balance. It makes her heart ache, her chest hurt, and she wonders if she'll ever feel normal again. She wishes, just for a minute, not to remember the loss of her husband. Not feel the weight of grief against her chest.

Bevie comes out behind the closed door. "Mrs. Brockmeyer, Dr. Cain will see you now."

In the sterile room, she sits on the chair against the wall as Bevie takes her blood pressure and her heart rate. "What brings you in today, Mrs. Brockmeyer?"

Heck if I know, she thinks quietly to herself because she doesn't remember making the appointment.

"Medication change."

Bevie nods and looks at Erla's chart. "Well, Erla, it looks like you aren't on any medication right now."

"That's right. We need to change that."

Bevie's eyes meet Erla's with a laugh. "All right then. The doctor will be in shortly."

"Thank you, Bevie."

A few minutes later, Dr. Cain walks in. Salt-and-pepper hair.

The last time she saw him, he administered a drug to Don that allowed his body to finally rest. Before he did it, he looked at Don and Erla and said, "In Dillon Creek, we take care of our own."

"Hello, Mrs. Brockmeyer. How are you doing today?"

Erla lies, "Doing just fine, Doctor."

She kept the appointment to see if the fine doctor might consider giving her the same medication he gave Don. Just so she can make her smooth transition to heaven. Planned. Well calculated. Less traumatizing for all parties involved.

This, she thinks, *is a possible alternative to the cement blocks, a rope, and Eel River.*

"What brings you in today?" He leans against the counter. "Looks like"—he looks down at her chart—"a medication change?" His eyes sit in question. "Erla, you're not on any medication."

"Yes, that's correct, Dr. Cain. But maybe I need to be?" She gives him a wink.

"I ... I'm not following."

"You know"—Erla winks again—"the medication we discussed in July."

He looks down at her chart again. "Erla, you haven't been to see me in a year."

Clearly, Dr. Cain isn't following Erla's lead.

"How are you dealing with the grief?" he says softer.

"Oh, the grief?" She pushes down the lump in her throat. "Fine."

Dr. Cain looks at her. "Erla, one thing you are not is a good liar. You are many good things, but you are not a good liar."

Tears start at the corners of her eyes and slowly make their way down her cheeks. "I'm not ..." she whispers and looks up at Dr. Cain.

Dr. Cain sits down next to her in a chair. "You did the right thing, Erla. Don gave you his wishes, and you followed them."

"Why doesn't it feel like the right thing?"

Dr. Cain hands her a tissue.

Erla dabs her eyes, the floodgates opening to all the sadness she's felt in the last few months.

"Because your heart aches. Sometimes, the right decision can feel like the wrong one when our hearts are invested in what we want and not what's best for the other. Don didn't want you to see him go down the path he was going. Now, he's free."

Erla nods, trying to soak up his words. "I miss him so much."

"And you will for a long time. Because heartache is the price we pay for love."

"Do you want to know something?"

"Yes."

"I keep his side of the bed, his glass of water that his lips last touched, exactly the same. I've left the same pillowcase on his pillow so that I still smell him. And when I've had a really tough day, I sleep with his T-shirt just to feel close to him."

Dr. Cain puts his hand on Erla's shoulder. "These are all normal things, Erla. Do you talk to anyone about this?"

"No."

"You should."

Erla looks at Dr. Cain. "Doc, I've spent most of my life in a happy place. Maybe it's just my turn to hurt."

"What about Mabe? Can you talk to Mabe?"

Erla shrugs. "I don't want to. I live it. Every day, I live with the grief. It's the last thing I want to do, Doc."

He nods and walks to the cupboard. Takes out a business card and hands it to Erla. "This is a grief support group in Eureka. They meet at noon on Fridays. If you need someone to drive you, I know Bevie would do it in a heartbeat."

"That's nice. Thank you." Erla takes the card and hangs on to it tightly as she stands.

"About the medication?"

"I don't need anything, Doc. Thanks."

"I figured."

As Erla makes it to her car, she realizes that Bevie didn't say anything about her blood pressure or heartbeat.

See, she thinks to herself, *you're just fine.*

She's just got a broken heart that's tired of fighting.

Patty meets Mabe out front of the Catholic church at fifteen minutes to seven, both dressed in scarfs, sunglasses, and big-brimmed hats.

"Are you ready?" Mabe asks.

Patty says, "I think so."

Mabe says, "What did you tell your husband?"

"That I was meeting with a group of drunks."

"Good cover." Mabe nods. "Did you drink today?"

"No."

"Did you drink yesterday?"

"No."

"How about the day before?"

"I haven't had a drink in six days, Mabe."

"And now, you're at your first meeting. I'm glad you have the courage tonight."

Mabe takes Patty's hand, and they turn and walk into the AA meeting.

"If I told you that you never had to drink again, would you believe me?"

"I don't know. However, I know, today, I don't *want* to drink again."

"That's good enough, dear."

And the two women, with forty years between them, walk into an AA meeting.

Because all they have is one day at a time.

18

Tess

I wake up to the pitter-patter of rain on the roof and remember why I'm naked.

The wind howls.

And the old house cries against the wind.

She's strong—I feel it in her bones. The beams have provided solace against winter months for years.

"Tell me a story, girl," I whisper in the cool, still morning air and wait for her response.

I slide my hand across the bare sheets beside me, and the old memories, the old feelings rise to the surface of my heart. A mix of emotions dwells somewhere deep within me at my memory of last night.

Emptiness that I'm alone again.

Longing for what we had as kids.

Sadness maybe.

And heat. I blush at the thought of our naked bodies lying next to each other. His arms that curled around my breasts—

a simple reminder of the intimacy Casey knows how to give without expectation in return.

Old feelings and new feelings, and somewhere in between.

It's Wednesday.

Shit!

I fly out of bed, unaware of the time but knowing Emmitt starts his work today.

Quickly, I grab some clothes. I run to the bathroom and jump in the shower.

"Hey." I hear Casey's voice.

I peel the shower curtain back and see his ruggedly handsome face, a smile, and a cup of coffee in the doorway of the bathroom.

"I figured you could use this." He sets the mug down on the counter.

He's dressed in a nice button-up shirt. Jeans that fit him too well in all the right spots, and here I am, praying to God that yesterday's mascara isn't making its run down my face.

Painfully aware of my own insecurities and the way he looks right now, staring back at me, I retreat back behind the curtain and say an uncertain, "Thanks, Case."

Hidden behind the curtain, I roll my eyes and mime the words, *Thanks, Case.*

"Hey," I call out before I hear the door shut.

"Yeah?" His voice is smooth, like his dress shirt.

"What time is it?"

"Ten after eight."

"I'll be ready before Emmitt gets here."

"Tess, I can handle Emmitt. Not sure he needs much direction."

My thanks is meager as I allow the hot water to run down my backside, and it reminds me of Casey's rough hands.

You're not going to last, Tess, I tell myself.

Still, I don't hear the door to the bathroom shut as I begin to wash my face. Pulling my face from the water, I ask if he's still there. When I peek out the shower curtain, he's not there, but a pink towel now sits on the sink.

He grabbed me a towel, and I smile with every single part of my body.

After I'm done drying my hair, I add a little eye shadow but not too much. Lengthen my lashes with mascara and put on some lip gloss. Down my coffee like it's life.

I walk out into the kitchen a half hour later to a quiet house. Voices trail from the downstairs. Banging hammers.

If Emmitt doesn't need my help on the inside, well then, I'll start on the outside. I remember the berry briars around the front of the house need to be cut back.

I grab a jacket and put it over my new Ketchikan sweatshirt. I find some gloves in the wood box outside but shake them out just to be sure there aren't any spiders. Throw a beanie on. Just as I'm about to head outside, Casey comes inside.

My heart doubles over itself, and I see his eyes scan my body.

"Hey," he says.

"Hey."

"Where you headed?" he asks.

"Clear the berry briars out in front of the house."

His subtle laugh is throaty, and I watch how his Adam's apple bobs.

"What?"

"You just don't give up, do you?"

I change the topic. "What are you doing?"

Casey looks back the way he came and pulls his thumb in the direction of the detached garage. "Do you know there's a ride-on lawn mower in there?"

But his question gets lost somewhere in the face he gives me. The way he used to look at me. When we were kids. It's a face I don't see him give anyone, except me, but then again, I haven't been around him in quite some time, so maybe he has. I try to ignore it and elbow him as I walk past. My face meets the cool weather, and the drizzle touches my skin.

"Mowing the lawn, Atwood?" I smile, putting on the gloves.

"Something like that," he says.

Toward the afternoon, after the berry briars have had their way with me, my hands are ice-cold, even with the gloves, which, I guess, aren't supposed to provide warmth, but at least it's a cover. Sweat drips down my back. I wonder why I even tried with the makeup, the hair today. I pull a strand of hair from my face as I stare down at the beautiful surroundings below me.

The view from the front of the house that overlooks the Tongass Narrows is breathtaking, but the water's rough movements remind me of a chaotic time, a time I can't really put my finger on; it creates a lonely feeling inside me, a sinking feeling. A feeling of fear.

A distant thought prickles in the back of my mind. *How can I have feelings for a place I've never been?*

"Hey, Morgan!" Casey calls from the garage. "You need food?"

I glance down at my watch. It's twelve thirty.

"I could eat," I call back.

Morgan. We're back to that?

Casey nods in my direction, his hands on his hips. He turns and limps back into the garage.

I wonder if the cold weather is harder on his body. The countless surgeries he's had. Laurel always had a way of keeping me up-to-date whether it was at Tipple Motors or at Nelson's or just downtown. I know she always had a soft spot for the two of us, even after Conroy and Tripp died. Maybe she knew the only person to console her son's broken heart was the one who had broken it in the first place. If she only knew what had happened between us, I'm not so sure she'd feel the same way.

I wipe the sweat from my brow and walk up toward the garage. Removing the gloves, I set them down on an old wine barrel just outside the garage.

"Shall we?" Casey asks.

"I hope we beat the rain. Should we grab an umbrella?"

Casey laughs. "Afraid of a little rain, Morgan? Never bothered you when we were kids."

"I'm smarter now, more prepared."

It's quiet as the drizzle slowly comes to a halt while we make our way down the hill.

"Which surgery is the limp from?" I ask. Blowing in my hands to keep them warm only for a second or two.

He shrugs. "ACL repairs. A broken femur. Take your pick."

"Is it the colder weather?"

"That, and if I don't keep active, the stiffness will sneak up on me."

We walk.

You ever think about walking away? My heart wants to ask. But I don't dare allow the words out of my mouth.

Every time Casey got on a bull, my heart would do a song and dance. He loves to ride, and I love—loved—him. It was that simple.

He knew it scared the shit out of me, but he always came back to me with a, "See, not so bad."

Then, he'd pull me in for a kiss, and I'd forget all the fear, the last eight seconds, because he was alive and there and nothing else mattered.

"What's good in Ketchikan?" he asks.

"No idea. Olive mentioned a fish and chips place. We could try that?"

Casey nods.

The stillness between us sits as we reach the bottom of the hill, and we veer onto Creek Street.

"There." I point to Addy's Fish 'n' Stuff.

"Sounds about right."

We make our way inside. It's a bar and a restaurant, and it smells like deep-fried everything.

Divine, I think to myself.

"Just two?" the young platinum-blonde waitress asks us.

"Just two," Casey says.

"Window seat?" she asks, eyeing Casey up and down like a piece of meat.

I roll my eyes. "Yes, please."

The waitress finally acknowledges my existence.

There are several flat screens throughout the dark restaurant/bar.

On one screen is basketball.

On another screen, football.

On another, of course, *Deadliest Catch.*

Platinum-Blonde leads us to the window seat. The same view from atop the hill, except no longer a bird's-eye view; we're at eye level.

Two big cruise ships sit out in the water. People of all shapes and sizes, bundled with warm jackets, make their way to and from with uniformity.

"Can I get you something to drink?" She eyes Casey.

Casey looks to me. "Morgan, what are you having?"

"Water is fine, thank you." I look up at her, but she's too busy ogling Casey.

"I'll have the same."

"Great. I'll be back to take your order."

I try not to laugh when she leaves the table.

"What?" Casey asks.

"Nothing." I look through the menu that is already on the table.

"What?" he asks again, opening the menu.

I shrug. "Nothing's changed. Women still throw themselves at you."

And the next thought makes my stomach drop. I think of all the women who have thrown themselves at him for the last eight years. My curiosity wants to ask how many women he's been with since us. But the answer makes me want to throw up. I don't want to know, and yet I do. It's like passing a car accident. You don't want to look, but your curiosity won't let you not look.

"How many women have you slept with? Since us, I mean." *Dammit, Tess.*

"You really want to know?" he asks, not looking up from his menu.

"Yes."

"A handful."

"Liar."

Casey looks up from his menu. "Believe it or not, Tess, I really had a hard time getting over us, and contrary to popular belief, cowboys don't fuck everything." He shrugs. "Doesn't mean I didn't mess around with some."

I allow his words to sink in as a wave of heat rushes through my body. I gain his stare from across the table.

"How about you?" he asks.

"One," I whisper. "A mistake. A drunk one-night stand."

"What's his name?" Casey's jaw grows rigid. Hard.

"I don't remember." I laugh. Tilt my head. Badly, I want to reach out across the table and cover his eyes, so he can't see the half-smile, feeling the vulnerability prickle my spin.

But the pain of that night comes back. The silent cries on our drive home. The need to hold something, anything, instead of feeling the pain I felt, that Casey felt.

The waitress returns with a notepad and a pen. "What can I get you?" she asks Casey first—of course.

But Casey looks to me. "Morgan?"

I scan the menu, as if there might be one more option other than the fish and chips. "I'll get the fish and chips, please."

"Okay, hon."

I snarl. Platinum-Blonde can't call me hon. Clearly, she's younger than me.

Casey also orders the fish and chips.

"Comin' up," she says and retreats back behind the counter.

A man who's in his late fifties stares at us from the bar.

"Guy at the bar has been eyeing us since we walked in. You didn't piss off any husbands, did you?" I kid.

Casey attempts to turn and look, but I stop him.

"Don't look now. It will make it painfully obvious that I said something." I take a sip of water just as the man, though hesitant, stands, leaving his beer at the bar, and approaches our table.

He's a bit shy. "Mr. Atwood? Casey Atwood?" he clarifies.

Casey stands and sticks out his hand because that's what Daryl always taught his boys to do. "Yes, sir."

The man extends his hand. "I'm sorry. I couldn't help but notice you and thought, *What the hell is Casey Atwood doing in Ketchikan, Alaska?*" He's a bit shaken by Casey's presence. "Name's Bob. It is truly an honor to meet you, and the boys and I are real excited to watch you ride these last four events before the finals."

"Thank you so much, Bob."

"Oh, excuse me, ma'am." He tips his trucker hat at me. "Could I ... could I take a picture with both of you?" Bob asks. "Hey, Rosie," he says back toward the bar to our waitress. "Can you come take our picture?"

Rosie—a bit perturbed says, "Can't you just let the man eat in peace, Bob?"

Bob looks back to our table. "He ain't eatin' yet. Is that all right?"

Rosie begrudgingly walks over to our table and snaps a picture.

"You're a lot taller in person," Bob says, looking up at Casey.

"That's what I hear, sir."

They exchange handshakes just as the PBR announcer from one of the televisions says, "And how about that Casey Atwood? Boy, has he had some fantastic rides this year. In fact, Jack, it's my prediction that he will win this year's World Finals."

19

Casey

Emmitt and his crew have started with the roof.

"Let's just go look at furniture," I say to Tess.

She gives me a smug look. We're out on the deck because inside is just too loud with all the pounding. "If we're going to sell this place, there's no need to look at furniture."

"I know. But if we stage it right, it will sell quickly."

A smile spreads across Tess's face. "Since when did you learn about staging a house?"

"Since I've done some research on Google."

She takes another sip of her coffee and eyes me curiously. I want to ask her about the picture downstairs that's been eating away at my free thoughts, but now is probably not the time.

"You have your flight booked?" she asks, taking in the view.

"Fly out tomorrow at four. Gives us most of the day."

"Are you nervous?"

I side-eye her.

She finishes my thought in her best impression of me, which isn't great, for the record, *"Nervous? No. Ready? Always."*

Tess shakes her head at the memory. It's the line I've used since we were kids.

She sighs, and before she puts her mug to her lips again, she says, "Casey, you've always been a champion. It's just that the world has the opportunity to see it."

I reach out and place my hand between her shoulder blades in the softest way possible.

A young kid, maybe eighteen, comes around the corner, holding some sort of dish.

"Tess?" he asks.

He's clean-cut. I can tell he's military in the way that he walks, his movements precise and with purpose.

Tess turns. "Oh, hey, Jacob. How are you?"

"My grandmother wanted me to bring you this. She says to warm it up in the oven at two hundred degrees. I say, add vanilla ice cream."

Tess takes the dish. "That is so thoughtful. I still have her last dish I need to return. Is she at the Visitor Center today?"

Jacob's nod is quick, one that's clipped and barely a nod but nevertheless an act of acknowledgment.

"Oh, Jacob, this is—"

But Jacob shoves his hand out. "Casey Atwood. Two-time bull-riding champion of the world. Contender for this year."

Tess rolls her eyes. "Don't do that, Jacob. This guy wants to go buy furniture, and I'm afraid his head won't be able to fit through the door if people keep treating him like that."

I smile. "Lucky, as Tess likes to put it. It's nice to meet you, Jacob. Military?"

"Marines."

"Thank you for your service."

"You ride this weekend, correct?"

"Yeah, leaving tomorrow."

"Good luck, sir."

"I'll need it."

Jacob turns to leave.

"Thanks again!" Tess calls.

"Nice kid," I say.

"Yeah, he is." A few seconds pass before she says, "I can't go to the furniture store. I need to bake a cake and make my mom's pasta dish. I'm going to run to the store."

"Maybe tomorrow?" I ask with an ulterior motive. I want this house to look like a home before we leave to go back to Dillon Creek eventually and not so we can sell it—so that Tess might not want to sell it.

She nods as she takes the dish inside. "Maybe."

I don't do well on idle. I have a hard time sitting during the day. I debate on asking Emmitt if he needs help on the roof, but I don't do heights, so that's out of the question. So, as Tess is doing her thing, I go downstairs and start going through stuff, like old boxes stored underneath the staircase.

Boxes full of newspapers, books, magazines, pictures.

"Ike didn't throw anything away." I stare back at all the boxes that somehow fit together like a Tetris game.

I take the first one and start to go through it.

It's full of old *Time* magazines, dating back to the magazine's inception in 1923. Carefully, I thumb through them. I call Michael, Ike's son.

"Hello?"

"Hey, Michael. It's Casey Atwood."

"Hey, Casey. How do you like the house?"

"It's beautiful."

"That's terrific! I'm sure you are both better off with it than I was. Just don't have the time. You know how it is."

"Yeah. Anyway, there are a number of boxes underneath the staircase downstairs. Looks like they're old books, magazines, photos, based on the labels on the outside. Do you want us to set these aside?"

He lets out an exasperated breath of air. "I don't give a shit what you do with them, Casey, quite honestly. My dad saved everything. I'd hate to waste your time, having you go through all of them. Just ... hell, I don't know. Maybe the photos would be nice."

I nod even though he can't see me. "All right."

We hang up, and I slide my phone back into my front pocket.

The next box is full of *Newsweek* magazines, also dating back to the magazine's start date in 1933. Ike was a keeper of information, but why would he have saved all of these old magazines?

Opening the next box, I notice leather-bound books and notebooks. The box is labeled *Books*. Inside are old classics, like *The Great Gatsby*, *To Kill a Mockingbird*, *Wuthering Heights*, *The Catcher in the Rye*, *Tess of the d'Urbervilles*. This book catches my eye. *Tess*. I set it aside. I continue digging. *Pride and Prejudice. The Call of the Wild. Crime and Punishment. Jane Eyre. Brave New World. In Cold Blood.*

At the bottom of the box, stuck under one of the box flaps, is the corner of a photo. I pull it out, and it's Tess. But she's with another man. Immediately, my response is jealousy. My heart starts to pound, and my hands grow sweaty, but as I look closer, the image is dated. Tess wouldn't be this age at the time this photo was taken, but the resemblance is uncanny. I stand and walk over to the photograph hanging on the wall. I hold up the photos side by side.

It looks just like the woman holding the baby in the photo. I walk back over to the boxes and take out another box. This one though has several letters. Maybe twenty or so.

The letters are from all over the world. Many were from Ike—to himself; to his son, Michael; to his wife, Agnes; and some to woman named Elizabeth but those all came back returned. I slide one letter out that's addressed to Elizabeth—to the same exact address as this house. A picture falls out.

Dear Elizabeth,

Your daughter is good. She's happy.

Tenacious. Hardheaded. Stubborn. But boy, does she have a kind heart.

I'll send more pictures when I can.

Best,

Ike

And this picture, no doubt, is the same little girl in the picture that the woman is holding in the photograph on the wall.

After several hours of digging, this is all I can find.

I shove the letter and the photo of the little girl in my wallet.

"Why the hell did you bring us here, Ike?" I whisper to myself.

Unable to stop thinking about Ike's letter to a woman named Elizabeth, I move the magazine boxes upstairs and into the garage.

The hammering on the roof was more muffled downstairs. Tess isn't inside when I peek in the kitchen, carrying the boxes, and I breathe a sigh of relief.

You don't have facts, Casey. This could all be just a misunderstanding, so don't go spouting anything that's not grounded in facts.

I take each box to the garage and cover them with a waterproof blanket. I take the box of letters and journals, most stemming from Ike's travels, and also put them under the waterproof blanket. I text Tess.

> *Me: I found a ton of Time and Newsweek magazines dating back to the 1920s. Maybe we can donate them somewhere?*

Several minutes pass.

No bubbles appear, so I shove my phone back in my front pocket and walk back downstairs because I wonder if there's something else that I'm missing.

I search every goddamn square inch of the downstairs.

Ike was a facts man. He was a newspaper publisher for as long as I've been alive. Longer likely.

Why the hell would he bring Tess and me all the way to Ketchikan for apparently no reason at all?

The nagging thought gnaws at me.

My phone rings. I slide it out of my pocket and see that it's Tess.

"Hey," I say.

"Hey."

I can tell by her tone that something isn't quite right, but I can't put my finger on it.

"You never call my phone. Are you all right?"

"Yeah, no. Fine. I'm … I'm just at the Visitor Center with Esther." She pauses.

"Tess?" Worry starts. "Do I need to come down there?"

"No, no. I'm just going to be longer than expected."

There's silent between us.

But I'm already walking down the hill, not even sure which way the Visitor Center is.

"Call me if you need anything." I attempt to make my voice sound normal, like I'm not hauling ass down the hill.

"I will."

"Okay."

And she hangs up.

When I plug the name of the Visitor Center into my phone, I realize I'm not far.

When I arrive, I peek in the windows and see a woman, who I assume is Esther, sitting with Tess at a table in the far-left corner.

They look to be in deep conversation.

Breathing a sigh of relief, I slide my phone back into my pocket. Guess phones are good for something. I ease myself down on the bench in front of the Visitor Center and watch as another cruise ship sails from Ketchikan. I blow out a sigh of relief. Tess's tone just wasn't right. I turn my head back inside to take another look.

They're both smiling.

Keep your mind busy, Casey.

I text my brother Cash.

Me: You gonna be fighting bulls at the finals?

I wait for a response, but I don't hold my breath as I see my last text never went answered.

It was like when Cash left Dillon Creek after Conroy died. He left everything behind. He didn't really have anyone tying him to town aside from his family and a woman named Scarlet. We—his brothers—knew that he had a thing for her. We'd never seen him act the way he acted or do the things he'd done when he was around her.

But Cash is the type of guy who doesn't need roots. He's a gypsy at heart, and maybe it was just easier, just like it was for all of us boys, to run. Besides, grief is easier when you're running, but I know, eventually, it will catch up to you, and it's just a matter of time before it does.

The bubbles appear under our text chain, like Cash is responding, but they quickly disappear again, only to reappear and disappear again. Maybe he's not fighting the bulls. Maybe he doesn't want to know I'm in the finals.

The last two times, he wasn't. Why would anything change?

But a text pops up.

Cash: No.

That's it.

Some things never change. Cash isn't really into conversations. Women and booze and anything that goes along with being great at what you do, help him cope. There are parts of him that make him a good brother, but I'd never admit that to him.

20

The Ladybugs

Winter is almost upon them, and the planning for the holiday fundraiser is moving right along.

Delveen and Pearl have been on their best behavior. Maybe Clyda scared the dickens out of them or they are really trying to do better. Either way, it's made their group time far more enjoyable and more productive.

"Colt said he'd donate a jersey," Delveen says. "I hope you don't mind, Clyda, that I asked him."

The group of women, aside from Delveen, are taken aback by her apology.

As far as they can remember, the last time Delveen apologized was in 1972 after an indiscretion that everyone talked about. But that's for another time, another book.

"Whaaaat?" Delveen asks.

Four sets of eyes divert to plants, books, the restaurant windows as they shake their heads, murmur, "Nothing," and shrug.

"Anyway," Pearl says, "the Talcombs said they'd donate a two-night stay at The Shaw Inn."

"Adam donated music lessons at The Steeple," Mabe says.

Clyda almost blushes. But what's more, Erla notices, is there's a twinkle in her old friend's eyes. Her husband has been gone for an awful long time, and Clyda has never taken up with another other man. "Carl donated a gift certificate from the Blacksmith Shop."

Now, Erla thinks, *that would be a couple—Carl and Clyda.*

Pearl Harvey lets out an awful scream that carries right out of Dillon Creek Pizza, down Main Street, and to the world's tallest living Christmas tree at the end of Main.

"What is it, Pearl?" Delveen's face is full of concern.

"Something just brushed against my leg, and I'm ... I'm too terrified to look!"

Mabe scoots back in her chair. "It's just Mayor Charlie."

He meows and wanders over to Mabe in search of treats.

Charlie is a tabby cat, and the unofficial mayor of Dillon Creek. He finds that it is his business to keep in everyone's business and beg for treats, all while keeping the town running smoothly as well as a cat can—hence the name Mayor Charlie.

Everyone loves Charlie.

Officially owned and well cared for by the Boyton family, Charlie is also loved by the community of Dillon Creek. In fact, one year, he was the grand marshal in the Christmas tractor parade.

"Shoo, Charlie. The Ladybugs are trying to get some official business done." Junie comes out, probably from Pearl's god-awful scream, and picks him up. "Sorry, ladies."

"It's no bother, Junie," Clyda says. "Us crazy, old ladies scare easy these days."

Pearl is clearly embarrassed. "Sorry, folks. It was just Charlie," she says, primarily to The Lunch Guys because they're the only other patrons in the restaurant. She takes a sip of her water and shakes her head. "Now, where were we?"

Delveen looks at the time. "I've got to run, ladies. I have a hair appointment with Pixie."

"You have your to-do list?" Erla asks.

"I do." Pearl puts on her coat.

"Watch out for furry felines. I hear they're ferocious these days!" Mabe calls as Pearl leaves.

But Pearl does something that makes the group of old women howl.

She turns around and flips them the bird.

Later in the evening, while Mabe is warming up leftovers, she sits down to read the *Dillon Creek Echo*.

After Ike passed away, which was a true tragedy in their town, there was no memorial service. Ike hadn't wanted one and made that clear to Michael, his son, who's taken over as publisher of the newspaper.

The headline in the *Dillon Creek Echo* made Mabe's stomach grow sour, and the blood drain from her face.

ANONYMOUS TIP AFTER EIGHT YEARS OF THE ATWOOD/MORGAN TRAGEDY

Chief McBride has confirmed that an anonymous tipster recently called into the Dillon Creek Police Department with information on the Atwood/Morgan tragedy.

When asked if Chief McBride plans to reopen the closed case, he declined to comment.

When asked what the new details by the tipster were, he declined to comment.

When asked if it was a reliable source, he declined to comment.

"At this point, we're just looking at the new details that are emerging," Chief McBride concluded.

Anyone with information is asked to call the nonemergency line of the Dillon Creek Police Department at 707-786-4225.

Ike never would have run this story.

Not in a million years.

He loved this community, and here it is, being ripped to shreds again by a journalist who thinks he knows how to run a paper like his father did.

Michael Isner should have known better, Mabe thinks to herself while trying not to get sick.

Mabe, too, thinks it's odd that neither Delveen nor Pearl said anything about it at the planning meeting. Maybe it is true that Clyda scared the living daylights out of both of them.

Oh God. What do I do now?

Her phone rings, and it makes her jump out of her own skin.

She walks to the phone on the wall. "Hello?"

"Hello, Mabe. It's Patty. Listen, we were invited to the Linfields' for dinner. I'm not sure what to do. Truby Linfield and I used to drink wine together, and I know she'll expect that. What should I do?"

"Take your own car. That way, you can leave when things start to feel uncomfortable."

"What will be my excuse if I feel the need to leave?"

"Tell them you're in Alcoholics Anonymous and you've got a drinking problem that you're trying to get help for and that you feel uncomfortable."

Mabe's words are met with dead silence on the other end of the line.

"Tell the truth," Mabe sighs. "Because lying and hiding aren't going to keep you sober, dear."

It is this moment that Mabe feels the heaviness of what she just said.

Mabe Muldoon isn't going to stay sober if she keeps this big, awful secret in her life. She's seen these things come to fruition in her short stint in AA, ones she's not supposed to talk about to protect the anonymity of its members, but she sure as hell doesn't want to drink again.

"Oh. Be honest?"

"Be honest."

"Okay. I'll call you tomorrow."

"Sounds good. Good-bye, Patty."

"Good-bye, Mabe."

Right as she hangs up with Patty, Erla calls.

"Hello?" Mabe says.

"Have you read the headline in the *Dillon Creek Echo*?"

"Yes." Her *yes* is exhausted. Tired. Twisted.

Erla says, "You know, Chief McBride came to my house, asking questions."

That's peculiar, Mabe thinks. *He didn't come to my house.*

Perhaps he knows more than he's letting on. Perhaps he knows, and he's trying to feel around Mabe's dearest friends. Catch her in a lie!

Now, Mabe Muldoon is many things, but she's not a liar, and now, she has to become one.

The boys' cries in the field that night still haunt her. She's going to be sick.

"The witness said to look for an older woman in her seventies. Whoever this person is ought to come forward. What a horrible, horrible person," Erla says.

21

Tess

Esther sits in front of me at the table. Her smile is familiar and warm and comforting. Her eyes, the shape of almonds and tilted downward, tell thousands of stories, accounts of real life, of human kindness and forgiveness, solace coming through like a wave that washes over me.

"I made my mom's favorite pasta recipe and a cobbler. I just can't thank you enough for the salmon and the casserole."

"You did not have to do that, Tess. It is very kind of you." Her hands—soft like pillows, the color of worn leather—rest on her arms. "I am glad you came here."

I try to settle in my own skin, but I can't. Feeling twisted up like a rag, unable to find comfort in my soul, I ask myself why I'm here.

"How long have you volunteered here, at the Tlingit Visitor Center?"

"Many years. My job, as an elder in the Tlingit tribe, is to educate others on our people."

Esther says *our* like it belongs to both of us.

"I would like to show you around if you'd like, Tess?"

She reaches across the table and touches my arm, as if we were old friends. Her skin is much richer than mine, more beautiful, more radiant. Mine is a dough white while hers is a decadent dark-chocolate mousse.

Esther stands, slow and steady, and I wonder how old she is. I almost want to help her, but I refrain. It's clear she's taken several trips around the sun, and she isn't feeble or weak; she just moves at a pace her body will allow.

We walk to a glass case.

"These are raven rattles. They are used for ceremonial purposes by chiefs and shamans."

My eyes trace down the bright blue ink or paint—I'm not sure which—and the brown zigzag line down the middle. "Is that a raven?" I ask.

Esther nods. "And bound together with cedar twine."

"The Tlingit made twine out of trees?" I look closer. "And a shark on the raven's back?"

"You have good eyes, Tess. Yes."

"What does it mean?"

"Tlingit carvers tell stories through their carvings. Some raven rattles don't have sharks, and some don't use the same colors. But this one tells a story, as they all do. In Tlingit culture, the raven is both a trickster and a creator. The rattles signify the relationships among people and animals. Look on the underbelly of the rattle. Do you see faces?"

I look at the underbelly and back to Esther. "Yes," I say, in awe of the incredible handcrafted work.

"In this particular story, the raven went down deep into the water and visited with the fish people because of a disagreement, teaching the men and women that fish are really like people. Fish, in other words, are just another form of humans. We must all work together. Alas, the raven and the shark, working in harmony in ceremonial dancing."

Esther's tone is something I want to rest in. It is soft and delicate and light.

She reaches out and touches my hand again. "Come. We have much to see."

Esther leads me to a totem pole.

"This is made of western red cedar and stands ten feet tall. A smaller totem pole."

The bright oranges, reds, blues, and yellows are mesmerizing.

"I see a wolf. An eagle."

"Totem poles are read from the bottom to the top."

"Is that a woman at the top?"

"Yes. There are two main moieties of Tlingit society—raven and eagle. Each clan has its own history, songs, totems. Can you guess which clan this totem came from?"

"Eagle?"

"Very good, Tess."

I see when Esther's eyes break, as if grief or sadness sit in the back of her mind, waiting for the right time to pounce.

"What about the woman at the top?"

"Ah, very good. How do you know it's a woman and not a man?"

I study the woman. "Her lips—they look more like a woman's than a man's."

Esther nods. "That is Fog Woman. A story for another day."

"What about the wolf?"

Esther pauses and looks into my eyes, as if waiting for me to understand, but I don't. "The wolf means powerful healing," she whispers. "Come." She changes the topic quickly. "There is so much to show you."

The rain is unforgiving and makes me wonder how long I've been here. "I'm sorry, Esther. I must have lost track of time. I need to get back to the Isner house to help the men."

"I see. Yes, it is well beyond our closing time at the Visitor Center." Esther reaches out and touches my hand again. "I want to give you something. Just one moment." She makes her way into the back and comes out with a blanket. She hands it to me. "This is a Chilkat blanket. It is used for ceremonies and dances. The yellow, blue, and green that you see used here are made from natural dyes. I would like you to keep this."

Overwhelmed by the moment, I tell Esther I can't take it. "This … this is much too precious. Surely, you'll find a more rightful person, someone other than me."

I see the complexity of emotion that moves through Esther's face. This time, her eyes fill with tears, and I'm embarrassed I've made her feel this way.

"I'm so sorry, Esther."

She shakes her head. "No, Tess. Don't be sorry. You have no reason to be sorry. But please, take this blanket. It would mean a lot to me if you did."

Why? But I don't dare ask.

Instead, I embrace her. Feel the warmth against her chest. "Thank you," I say and then quickly pull away, hoping the hug did not make her feel awkward.

"I'm sorry. I didn't mean to make you feel uncomfortable," I say as I see the shock register on her face.

She pulls me back for an embrace, and I feel like a little girl again, rested and comfortable and at ease with life against her grandmother's bosom.

Finally, she lets go.

We stare at each other for a long moment.

"Do you have a bag I can put this in, so it doesn't get wet?" I think about the walk home.

"Yes, yes." She walks behind the front counter and gives me a plastic bag.

Part of me doesn't want to leave Esther, but I know I should.

"I would love for you to come back, Tess. To visit."

A smile spreads across my face. "I'd like that very much, Esther."

She takes my hand again. "It has been with great pleasure to spend some time with you, Tess."

She takes my cheeks in her hands, her eyes exploring my facial features, as if comparing two different time periods.

She lets go, and I retreat toward the door, only to see Casey sitting out front.

I turn back and wave to Esther, who kisses her hands and points them in my direction.

I walk outside. The rain drums down on the awning.

Casey stands. "Hey, you all right?" He looks through the window behind me. "Your voice just didn't sound right on the phone."

"No, I'm fine."

We stand there.

"What's in the bag?"

"A long story. I'll tell you on our walk home."

I start at the beginning as the relenting rain ceases enough for us to begin our journey home.

"I don't know, Casey. She looked as though she knew me. Like she'd missed me. I know ... I know that's weird to say, but it was something in her eyes, her touch, the way she reached out for me—something familiar and something I've longed for. I ... I don't know. The whole thing was just surreal."

"And the blanket is a Chilkat blanket?" he asks. "What does it mean?"

"I have no idea, but I'm going to look it up when we get home—er, to the house," I quickly correct myself, not wanting Casey to think anything more of the house than a business transaction.

Regret about last night drips into my mind like slow-fed poison. I let it get too far. I should have said something. Stopped us. And although we didn't have sex, it feels like we did. I suppose those feelings are just a decay of old memories.

It's after five in the evening when we arrive back at the Isner house.

Emmitt and his crew are gone, only, a medium-size shipping container to the right of the garage, probably somewhere to put the bigger tools.

The rain starts again just as we walk inside.

"Does it ever stop raining here?" Casey asks, walking to the wall of windows.

"Come on. Home isn't much different," I say, carefully placing the blanket on the kitchen counter.

"Yeah, but home, we have slow and steady rain. This is a downpour every five minutes."

I look up and study Casey's silhouette in the window.

"Hey, Tess?"

I jump at the mention of my name, caught up in thoughts of him. Of us. "Yeah?" I pretend to busy myself in the kitchen, start dinner, move pots, do dishes.

"Never mind." He's still staring out the window.

I stop pretending to do things, stand, and stare at him. "No—" I start, but fear confines me, holds my words, my heart hostage.

Was he going to ask about the night we both left big pieces of our hearts in Oregon?

Was he going to tell me a memory of our brothers?

Was he going to ask about us?

It's better this way, I try to convince myself to hide underneath the blanket of lived existence and keep the memories to myself so my heart might somehow find temporary peace.

"I'll make salmon tonight for dinner," I say, hanging up the conversation we didn't have.

Trying to act casual and tread lightly against the gray between us, he makes his way to me and touches my hand to stop me. Meets my eyes with his. His stare reaches into parts of my body that scream for him and only him.

"The framed photograph on the wall downstairs, have you … have you seen it?" he asks with trepidation.

Oh. I breathe in a sigh of relief. "Yeah, the one with Ike, Emmitt, Esther and Martin, the young woman and the little girl?"

Casey nods.

"Yeah, sweet picture."

But something deeper is in Casey's eyes. A thought. An emotion maybe.

"What of it?"

In this moment, I see him throw up his white flag in surrender as he studies my face, as if he's given up. I want to push for more, but I don't.

"Nothing," he says.

His grip tightens around my hand, and I feel a bolt of electricity course through my veins.

There's a knock at the door, which makes us both jump.

Casey says, "I'll get it."

I hear a conversation at the door.

"Stanley, I presume?" I hear Casey say. "Thank you. No, no, it's working great."

I grab the bottle of Pendleton from underneath the counter and follow the voices to the front door. I hand it to Stanley. "I can't thank you enough, Stan."

His face full of surprise, he graciously accepts the bottle. Tips his hat. "Thank you, Ms. Morgan, but you really didn't have to." Stan turns to walk away. "Let me know if anything comes up."

"Will do, Stan. Thanks," Casey says, and we watch him disappear into the rain.

Casey shuts the door behind him. "We need to talk."

22

Casey

I've started and stopped so many times.

Just fucking tell her already. What are you so scared of? I ask myself. Maybe of pushing her away. It seems like we're making headway, and I'd hate to scare her. But we were friends first. Friends before sex came into the picture. Friends before she stole my heart. I've tried to put myself in her shoes several times from the time we left the Visitor Center until now—and I keep coming back to, *Ask her about the picture.*

In the doorway, we stand.

"What?" she asks.

I run my hand through my hair. "That picture downstairs, doesn't the woman holding the child look just like you?" Holding my breath, I wait for her answer.

Tess's eyes search mine and then the decaying floor that our feet are planted firmly on. She doesn't speak, but her eyes meet mine again. "I … I don't know. Maybe. I guess." She laughs.

Her laughter fills me with relief. *Thank God.* I felt like I was carrying this big secret around with me. "It's crazy, right? That I thought that? Just a coincidence?"

Tess laughs again. "I think you watch way too many investigative shows." She turns on the ball of her feet and starts dinner.

I watch her as she seasons the salmon with lemon, butter, olive oil, basil, thyme, parsley, and garlic, and then my phone rings. "It's Garrison. I'm going to take the call."

Tess nods.

"What's up, buddy?" I answer.

"Tell you what. There's no shortage of women in Detroit." He laughs a salty laugh. "You flyin' in tomorrow?"

"Tomorrow. Late." From the darkened living room, I look back at Tess and watch her make a salad.

"Eddy and I rented a car, so I'll swing by and pick you up."

It's quiet for a moment.

"So, what's up with you and Tess?" Garrison has heard about Tess for years. "You shacking up in that little place in Alaska?"

"Nothing like that. A business venture."

Garrison lets out a howl. "A business venture? Is that what you're calling it now? Come on," he says. "I know that girl has had your heart since way before we were friends. Just time you stop lying to yourself, bro."

"Whatever. Anyway, pick me up tomorrow. I'll text you the flight time."

"Yeah, okay."

"Hey, Garrison?"

"Yeah?"

"Thanks."

"That's all right."

We hang up, and I return to the kitchen and see two glasses of wine poured.

"For me?" I ask, motioning to the wine.

"For you," she says.

Not sure how much more wine I can take, but I don't have the heart to tell her wine isn't my favorite, so instead, I chug it down like a cowboy would. Quick.

"So, who's Garrison?" she asks, curious, sitting down on the stool.

"Travel buddy. Started the circuit together. He's more of a loose cannon, an in-the-moment kind of guy, guess you could say. But a damn good bull rider." I set the glass by the sink and grab a Coors Light from the refrigerator.

I see her grow uncomfortable under my stare.

"What's wrong?"

She sighs and puts her wineglass to her lips. "This—I don't know—seems to be our MO. We make dinner, drink some. Then, the night sits upon us, and the alcohol takes control. Then, we do things that—I don't know—maybe shouldn't happen among business partners."

I eye her and take a long swig of my beer. "Business partners?"

Tess nods.

I shake my head and move so close to her that her only choice is to stand from the stool.

"Business partners?" I whisper.

With her chest to mine, I can feel the power with each beat—either her heart or mine.

I can't do this anymore. I can't pretend, and I can't walk away anymore.

"Let's just get it over with and see where it goes," I say.

And with that, she takes my face in her hands and gives me her mouth.

I take her ass in my hands and lift her up. Her legs wrap around my middle.

Like we've done this before.

Like our bodies are only meant for each other.

"What about dinner?" she asks against my lips.

"There's only one thing I want right now, Tess—and it's not dinner."

I hold her against me, and she feels me harden. She quietly whimpers.

Our mouths explore each other's as if we'd just met.

She nips at my neck, and I melt under her taste.

Holding her against me, I walk us to the back bedroom—her bedroom—and lay her down on the bed.

After unbuttoning my shirt, I take hers off, and I see the lace of her bra and her panties as she shimmies off her pants and I put my body to hers.

"Pants," she says as she paws at my belt buckle.

I almost crumble under her touch as I spring to attention in my boxers.

She tugs me to her, and I groan in her ear.

"Tess, I'm not sure how long I'm going to last."

I rest my head against her chest but can't help myself. I take her breast in my mouth and tug at her nipple with my teeth.

Her legs loosen around my hips.

Tess reaches down and attempts to take my boxers off, but I stop her and moan.

"Are you sure?" I pant. "Tess, this is what you want, right? The aftereffects of who we are too."

I look down at her. Her dark hair is sprawled across the pillowcase. She looks up at me with the same green eyes she did when we were kids and the first time I made love to her.

"Yes."

Thank God.

My mouth falls to hers as she finishes the job of getting my boxers off. Taking myself in my hand, I sit back on my knees and stare down at her.

Her cheeks pink. I stroke myself and watch her as she takes her breasts in her own hands and watches me.

I was good and hard before, but now, I'm aching for her. I move inside my hand as I watch her.

"I'm afraid I'll lose my shit, Tess, and I won't get this view back again."

Pushing myself into my hand again, I gaze down at her. I run my free hand against her stomach and lower it to her middle.

"Is that for me, Tess?"

She's completely wet.

Tess pushes against my finger, which has made it into her folds.

Before I dare give myself pleasure, I watch her shudder under my touch. I remove my hand from my shaft and bury my mouth between her legs.

She calls out as I take all of her in my mouth. I flick my tongue against her knot, unhurriedly at first.

I grow harder, and it hurts, listening to her pant.

Tess takes the sides of my face and holds my head.

Just at the peak of her arousal, I stop and only put the tip of me inside her. I slowly push in and out, only giving her a small taste of what she needs.

She pulls her knees to her chest so that I have full access.

Again with my tip, I tease her, and her eyes burrow into mine.

"Oh God," I say as I watch. "Wait. Wait. Wait." I sigh, as this feels way too good, and when we orgasm, I want it to be from being inside her.

She lays on her side. "Enter me like this. Wait. Wait. What about a condom?" she asks, and it almost kills me.

I know why she wants the condom, and it isn't because she doesn't trust where I've been.

I grab my wallet from my jeans, and she takes it from me, opens it, pinches the top, and rolls it on while I kiss her mouth.

She assumes her position on her side and opens herself up from behind, and I slide inside her.

"Casey!" she calls out against the pillow.

"You're so wet, Tess," I hiss against her hair.

Reaching around her, I get my fingers inside her folds and lightly rub the knot.

I need to watch her when she comes, so I pull out. She moves to her back, and I slide inside her again.

We watch each other move and break and bend. We make love against the night, against everything that's wrong and everything that's right.

Friday morning comes too quickly. I feel for her in bed, but there are only cold sheets, remnants of our lovemaking.

"Tess?" I sit up, only to find an empty room. I rub my eyes, trying to cling to the memories we made last night.

I get out of bed, throw on my boxer shorts, and walk out to the kitchen.

In my shirt, she's making breakfast, and I allow my heart to fall even harder. She looks beautiful.

"What on earth are you doing?" I smile, walk toward her, pull her hips to mine, and give her a long, slow kiss.

"Waiting for you," she says as I pull away. She eyes me up and down. "Looking good, Mr. Atwood."

"I could say the same to you, Ms. Morgan."

"Coffee?" she asks.

I nod as she makes me a cup and slides the mug to me as I sit at the island.

"I remembered all the little things," she says.

"Little things?"

"I remember all the little things you used to do for me. Like bring me a coffee when you knew I was working late at the Dillon Creek Movie House. Or walk me home at night if I was helping out at The Whiskey Barrel." Tess laughs. "It was Dillon Creek, and I was quite safe to walk alone, but now, I know why you did it."

I take a sip of coffee. Smile against the memory.

"I remember the night after we made love for the first time." Her voice grows hoarse. "You took a fall off a bull that cost you a sprained ankle."

I remember.

"And now, I can't believe I did this to you, Case. You're preparing for the finals, and I can't be the mistake that allows it all to slip away."

Wait. What?

"Mistake?" I blurt out because I'm pissed she'd use a word like that to describe us.

"We can't let that happen again, not until you're done with the finals. I can't—" But she can't finish the sentence. I see the tears fill her eyes and the vulnerability. "I can't lose you this time, Casey. No matter how we feel, we lost—"

Before she can finish the sentence, I come around the corner and take her into my arms, and she melts into me.

"Nothing's going to happen to me, Tess."

But truth be told, something could, and it might.

23

The Ladybugs

Erla is up early, as she always is. She's up before the sun and in bed well after she should be.

It felt good to talk to Dr. Cain. Just to talk to someone. Millie, the dog, knows far too much for her own good, and she's a good listener. She's curled up in Don's chair when Erla comes out to the living room, coffee in hand.

She sees the card the doctor gave her from the grief group next to her chair.

"Good morning, old girl." She gives Millie's head a pat and then makes her way to her chair.

It's been a few weeks since she talked to Doc. Since then, bright yellow sticky notes—reminders, as she likes to call them—adorn the refrigerator, the coffeepot, cupboards, countertops, canisters, and stove.

Two nights ago, she left the stove on and wondered why her house was burning hot when she got up in the morning.

Erla retrieves her yellow legal pad from the small shelf underneath the table that separates her and Don's chairs.

Dying, most days, just seems like a better option.

But Scarlet and Devon—what would they do without her? It would break Scarlet's heart, but eventually, she'd move on; she's young enough. Devon? Erla isn't so sure. She is already angry with Erla for not telling her that Toby Lemon is her biological father. She was so furious with Erla that she didn't even attend Don's service. But Erla also knows her daughter, and regret is an awful thing to carry on one's shoulders.

There's a million and one ways to die, but Erla wants to be discreet, cause the least heartache, in making her exit from this world. Erla likes the drowning idea, as morbid as it is.

1. To do before accidental drowning in Eel River.

—Find car that no one can trace back to me.

—Cement blocks.

—A rope.

—Pay up all bills to the first of the month.

—Update will with Twila.

—Donate all junk to Tabitha's.

Tabitha's is a Seventh-day Adventist thrift store in Fortuna, but she knows her church, her pastor, would understand. Everybody knows there's one God in religion—for the most part. And besides, First Christian Church doesn't have a thrift store, so Tabitha's is the next best thing.

Erla runs into a problem. Eel River gets fairly low in the summertime, and she could get found out. They'd know it was a suicide when they discovered the cement blocks and the rope. But maybe by then, when the river begins to dry, all that will be left of Erla Brockmeyer is a pile of bones and no DNA to trace back to her. What if her DNA was left behind though? The whole town would be talking about Erla's suicide. And she sure doesn't want to be one of those souls that gets stuck between the real world and heaven because of unfinished business.

Erla winces. *And not to mention, suicide is a sin! Oh Lord. Wouldn't that be just her luck?*

All she wants is to be with her husband again.

As the sun begins to rise, Erla realizes this plan must have every inch of detail covered, and if she can't, then she ought not carry it out.

Her phone rings, and it scares the wits out of her. It's just after six in the morning. *Who could be calling her at this hour?*

"Hello?" Erla whispers into the kitchen phone.

"Hello? Erla? Why are you whispering?" Mabe asks.

Erla isn't sure why she was whispering.

"Are you in bed?" Mabe asks.

"No."

"Are you up?"

"Now, I am."

"Were you up before I called?"

"Yes."

"Did I interrupt you?"

What in the world would Erla tell Mabe if she asked what she'd interrupted her from?

So, she lies instead, "No."

Boy, she has really been pushing it with God lately.

"Can I come over for coffee? I can't sleep."

"Sure."

It's not five minutes later that Mabe arrives in the dark.

Mabe takes one look at the kitchen. "Why do you have sticky notes everywhere?"

Erla panics. "Reminders."

Erla pours Mabe a cup of coffee, praying she won't ask any more questions. She adds a splash of creamer, just like Mabe likes it.

She hands the cup to Mabe, and they go into the living room.

Thank goodness Erla hid the legal pad back in its rightful spot.

Mabe picks up Millie, sits down in Don's chair, and sets Millie back down on her lap.

"Why can't you sleep?" Erla asks.

"A lot on my mind, I guess."

Mabe really can't sleep because she's convinced Chief McBride knows it was Mabe out there in the field that night. She should turn herself in. But did she really do something wrong? Sure, it was despicable, what she did. Selfish. Awful really. But the nightmares that arrive every night are Mabe's punishment.

Could she go to prison?

She was on the scene, yes. However, she wasn't driving the Jeep. She might know more than most know. There was a third person, and that person was driving—the person who was never discovered after the accident, who walked away from the scene somehow. But in order to come clean with all this, Mabe must face the music.

That she was there.

That she's the one who walked away.

The whole town would blow up in smoke. An idea, a split between town—who was driving the night and who wasn't. Quietly, sides were taken after the accident. The Morgans blamed the Atwoods since it was assumed that Conroy was driving because it was his Jeep. Mabe didn't really make out the third person, but she definitely noticed the features were more womanly than manly.

Millie's movement in the chair brings Mabe to the present moment.

"Four hours of sleep is my limit these days," Erla sighs. "I'm tired, Mabe. Do you ever feel like you're exhausted from life and all you want is to go to sleep and not wake up?"

Mabe is quiet for a moment. "Yeah," she says, remembering what it was like when John and Francine died. Most days, she just wanted to die too. But a quiet voice inside her kept saying, *There are big plans for you. You need to stay put.*

"It's been a good run. I've had a great life, but I'm awfully tired."

Mabe is hesitant. She needs to tell someone. Someone she trusts. Someone who won't breathe a word to anyone else. Mabe thinks maybe this, her telling Erla, could be a practice run for if and when she talks to the chief. But everybody will know that Mabe Muldoon let the boys die in the field that night. Her heart becomes overwhelmed with sadness. Guilt.

"Do you think that we make it to heaven even if we made some wrong turns in life, Erla?"

Erla feels the panic begin to build. *Does Mabe know she's contemplating suicide?* She must know or else why would she have asked such a real question?

"I don't know. But I'd like to think so." Erla feels as though she might be sick. "Excuse me, Mabe." And Erla goes to the bathroom.

Mabe takes this opportunity to set Millie back down on the chair. She walks into the kitchen to read Erla's sticky notes.

Pay water bill on the 25th of each month.

Did you turn off the oven?

Does Millie have food?

Is your car in the garage?

Derrick is the name of the guy who mows your lawn. He drives a red pickup truck.

Pay the cable bill on the 15th of each month.

Pay the mortgage on the 1st of the month.

Have you taken Millie out to go potty?

Give Millie her flea pill on the 10th of each month.

The Ladybugs meet on the last Tuesday of the month.

And when Mabe reads the last sticky note, she knows there is something awfully wrong with Erla: The Ladybugs meet the *first* Tuesday of every month at noon sharp.

When Mabe hears the door open, she quickly walks back to the living room and scoots Millie over, and when she leans to the left, she sees a legal pad of paper underneath the table. *Accidental drowning in Eel River* with notes below it.

Dear God, Erla, what are you doing?

Mabe feels her heartbeat accelerate. Her mind begins to spin with questions.

Would Erla Brockmeyer off herself?
Does she have a drinking problem too?
Was it written by someone else?

Erla comes back into the living room, sits down, and sips her coffee.

Would a normal person in their right mind sip coffee after writing something like that?

Mabe's face grows hot when she thinks about asking Erla about it. She reflects on a time when Erla helped save Mabe's life.

"Erla?" Mabe says.

"Yeah?"

Silence sits between the two old women like fog. It hangs, looms, hovers.

"Never mind."

Mabe knows better than to ask Erla this. Of course it isn't Erla's legal pad. It didn't look like her handwriting.

"Your coffee is getting cold," Erla says.

Mabe already asked once about the sticky notes. She'll wait for Erla to say something about it—if she does. Mabe sips her coffee and waits for the world to light up once again.

That's what Erla needs, Mabe thinks to herself. She just needs some light.

Later that day, Mabe is pruning her prize-winning flowers when the phone rings.

"Hello?"

"Hello, Mabe. It's Patty."

"Hello, Patty."

"Listen," Patty says. Her voice is so soft that a church mouse can squeak louder. "My husband wants to take me on a getaway for the weekend."

Mabe listens.

Patty finally says, "What shall I do?"

Perhaps this is a trick question, but maybe it's not. "Well, honey, I suppose you'd go."

"What about taking my own car?"

Mabe wants to laugh. Patty really is quite literal, and Mabe enjoys this about her. "Your husband wouldn't drink to the point where it makes you uncomfortable, would he?"

"Oh, no. Ron isn't a real drinker."

"Wonderful. Then, go."

"You think it's all right?"

Mabe thinks on it. "Do you want to go, Patty?"

"I do. But, well, it's just … I wonder if Ron will expect something from me."

"He is your husband, right?"

"That's right."

"So, why would it be wrong, Patty? People consummate their relationships all the time. Every day in fact."

"What?"

Mabe sighs. "Sex."

"What?" By Patty's tone, Mabe can tell she's taken aback.

"What exactly are you talking about, Patty?"

"To drink, of course."

Now, Mabe is taken aback. "Oh. Doesn't Ron support your endeavors not to drink?"

"Well, I haven't really told him."

"What do you mean, you haven't told him?"

"I haven't told him that I think I'm an alcoholic."

"You mean to tell me, you haven't been drinking for some time now, and he doesn't know that you're going to AA? What do you tell him when you meet with me?"

"Ladies' luncheon."

"Well, Patty, the first thing you need to do is get honest with your husband, and this weekend seems to be the perfect time. Call me when you return home." And with that, Mabe hangs up the phone. She hasn't really needed to get tough with Patty, but sometimes, that woman worries her.

Just as Mabe sets the phone back upon the stairs, Chief McBride's police cruiser pulls up to the house.

Mabe's heart seizes. Her entire body goes numb.

I'm going to prison, she thinks in her head. *Somebody finally identified me.*

"Ms. Muldoon," Chief McBride says, making his way from his car and down her walkway.

Mabe thinks *Ms.* is probably acceptable, being that it has been quite some time since her husband, John, passed.

"To what do I owe the pleasure?" floats out of Mabe's mouth, like a tongue slithers from a snake. Mabe slips off her gloves. "Would you like some iced tea?"

"Yes, that'll be wonderful."

Mabe retrieves the iced tea from inside, shaking like a leaf, and returns to her porch, where Chief McBride is sitting in one of the old rocking chairs.

"Sunny days don't come too often in the fall," the chief says. "Thank you."

Mabe sits down next to him, setting her tea down on the table that separates them. "No, no, they don't."

Don't panic, she tells herself.

But her hands and insides are vibrating so bad that they're liable to vibrate right out of her body and dance into the sky.

"Listen, I'm sure you've heard, but there was an anonymous tip that came into the police department about a woman in her seventies or so being on the scene the night Tripp and Conroy died. You wouldn't happen to have heard anything about that, have you?"

God, Mabe feels, has put her at a crossroad. She could tell the truth right now and clear the awful air that's been following her, eating at her conscience for eight long years, or she could continue to lie because the fear tells her she must.

"No, I haven't. But it sure is awful," pours from her mouth.

Chief McBride takes a sip from his iced tea. Sets it down next to Mabe's. "I think the person was just stuck. Saw what happened and panicked. Don't you?"

The blood rushes to Mabe's face. *Say something, Mabe.* "Maybe." She tries to act casual, but inside, her body is absolute chaos. She wonders why she hasn't already dropped dead from a panic attack—or worse, a heart attack.

People can die from those.

"Anyway, I best be on my way." The chief stands. "Let me know if you hear anything, Ms. Muldoon?"

Yes, if Mabe Muldoon doesn't die first.

24

Tess

After Casey leaves for the weekend, I feel like a small piece of me is gone, and I hate how this sits with me. It brings back old feelings of grief and loss and loneliness.

We came back from Oregon.

Our brothers died.

Casey left.

And I lost myself.

Emmitt and his crew are working on the roof, and thankfully, it's almost finished. Amid the hammers and tools and working at warp speed it seems, I decide to make dinner for the crew before they go home. Mostly, it looks like younger single guys on his crew without a pot to piss in.

I look down at my watch. "It's too late to make dinner." I reach for my phone and notice a text message from Casey.

> *Me: Lock the doors at night. I'll be home late Sunday night. I love your hair.*

I laugh out loud. When Casey and I were young and exploring each other's bodies, learning about each other intimately, we knew *I love you* was a big statement. We somewhat knew the ramifications of love, the price we'd pay for love, but we really had no idea. Anyhow, instead of *I love you*, it could be:

I love your jeans.

I love your hair.

I love the way you move.

Casey though was the first one to say it.

I love you, I say the words in my head and then out loud. I smile as the statement presses against my chest, lies like a piece of lace, dainty yet sturdy. And for just a moment, I allow my head to play out a future with Casey.

Us.

Holding hands.

A front yard.

A white picket fence.

Children.

And the thought fades quicker than it appeared because I can't go there yet. Guilt twists in my gut like a rag.

And home. Where is that? Is that in Dillon Creek, where my parents despise his parents? Where everyone knows our past? Where our brothers died and everyone cried and the whole town mourned? Where a town divided right down the middle and the people moved with it, silently taking sides?

Or is home here in Ketchikan, where no one really knows us? Where grief doesn't plague us at every corner we turn? Where we're not remembered as those who lost their siblings? We'd just be a young couple who've taken to a beautiful place.

The wind starts slowly, and the whine of the old girl—the house—brings me out of my thoughts.

"Didn't like that much?" I say to her.

I text Casey back.

Me: I love your walk, and will do.

I think about adding a heart emoji but delete it at the last second.

I text Olive, as I can't prepare a dinner quickly enough before Emmitt and his guys have to leave.

Me: Hey, Olive. It's Tess. Where's a great place to get pizzas?

She texts me back.

Olive: Paul's Pizza Shack. ;)

Me: Thank you. ;)

I grab my purse, a raincoat, and head out the door.

Before I begin my descent down the hill, Emmitt calls from the roof, "Hey, Tess! Please, take my truck. We'll be done here in an hour." He tosses the keys down to me. He laughs. "We've been watching you two walk downtown. Winter's coming. Come the beginning of December, you won't be able to make the walk up that hill with all the snow."

"Are you sure?"

"You gonna steal it?"

I laugh. "No."

"All right then."

I nod, shove his keys in my pocket, and head downtown in his truck.

As I wait for the pizzas, Paul's Pizza Shack is everything it advertises. It smells like fresh dough, and when the wind blows, the pizza shack shakes and shimmies.

I try to stay away from the thoughts that have been stewing in my head most of the day. The woman in the picture that Casey swears I look like. Emmitt's words when he asked if I remembered the winters. The familiar scent of the Isner house. *It's all just coincidence, right?* That's what I tell myself. *But why do I keep sitting in these thoughts? Thoughts I can't seem to let go of. Why would Ike bring Casey and me here? Why would he give us this house free and clear?*

Against my better judgment, I text my mom and ask her to send me some baby pictures, just to prove Casey is being overly cautious.

"Tess?" I hear my name being called.

I take the five pizzas and head home.

"You didn't have to do this, Tess," Emmitt says, taking a slice from the box.

The rest of the guys eat hungrily, shaking their heads.

After they finish, I thank them again. The guys are up ahead, loading into their trucks.

Emmitt turns to me. "Thank you, Tess. That was really nice of you."

"It was my pleasure, Emmitt."

He starts to walk away again, his age resting in his bones. He stops and turns. "Oh, I'll stop by tomorrow morning. A little something for you and Casey. It's not much, but it'll get you through."

"What is it?"

He tips his hat. "You'll just have to wait and see," he says and disappears into the dusk.

After I clean up the kitchen, I grab a glass of wine, my laptop, and think to myself that we might possibly need internet. I can use my phone as a hotspot, but also, it might make more sense for us to pay the monthly fee for Wi-Fi.

I double-check the chimney with a flashlight before I start another fire, just for good measure.

The wind begins to kick up, and the rain dances against the roof.

"Why is it so windy here?" I say out loud, partly to her—the house with bones of steel—maybe for an answer, but maybe just so that she knows how strong I think she is.

Her bones whine against the wind. The roof withstands the rain, even in the process of getting a new one. Maybe her way of saying, *It's what I needed, and thank you.*

I sit down on the sofa, and my mom finally responds to my text from earlier.

Mom: Hey, babe. Why would you need pictures?

My mother loves my baby pictures—any pictures for that matter. She's always first to share with anyone who will look, so this response is odd to me.

My mother has a way of sniffing out things and getting herself involved when she doesn't need to, so in an effort to keep her nose out of my business, I lie.

Me: I was invited to a baby shower, and the host needs pictures of us for some game.

She always likes when I make new friends.

Mom: Oh, that's wonderful! I'll e-mail them now.

E-mail? Why e-mail?

Me: Why e-mail? Can't you just take a picture of the picture and send them over text?

Mom: You don't want them to look pixilated, do you, when you print them for the game?

Oh shit. Right.

Me: Right. Thanks, Mom.

Mom: Call me tomorrow, so we can catch up?

Me: Yeah.

Mom: I love you, baby.

Me: Love you too.

I pull up Google on my laptop with a hotspot on my phone and type in *Chilkat blankets.*

It talks about how they're made with goat's wool and cedar bark weft and hand-dyed with wolf moss. A man created the design utilizing clan symbols, and a woman wove the blanket with her hands on a loom. The blankets were used for special occasions, dances, ceremonies, honored guests, a death of a chief or a person of high-ranking Chilkat Tlingit society. It takes a year, sometimes two, for a person to make the blanket and it's *only given to those with Tlingit bloodlines or those who an elder trusts."*

I roll this sentence over and over and over in my head.

Tlingit bloodlines or trust.

Tlingit bloodlines or trust.

Tlingit bloodlines or trust.

Esther doesn't know me from Eve. But the visit—the feelings return to me, the feelings of home and comfort, and her scent rushes in. Like we've met before. But my mind cannot rationalize this.

How would I not remember meeting Esther before I came here?

Why would she give me this beautiful, handcrafted blanket that is so important to their tribe?

The questions sit in my mind like a fire being stoked.

Quickly, I run downstairs, maneuver around Emmitt's tools and supplies, and grab the picture from the wall. I run back upstairs and head back to my laptop, setting the picture down next to me.

I check my e-mail and notice I've received one from unemployment.

Unemployment.

As in I'm no longer employed. I no longer have a job. I'm no longer needed.

The lump in my throat is swallowed and sits in my stomach as I fill out the forms the unemployment office needs and e-mail them back.

The memory of the video of the little boy and Casey pops into my mind.

Casey would have made a great father.

What were Casey's thoughts when he was looking into the eyes of the little boy?

Does Casey know he'd be a good father?

Do I know if I'd be a good mother?

Push your tears down, Tess.

Regret starts to creep up my throat.

Allow it. After all, this is a fallout of your past decision-making.

I try not to unpack the memories, force them to stay down but I can't, so they slowly start to unfold.

Ten little fingers and ten little toes and the little round face.

They took him almost immediately.

I begged for just a moment with him, with us.

"It's not a good idea, dear," the nurse softly whispered into my ear. "Begin your healing."

Never had I felt a hole so deep inside me.

Never had I wanted something back so bad in my life.

Tears began.

The deep ache in my heart formed.

And my body shook with sadness.

I'm jolted awake by the wind. No, not the wind—the old girl's reaction to the wind. I sit up and feel the darkness around me, except for the small embers from the fireplace that keep breathing.

It was a loud bang.

Maybe something fell downstairs.

Maybe something fell off the roof.

Looking behind me, I see something in the shadows near the kitchen.

My heart begins to pound.

My breathing become tiny and small so as not to disturb the quietness. I tiptoe to the fireplace, where the embers still burn. I take the fire poker and turn to the kitchen.

I'm a rather-not person. The women in the movies who ask, "Who's there?" are not my people. I'd rather not see the perpetrator. And what are the odds that the bad guy actually comes forward? Never. They never do.

My hands tighten around the iron weapon. I step to the kitchen and peek over the counter.

It's then that beast unfolds itself, and I scream as the raccoon jumps from the counter and scurries out of sight.

I try to catch my breath as I run to the front door and open it, praying to God the raccoon doesn't have rabies or some awful mutated disease.

Breathlessly, I whisper, "Hey, here's a way out."

After waiting a few moments, I carefully sneak to the last location I saw the raccoon.

I hear it before I see a black-and-brown ball of fury take off toward the front door, and just in time, I watch as its tail is the last thing I see heading outside.

25

Casey

"You've setting a precedent, Casey, but no pressure, right?" Garrison rubs some clear gel on his shoulder.

"What is that, old-man shit?" I laugh, grabbing my rope for the first ride. I drew Top Ten, a bull that's new to the PBR but is quickly gaining a reputation for being a force to reckon with.

"Hey, don't knock it till you try it. Makes me feel like I'm eighteen again." Garrison throws the gel shit in his riggin bag. "So, what about Tess? You guys shacked up or what? Building a future together and all that shit?"

I'm not sure Garrison will ever settle down. Hell, I'm not sure he'll ever mature past the age of twenty-two. But he's loyal.

"I don't know," is all I say.

"Come on. You don't expect me to believe that bullshit, do you, man?" A low whistle escapes through his teeth, and a slow laugh follows. "You're different. You're different in a way I've never seen you. You're actually packin' that damn phone around now. Checking it. You've got this stupid love-drunk face you wear. Ain't my first rodeo, Atwood."

I laugh out loud. "Love-drunk?"

Garrison nods. "Love-drunk. Look, I don't really know too much about your past—like, your childhood and shit. But I've seen a lot of buckle bunnies come after you—some really hot ones—and you've always had this wall up between them and you. Like some shit is holdin' you back. Anyhow"—he stands from his sitting position on the bench—"you ever want to talk about it … don't bring that shit to me."

I let out a slow, easy laugh.

Garrison does too. "Kiddin' aside, man. I ain't ever been in love, but if you do want to talk, I'm here. Not sure I can help much in the love department, but I'm here." Garrison slaps me hard on the back. "Let's ride, cowboy!" he yells.

"Garrison!" Travis, a PBR official, comes into the locker room. "You're on next!"

"Let's go!" Garrison slaps his own face.

I prefer the arena when it's quiet. When it's just me, the smell of cow shit, the dirt, and the sound of the bulls pushing themselves around in the bull pens behind the chutes. I make it a ritual to get to the arena early, way before the staff, the crowds, the cowboys, before the lights come on, and before the arena is staged.

I get right with God.

Visualize my ride on the chosen bull for the event.

Dance through the steps.

He leads.

I follow.

Balance.

Left hand up.

Roll the hips.

But right now, it's nothing like that.

The arena is jacked.

The lights are bright.

The music is loud.

And the bulls are ready.

I take a seat on the fence behind the chute, so I can see Garrison's ride. He's still in the chute, readying himself, everyone waiting for his nod.

"Hey, stranger." A woman's voice sounds.

Oh shit.

"Hey, Riley."

She climbs up on the fence next to me.

"Been a while, Atwood." She bumps my shoulder and bites her lower lip. "If I were a betting woman, I'd bet ten thousand that says you've been avoiding me."

I let out a slow chuckle. She'd be right. If I couldn't have Tess, Riley might be a close second.

"You've had some real good rides, cowboy. Hear you're a contender in the World Finals."

Riley's long, dark hair rolls down her back.

"Can't say you've had a bad year chasing those barrels either."

She smiles. "I've done all right."

"Don't be modest, Ri."

Garrison gives the nod.

The commentator explodes with words. "Garrison is on the bubble, folks, for a spot in the World Finals. These next several weekends will decide his fate. Look at him go!"

The bull jumps, twists, turns, and bucks. But Garrison is in a zone all by himself.

Jump.

Twist.

Turn.

Buck.

Twist.

Turn.

Jump.

Buck.

The horn sounds, and I stand and throw a fist into the air as Garrison does the same after he dusts himself off.

Riley is standing up, cheering next to me.

"Hey," she says, "can I talk to you?"

Fuck.

This is it.

She's going to ask why I've been avoiding her.

We had sex. I don't know … we were kind of together, but I couldn't fully commit.

I jump down behind the chute and help her down.

"Look, Atwood, to be … to be quite honest, I would wait forever for you. But I'm not sure you can say the same. It's like we were in a relationship with calls and texts, dinners and dancing, and then you made love to me for the first time. Then, you were just … gone. I had to hear from Garrison that you went back home." She pauses for a minute. Looks down at her feet and then back up at me. "I will be okay if you just tell me what the hell is going on." Her voice is calm, even-keeled. Steady. "And then I see the pictures of you and Ava online …" Her voice grows to a quiet whisper.

I won't make excuses. She's right.

"Casey, I fell hard for you, and if you don't feel the same, then let me go. But you can't text me anymore. You can't call me anymore. I need a man who's willing to be there for me in all aspects of my life."

"Atwood!" Travis calls down the row of chutes. "You're up next!"

Riley looks up at me with her doe eyes and long eyelashes. "Atwood, you've always had walls up, like you're trying to protect yourself from the world, and I think you hide behind the bulls, the eight-second rides, the excitement, just so you don't have to deal with life," she says with sincerity and truth as tears begin to form.

"Come on, Ri. Don't do that." I pull her in for a hug. "Please don't cry."

She laughs against my safety vest.

"Why do you have to be such a good cowboy and be broken in ways that people can't see?"

"Atwood! Let's go!"

Her words fall directly against me, hitting me in the chest, the gut.

I pull away from her. "You're right. I suppose my heart is a bit broken."

I leave Riley standing there, just like I did months ago. She's a beautiful woman.

She'll find her happiness, I told myself then and I tell myself now.

"Why do you have to be such a good cowboy and be broken in ways that people can't see?"

I let Riley's words fester inside me as I climb into the chute with the bull.

I feel the beast breathe underneath my thighs.

Top Ten feels my tension.

He head-butts the gate. Stomps his hoof.

I tighten the rope around my hand and get right in my position.

And I can't stand these feelings, and the only way to escape them is to latch on to the adrenaline.

"Okay, boys!" I nod.

Top Ten launches out of the chute on a tirade.

Angry, he spins.

Buck.

Twist.

Kick.

Spin.

Angry, he moves with speed and precision, a method.

Each time his front hooves make contact with the ground, I feel his force throughout my body.

I breathe and dance with Top Ten as if he were the wind and I were the silk.

Move.

Follow.

Move.

Follow.

Move.

Follow.

As if we were one muscle working together.

The loud horn sounds, and I release myself from the bull, only to come up facedown in the dirt.

Just as I look up, I'm face-to-face with the bull.

A few feet away from one another, we lock eyes.

Just me and the beast.

My breathing is the only thing I hear. It's loud, and it ricochets off the cool, hard dirt. Pulsates in my ears.

He could kill me right now.

One step on my skull, and I wouldn't make it.

Tess would be alone.

My parents and brothers would grieve another son, another brother.

There are moments in life where we're pressed with decisions, ones that could change the trajectory of our lives.

Follow your heart and make the right choice, or follow your ego, and you'll play Russian roulette.

The snarl of the bull's stare eats at my insides—maybe his way of saying, *You're close to meeting your maker. Stop this. Do something different. I'm giving you a chance to live. Do it right.*

The bullfighters pull at my arms as another bullfighter jumps in front of the bull.

What seemed like several minutes has only been several seconds.

With help from a bullfighter and with one swift movement, I run for the fence.

The crowd erupts, and I turn to see the sea of people on their feet.

"Boy, oh boy! That was one heck of a ride by veteran Casey Atwood! Whoa! I haven't seen a ride like that since … well, I'm not sure. But this one—this one—was *incredible!*"

I try to catch my breath while attempting to wrap my head around not the ride, but the moment between the bull and me. When the arena fell silent and all that made sense was me and Top Ten and his eyes, the way they burrowed into mine. Safely up on the fence, resting my head against on a board, I close my eyes.

"Come on, cowboy!" one of the bullfighters calls to me, his hand hits my vest. "Hell of a ride!"

"Folks"—the commentator's voice gathers with excitement—"a well-earned score of ninety-four!"

The arena explodes, and it takes everything in me to let go of the fence, turn to the crowd, take off my hat, and wave.

The commentator's voice is muffled because the roar of the crowd is so loud.

Cowboys, bull riders, PBR officials smack my back, congratulating me on the way out of the arena as they gear up for the next ride.

Garrison meets me at the gate with a push. "That's how you do it, cowboy!" he says as we make our way to the locker room.

"Hey," I whisper into the phone.

"Great ride, cowboy," Tess says, and I feel her words meet my heart.

"How are you?" I ask. My towel wrapped around my middle, I sit down on the bed.

"Good. Just finished dinner, and now, I'm sitting by the fire with a glass of wine."

"Wish I could be there."

"Me too."

"Is it raining?"

"Yep."

"The wind howling?"

"Surprised you can't hear it."

I smile into the phone. "I miss you, Tess."

"I miss you too." But I hear it in her tone—the worry. "That … that was a fantastic ride, Casey."

"Yeah?" I don't care about the ride right now. All I care about is Tess and hearing her voice after all the chaos of the previous two hours.

"Yeah."

We're quiet for another minute.

"It's late there."

"There was a lot of fluff shit I had to do afterward. Publicity and whatever. Make the sponsors happy."

"You didn't go out and celebrate?" she asks.

"No, I just want to get home to you." I stand and remove my towel and walk to my overnight bag. Pull out underwear.

"What are you doing right now?"

"At the moment, I'm standing in the middle of my room, naked as a jaybird."

"Mr. Atwood, I'm certain almost half of America would love to see that sight after your ride tonight." Her tone now is flirty, not as guarded or worried.

"Well, there's only one woman I need." I barely hear it, but I hear her breath hitch, like it's caught. "Tess, you all right?"

No answer.

"Tess?"

"I'm here." I hear her smile in the way she whispers. "Hey, Case?"

"Yeah?"

"Promise me you'll be safe? I know … I know that's hard to do, but I'd really like you to come back to Ketchikan in one piece, okay?"

I smile. "I always do, Tess."

"Oh," she says.

"What?"

"Anna is calling on the other line."

"Talk to her. It might be important."

"Are you sure?"

"I'll call you tomorrow."

"Okay. Good night, Casey."

"Good night, Tess. Hey."

"Yes?"

I think for a minute. I don't to want to rush this with Tess. I want to start out right. Whatever is happening between us, it's different, and I don't want to change a fucking thing.

"Never mind." So, instead, I silently whisper, *I love you.*

26

The Ladybugs

It was the drinking bender Patty went on after she and her husband, Ron, returned from their getaway that took away Mabe's fear about the whole Chief incident.

It was Ron who called Mabe, and it was Mabe and Betty who drove to Patty's house in Fortuna.

Two old ladies with some sobriety behind them made for hell on wheels.

"How did you know to call me, Ron?" Mabe asks when they're met at the front door of the Patty's residence.

Ron shrugs, and Mabe sees his heart is broken just by his eyes.

"I noticed Patty would make calls in the closets or downstairs, go to ladies' luncheons when she thought I was busy doing something else. I thought she was having an affair until, one day, when she left her phone on the counter after she returned from the pantry closet. I went through the phone and looked at the last call made. I saw the name *Mabe AA*. And then I found *The Big Book of Alcoholics Anonymous* in her nightstand." He pauses to collect his thoughts. "I ... I always knew she drank differently. I just didn't want to believe it was this bad."

"Where's Patty now?" Betty asks.

"Bedroom. Upstairs on the left."

Betty makes her way upstairs.

"Did you know all along?" Mabe asks.

"That she has a drinking problem or that she was going to AA?"

"Both."

"Not until she admitted it, no. But these past few days, I can't get her to stop. That's why I called you. Why can't she stop, Mabe?"

"An allergy of the mind," comes out of Mabe's mouth. "She can't stop because her mind is telling her that just one more drink will take her to places she needs to go."

Ron nods. His eyes fill with worry. "Will she be all right? I mean, if she stops, she'll be okay, right?"

"I don't know, Ron." Mabe pats Ron's hand and follows Betty upstairs to the bedroom on the left.

Patty is lying on her bed in her Sunday church clothes. It's a Tuesday, so Mabe isn't quite sure why she's still dressed in her church clothes. Betty is at her side.

When Patty catches Mabe's eyes, her face turns sour, and she begins to cry. "I'm sorry, Mabe."

Her apology makes Mabe's heart ache. She's been here several times, and Erla is the only one who gave her the truth, even when she didn't want to hear of it.

"You owe no apology to me, Patty," Mabe says.

"You want to get sober and stay sober?" Betty asks. "Put the plug in the jug?"

Patty picks up her head. "I'm sorry? Plug in the jug?"

Mabe knows Patty is very black and white and will not understand.

"Get sober and stay sober, Patty. Would you like that?" Mabe sits down next to Patty.

"Yes."

"All right then," Betty says. "You'll go to Mabe's house for a few days to dry out, and I'd better see you both at a meeting in Fortuna tonight at the Adventist church." And with that, Betty stands, gives Mabe a nod, and lets herself out.

"I-I'm not sure what happened, Mabe, but my drinking got more awful. I couldn't hide it from my family anymore."

"When's the last time you changed your clothes?" Mabe can smell the fermented alcohol oozing from her pores.

Patty looks down at what she's wearing and looks back at Mabe sorrowfully. "I don't remember."

"Come on. Let's get you in the shower. Then, we'll talk about next steps."

Mabe helps Patty undress and step into the shower.

There are two sets of eyes behind her, watching their mother step into the shower.

And then Mabe's heart hurts all over again when the taller one asks, "Are you going to make our mom better?"

Mabe's chances of being a grandmother disappeared when Francine died. Mabe had big plans for her grandchildren. She was going to teach them how to play poker, how to use cuss words appropriately, love them, but she never got that chance.

Mabe takes the children back into their parents' room, out of the bathroom so that Patty can shower by herself.

When Mabe looks at these children, it's as though she were looking into the eyes of God, the innocent ones affected by a seemingly hopeless disease.

The smaller of the two says, "Are you a grandma?"

Mabe laughs. "No, but I suppose if you need an extra one, I could be that person."

"Why is our mom acting like this?" the older one asks.

The younger one says, "I just want her better."

Mabe wonders how on earth she'll be able to explain alcoholism to two young children, but she tries.

Tess

"Just so you know," Anna says, "Colt and I didn't know that Casey received a letter, too, until the day before he left."

"It's okay, Anna."

"It is?"

"Yeah."

"So, have you guys ... come to an agreement?"

"Yeah."

"Have you had sex?"

"Yeah."

The line grows extremely silent.

"Anna?"

"I'm here."

"Are you all right?"

"Are you?"

I laugh.

So does she. "Is this a good thing?"

I think about Casey and our past and everything in between. "It won't happen again."

"Why not?"

"So many reasons and too long for a phone conversation. More of an in-person conversation. Anyway, how are you guys?"

"Do your parents know?"

"That we had sex? God, no."

"No." She laughs. "That Casey's in Ketchikan."

"I have no idea. My mom hasn't said anything."

"Do you think she'll blow a lid?"

I shrug. "Anna, she'd blow a lid if I were wearing white pants past Labor Day."

"Ah, good point."

I can feel her next question coming on.

"Was it good?" she whispers.

"Amazing. Quite honestly, now, I know why sex with the other guy was just okay."

Anna giggles. "I have news."

"What?" I put my wineglass to my lips and take a sip.

"I'm pregnant."

I jump up off the couch. "No way! You are? Anna!"

"I'm only a minute pregnant, so we're going to wait until after the twelve weeks to tell anyone."

"Anna! I'm so happy for you guys! How did it happen?"

"Uh, well …"

I roll my eyes. "I mean, were you guys trying?"

"Yes. I was just nervous it would take some time."

"Clearly, it didn't."

I walk to the window and stare out at the old red truck that Emmitt brought over earlier today. Said it would get me where I needed to go. I tried to give him money, though I couldn't afford much, but we do need a car as winter approaches. Old feelings start to resurface, but I swallow each of them, allowing them to fester in my gut.

"How did you tell Colt?"

"What do you mean?"

"Well, isn't there some sort of fun way to tell your husband you're pregnant? I think I've seen it on Pinterest or something." I let the curtains fall back into place, which reminds me, we'll need to buy new curtains if we want to sell the house. I think it's called staging, as Casey put it.

"Oh, no. I just handed him the pregnancy test."

Typical Anna. There's no fluff. No surprise. Just the facts. "And?"

"He couldn't believe it."

"Well, did you tell him that's what happens when two people have sex?" I laugh.

"He's still in shock. But I think he's silently hoping for a boy. Probably because he wouldn't know what to do with a girl as long as the baby is healthy."

Her words resonate in my bones. *As long as the baby is healthy.*

Deafening silence is what we heard all those years ago. Deafening silence fell on our ears when cries were begged for. Just a cry to remember. A sound to tuck into our hearts and keep when the silence of the world got to be too much.

"Earth to Tess."

"Sorry, yes, I'm here. Heard something outside." I'm not lying. Because the wind and rain are all I've heard for the better part of the day. "So, when are you due?" I walk back over to the sofa and sit down.

"We haven't met with the doctor yet. I'm at eight weeks. According to my calculations, I'm about six weeks pregnant."

"That's exciting, Anna. I couldn't be happier for you and Colt."

"Any bites on the house?" she asks.

"Still fixing things. Emmitt, the general contractor we hired, said he should be done with the work before Christmas."

"And then you'll sell it?"

"That's the plan."

"What about ... what about you and Casey?" Her voice is quieter.

"I'm not sure."

She sighs.

"What?"

"I'm just not sure why you two haven't figured out you're meant to be. I mean, sure, your parents will be pissed. But they'll eventually get over it. Especially when you guys start having kids. They'll have to, right?"

My heart sinks and falls to a puddle on the floor.

Anna and I always dreamed of marrying the Atwood boys when we were younger. Having babies. Living next door to each other. Celebrating Christmases and birthdays and Easters together.

We never planned on losing brothers.

We never planned on family feuds and broken families.

But we also never planned on unexpected miracles, as Clyda always used to put it.

"Maybe."

I want to tell Anna what happened, but I'm too afraid all these emotions I've held on to for so long will make me cry uncontrollably.

Besides, I need to talk to Casey about that before I talk to anyone.

"Well, I love you, Tess."

"Love you too. And I'm so happy for you two."

"Thank you. Good night."

"Good night."

I hit End just as an e-mail comes in from my mom. It's some of my pictures I asked for earlier. She finally sent them.

> *Hey, honey.*
>
> *Here are a few pictures I found. My favorites.*
>
> *How's it going there?*
>
> *Anyhow, I love you very much.*
>
> *Love,*
>
> *Mom*

This is not my mother.

My mother has always made a concerted effort to intervene herself in my life. Meddle. Save the day, if she can. I haven't called her very much since I've been here, and she hasn't called me much. Hell, she has to know Casey is here, too, and she hasn't said a damn word. I mean, it's Dillon Creek. I'm certain when I left, Delveen submitted an op-ed piece to the *Dillon Creek Echo* about my leaving. Nevertheless, it's odd behavior for my mom to act ... well, normal. I know she meddles because she cares deeply. I know she does it because she's terrified of losing me, like she lost Tripp. I know she partly feels every inch of Tripp's death daily. Maybe she feels she could have prevented it.

I wake up every day and wonder the same thing.

If I had been home ...

If I hadn't gone to Oregon with Casey ...

If I had stayed put and not made decisions that would haunt me and Casey for the rest of my life ...

What I wouldn't give to hear my brother's voice again.

Why didn't I save his voice mails?

There are four attachments in the e-mail, and they're clearly labeled—age four, age five, age seven, and age nine.

I get up, go into the kitchen, and grab the framed photo. I open each photo my mom sent—one of me by a tree, eating a popsicle; one of me in my Sunday dress at age five; another one of me on the first day of school with a rainbow-colored sundress and no front teeth to speak of; and one of me at age nine when I got my first real big-girl bicycle with hand brakes. I remember that day because three hours later, I crashed it into a parked car. Time seemed slow and life was simple and I didn't understand the complexities of the world. But all of these photos don't look like the little two-year-old in the photo.

I don't know how Casey thinks I might look like the woman, even the little girl—I mean, sure, if I compare the two, but all two-year-olds can look similar if they have the same hair color. But a lot of change happens between two and seven. I saw it in my students—the changes.

Feeling relieved, I e-mail my mom back and ask her how she's doing. I give her a rundown of the renovations, the people we've met. I don't touch on Casey because that's a conversation better had in person. At the end of the e-mail, I ask her for pictures when I was an infant.

Waiting for her response, I sip my wine and watch the fire dance. I think about the truck that Emmitt allowed us to borrow and how kind it was of him. I think about Esther and the Chilkat blanket she gave me. I think about Olive. I think of the kindness people have extended to a woman they don't know.

The wind begins its nightly ritual, and the old girl gives back, creaking and whining and letting the wind know she's not giving up the good fight. She tells the wind of her new roof, the new floors she'll get soon get, that she has new owners now, and that she's content.

For the first time in a long time, I feel like I'm in the right place at the right time. As if this old house needed rescuing and I was the only person for the job.

Now, I'm not scared to start a fire by myself. I'm not scared of chimney fires. I'm not scared of the wind or the rain. And I'm not scared of Casey.

I welcome the thought of a new life. Maybe teaching isn't my calling. Perhaps it's something different, but I don't have to know tonight or tomorrow or next week.

Breathing the old, musky smell in, I rest in ease. For the first moment since Tripp and Conroy left our lives, I am content. Even as a child, I felt restless. I remember never wanting to be left alone. I was anxious. I wanted my mother at all times.

It is now that it dawns on me.

I needed my mother at all times as a child, like an old memory I grabbed from the sky like a fleeting thought. *Oh, here you are.*

I needed her next to me.

I needed to feel her hand in mine.

I needed her.

And then, one day, I just didn't.

I grew up maybe.

And she still needed me as a little girl.

Maybe she had a harder time with the transition.

Isn't that what mothers do? But how would I know?

Emotion sets in my chest like cement, so much so that it becomes hard to breathe.

But then the old girl lets me know she's here with a quick shudder with the wind.

"I know," I whisper.

Is it crazy, I ask myself, *that I talk to an old house?*

Finally, an e-mail comes through from my mom with a *ping*.

Hey, honey.

For whatever reason, I'm having a hard time finding your infant pictures, but I'll keep looking.

It's in my gut that I feel a tinge of turmoil start to twist and turn like a hurricane, a slight and unsettling feeling that lives somewhere between my throat and my stomach.

All that was right in the world only seconds ago has tilted.

My mother has never had a hard time finding anything.

The green spatula from 1972? Third drawer down, next to the ice cream scoop.

The Little Golden Books from my childhood? Attic. Right side, under Tripp's baseball cards.

The video of my first Christmas recital? The entertainment system. Left side, back row.

My mother has never misplaced anything in her entire life, and this thought is so unsettling that my heart starts to beat quicker.

Something isn't right, and this scenario isn't adding up.

I reply.

Okay. Thanks, Mom.

I love you.

I set my phone down on the coffee table and begin to ponder what the hell is going on.

Why has the world led me to Ketchikan, Alaska?

28

Casey

"Can I talk to you for a minute, Ri?"

Riley's coming down the path between the bull pens with her horse, and she stops in front of me.

Our conversation played in my mind so many times last night.

What I should have said. What I should have done. And all I did was sit there like a coward.

"Look, I'm really sorry for the way I handled things between us. It wasn't right. I never wanted to hurt you."

The corners of Riley's mouth turn upward. "I knew, Case. I knew that you didn't love me the way I loved you. There was always—I don't know—something that I saw in your eyes that told me you were miles away from where I wanted you to be. But I tried. I tried to keep you in that saddle. Tried to make you love me the way I wanted you to love me," she sighs. "Ain't nothing right until it's right."

I rub the ears of her horse, Storm, study the lightning bolt on her head that runs into her mane.

"Truth be told, Casey. I should have ended it before it ever really got started."

Cowboys and cowgirls are making their way past us, saying, "Hey."

A few slaps on the shoulders from other bull riders and cowboys congratulating me on my ride last night.

"Where to next?" Riley asks.

"After tonight?"

"Yeah."

"Ketchikan, Alaska."

"What's there?"

"My future."

"Huh. I thought you were from Dillon Creek."

"I am."

"Is it that Tess girl you grew up with?" She shakes her head and smiles. "I always knew it was that girl."

I look down at Riley. "I'm really sorry, Ri."

"There's always another cowboy, Casey. Maybe not one quite like Casey Atwood, but there's one for me. I hope you find what you're looking for, Casey. That Tess is a lucky woman." Riley gives a gentle pull on the reins to Storm, and they walk away.

Shoving my hands in my pockets, watching her walk away, I think to myself that I could have built a future with Riley. She was a close second to Tess. But the heart wants what the heart wants.

Garrison walks up and slaps me on the back. "You ready, cowboy? Get ready for our rides?"

We walk back to the locker room together.

Blaine, the athletic trainer, tapes my ankles, knees, and wrists while Garrison hops on the stationary bicycle and waits his turn.

Garrison is quiet, I notice, which isn't like him, but he's preparing for battle. He's on the bubble of making the World Finals. These next few weekends are crucial for him. He's drawn What in Tarnation for tonight, one of the toughest bulls in the PBR right now.

"Cat got your tongue, cowboy?" I ask.

"Just gettin' centered, man."

"All right, man. I'm gonna go do my rope."

I grab the rosin from my riggin bag, my rope, and head outside. I tie my rope up to the fence and begin removing the old rosin with a wire brush. I think about Top Ten and the way the bull stared me down; it was like I was looking death straight into his black eyes and he let me live. Gave me a chance.

Do we get second chances in life? Do we get do-overs?

Branson—another PBR rider, a father, a husband—didn't get a second chance at life. His bull didn't give him another chance.

Raised in the church, I know what God is. I don't use him as often as I should, but I pray before every ride. Maybe, with Top Ten, God was trying to get my attention. Hell, I don't know.

But what would God say about Branson? He had a family. Why did he die while the rest of us go on living, go on setting ourselves up for death night after night?

After the old rosin is removed, I throw my brush back in the bag and grab a rock of rosin, break it against the fence, and then forcefully slide it up and down the length of my rope.

Everybody has a plan, I guess, some way they'll live and die, and that's it. When I was younger, I always pictured myself riding bulls until I was old. But as I've gotten older, the self-centeredness that I had as an eighteen-year-old kid has changed. I started to think about how Conroy's death had changed me, my family. Life was a luxury no more. It was no longer promised or guaranteed. I started to think about my mom and dad, and as they get older, how they'd handle the ranch, the land. I started to think about marriage and a family and Tess. All that shit that I'd pushed down for years slowly began to creep back into my life. I sure as hell don't want to be selling old-man gel on television because I have to make ends meet or because I don't have a choice. I want to end up on top. To walk out of the arena for the final time and have options.

After the rosin is applied, my phone sounds from my bag.

It's a text from Tess.

> *Tess: I wanted to call, but instead, I decided to text you, only because your focus is most important to me. Ride like hell, Casey Atwood. Ride like hell.*

Knowing it's hard for Tess to watch these events, I always feel the need to reassure her.

> *Me: I'll see you tonight, Morgan. Save me a spot next to you in bed. ;)*

I wait for her to respond, but she doesn't, so I throw my phone back in my bag along with all my shit.

The announcer takes to the microphone. "Now, this cowboy is no stranger to the PBR, and he's had some really great rides this year. Garrison is your next cowboy."

I throw my bag over my shoulder and head to the arena to catch Garrison's ride. I climb up the fence and sit, having a clear shot of the arena, next to Cody and Lou and a few other bull riders.

"Miss anything?" I ask.

"Nah, just gettin' started," Cody says, chewing tobacco in his lip.

"Man, Atwood," Lou says, "you've had some rides lately." He shakes my hand.

Garrison gives the nod, and the chute flies open.

The bull takes off in a fury of jumps, kicks, and spins.

Then, he switches direction. Something I know Garrison didn't plan for.

What In Tarnation isn't known to switch directions.

And then it happens.

Garrison loses his seat and gets sideways on the bull.

He tries to gain his seat back, but it's no use.

"Fuck," I whisper.

With one massive buck, Garrison flies into the air, but he's caught up. His rope is stuck on the bull.

The bullfighters try to distract What In Tarnation, but it's no use.

One bullfighter reaches from the back of the bull, trying to loosen the rope.

He bucks and spins as Garrison's arm is still attached to the bull. What In Tarnation back hooves land on Garrison's calf.

I stand.

Finally, the rope comes loose, and Garrison falls to the ground, limp.

The entire arena grows eerily silent as Garrison lies there.

I jump off the fence and run to him, but I'm pushed away by medical personnel who've made it to him quicker than I did.

My heart is pounding out of my chest.

"Come on, Atwood." One of the bullfighters takes me by the shoulder and leads me to the fence, but I don't take my eyes off my friend.

The stretcher comes out, and with a neck collar on him, they load him onto it.

"I'll meet you at the hospital. Which hospital?" I ask the medical personnel as they walk past with Garrison.

"Fuck that shit, Atwood." It's weak, but he says it. "Get back on that bull. You ride that son of a bitch."

I have to smile. Laugh. "I will, man. I will. I'll be there soon."

He gives me a weak thumbs-up.

We take falls off bulls, we heal and recover and come back to the PBR only to do it all over again, separates the boys from the men. But watching buddies never come back because they're six feet underground or sitting somewhere on someone's mantel, like my brother sits on my parents', that's finality.

"Atwood! You're up next!" Cody yells.

I put my hands on my waist, drop my head, and do what Garrison asked and get back on that bull.

When I'm in the chute, the adrenaline courses through my veins like power. It's payback.

An old bull rider once said, "Never get on a bull with revenge in mind. These bulls out here aren't out to get anyone; they're out to get riders off their backs. Respect the bull, and he'll respect you."

But the old bull rider's words disappear with my rage.

Before I give the nod, I say a prayer. *Please, God, I don't ask for much, but watch over Garrison.*

I nod.

The chute opens, and the bull comes out with the same vengeance I feel for him.

He bucks.

I sit back in my seat.

He kicks.

I balance.

He spins.

I stay upright and loose.

We dance.

He leads.

I follow.

He jumps.

I stay.

We do this deal for eight fucking seconds.

The buzzer sounds, and that's when I realize I'm hung up. My rope is stuck.

I'll ride through the World Finals, and I'll hang it up, I tell myself, *if I make it out of this one.*

I drop by the hospital. Garrison is in the emergency room still, but they let me back there. I told the front staff that he was my brother.

In a lot of ways, I guess he is.

But in the direction the nurse told me to walk, I hear howling from behind the curtain.

"Please, God, make it stop!" Garrison says.

And then silence.

I pull open the curtain, and a young doctor is moving his shoulder.

Garrison is still in his vest, his clothes.

"Ma'am"—I tip my hat—"I'm his brother."

Garrison laughs. "My brother. That's right," he says, still wincing in pain.

He looks like hell. A swollen left eye. Bumps and bruises to his face. But everything looks to be intact.

"Dislocated shoulder, a torn Achilles', a mild concussion, but he should be okay," the doctor says.

Garrison looks lovesick for the doctor.

"We'll keep him overnight for observation. I'll get him admitted." And with that, the young doctor leaves.

Shoving my hands in my pockets, I walk closer to his bedside.

"How'd your ride go?"

"How's the head?"

"Shut up, man. I'm fine. How'd the ride go?"

I shrug. "You told me to get on the bull. Tess told me to ride like hell, so I did."

"Score?"

"I did all right. You scared the living shit out of me, asshole."

"Scared the shit out of myself."

"Keeping you here overnight. Need me to stay?"

"And interrupt my time with the beautiful Dr. Harper? No, thank you, sir."

"You realize when you leave the ER, she stays here, right?"

Garrison's eyebrows barely waggle with the swelling. "Garrison always finds a way."

I laugh at my friend, damn glad he's okay.

29

The Ladybugs

At Mabe's dining room table, Patty sips her tea and stares out the window. "I wasn't always an alcoholic drinker," she says quietly.

"I don't think the majority of us start out drinking alcoholically," Mabe says.

"When did you realize you were an alcoholic?"

If Mabe's' being honest, it took some time.

In meetings, in the beginning, she used to say, "I'm Mabe, and I want to quit drinking."

Betty leaned over one day and whispered, "Mabe Muldoon, there's no in-between, just like with pregnancy. You either are or you aren't. You're either an alcoholic or not. Now, shit or get off the pot."

Mabe smiles at this memory.

So, what did Mabe do after that?

She started to say, "I'm Mabe, and I sure as hell don't want to drink again."

And that suited the group just fine for a time.

And then, one day, Mabe couldn't deny it anymore. She was absolutely an alcoholic.

But she gives Patty the truth. "After my husband and my daughter died. That is when I knew I couldn't stop."

Patty watches a sparrow out the window take a bath in the birdbath.

Patty turns her head and looks to Mabe. She goes to speak but quickly dismisses the words that lie against her tongue and takes another sip of tea. Another moment goes by. "Have you ever experienced something that you'd rather not remember?"

Mabe nods, sips her tea, and realizes there isn't enough sweetener, so she adds another packet and pushes all the awful memories away from that night eight years ago. Pushes thoughts of her husband's last breath, the call she received from Francine's partner when she died. Those are memories she'd rather not have.

A single tear slides down Patty's face. "Do you ever wish so badly that you could take away one single decision, one bad choice, that sits with you day and night and the despair of that choice every single day?"

Mabe's eyes fill with tears this time. "Yes."

Patty meets her gaze and nods, as if taking Mabe's yes as a confession.

Patty runs her finger along the ceramic mug, weighing what she'll say next.

"What's holding you down, Patty?"

"Every night, I wish I hadn't made a choice to leave. I wish I had called my parents instead." Another tear slides down Patty's cheek. "I still remember their loud cries that only got softer and softer as each minute went by." Tears are streaming down Patty's face. "Somehow, I escaped alive. A few bumps and bruises. I wore an old safety harness I'd found between the seat cushions.

"I saw headlights coming down the road. I panicked. I didn't know what to do, so I left the scene. Through the field, I followed Eel River home and up to town. I made it home that night. I left two lives in the field to die that night."

The pain in Patty's face from years of unwanted memories and sadness are met in this moment. She begins to cry and cry and cry, and so does Mabe.

"I was driving, Mabe. I wasn't drinking. But Tripp and Conroy had been. Tripp and I had been seeing each other at the time. The headlights went out, and I couldn't see. Everything was dark, and the speed accelerated under my foot," she pants. Fearful if she doesn't tell everything to someone now, she'll never tell the story.

Mabe comes over to Patty's side of the table, and she buries herself into Mabe's chest.

"I'm so sorry I left, Mabe. I'm so sorry I left."

In all the ideas that Betty has had, Mabe knows now that it isn't Betty who put this pair together; it was God's divine work.

Mabe needed Patty, and Patty needed Mabe.

"Can I tell you a story?" Mabe whispers, attempting to wipe her own tears.

Patty whimpers a weak, "Yes."

"Once, there was an old woman with not-so-great eyesight. She knew she wasn't supposed to drive at night." Before Mabe says the next sentence, she takes a big breath in and releases it. "She'd been drinking. She took Waddington that night because she didn't want to go through town. She saw the Jeep ahead of her, but it sped up. Then ... there was an explosion of sorts, fire, and then everything fell silent."

Patty lifts her head and stares at Mabe. "You were the headlights?"

Mabe's eyes fill with tears. "And I left too, Patty. I left the scene because I'd been drinking and I didn't want to get caught."

Mabe knows the right thing to do. She knows they both need to go to Chief McBride and tell him what happened. Even if it costs her everything, the families need to know, and in order for them both to stay sober, they need to clear away the wreckage of their past. But she won't bring this up with Patty yet. She's still trying to get off the booze. All of it would be too much for Patty to face right now, so she holds Patty the way she held Francine when she was just a young girl.

30

Tess

I watch the ride and panic as I see Casey is hung up.
Two bull riders in a row?
Too much rosin?

Fear tickles the back of my throat and my insides.

"Come on, Case. Come on," I shout to myself in the stillness of the old house. "Please." My hands begin to sweat, and my stomach grows into a fit of nerves.

The bullfighters step in while Casey struggles with his own rope.

"Please, God, take care of Casey." I sit forward on the sofa and bite my lip. "Someone, help him!"

Finally, he releases himself, and with one last buck, Casey lands nearly on his feet, but I can't breathe. It isn't until he looks at the bullfighter and then to the crowd and waves that tears gather in my eyes as a sob chokes my throat.

"Dammit, Casey."

I don't dare turn off the event from my phone because they might interview him. Or what if he passes out once they get him behind the chute? My cheek, now raw, puffs between my teeth.

My phone rings almost instantly.

"Hey," I say breathlessly, trying not to allow my emotions to get the best of me.

"I'm okay."

But I cover my mouth as the tears start to fall. Feeling the pressure in my chest, I try to speak, but I can't.

"Hey, I'm fine, Tess. I just wanted you to know I'm fine, okay? And …" He grows silent. "I love you, Tess. I've loved you for as long as I can remember. You're my first wet dream, my first boner—I'm certain. You've always been the one." He lets out a breath. "Look, I've tried to move on, but I can't. Not without you. No matter the cost, I'm willing to wait. Whatever you need."

"When you got—" I pause, trying to contain my love and fear at the same time. "When you got hung up, I panicked, Case. I couldn't breathe. I couldn't do anything. I realize that now, I'd rather have you in my life than not have you."

It's quiet for a long moment.

"Well, Tess, I'd say we have a predicament then."

"A predicament?"

"We can't be business partners and lovers at the same time. But we can be lovers working on a house."

I hear his smile through the phone. I know what his smile feels like when he kisses me, what it feels like against my backside, against my heart, my breasts.

"Come home?"

"Home is anywhere with you."

A tear falls again.

"I need to check on Garrison real quick before I fly out."

"Give him my best, will you? He's okay, right?"

"I hope so. Gave me a thumbs-up and some words of advice before they hauled him off."

"I love you, Casey," comes out of my mouth so quickly. That could have been Casey, and if I hadn't said it now, I'm afraid he never would have heard it.

"I love you too, Tess Morgan."
"See you when you get here."
"See you then."

I hear the front door rattle.

Could be the wind, I think to myself, sitting straight up in bed.

Quickly, I creep from my bed and down the hallway just in time to see my cowboy come through the door.

I run to him, jump into his arms, wrap my legs around his middle, and hold him tighter than I've ever held anyone in my life. Emotion reaches my throat.

Casey's arms wrap around my middle, and he sighs into my hair. "Hey, baby," he says as if I am the most important thing in his life, and I feel it in every inch of my body.

Placing my hands on his face, I trace the outline of his facial features against the silhouette of the moon—a rare occurrence in Ketchikan. I think about the road he's traveled to get here, that we've traveled to get here, many times alone. Both set out on paths in search of the easier, softer way, the road of less raw love, less feelings, less emotion—only to find each other again and know it is exactly what we needed the whole time.

He rests his head against mine and slowly puts his lips to my lips.

At first, it's gentle.

And then I feel like I become a need so deep within Casey that I feel it in my toes. His mouth enraptures me, and I fall to pieces.

The walls come down.

The walls of sadness.

The walls of madness.

The walls of guilt and the walls of hurt.

I let them all fall down like toy soldiers.

His mouth moves to my chest, and I feel it in my heart.

I pull his mouth to mine again, not wanting to waste another minute.

We pull away only for a second so that we can both agree to steal the rest of the late-night hours from the moon, loving each other.

I feel his power between my legs.

"I know ... I know I said we couldn't do this anymore, Case," I say breathlessly, "but I can't *not* tell you how much I love you without my body."

I can only make out pieces of Casey's face because it's so dark as he carries me down the hallway.

And when the light from the moon meets his face again as we enter my bedroom, the only thing he says is, "Show me."

He lays me down on the bed in just his T-shirt that I grabbed from some clothes he'd left here before I went to bed tonight.

Casey smiles when he notices the design. "That's mine," he says as he crawls on top of me.

"Listen, I can't sleep without you. I've spent the last eight years searching for a man just like you, but now that I'm with you, I never want to spend a single night without you." I pull his mouth to mine and kiss him with recklessness and love.

I could have lost Casey for good tonight.

"Great ride, Mr. Atwood," I whisper when I pull away and pull his T-shirt off my body.

"Your ride is always the best, Ms. Morgan." He pushes off my body as I lie here with just my panties on.

He takes off his button-up shirt, exposing his scars—two on his left shoulder, one on his abdomen, and one just below his right pectoral muscle—the proven fight to do what he loves. Casey removes his jeans and socks and then his underwear.

My insides grow warm as I see all of him standing in front of me.

The most vulnerable we can be is when we allow others to see us just as we are. No makeup. No lies. Just nakedness and hearts and all the push in between.

Casey gets up, walks down the hallway, comes back with a condom.

He knows this simple act can ruin the mood for both of us, but he also knows it's the right thing to do.

And in this moment, I know he's thinking more of me than himself—the way he's always done things. I just never saw it.

Casey slides the condom on and pushes into me with one shot.

He doesn't take his time, nor is he slow about it.

He opens me up, and I call out.

Casey puts his mouth to my breast as he pumps into me. "I'm not going to be gentle with you tonight, Tess. I can't."

"I don't want you to be gentle, Casey. Take what you need."

He stares at me. Takes his hand and sweeps a strand of hair from my eyes. "I'm in love with you, Tess Morgan. I always have been."

"I'm only sorry I didn't see this sooner. I'll take the rest of your tomorrows, if they're available?"

Casey stops moving inside me. His stare twists and turns, and I can't understand what he's thinking.

"Case?"

He drops his head to my chest and sits at my side for a moment, unable to speak.

"Casey, did I say something wrong?"

Sharply, he looks up at me. "No. Because that's exactly what I want." He's holding something back.

"Casey, what is it?"

"We ... we need to talk about what happened, Tess, what set all of this shit in motion. And if we don't, I'm terrified we won't make it."

The loneliness and every last bit of sadness meet in my gut.

Tears start to build in my eyes.

He pulls me to him, our naked bodies entwined and tangled, and it feels every bit of wonderful that I spent the last eight years dreaming about.

It's just Casey, me, and the moon. There is no rain tonight; there is no wind.

It's quiet for a long time before I say, "Do you think about his name? What ... what they named him?" My voice grows uneven.

Casey kisses my head. "Every day."

"I think about ... I think about what his favorite cereal might be and what his teacher's name is." Tears start to stream from the corners of my eyes, meeting Casey's chest. "Does he sleep well at night? Does he have your eyes? Does he know that he has two people who love him more than anything?"

My body begins to shake as Casey holds me and allows my tears, the anguish, and all the years of questions I've had.

"We can meet him, Tess. We ... we don't have to say who we are. I mean, the adopted parents can know, obviously."

Meet him?

Fear and panic collide in my stomach. "Tripp Conroy Atwood is what I secretly named him in my head. TC for short. Because CT would have been weird as a nickname." My eyes sting from the tears that fall. "I keep thinking about when he comes to a certain age, he'll want to know us. If his parents tell him, right? He'll want to know who we are and why we gave him up."

"A wise man once said, 'The truth is the only option.' Tess, we did it for his sake. We were young, barely learning to care for ourselves."

But I know this is Casey's way of making me feel better. The moment Casey knew our baby was a boy was also the same moment that they took him away. Casey would have kept him if that was what I wanted, but I never knew how bad this choice would feel later. I can only imagine what our little boy will feel the day his parents decide to tell him—*if* they decide to tell him. And this is what breaks my heart into a million little pieces.

"I've felt a pit of despair for so long, Case. Maybe my choice to become a teacher was my way of giving back the love to other kids, but maybe it was for myself, for my own selfish reasons."

Casey tips my chin up so that I'm looking him in the eyes. "You are not selfish, Tess. You made the decision for our son so that he could have a good life. Do you understand me?"

I try to will myself to believe Casey's words. Swallow them, allow them into my heart so the sadness might just fade eventually.

"What do we do now, Case?"

"We walk through it, Tess. We feel through it all and allow all that shit to come in and go and let it move through us, so we can finally let go."

"What if I can't?" A sob escapes my throat as I try to hold back the tears.

In this moment, I realize I'm still holding back. It's hard when we condition ourselves to live a certain way for so long, and when we try to do something other than what we've conditioned ourselves to do, we think we can't.

"I-I feel guilt for only going to the doctor a few times while I was pregnant, too scared someone would find us out. That was selfish too. I put my ego above my own child's welfare, Case." For once, I let it out. "I feel guilt for giving up on our child. And his silent cries when they took him away, as if he needed his mother, and I couldn't be that person for him." I weep.

Casey holds me tighter and doesn't say a word.

"I let him go, Casey. What kind of mother does that?"

"One who saw what was best for her child."

3I

Casey

Tell her, Casey. Tell her what you fucking know. Tell her what you did.

It's been several minutes before anyone has said anything.

"Tess," I whisper. "I need to tell you something. Tess?"

But she's fast asleep on my chest.

I kiss her head and stare at the ceiling as I try to contemplate all the scenarios of what will come of Tess and me once I tell her.

One thing I've never been is a liar.

I feel her hand slide around my length, and it turns hard in her hand as she moves to my mouth.

"Tess," I try to speak, " I need to tell you something."

She shakes her head in the darkness. "No, not right now. Just make love to me, Case. I need it. I need you. I need to not feel for just a little while."

I pull her face toward me and take her mouth with mine.

Her hand grips tighter and she strokes my length.

"God," I whisper through our kisses.

Slowly, I move her to her back and slip inside her.

Our mouths move like we're hungry and hurting at the same time, wanting more of each other, as if this space we have isn't close enough.

Her hands are slow.

I break away from our kiss and look into her eyes; they're glassy and full of tears.

"Tess ..."

"Don't worry; they're good tears."

I nod as I move my mouth to her breast. I take the full, hard nipple into my mouth and tug.

Quietly, she whimpers as my finger moves against her knot. "Is this what you want?"

"Yes." She sucks in air as if her life depends on it.

"Tell me." I stop moving as I watch her on the bed, her chest moving with anticipation. "Do you want this?" Touching my mouth between her legs, her sweet smell around me, I open her folds and toy with her, my tongue moving and teasing.

Her entire body shivers as she calls out, "Casey ... more." Her pelvis thrusts toward me.

She hides her face in ecstasy.

Again, I stroke her with my tongue, this time applying pressure as her thighs begin to quiver.

Sliding my finger inside her, I watch her begin to unravel.

The condom still on, and with one last tease of her knot, I move my body on top of hers.

"Please, Casey," she pants.

And it's when our eyes connect that I push myself inside her.

I watch our childhood memories play through her face like reruns.

I watch as she devours this feeling I give her with euphoria.

I watch her eyes close as she takes her breasts in her hands and tugs at herself.

She pulls me to her and kisses me deeply, bites at my lip, holds me closer, as if she could.

Afraid I'll end this party early, I stop. Stare down at her.

"Are you all right?" she asks.

"I am." I delicately kiss her lips. "But this feels too good, and I need to slow down."

Gently, I push into her again and begin to move. She holds me in the spot she needs me, and I watch as her face begins to lose control.

"I want to watch you fall, Tess. Just fall." And when I say this, she screams.

And I push into her one last time.

We fall together, and for several minutes, we lie in the darkness.

"Tess?"

No answer.

With our bodies intertwined, wrapped in each other, she's fallen asleep.

The nagging thought returns to my head. *Tell her, you asshole. You have to tell her before it's too late.*

Maybe I should wait to tell her. I'm afraid she'll push me away and not allow me to help with the house financially. And then she'll really be in a bind because she's so damn stubborn.

But she deserves to know.

After the house is done, I tell myself.

It's the next morning. Tess and I made love once more in bed and then in the shower.

Emmitt wipes his brow in the early morning sun peeking through the downstairs window, and I'm brought to the present moment.

"The floor is rotten down here too. So, we will need to move all this stuff out and redo the walls and some of the Sheetrock."

Tess and I exchange glances.

"Will this put us behind schedule?" she asks.

"Just a day or so."

Tess says, "I just worry about you working in the cold, Emmitt."

Emmitt chuckles. "I appreciate your concern, Tess, but I'll be fine. I might be old, but I ain't dead."

But he looks at her differently. Not like a woman who's hired him to repair her house, but like a child, I guess. Someone he takes care in knowing. Someone who's both proud of her empathy and concern for his welfare.

Emmitt says, "So, if you guys could move all this stuff to the outside garage for the time being, that would be wonderful." He turns to walk away but stops quickly in his tracks. "Oh, Casey?"

"Yeah?"

"Great rides this weekend. The guys were taking bets on how well you'd ride. Not too shabby."

"Thank you. Appreciate it."

He whistles through his teeth. "But when you got hung up, that whole damn bar about died."

I look at Tess to see her body tense. "I like to make things exciting, Emmitt."

Tess gently pushes me. "See, you jump-started everyone's heart."

Giving her a quick kiss on the head, letting her know I'm not going anywhere, I say, "Who won bets?"

Emmitt says, "Me."

"I wouldn't have taken you for a betting man."

"I only bet when I know I'm going to win." And with that, he walks upstairs to the outside to roust his men.

The rainy afternoon is spent moving boxes from the lower level to the outside garage. Once we're done moving boxes, we start to dig through them. What to keep, what not to keep, and what to give to Michael, Ike's son.

"Man, Ike really liked to write," I say.

"Look at this, Case. It's an old typewriter."

"Might want to save that. Could be an antique one day."

"Save it? I'm going to use it." She slips her phone out of her back pocket and takes a photo. "I just texted Michael to see if he wants it."

Her phone chirps almost immediately with, I assume, a response.

"Said I could have it." Tess inspects the typewriter. "Might just need a new ribbon, but other than that, it looks good."

A strand of hair falls in Tess's face, and instinctively, I push it behind her ear.

God, I've wanted this for so long. Her. Us.

She drops her head to the side. "What?"

But it's not the right time to tell her. Not yet. For her own sake.

"Just thinkin' about how lucky I am." I move my hands around her waist and pull her close to me, kissing her lips lightly.

She stands on her tiptoes to kiss me. "That's funny," she says, "because I was just thinking that same thing."

Tess seems lighter. Like the weight of her mind from last night is somehow less heavy.

"How do you feel?" I ask.

She nods. "A little better."

But I still see the contrition she keeps. I'm not sure that will ever go away. I see the haze behind her bright smile, the one she gives everyone. I see Tess for Tess. Not for the woman she portrays to be. I suppose she sees me for me and not the man I portray either.

"What's that box? Last one?" She's looking behind me, and I turn.

It's a small box, and she lets go and walks to it. Opens it.

"Letters." She laughs. "Go figure."

But when she looks more closely at them, her face changes.

"What is it?" I walk closer to her.

She holds up the letter to read it better. "These … these are letters from Dillon Creek. From … my mother." Tess looks up at me.

32

The Ladybugs

Admitting what Mabe did to Chief McBride has never been on the top of her to-do list. Not ever.

But she once heard a motto that says, "How free do you want to be?"

For one thing, Mabe didn't want to drink again, and she surely doesn't want Patty to drink again either.

They've both harbored enough guilt to drop an American hero square in his tracks. It is time to let go.

First, Patty tells her husband. It was before they were married and Patty was barely an adult, barely eighteen, sheltered, Patty explains but does not hide behind those excuses. She snuck out that night from her home, and it changed everything.

Mabe, Patty, and her husband, Ron, talk frankly.

Ron simply said, "Honey, I don't want you to drink again, and if this is your way to freedom, we need to do it."

Nobody knows if Mabe or Patty will do prison time. But they have to trust God.

So, here they both are, outside the chief's house on a Sunday after church, staring at the McBrides' red front door.

"Are you ready?" Mabe asks.

"Ready as I'll ever be, I suppose," Patty says.

Mabe takes Patty's hand. "Even if we go to prison, Patty, at least our souls will finally be free, and maybe we'll get stuck in a prison that makes the best pudding west of the Mississippi."

Patty thinks about her children, and her heart begins to ache. *But what's the alternative?* Patty asks herself. *If we don't confess and I can't be free, this awful choice I made all those years ago will haunt me forever.*

Even if Patty and Mabe go to prison, at least she'll get out someday. Maybe.

Mabe knocks.

Patty holds her breath.

The chief answers. "Well, hello, Mabe! To what do I owe this pleasure?"

"I'm afraid it's official business, Chief. May we come in?"

The chief's face falls in concern. "Absolutely."

They sit in the living room, and Mabe introduces Patty to the chief.

Patty begins her story.

The chief listens.

Mabe starts her story.

The chief listens.

"And I'd been drinking that night, Chief. That's why I left. I didn't want to get into trouble. I didn't want rumors to spread around Dillon Creek, so I took the cowardly way out."

The chief sits back in his recliner, his fingers creating a steeple. He thinks.

Patty tells him about her drinking and her alcoholism.

"And how old are you now?" he asks.

"Twenty-six, sir."

"Do you have a family?"

Her eyes flood with tears. "Yes, sir. Two children and a husband. We live in Fortuna."

The chief knows that there is absolutely nothing that Mabe or Patty could have done for those boys that night. But the chief's concern is the acceleration of speed toward the tree. Was it murder? No, probably not. But if the chief wants to sleep at night from this point forth, he's got to investigate all the evidence again. They never tested the engine for any issues. The boys' blood alcohol level was enough to prove they had been drinking and driving—until Patty stepped into the picture.

The chief leans forward. "As an officer of the law, I need to make sure all leads are investigated. With that said, I am going to make some calls, and I will get back to you. What you both did today was brave. However, I wish that this had come to fruition sooner."

"Thank you, Chief. I look forward to receiving your call. Are we ... are we free to go?"

"Yes, you're free to go. But don't run off to Mexico or anything."

Patty and Mabe barely smile.

"No, we wouldn't do that, Chief."

"I know. It was a joke."

33

Tess

I examine the handwriting. In the middle of the envelopes, they're both addressed to Ike at his address in Dillon Creek and in Ketchikan.

My first thought is, *They were having an affair, but my mother is quite a bit younger than Ike was.*

"What's the letter say?" Casey asks.

I look at him as if he'd asked me to tuck in the moon. *This is odd, but there's got to be a simple explanation, right?*

When I take out the letter, a picture falls out.

It's me.

Tess, age four, it reads on the back.

A prickle of chills waves through my body.

I unfold the letter.

December 1998

Dear Ike,

Sometimes, I look back and wonder how we got so lucky with our Tess. I suppose everything happens in God's time.

I know he's got a plan, but with the wind, so to speak, sometimes, it's hard to see.

And we did as you'd requested. We changed her name to Tess, as I'm sure you've heard.

Could you pass this picture on to Esther and Martin?

Hope all is well with you in Ketchikan.

Best,

Mavis

Slowly, I hand Casey the letter. "How ... how does my mother know Esther and Martin? And what does she mean by changing my name?"

I take out the other letter. This one is addressed to Ike's address in Dillon Creek. Another picture falls out—*Tess, age 5.*

December 1999

Dear Ike,

Here's a picture of Tess in a dress. You cannot get this girl in a dress if her life depended on it.

Give it to Esther and Martin when you see them.

Best,

Mavis

I take out another letter along with another picture—*Tess and Tripp*.

December 2000

Dear Ike,

Here's a picture of Tess and Tripp on our way to get Christmas trees at Fisher's Christmas Tree Farm in Hydesville.

Can you believe we got snow this year?

Tess learned to ride a bicycle and started dance and learned to tie her shoes.

Truth be told, she has two left feet, but I think she enjoys it, and that's all I can ask for.

Best,

Mavis

P.S. Give Esther and Martin our best and the picture.

I sit down on a bucket that's close by and attempt to wrap my mind around this as I pull out another letter, handing the one I just read to Casey. Instead of opening the next one, I count the letters that are in the box.

"There are nineteen." I stare up at Casey. I'm sure his mind is spinning too. "Why nineteen?"

My mom could only send me pictures dating back to age five. I tell Casey the story about the phone conversation with my mom and the response that I received from her.

"She said she couldn't find them, Case," I say in disbelief.

Casey shakes his head. "Your mom is the most organized person in all of Dillon Creek."

"I know."

I read the next letter.

December 2001

Dear Ike,

I hope this note finds you well.

It's official. Tess hates dance, so you won't see her in The Nutcracker performance this year at the Dillon Creek Repertory Theater. But she's made some wonderful friends. Anna Cain and Casey Atwood. Mark my words, Ike, she's destined to marry the Atwood boy. He's such a well-mannered young man. There's no doubt, Daryl and Laurel did a fine job with those boys.

Anyhow, here's a picture of the three of them. They're all tanned from the heat wave we had this summer. I think it's odd to have a heat wave in Dillon Creek. Maybe Gore is right about global warming.

Anyhow, I digress.

All my best,

Mavis

I don't know if it's my mother's words or the picture that makes my eyes prickle with tears.

The *before.*

Before the storm.

Before the hurt.

Before the death of two young boys.

The tragedy that sits between us is like new grief.

Casey watches me as I hand him the next letter, the next photo. I breathe in the cool, crisp air from the open garage. He sets down the letter, pulls me to him, and holds me.

My mind spins.

With my ear against the thumping of his heart, I wonder why it beats so hard. Perhaps it's for me. Maybe he's feeling my unresolve, my nerves, but instead of asking, I allow his heartbeat to give me rest. I find mood in the beat. We sit here, in the middle of the garage, and give ourselves this moment of uncertainty.

"I need to go talk to Esther," I whisper.

"You might get the answers you're looking for. Do you want me to go with you?"

I pull away and look up at Casey. Marvel at his ruggedly handsome looks but mostly his heart. That is a side that many don't see—except in the viral video with Mr. Austin. I think that's the day that America fell in love with my Casey.

"No, this is something I need to do alone."

He nods and kisses my mouth for a few seconds too long. Because we both feel the heat between us, I'm barely able to pull away.

I drive down to the Visitor Center with the box of letters.

What's the worst that can happen? I ask myself as I stare up at the Visitor Center.

But when I look closer, it looks darker than I remember. *Are they even open?* I grab the box of letters, my heart pounding, and I approach the two-story building, but it's dark inside. It's locked when I give the door a pull. I peer through the tinted windows, and it's still.

I don't have Esther's number.

I walk back to the truck, get in, and pull the door shut. I stare at Tongass Narrows as a bald eagle lands on the hood of the truck and stares right back at me.

Taken aback, I stare at its sharp features and regal look. Its stunning, sleek feathers put me in a trance.

And then the eagle unfolds its wings out to where its wingspan is longer than the front end of the truck.

I've never witnessed anything more beautiful than what I'm seeing right now.

It lets out a high-pitched whistling while staring right at me.

Of all the places this eagle could land, why on a borrowed truck while I'm sitting at the Visitor Center?

It calls again, as if willing me to understand what it's trying to say.

"What?" I whisper. "What do you want?" Chills shoot through my body.

With a loud whoosh, the eagle moves its wings and takes flight, and I stare up through the top of the windshield.

In disbelief, I fall back to the seat when the eagle flies out of sight.

Look up, the quiet voice inside me says, and when I do, there's a woman on a bench overlooking the same view I am, except closer.

She's petite, little, with dark hair. I follow the inner voice inside me that tells me to get out of the truck and walk toward the woman.

So as not to startle the woman, I walk to the other side of the bench.

It's Esther.

I breathe in a sigh of relief.

"I've been waiting for you," she says. She smiles and reaches for my hand.

It dawns on me that I forgot the box of letters in the truck.

"You're here about the letters," she says, still staring out to the body of water in front of us. "Sometimes, if we just sit and wait for the Great Spirit, we see the most striking things life has to offer."

For the first time, I'm able to see her almond-shaped eyes as my own, similar in shape and color but far more experienced and well-versed in life. "Yes, I'm here about the letters. How did you know?"

"I knew this day would come."

Looking down at our hands, I realize, aside from color—hers the color of milk chocolate and mine a pale pink—and age, they look identical.

"How come we have the same hands, Esther?"

But she doesn't answer. She only stares straight ahead.

Finally, after several moments, she says, "It is not for me to explain, my dear. It is not my place."

"Whose place is it?"

"This needs to come from your mother."

I'm slow to speak. "You aren't my mother?" A question I've pondered for several moments.

We do look alike in different ways.

Her answer, "No," gives me both a feeling of sadness and relief at the same time. Sadness because I feel a deep connection to Esther, a wise woman with profound comfort of who she is, and relief that I don't have to feel through another upset.

"But please know, Tess, that if we had to do it over again, we'd do the same," Esther says and reaches for my hand.

I'm not sure what this means. "Do what over again, Esther?"

"You must go now, Tess, and find the answers you're looking for."

At first, I'm reluctant to let go for reasons I can't explain—I only feel it deeply within me—but I do what she asked me to do.

I stand. "Can I come tomorrow and see you?"

"My hope is that you will come every day to see me, Tess." And with that, her wide smile spans the distance of her face, and her eyes light up.

"Same time tomorrow?" I ask.

She smiles. "Same time tomorrow."

I walk away from Esther, feeling a little peace. With all the unanswered questions, I should feel indifferent, but I don't.

When I get back to the truck, I look down at my phone. It's an unknown number who's called, so I call it back.

"Hey, Tess. It's Jacob." His voice is slow, almost sad. "I ... I just need to tell you that my grandmother passed away this morning in her sleep."

The air that I breathe suddenly stops. It stands still, unable to reach my lungs. I gasp, jerking my head up to look at the bench, but there's no one there, except the eagle resting on the back of the bench.

"What?" A loud ringing in my ears starts.

"I wanted to tell you in person, but you weren't at the Isner house, so I got your number from Olive."

"But ... I just talked to her."

My sentence is met with silence on the other end of the line.

"That can't be, Tess. She died this morning."

"No, no. She—" I climb out of the truck and begin searching for her, walking to the bench. My eyes swiftly searching for Esther. "Jacob, she was right here. I just spoke to her."

A sigh sounds. "I came home on leave to say good-bye to my grandmother, Tess, and to help my grandfather. She had cancer. She didn't want anyone to know. She didn't want pity."

I ask him the words that are dying deep inside my chest. "How am I connected to your family, Jacob?"

"Huh?"

I tell him about the letters from my mother to Ike.

I tell him about the picture downstairs.

I tell him about the way Emmitt looks at me, treats me.

I tell him about the familiarity of the Isner house. The smells. The insecurity I felt as a little girl with my own mother.

This starts to spew from my mouth, and I cannot control it.

When I'm done, there's only silence on the other end and then an apprehensive sigh. "I have no idea what you're talking about, Tess."

34

Casey

I *sure as hell can't tell Tess now.*

She's trying to navigate the waters of this whole thing with Ike and her mother. This is the last thing she needs.

But Tess comes through the door just as I'm making a fire for the evening, and she looks like she's seen a ghost.

"You all right?"

Slowly, she moves her head to face me. "I'm not sure anymore, Case." She shuts the door behind her, shock registering on her face. She hangs her coat up, walks to the sofa, and sits.

I sit next to her, and she begins to unravel a story about an eagle and a conversation with Esther, who just passed away, and Jacob and how the answers to all of this lie with her mother, Mavis.

"What about Martin?"

Tess shrugs. "I'm sure he knows, but I don't think he'll tell until I talk to my mom." Tess stares at the flames, and darkness begins to fall outside. "I felt close to Esther, you know, like I knew her. Like something of me was connected to something in her. Some sort of mentor or spirit guide maybe. I don't know." She laughs. "This all sounds so crazy, right?" She looks at me, trying to be brave.

Shaking my head, I push a strand of her hair from her face. "I used to ride bulls with a guy named Pauly Calhoon. His mother was Native American while his father was a little everything. Anyway, he said that to the Native American culture, the eagle means sacredness. Since they fly so high, they believed that they were closest to the Great Spirit. That the eagle delivers prayers to the Great Spirit. He said that the eagle means strength, wisdom, and courage." I stand and walk to the counter. I grab my cowboy hat and walk back to the sofa and sit down. "Pauly gave me this before his last ride. He was a real spiritual guy." I pull out the eagle feather he gave me all those years ago.

"He died?"

"No, no. His father did though, so he moved back to Montana to help his mom with the family ranch."

"May I?" she asks.

I hand her the feather.

"Maybe the eagle came to you as a symbol of strength. That no matter what comes of all of this, you will be okay, no matter what, and that you need to keep moving forward."

Tess takes her attention from the feather and moves it to me.

"Look, on a whim, right before winter, you moved from our small-ass town to an old fixer-upper house in Ketchikan, Alaska. You left everything behind. Now, you're here, I'm here, and we're back together." But when I say this, her face grows in question, her stare still on me. "I mean, if you'll have me. We haven't made things official."

"I'd like that, Case."

"The feather also represents freedom," I say as I pull her to me. Her head falls to my chest, and I kiss the top of it. "Maybe it's time to be free, Tess."

The rain starts. The wind starts. The fire crackles. The old house begins its groans. There's absolutely nowhere else I'd rather be.

As if everything in the world is finally right in so many fucked up ways.

Like the Great Spirit and God agree that I finally got things correct and my job is to get Tess there too.

I reflect on my time with Top Ten, how he let me live and how that ride was the ride that gave me purpose outside of bull riding.

"Case?" Tess asks, still holding the eagle feather between her fingers.

"Yeah?" I take in the scent of her hair.

"What do you think our little boy is doing right now?"

I feel the ache of lies in my chest. "I think he's getting all the love he needs at this very moment."

It's been two weeks. There wasn't a service for Esther, but Tess and I walked down to the water and threw roses in the ocean.

The upstairs floor is finally done. The house is almost finished. Tess and I purchased furniture, and she redid the bedrooms and the bathrooms. We updated the house with new appliances, beds, rugs, and a living room set. We changed the downstairs into a recreational room with a pool table and a big screen TV. We even added a mechanical bull, which Emmitt had come across when he was in Fairbanks.

The house looks brand-new, and yet there's a connectedness to its past with pictures we found in the basement, dating back to the early 1900s. She created a picture montage between the living room and the kitchen.

Tess has a knack for decorating. And I see the joy on her face when she finishes a room.

We've broken in the house with our lovemaking.

The kitchen.

The shower.

Downstairs.

I give her what she's needed from me these past eight years, and she gives me what I've needed. We've made up for lost time and then some.

And Tess still hasn't called her mom. I don't want to rush anything, but I can see the worry in her eyes when she's smiling. I see the fear on her face when she thinks about it.

"The finals are next weekend," she says, trailing kisses down my stomach.

I groan, pulling her to my mouth. I kiss her and then pull away. "Tess, I'm not having sex with you until you talk to your mom."

"*What?*"

I smile against the pillow. Smile. "Nope, I'm shuttin' shit down. No free rides from this guy anymore."

She climbs on top of me, giggling and naked and beautiful, and I know I'll cave—I always do for her.

"Is that right, Mr. Atwood?" She leans down, pushing my arms above my head. "You realize I've ridden a bull too. And he was like butter in my hands."

I laugh out loud.

She does too, and she doesn't cover her face. I see the little girl inside her that I saw all those years ago even if it is only for a moment. She falls against me, resting her head on my chest again.

Tess sighs. "I guess I'm scared, Case. I'm scared of what she'll say."

"What could be scarier than losing your brother and a child in one day?"

Tess's body grows extremely still.

"Baby, we can do it together."

She pulls her head from my chest and looks down at me. "You'd do that?"

"I would do anything for you, Tess."

"After the finals." She nods.

"No, Tess. Now."

She sighs. "You're a real pain in my ass, Atwood."

"Same, Morgan. Same."

I pull her to me and make love to her once more because I can't spend another second without her.

I flip her over and push inside her from behind—the way she likes it.

It's quick and hard, but we will make up for it tonight.

We both climax together.

Tess is on the phone when I come back inside the house from stacking firewood. It's starting to get real cold here with daily temperatures into the teens. I think of investing in warmer jackets for Tess and me.

Is it her mom? I think to myself as I sit down at the counter on one of the new stools we purchased. I slide my phone from my pocket.

"Wonderful. Thank you so much, Mary Jo. That will be great. See you tomorrow. Bye." She hits End. "That was the real estate agent that Emmitt had recommended. She's going to come by and take a look at the house tomorrow."

"You still want to sell?"

"Don't you want your money back and then some, Case? I thought that was the plan. A business deal. Besides, you fulfilled your end of the deal, as I did mine. We never talked about a draw—if we both fulfilled our end of the bargain." Her eyes find mine.

"What if ... what if we keep the place?"

"Why would we keep it? Casey, you put a lot of money into this place. You need your money back."

This time, I stare at her straight in the eye when I say, "This place, Ketchikan, will always be the place that rebuilt us, and I don't know about you, but that's worth a whole hell of a lot more than just money."

Tess drops her shoulders and smiles. She turns a little pink in her cheeks.

"Besides, Grandma Clyda always says, 'You ever seen a U-Haul behind a hearse?'" I smile at her and pop a carrot into my mouth from the bowl on the counter. I shake my head. "We can't take money with us when we die."

Tess looks around at her work, our work, Emmitt's work. The white-tiled backsplash that we splurged on. The granite countertops that we installed with help from Stanley.

"So, we keep it and then what? Use it every ten years, like Ike used to do?" Tess asks.

"I don't know. I haven't thought that far. What if we rented it out?"

Tess bites her lip, crosses her arms over her chest, and thinks. "Let's meet with Mary Jo and see what she thinks. Then, we'll weigh our options."

I shrug. "Up to you." Then, "Did you call your mom?"

I watch as her face shifts to nerves and apprehension.

"No."

"Okay, here's the plan. I booked us two one-way tickets home. You'll ask your parents all the questions, and then we'll fly together to the finals."

Her demeanor changes and grows uneasy. I see the shift. I see the mood.

"You can't keep running, Tess."

"I'm not running. I'm thinking."

"Is that what you call it? When the color drains from your face and you bite your lip?"

She tries not to smile. "What date are the tickets for?"

"Monday. I'll fly here on Sunday to get you, and then we'll fly home on Monday. That way, we'll have two weeks in Dillon Creek before we leave again. Gives you plenty of time to figure things out with your parents."

She shakes her head. "After all they've said about your family, the way they've treated you, how can you be so kind, Case?" She reaches over and puts her hand on top of mine.

"I might not have a relationship with them, but it's real important that you do, Tess. Don't worry. They'll come around eventually."

"Have you met my mom?"

I laugh. "I said, eventually. Besides, I'm a grown man, Tess. I can look out for myself. I have three brothers, remember?" And both of us share a moment as the grief washes over us. "Do you think Conroy and Tripp would let that shit continue? They'll make it right. The truth will come out one way or another."

"Can I tell you something a little morbid?" she asks.

"Yes."

"I keep Tripp in the same white plastic container I brought him home from the mortuary in. He's in my bathroom linen closet. And I specifically didn't bring him with me to Ketchikan, so I'd stop talking to him as if he were really still here." Her voice dies to a whisper.

I stand and walk to the door. I grab my cowboy hat, bring it back to the kitchen, and sit down on the stool again. From the inside of my hat, next to the eagle feather, I pull out a photo of Conroy and me when we were little boys. "I won't ride a bull without him." I hand the picture to Tess.

Her eyes fill with tears. "Do you realize we don't talk about them? Ever?"

I nod, watching as Tess takes in the photo when my phone rings from my pocket. Pulling my phone from my pocket, I look at the screen. It's Cash. I roll my eyes. Because the one thing I learned with Conroy's death is, you always pick up the phone when someone calls. It might be the last time you talk to them. Conroy called my phone the night he died, and I let it go to voice mail because I was more caught up in getting to Oregon, so Tess could have the baby, and we could give him to a rightful home. I thought I'd be able to call him later.

Life had other plans.

I answer. "What?"

"Brother!" he yells.

I can tell he's drunk.

"Hey, you need to settle a dispute." His speech is slow, slurred.

"What?"

"There's a newspaper reporter here in Dallas, and she is hot! She says you have a fucking kid, and I told her she's fucking crazy!" He laughs into the phone, and my heart falls from my chest as my eyes meet Tess's.

35

The Ladybugs

Mabe hasn't eaten in days. Patty went home to be with her family in case their time together disappears.

Mabe's phone rings, and it sends a shock wave through her body.

She came clean to Betty. Told her everything.

Betty told Mabe it was the perfect time to serve a prison sentence.

Mabe thought Betty had fallen off her rocker. That the cheese had slid from her cracker.

"Your only living relation is a seventy-something woman. Your house is paid for. Your car is paid for, and The Ladybugs will survive without you," Betty explained the other day.

But the truth is, Mabe is more concerned for Patty. Mabe had made a decision that night, but her decision, she decided, didn't involve breaking the law.

"Hello?"

"Hello, Mabe. This is Chief McBride. Listen, I need to meet with you and Patty today if possible."

Oh dear. In person. This isn't good, she thinks. She pictures herself in a bright orange jumpsuit.

"Yes, Chief. What time works best for you?"

"An hour?"

"Yes, that will be fine. Would you like to come here?"

"That'll be fine."

"See you then."

After she hangs up with the chief, she calls Patty, and what usually takes seventeen minutes—the trip from Fortuna to Dillon Creek—only takes Patty eleven minutes.

At fifty-nine minutes since the phone call, there is a knock at the door. Mabe squeezes Patty's hand and answers the door.

"Chief, thank you for coming," Mabe says.

"Not a problem."

Mabe, Patty, and the chief sit around Mabe's dining room table.

The same sparrow takes a bath in the birdbath, and Mabe can't quite understand why the sparrows are out, being that it's winter and all.

The chief is slow to begin. "Your story matches up. We even dusted for prints after all these years. We hadn't in the initial investigation because there wasn't a third body or a third person—or so we'd thought. Your prints came back as a match. I had an unbiased mechanic from down South come to Evidence at the station in Eureka. Apparently, the spring had broken from the throttle body. The mechanic found the spring under the hood, next to the carburetor, on the intake manifold. And we'd never tested any of this because we didn't have reason to."

"I have no idea what an intake manifold is, but, Chief, that sounds like it's a good thing?" Mabe asks.

"It's a very good thing. Basically, it means that Patty is telling the truth. You didn't kill those boys that night, Patty."

Patty's eyes start to leak tears, as do Mabe's.

"Now, I have to ask you this, only because I need to make sure all my bases are covered."

Patty nods.

"Were you drinking that night?"

"No, Chief. I … I drank alcoholically after that night and maybe because of that night. But I did not drink that night or before that night."

The chief stares Patty down, reading her body language, her facial expressions, anything that might give a signal of dishonesty, but there is none that he can see.

Tripp and Conroy lost their lives that night not because of who was driving or who was drinking, but because of a faulty vehicle.

"Being drunk isn't a crime. Being the designated driver in a faulty vehicle isn't a crime either. The way I see it, Patty, you've served your time, which has led you down this beautifully broken road."

"You both will have to live with what you saw that night and your decision to leave, but remember, there is nothing you could have done to save those boys. They were both way beyond human aid."

Mabe and Patty sit with the chief's words and allow them to fester inside them.

"I should talk to the families though," Patty whispers. "Tell them the truth."

Chief McBride gently places his hand on Patty's. "You know, I've been doing this job for a long time. Seen a lot of heartbreak, a lot of death. So, I want to ask, before you do that, think about the heartache that will surface again. They'll have to relive their deaths all over again. They'll have to relive that night. Before you do that, are you doing it for yourself or for them? Because what would be the outcome? Will it change anything? Will it bring back Tripp and Conroy? Will it fix anything?"

This hits Patty straight in the teeth, in the gut. The truth can be an awful pill to swallow. "Myself."

"What's next?" Mabe asks.

The chief shrugs. "Nothing. Case closed." He stands to leave.

And as Patty and Mabe watch the chief drive away in his patrol car, they both know they'll have to live with what they heard and saw that night and the decisions they made, but they both are finally feel free.

36

Tess

Casey hangs up the phone, and my heart sinks.

Seeing the pain in his eyes is almost harder than listening to Cash spew the secret we've kept for eight long years.

"I swear to God, Tess, I never told a soul."

I shake my head as the tears begin to well in my eyes. "We should—" My voice breaks. "We should have known that with you in the public eye now, we couldn't keep this secret forever."

But there's more in Casey's eyes. More that he's not telling me.

"What is it, Case?"

But he shakes his head. "Nothing. How the hell did a reporter get ahold of this information?"

I stare down at my hands, feeling numb, as though I were in a bad dream.

"We can't hide from the truth, Casey."

And when these words fall from my mouth—words that have entangled themselves, embedded themselves in the back of my mind—I realize we need to come clean.

"What about our little boy, Casey? He's eight. He knows how to read. What if he sees this story on a cover of a magazine? What about our families? I don't want them to find out this way."

Fear fills all of the dark pockets of grief that I've held on to for so long.

Casey calls his brother back, and Cash doesn't pick up. I see the anger on Casey's face, not just from Cash not picking up, but also all the past disappointments that he's caused Casey.

The lies.

The missed birthdays.

Missed holidays.

The selfishness, self-centeredness.

The ego.

His reckless ways.

His ignorance of truth.

Casey leaves a message. "Get that reporter off your back, Cash. Fucking leave it alone. Please."

He hits End.

"We should go home sooner, just in case." I try to conceal my sadness that has now turned to anger.

"Tess, whether we go home sooner or after the weekend, it won't make a difference. If this story goes live, we're still going to look like we've hidden it if we tell them now before the story runs or after."

He's right.

"Besides, she doesn't have proof. I wasn't, you know, where I'm at now, so there wouldn't be pictures or anything to trace all this back to us. The only thing is the birth certificate—"

And we both hold our breath.

I let out a sigh. "We have one copy, and the adoptive parents have a copy. That's it. The adoptive parents would never put this out there if they loved their child," I say. "No way in hell they'd start a media frenzy like this."

"We found a private agency for unwed mothers. There's no way the outfit would have leaked this," Casey says. "Just need to face the music."

I longed for Casey when he left over the weekend, not because I needed him, but because I wanted to be with him.

Nothing, thankfully, ran in any magazine, tabloid, newspaper, as I spent hours searching the internet.

Mary Jo said we could sell the house for an easy $872,000. The truth is, I need the money from the house. I haven't been working, and my ego won't allow me to admit this to Casey.

"With these views and the easy access to town and the ocean, you'd better believe this house will be snatched up quickly," Mary Jo had said.

And on Monday, as we board the plane for Dillon Creek and ponder the house price, telling the truth, and finding truth, I receive an e-mail from *Touch* magazine, an e-mail subscription I signed up for in my quest to find anything on our story bleeding across the pages.

I read the headline.

ATWOOD FATHERS BABY

When shock and grief combine itself, it's a recipe that makes one almost go mad. Without air in my lungs and with a sinking feeling in my stomach, I look to Casey and show him my phone.

We take our seats on the airplane, and he takes my phone and opens the article.

He reads.

I'm too scared to look.

He's quiet.

I can't speak, as fear gathers in my body.

My hands begin to sweat, and I feel as though I'm going to throw up.

The other passengers board the plane like it's a normal Monday, and it is to them. They laugh and joke and read and go about their day as if nothing were wrong in the world, and it isn't for them.

"Please, Case," I say breathlessly, "tell me what it says."

He continues to read the article as if he hadn't heard me.

It feels like years pass before he looks up at me.

I let out a loud sigh that is broken down by a muffled cry. "What?" I whisper and peek over his shoulder.

Disbelief is all over Casey's face.

Unidentified child.

Eight years old.

Undisclosed source close to the adoptive family.

Cash Atwood.

Those are the phrases I pick up from the article. "Cash Atwood?"

"Cash," he says and stares through me. "Cash said it was his baby."

"Mr. Atwood, sorry, I hate to interrupt, but would you mind signing this for my nephew? You're his favorite bull rider." A man in his mid-fifties stands in the aisle, a pen in one hand, a piece of paper in the other.

Automatically, Casey takes the man's paper and pen and signs it. "Thank you, sir. Appreciate the support," he says, like a practiced line that he repeats over and over and over.

A plastic smile spreads across my face as we sit somewhere between disbelief and reality, and I still can't get used to *this* Casey. I'm not used to women fawning all over him or the people asking him for his autograph or to take a photo.

The man thanks Casey and walks back to his seat. Casey hands me back my phone, a blank stare on his face.

"I'm not sure if I should be thrilled or curious about why Cash did this," I whisper to Casey.

Casey shakes his head, unfit for words—I can tell by the way his jaw is tight and his stare is hard.

When we arrive in Dillon Creek, it's late in the day, and the sun is setting behind the wall of redwood trees that serve as the backdrop to town. Calder left a truck for us at the Arcata Airport.

As we drive down Main Street, Casey slides his hand between my legs and looks at me longingly. "You okay?"

I look back at him. Nod. "I will be. I just want this to be over with now. I want to get on with our lives."

But for me, there's a stain on Dillon Creek now, which was once a place I sought refuge from the outside world, a tiny well-kept town that sits just past the State Route 211.

Old feelings of inadequacy return.

I couldn't hold on to my job.

Not that I wasn't good enough. I know I was—am.

It's the politics.

School should be in session now.

My kids have a teacher who should have retired years ago.

And here I am, twenty-seven years old, still trying to figure out life.

"Home?" Casey asks.

"Yes."

The porch light is on.

Anna must have done that. I inwardly smile at the thought of a hug and a late-night chat about boys with a glass of wine with my best friend.

"Do your parents know we're coming?"

He uses *we* like I will let him come to my parents' with me. Let him endure the blameful looks from my parents. The heated words that might spew from all of our mouths.

I shake my head.

"You didn't tell them?"

I shake my head again.

"Tess," he sighs. "Why not?"

"I don't want them to be prepared, Case. I want all of this to happen naturally. Come on. You know my mother."

He pushes strands of my hair behind my ears. "You know it's Dillon Creek. It'll make the paper tomorrow. I'm sure the truck was seen driving through town."

"There are four Atwood brothers. How would they know it wasn't just Calder or Colt with one quick glance?"

He shrugs. "Could be right. When do you want to go over to your parents'?"

"Tonight."

Casey sighs again. "Let me go with you, Tess."

"No, there are some things I need to do alone, Case."

He gives a half-laugh. "Reminds me of when we were kids. Remember when Branch Thompson stole your backpack, just to be a shit ass. You told Anna and me that you were going to go to his house and get it. Hell, we weren't older than maybe eleven or so. When we grabbed our bikes, ready to go, you told us we couldn't. That there were some things you needed to do alone." He laughs. "But we followed you. Heard you yelling at him on his front porch about wetting the bed and sleeping with his favorite blanket and that all this dirt you had on him came from a reliable source. And then"—he laughs—"you said, 'Give me my backpack, and I'll let you live.' "

We both laugh.

"That kid ran inside so quickly and grabbed your backpack."

We're still laughing when we pull in my driveway.

Home.

"I've never doubted your abilities, Tess. I know … I know our son is just as tough as his mama, and I know you can do this alone. But if you don't want to do it alone, I'll be here." Casey leans over and kisses me lightly on the lips, and I feel it in my toes.

He pulls away. "Call me when you're back home? I'll come stay the night."

My stomach erupts with butterflies at the thought of having Casey in my bed tonight. Between my sheets. Under me. Inside me.

"That sounds wonderful." I kiss him once more, and he jumps out of the truck, grabs my bag, and carries it to my front door.

"Thank you."

Casey turns to leave. "Tess?"

"Yeah?"

"I love you more than bull riding and the stars and the moon, and I've never stopped loving you."

I feel his words in my heart. "I love you too."

I watch as he drives away, taking tiny pieces of my heart with him.

The porch of my parents' house is decorated to the nines for Thanksgiving. My mother has an impeccable decorating style. I just hope she's not several glasses into her nightly ritual.

I close my eyes and pray as my heart begins to pound.

I knock and open the door.

"Hello?" I call out.

Thump.

Thump.

Thump.

Thump.

My heartbeat is so hard that I hear it in my ears.

My mother peeks around the corner, and her jaw falls open. "Tess!" she calls out. "Dad! Tess is home!"

But she sees the look on my face.

"What is it? What's wrong?" She grabs me by the shoulders.

"We need to talk," I say as I walk past her. I ease myself down to the sofa, letting my purse strap fall off my shoulder.

The letters are in my purse, so I keep it close—proof that something isn't right.

My dad comes downstairs.

"Tess, my sweet girl," he says.

I stand, and he pulls me into a hug.

My father takes a seat next to my mom.

"What is it, honey?" my mom asks.

I let out a deep breath and allow my shoulders to fall into a restful position, knowing they'll creep up to my ears before this is over. Rehearsing the conversation over and over in my head only cluttered my thoughts.

"Did you find my baby pictures, Mom?"

She's silent, toying with her hands yet looking at me straight in the eye.

"Please, just be honest with me. That's all I want."

"No," she whispers.

"Do you have any baby pictures of me?"

"No," she whispers again.

My dad's eyes grow sad. "What's this about, Tess?" He puts an arm over my mom.

And in this moment, I'm glad they have each other.

"You don't have my baby pictures because you didn't have me when I was a baby. Is that right?" The words fall from my mouth, and even I have a hard time believing them.

My mom's head drops to her lap as tears begin to fall.

Knowing I'm on the right track because Mavis Morgan does not cry, I reach down into my purse and pull out her letters to Ike. I set them on the coffee table. "Mama, I just need the truth. I need the rest of the story."

37

Casey

Calder, Colt, Anna, Mom, and Dad are all gathered around the dining room table, laughing and joking.

The pile of Australian shepherds are passed out in the living room by the fireplace.

But the back door—the door our good friends and family know to use—opens.

It's Cash.

My mom calls out, "Cash?"

She stands automatically and runs to her son. The one who only comes home when he needs something or needs time to think, to come back to his roots. The reckless kid who always stands out and shows off with unexplainable athleticism.

My father, not as forgiving, still stands and walks to his son. Wraps his arms around him. "Been a long time, kid."

Anna whispers to Colt, stands, and attempts to leave, maybe to give the family time to process the ghost who's just walked through the back door.

"No way in hell, Anna Atwood." My mom grabs Anna's hand. "You are as much a part of this family than these boys," my mother says in her motherly tone.

Anna turns and laughs. "Yes, Mrs. Atwood."

Mom pulls Anna in for a hug. "Besides, it's about time. I've been outnumbered for years. Even our dogs are boys!"

Calder and Colt stand and walk to Cash.

" 'Bout time, brother," Calder says, pulls him in for a hug. Colt does the same.

But I sit here and stare hard at the brother who just walked away. The brother I idolized for so many years, growing up, before he turned into an asshole. The brother who taught me to whittle wood and break a colt, who taught me the basics about bull riding. Guess to fight them, you've got to know how to ride them.

Everyone looks at me and Cash, waiting for something, anything.

And to my surprise, he doesn't look like a train wreck. Even if the last time he called me, he was drunk, which isn't anything new.

"Now, you decide to show up?" My words cut through the silence of the Atwood ranch, ricocheting off the surrounding mountains, the soil, the cattle, the walls that have held the Atwood house up for the past one hundred years. "Of all times, now? Well, cowboy, you weren't needed then, and you're not needed now."

Cash stares at me long and hard. Tips his chin up. "Suppose I deserve that." He rubs his jaw with his fingers.

Nobody says another word.

"You think that you can just come in here and act like nothing happened? Like you didn't go AWOL and worry the shit out of Mom and Dad?"

"Where were you on the night that Conroy died and I had to hold up Mom?" Cash's words slither to me.

I see red. "Shut the fuck up, Cash." I allow the anger and the regret and the sadness and the guilt to surface like boiling water.

Cash says, "Where were you, Casey? In fact, where was Tess?"

He knows.

My fists become balls, and I feel the anger coursing through my veins.

"That's enough, boys," Mom says.

"Why'd you take the blame?" I seethe. "Why'd you tell the reporter what you told her?"

Mom interjects, "What are you talking about, Casey?"

Cash smiles. "Tell them, Case. Why don't you tell the family your deep, dark secret? Because God knows I'm tired of hanging on to it."

With everything I have, I land a punch across his nose.

Calder and Colt jump in and hold us back as we struggle to free ourselves, staring each other down with momentary hatred.

"Casey, please. What are you talking about?" my mom begs.

"Let me go, Calder!" I yank my arms free and storm outside, not sure where the hell to go.

I walk toward the fence line through the darkness and scream out the most horrendous yell I have ever let go.

Resting my hands on the fence, I drop my head and stand here in the night as I listen to the stillness of the night.

Brooks, my dog, is at my feet, looking up at me, whining.

I've missed him, and I drop my hand to give his head a scratch. He tucks his ears in, knowing I'm not happy. Knowing that something is wrong.

"It's all right, boy."

Twenty minutes pass, and the red I saw earlier slowly begins to fade.

I hear footfalls behind me.

"You done?"

But it isn't Calder.

It isn't Colt or my dad.

It's Cash.

Sighing, I keep my head where it's at, my hand on my dog. "You've got balls, coming out here, Cash."

He laughs. "I come face-to-face with one-ton animals three nights a week. There's no question about my balls." Cash comes to the fence and stares at the ranch that's illuminated in the moonlight. He's holding a towel to his nose.

I don't apologize for the nose yet. With disdain in my tone, I say, "Why'd you tell the reporter it was you?"

"Why does it matter?"

"Because I don't want to feel like I owe you, Cash. Fuck. I don't want to feel anything toward you because you never, ever make right on your word, and I don't want to feel the fucking guilt because I'm fucking angry with you."

"Look, I know I'm an asshole, and I know I've screwed up a lot." He laughs and then pauses to gaze out into the darkness. "Too many times to count. Guess I just wanted to get it right, just once. You're going to the finals. I … I just didn't want that burden on your shoulders. And people expect that of me—that type of behavior—but not you and certainly not Tess."

I whip my head around. "How do you know it was the truth?"

He smirks. "Come on, man. I know you. The second you paused on the phone that day, I could tell that it was true. And I know that's why you and Tess weren't there on Waddington when Conroy and Tripp were killed. I know you went to Oregon."

"How? How do you know all this?"

"Fed the reporter drinks. Got her drunk. She knew some pieces, but I filled in the rest with what was left—in my head, of course."

"Suppose you fucked her too." I shake my head.

"Here nor there." Which means he did. "Have you told Mom and Dad?"

"No," I say sharply. I need to tell them. There's a lot I need to talk about with Mom and Dad … and Tess.

"You should be honest."

I let out a loud howl of laughter. "You, talking about honesty?" I give him a side-eye.

"We're built different, Case. It's expected of me to act a certain way. But you? The expectations for you are different. Besides, sometimes, it's easier to fit the mold we're given."

"For you."

"Yeah, for me," he sighs.

Footfalls sound again. Several this time.

Cash and I look back to see both of our brothers coming toward us.

There's only one missing. There's been one missing for the past eight years.

"You two figure it out yet? Or are we going to have to put you in the barn for twenty-four hours to figure it out?" Colt laughs as they join us at the fence.

I'm still pissed off at Cash. Maybe I'm taking other shit out on him that isn't his shit to own, but on the other hand, it feels real good to have the four of us together again.

Colt starts to laugh.

"What's funny?" Calder asks.

"I thought"—he laughs more—"you were going to rip Cash's face off."

Then, Calder starts to giggle. Then Cash and finally me.

Cash's nose is still swollen and red when he removes the towel because, now, he's bending over, laughing so hard that it's uncontrollable.

We all are.

I don't remember the last time we did this, but I know it was before Conroy died.

And it feels real good and real sad, all at the same time.

Once the laughter dies down, I tell my brothers about the baby. How well Tess hid it. I tell them about the little boy that Tess and I had. Gave up for adoption. I tell them the truth about why we weren't there when Conroy and Tripp were killed.

I hold back on Tess's story with her parents. I know her story has yet to be finished, and she'll tell it when she's ready.

Calder looks at Cash. "You stickin' around for the holidays? Could use the help."

"Yeah," Cash says, lightly rubbing his nose with his fingers.

"Broken?" I ask.

"Nah, I've had plenty of those. Bone is still intact."

I nod. "Suppose you deserved the others, but you didn't deserve this one."

"We good?" Cash asks.

"I don't know, man."

I'm not sure anything will ever be right with me and Cash. Maybe if he can stick around long enough this time, it might be.

But Cash's MO isn't sticking around too long for anything.

He's broken hearts all the way across America and into Brazil. I know it because I have to hear the sob story afterward. Women asking about him at events, wanting to know why he is the way he is. Why he can't just commit and settle down. Why he drinks too much and sleeps with way too many women. Why he goes from zero to a hundred with anger.

Pent-up anger and grief.

But for the first time in a long time, everything feels like it's beginning to finally fall into place.

Tess.

The truth about our son.

The finals.

My family, my brothers, our mom and dad.

But there's still one thing I have to tell Tess, and all of this good might just explode in my face.

38

The Ladybugs

Erla has decided and planned how she'll die. She's decided to drive to Garberville, forty-five minutes south of Dillon Creek, in a rented car with her cement blocks, her ropes, and all of her grief. There's a deep spot in Eel River that never gets below twenty feet, even in the summertime. She'll go late at night. It's foolproof. Even if the police find the car, she rented it under Larry O' Donnell in Eureka. Why they didn't ask for Erla's driver's license was a sign from God that she was doing the right thing. How on earth anyone could rent a car without showing proof of a driver's license is beyond her. And when the employee mentioned she was new at the rental place, well, Erla just squealed at her luck.

"To what do I owe this pleasure, Erla?" Twila asks as she sits down at her desk across from Erla.

"I need to update my last will and testament, Twila."

"We can do that." Twila types something into her computer. "How are you?"

Her look is a bit sad, maybe a little forlorn, and Erla knows what she means—without Don. *How is your life without Don?*

"It's moving forward," Erla says. "Always moving forward whether I'm ready for it or not." Erla chuckles lightly, trying to break up the slow sadness that has just overcome the office.

"And what's your date of birth, Erla?"

"September 2, 19 …" *Oh, no. What year was I born?* "Um, 19 …" Erla says again and then tries to laugh it off. "Why, I can't remember! Can we just write 19 something?"

Twila pulls out her calculator. "If you don't mind me asking, Erla, how old are you?"

"Seventy-six," she lies because, really, she stopped keeping track of her age at seventy.

Anything over seventy is considered old, so anytime anyone would ask, she'd reply with, "Old."

Twila does the calculation on her calculator. "Does 1942 sound right?"

"Sure." Erla Brockmeyer has been forgetting more and more these days.

Her house is an array of colorful sticky notes. She prays nobody will come over unexpected because she'll have to lie again. Boy, Erla wishes that God will give her a pass to heaven even though she's been doing the devil's work with the lying. And to be quite honest, she isn't sure how God feels about suicide. Though it's noted to be a sin in the Bible, she really hopes he'll see all the work she did before she came home for good.

In fact, just to remember this appointment, she made a line of sticky notes against the wall from her bedroom to the coffeepot and wrote *Twila: Will* and the date. There must have been forty of them! But all Erla has these days is time on her hands.

Time and silence.

Twila goes over the last draft of the will with Erla, and they make the necessary changes.

Before Erla goes, she hugs Twila, knowing it might be the last time she sees her. "Thank you for all you've done for Don and me, Twila."

"Oh, you're welcome, Erla. Truly, it's no problem."

Erla begins to leave out the back door.

"Uh, Erla? Main Street is this way." Twila points in the opposite direction.

"Oh, that's what I meant."

Erla reaches into her purse for her keys, and she feels a piece of paper next to them. She pulls it out and reads the piece of paper.

> *You are parked next to The Flowerpot. Also, you have seeds that you found in the garage that are in the trunk of the car. Donate those.*

Mabe tried to convince Erla that she could use her phone for reminders, but Erla has never been one to trust technology. Besides, a pen and paper have never steered her wrong, so no need to start using technology now.

Her phone is great for making calls and taking pictures, but that is about all she uses it for. She checks her e-mail on the computer and pays all of her bills with a good old-fashioned check, stamp, and envelope, which reminds her that she'll need to write out directions for Scarlet about Don's retirement checks.

When she looked at the retirement paperwork when Don first got sick, Erla could receive the checks, but once she passed away, there would be no more.

Erla pulls her coat tighter around her. She forgot it was winter in Dillon Creek. The changing of the seasons has always been her favorite.

This will be the last one, she thinks quietly to herself as she makes her way down Main Street.

Before she begins to cross the street, Bo Richards stops his truck for Erla and calls, "Mrs. Brockmeyer!" He waves from his truck for her to cross.

"Mr. Richards!" She makes her way across the street and waves a thank-you.

Erla feels relief. As if life has become a burden, and now, she's going home to the big house.

After Erla gets the flower seeds from her trunk, she makes her way into The Flowerpot.

"Good morning, Mrs. Brockmeyer. It is so lovely to see you."

"Likewise, Juniper. Listen"—she sets the box of seeds down on the counter—"could you use these? I simply just don't have the time or the use for them."

Juniper doesn't even look in the box. "Of course. I'm certain I'll find a home for them." Juniper is as sweet as pie even if she is a little earthy. "Interested in new seeds? I got some hybrids in that I thought you'd enjoy."

And it hits Erla like a pile of cement.

She won't be around tomorrow.

She won't be around ever again.

39

Tess

Mom's eyes are bloodshot.

Dad looks lost.

She holds her breath before she starts, staring deeply into my eyes. "We ... we wanted another child so badly." She uses the tissue to wipe her nose. "We couldn't conceive, your father and I. Tripp was getting older, and our time was running out. He'd run around the bar, happy as a lark, asking about a baby sister day after day," Mom says, remembering. "Maybe he knew something we didn't." Mom looks around the living room, as if watching a day and time come alive that no longer exists, only a moment that has burdened her waking thoughts. "It was no secret that we wanted another child. We should have been grateful for just one healthy baby, but"—Mom reaches for my hand—"I think I felt something that was bigger than your father and me, something that we were supposed to do, but I couldn't quite put my finger on it." Her hand tightens around mine.

"Anyhow, Ike saw something at the bar that day. He called me the next day," she sighs and holds her memories at bay only for a minute to regain her composure. "He said there was a beautiful little girl that he knew who lived in Ketchikan. That her mother couldn't take care of her and that her grandparents felt it was best for her to go somewhere far away from Ketchikan."

Mom pauses for a moment, and I move to the sofa to put my arms around her, feeling every minute of her pain.

I was that mother. Too young to take on the responsibilities of a child for an act I'd done.

The pressure from my heart fills my chest.

"Your biological mother's name is Elizabeth Walters."

Reality collides with the truth I've believed for years.

Esther and Martin are my grandparents.

My arms fall from my mother's sides because I'm unable to slow the thoughts, the pieces of the story down.

"She couldn't take care of you because she was involved in drugs and just couldn't get clean."

The feeling of chaos, I think to myself, never wanting to leave my mother's side once I came to Dillon Creek.

"The final straw came when your grandmother, Esther, came to pick up Elizabeth for dinner one night, only to find you at home alone. You told Esther that your mommy had been gone for a long time and that you missed her." My mom chokes back tears. "You were so innocent and so young, Tess."

I can't breathe because the story she's telling is one that I remember, looking deeply inside my subconscious mind. I just needed someone to breathe life into a feeling I still feel today.

"She said she'd be right back. And the sun set, and it was dark. I crawled into her bed and hid under the covers until the sun rose again. She didn't come home." My stomach begins to tie into knots, and I think I'm going to be sick.

This time, my mom puts her arms around me.

My father strokes my cheek, tears in his eyes.

"There was no way we could let you go, Tess, after Ike told us that story. You were ours if Ike could legally get you to us."

"That's why you don't have baby pictures," I say. I look into my mom's eyes. "Esther passed away." I shake my head and bring my eyes to the hardwood floor. "She gave me a Chilkat before she died." I cover my mouth, now understanding that I am the family member, not a trusted close friend.

"What?"

"Cancer, and I had no idea. I got to meet with her, and she worked until days before she died."

My mother smiles through her tears. "That was Esther." She picks up one of the letters on the coffee table. "We knew this day would come, Tess. I ... I suppose your father and I just didn't want you to feel unwanted if we told you. God, you're our daughter. And when you said you were going to Ketchikan, that Ike had written the letter to you, we knew." She nods and looks at my father. "We knew you'd eventually put the pieces together. Maybe it was the wrong decision not to tell you ... maybe it was the right one. I don't know. But"—she takes both of my hands into hers and looks down at them—"you belong to us, and I never wanted your biological mother to hurt your heart again. I'd seen how her drug abuse affected you. Her absence sat in your heart. When you were little, you were—"

"Terrified of you leaving my sight," I finish her sentence.

All of a sudden, I'm four.

Ike was beside me, holding my hand. He said, "Elizabeth, these are the Morgans. This is Bruce and Mavis and Tripp."

Tripp marched right up to me, a stuffed animal in tow, and hugged me. "Sister," he said and kissed me on the cheek.

My mom got down on her knees in her pantsuit, her impeccable hair, and it was the look in her eyes, filled with empathy and unconditional love, that made my two little legs move toward her. But mostly, it was the tears that started to fall when I took those steps. She held open her arms, and I fell into them.

"Welcome home, baby girl," she whispered softly into my ear.

"You changed my name," I manage to say in the present moment.

"I hope that's all right, Tess. Ike recommended we do it, per Esther and Martin's request."

"That ... that's my middle name. Tess Elizabeth Morgan."

"We didn't want you to lose everything," my dad finally says.

My mom says, "Please know, Tess, that while your biological mother couldn't take care of you, she was your mother, and she loved you with all her heart. That love never goes away."

And that's when all the guilt of the last eight years comes to a head.

I fall to pieces on the floor.

I cry for our son.

I cry for our son's adoptive parents who received the gift that my parents received when they adopted me.

I cry for the little four-year-old girl inside me who had a wonderful childhood because of my mom and dad. Because of Esther and Martin and because of Elizabeth.

I cry for the years I spent in guilt, wondering if giving up our child for adoption was the right decision or not, the unjust anger I felt toward Casey for all those years.

I cry for the unanswered prayers I never knew I had.

Quickly, I realize that our little boy has a great life, and I know this because we were the Ike Isner in his case. Because I was adopted, I was given this beautiful life.

We were given names of families who wanted our unborn child more than everything. Given résumés and videos and answered questionnaires.

Only given first names of potential adoptive parents.

And finally, we chose one family.

At last, I am free.

And when my tears of freedom finally settle, I say, "There's something I need to tell you."

I tell them the story of how a little boy and little girl fell in love.

It is an unconventional love that started with daisies and cow pastures and bull rides. It was a love that went unrecognized for years until one day, they both made a choice that changed the trajectory of their futures—a choice that would stay with them for years to come, along with the feelings of wrong. And little did she—I—know, the story would come full circle.

When I'm done with the story, my parents are on the floor with me, crying.

On this day, I know our relationship has changed forever. We not only have the common bond of family, but now, we are also able to see both sides of the coin. And what a freedom it is to know that.

Until it's late, we talk and hug and remember.

I tell them about Casey.

Ultimately, I tell them I need to go.

My mom takes me into her chest, just like I'm four again. "We've lost one child. We can't afford to lose another," she says through stiff lips.

I'm unsure of what that wholly means, although I have some understanding, which is, *Whatever it is that makes you happy, it makes us happy.*

"Besides," my mom says, "we've always known you two were just one letter away from falling in love. Guess you finally got the right letter."

The truth is, moms always know.

I say my good-byes and drive home.

Casey is already inside, and it's late, but he has a plate of dinner ready for me on the kitchen counter.

"How'd it go?" he whispers from the kitchen counter.

"How much time to do you have?" I ask.

"All the time in the world, baby." He kisses my head.

I pull away and look into his eyes, and I realize if I had never been adopted, I never would have moved to Dillon Creek. I never would have met Casey Atwood, and we wouldn't have had the experiences we've had.

"I love you," is all I say.

I sit down and eat, and I begin to tell him the story of Elizabeth Walters and me.

When I'm done, I expect the unease to go away on his face, but it doesn't.

"What's wrong, Case?"

He sighs. "I met our son, Tess. His name is Mr. Austin."

40

Casey

"I couldn't, Tess. I couldn't not know who he was." My voice quivers.

Tess is silent, in shock, staring down at her plate in disbelief.

"I went back to Oregon months back. Said that I wanted a make a little boy's day. Explained I was a bull rider. I didn't ask the adoption agency to give me information about the parents, but I provided tickets for that weekend. I just … I wanted to hold his hand." I choke back tears now at the memory of his firm little handshake. "He has your eyes," I say to Tess.

And this makes her whole body shake.

I reach for her.

"No." She finally looks up from her plate, her stare sharp. "How could you? How could you reach out to our son and not tell me about it?" she barely whispers.

"I-I'm sorry. I didn't know if I'd ever have the chance to meet him again."

Still, she's silent.

I can see that she's tired. She doesn't have the fight or tears or anything left in her.

My timing was real shitty.

"Tess …"

I reach for her again, but she slowly shakes her head.

"We need to sell the house in Ketchikan and part ways. It's for the best."

"What?" Doubt stains my tone. "Tess, come on. This is a little much, don't you think?"

Slowly, she brings her eyes to mine. "Good-bye, Casey. You can let yourself out."

And with that, she stands, leaving her plate at the table, and quietly walks to her bedroom, shutting the door behind her.

I sit down at the table, place my head in my hands, and try to figure out how to make this right.

From my pocket, I pull out a little white box with the diamond ring in it. There are rose petals and candles lit in Tess's room.

I should have told her sooner about Austin. Maybe I should have told her before I made the move to bring him to the event. I was ready though, and she wasn't. I knew she wasn't. But maybe I should have waited until she was.

Instead, I walk to the counter, grab a piece of paper and a pen, and begin to write.

> *Dear Tess,*
>
> *I'm sorry.*
>
> *I'm going to make mistakes. I'm human and imperfect in every way a person can be. But one thing is for sure: I'm in love with you, and I have been since I met you when we were barely out of diapers.*
>
> *I won't get it right all the time, but know that in my meeting Austin, my intentions were true, and all I wanted was to see him. Maybe that was wrong or right, but I know it was hard.*

If you never want to hear from me again, I'll understand. I'll have to.

But if you find it in your heart to come back to me, bring this ring with you because it's a symbol of my commitment to you forever.

You're my night sky.

My bright, sunny day.

My refuge from a fight.

My soft place to land.

My clearing on a dark day.

You're my home and my whole heart.

I love you, Tess Elizabeth Morgan.

And I'll wait for you for forever, no matter what it takes.

I'm not walking away this time.

Love,

Casey

I set the note next to the ring box on the kitchen counter, so she sees it. Then, I put Saran Wrap over the plate of food and put it in the refrigerator.

Before I leave, I walk down the hallway to the bedroom, and through the door, I say, "Tess, don't forget to blow out the candles before you go to bed. I love you."

When I get home, Cash is the only one awake.

"How'd it go?" he asks. Only one black eye has started to form.

I told my family about Austin before they had to read something else in the media.

"It didn't." My words are short, clipped, as I walk to my old bedroom and quietly shut the door.

I need to get my own place, I think to myself as I fall on my old twin-size bed.

"Hey." I hear Cash say through the door. "If Tess isn't going to the finals with you, I'll go with you."

That's it, and then footfalls go down the hallway and back to the living room.

Let her go, I hear Conroy's voice in my head. The same advice he gave me when I was fifteen when Abrams Locke asked Tess out. *She'll figure it out, Casey. She'll either find a way back or she won't. And either way, you'll have to accept it.*

I roll onto my side and try to allow the night to take me to sleep.

"You're quieter than usual. Not as loud. Or drunk," I say to Cash, who's sitting in the seat next to me, sunglasses on to cover up the full black eye I gave him.

First class gives us more leg room, so those are the tickets I asked the PBR to book.

Cash pushes his backpack underneath the seat.

He doesn't say anything, except, "Did you tell Tess you were leaving?"

I shake my head. "I'm sure she doesn't want to know."

"What makes you say that?"

Three women about our age approach us and are fit to be tied.

"What are the odds we have the number one bullfighter and a bull riding champion together—and brothers at that—on the same flight as us?!" one says, and they all squeal.

One of them thrusts a picture of me on Ridiculous about five years ago and a black pen. "Will you sign this, Casey, please?"

Another one pushes a picture of Cash toward him.

"Are you guys headed to Vegas for the finals?" the chatty one says.

"Yes, ma'am," we say in unison.

And they fan themselves with the pictures we just returned.

"Ladies, if you could please make your way back to your seats, the captain is ready for departure," the stewardess says, gently guiding the women back to their seats.

Cash barely smiles.

"What the hell is wrong with you, man?" I ask, trying to ward off my own troubles, trying to get my mind right for this weekend, trying not to die, trying to pray, trying to get centered. "You would have taken one—or all three—in the restroom and joined the Mile-High Club."

Cash rubs his good eye with a balled fist, sighs, and then proceeds with caution. "Bullfighter One asked me—no, told me that I'm on leave for at least six months. Get my life back on track," Cash finally says.

A few moments pass before I say, "What's the problem?"

He shrugs and stares out the window, searching for something he's not really looking for. "They said I drink too much. That I'm becoming a liability for the brand."

"Yeah"—I nod—"I can see that."

Cash continues to stare out the window, pretending to ignore me. A smile starts across his face.

"What?" I ask.

"You're the only one who can say shit like that and get away with it."

"Because you know it's the truth." I push my backpack underneath my seat.

"Probably right," he sighs.

"After the six months, then what?"

"I don't know."

The stewardess comes over the loudspeaker. "Please take your seats, ladies and gentlemen, and buckle your seat belts. Welcome aboard flight 223."

Cash wads up his jacket and makes a pillow against the window. "Wake me up when we get there."

"I don't know how you can just fall asleep anywhere."

Cash looks at me and pulls his head up from his makeshift pillow. "Why? It's easy. Close your goddamn eyes."

I shake my head and pull out my phone. My screen saver is of Tess and me. A picture we took down by the Tongass Narrows.

"You sure as hell aren't gonna win her back by staring at her picture," Cash says.

"Are you offering relationship advice? I thought you were sleeping."

He laughs. "Whatever, man. Wake me up in Vegas."

The words *let her go* keep playing in my head. Maybe time is the only thing that will fix this. Maybe then she'll see my side of things. I didn't do it to hurt her. Did I do it for selfish reasons? Yeah, probably. But we weren't even together at the time. Hell, I didn't know if she was coming back to me. But either way, she's hurt. That's what she's running on—heartbreak—and time is the only thing that will help heal those wounds. Maybe my timing could have been better. It felt like the honest and good thing to do at the time, but now, I'm not so sure.

In the picture, the back of her head rests against my chest. Loose strands of her dark hair dance across her face and are captured in one single moment. The smile she wears reminds me of a different time—when we were younger, carefree, and full of life and dirt and love. When we didn't know what sarcasm was or sex, grief, or real sadness. We were innocent, and our biggest burdens were chores and finishing our entire plate of food at dinner.

Time has passed, yet I catch glimpses of her from all those years ago, and I see contentment.

I appreciate in this moment that saving Tess isn't my job; it's her journey to save herself. She'll get right with God and her heart. But for now, it's her time to hurt because that's what life is all about.

It's beautiful.

And then it's sad and hard.

And then it's right again, somewhat boring. Routine. Scheduled.

But then something happens, and then it's beautiful again.

And what we realize is that we know only a little about life.

One day, when our lives have come to a close and we're ready for the stairway to heaven, I think we'll realize that the highs and lows were all worth it, that life was worth it—the heartbreak, the sadness, the beauty, the hard, the good, the brilliant—that our life is a journey to begin with, a story.

Whether Tess and I end up together or not, whether our story has a happy ending or an ending we don't foresee, we're better people for having experienced all of it.

I love this woman with all my heart, and if she sees that, then she'll come back, but if she doesn't, well then, I'll have to accept this piece of our lives as part of the broken journey of life.

41

The Ladybugs

Erla washes her face and brushes her teeth.

Some days, Erla barely remembers her own name. Some days, she does, but those things are easier to hide when you live alone.

No one to call your bluff or pull your cover, she thinks as she blends Mother Ann's cold cream into her skin.

Erla thinks of calling her granddaughter to tell her good night. Erla looks at her wristwatch. She could, she supposes, as it's only a quarter to nine. She does. But the call goes to voice mail, so she leaves a message.

"Hello, Scarlet. I just wanted to tell you how much I love you and how proud of you I am. I wanted to say good night, and I'll talk to you tomorrow."

Erla feels a little sad, like she wishes she had been able to speak to Scarlet. The pain in her chest returns, but it's sharper this time, and it stops her in her walk back to the bedroom. The shortness of breath seems to quickly follow when this happens, so she waits for it all to pass.

When it does, she carefully makes her way to the bedroom, to her side of the bed. Sits down. Says her prayers and thinks about tomorrow.

She'll drive down to the Garberville tomorrow evening. Erla kept the rope and cement blocks in the car after paying the neighbor kid, Meyers, to put them in there for her. Now, how she'll get the cement blocks out of the car once she is down by the river she hasn't quite figured out yet, but it will come to her.

She updated her will so that Scarlet will be the executor, and she'll leave everything to her and Devon.

With these chest pains and shortness of breath she is experiencing, Erla can't stand the thought of someone finding her body. She doesn't want them to live with the lasting memory. It makes her sad to think about. So, if there is no body, nobody will be traumatized, and those who loved her can just remember her as an old woman with a full life, who just fell off the planet, and not the way they found her.

Erla can trust in that. Her well-thought-out plans, except for the cement blocks from the car to the water's edge tomorrow night, which she'll figure out.

And with this lasting thought, she closes her eyes for the last time and dreams of Don.

"It's well past nine," Mabe says to Clyda on the phone. "Erla hasn't slept since Don passed away. Something's wrong. I'm going over there. Are you coming with?"

"I'll meet you there," Clyda says.

Once at Erla's house, they slowly open the door.

"Erla?" Clyda calls behind Mabe. "You here?"

As they make their way inside, they see sticky notes everywhere.

On the coat rack: *Don't forget your coat.*

On the front door: *Don't forget to shut the door.*

On the floor: *Don't forget to take off your shoes.*

On the wall in the entryway: *Don't forget to close the garage.*

On the walls: *Don't forget to pay the water bill and the gas bill* and *Don't forget to get creamer.*

Every surface, everyplace, there is a sticky note.

"Oh my good word, what the hell happened here?" Clyda says. "Looks like a damn flowchart threw up in here."

Mabe, too, is speechless. The last time she came over to Erla's, the sticky notes just lived in the kitchen. Her heart seizes when she sees all the notes.

Erla never would have let this happen to me, she thinks. *She would have checked on me. Called me out. Told me to get help, like she did.*

They make their way around the house and finally to the bedroom.

And there, in bed, on her back, is their old friend, eyes closed, fingers intertwined across her stomach.

Clyda and Mabe are flooded with relief.

"Goodness' sake, scared the daylights out of me," Clyda says as they both walk over to their friend.

"Erla, wake up." Mabe sits down next to Erla.

But she doesn't stir.

"Erla, honey, it's time to wake up," Clyda says.

Mabe touches Erla's hand, and she grows dizzy when Erla's hand is awful cold.

"Oh, oh, oh," is all Mabe says.

Clyda touches her old friend's skin. "Oh, dear God."

Mabe freezes into a panic, and Clyda moves her fingers to Erla's wrist, feeling for a pulse. Quickly, she moves to her neck, praying to find something that signifies life.

Mabe is already on the phone with Dr. Cain.

And the rest is chaos.

Mabe remembers the legal notepad between the chairs in the living room before the coroner takes the body of their old friend. But when she peeks between the chairs, the notepad is gone.

But the truth is, Erla did not succeed in taking her own life. Although she thought she had her best-laid plans, God had better ones. For He brought Erla home because it was her time and she was tired. She died with dignity and grace and with a broken heart. But it wasn't a bad heart that brought Erla home; it was the loss of her own true love.

Erla Brockmeyer died of a broken heart.

42

Tess

It's the day of the finals, and I'm nervous and sick. I regret the way Casey and I left things. Fixed emotions sit in my heart and stagger the beats, leaving me empty and hollow and numb.

Mary Jo calls on my phone. At first thought, I don't want to answer it, but I need to. If we want to sell—I'm not sure I want any memories of Ketchikan at all anymore—we should act quickly.

I've watched the video with Casey and our son, Austin, and I haven't been able to do it without crying.

The beautiful moments inside the forty-second clip have now changed my insides.

I've traced Austin's face with my finger. His little hand when he shakes Casey's. It makes love all the harder to navigate.

Questions dance through my head—not just about Austin, but also where I stand and how I feel about being adopted, trying to do what's best by Austin and not my heart.

Mary Jo's call goes to voice mail. I listen to it.

"Hey, Tess. We have an offer on the house that's far beyond asking price. It's a company out of Seattle. They're offering—are you ready for this?—1.2 million dollars. Call me as soon as you can."

"Oh my God." Relief shudders through my body.

If we sell, money won't be a problem. But the memories and the reason Ike gave us this house, my memories as a child that are slowly starting to come back, I will never be able to relive them again.

What about the history of the Isner house? The house has been a staple in the community for a long time. If we sell to some sort of corporation, surely, they'll demolish it and build what they want. Really, they're probably buying the house for the property.

But if we keep the house, maybe we can create new memories and erase those that make my stomach turn, ones I can't quite put my finger on but assume it's my biological mother's doing. It's been researched that children, even in the womb, take on their mother's feelings. Maybe these feelings aren't my own, but my mother's.

I don't want to call Casey for two reasons: one, he's got a big weekend ahead of him, and two, I don't want the uncertainty of us in the forefront of his mind when he takes to the bulls this weekend.

So, instead of calling Casey, I call Mary Jo.

"Can you believe it?" she asks when she picks up. "They offered 1.2 million dollars."

"I can't, Mary Jo. That's a lot of money. But I can't make a decision without Casey. He's in the finals this weekend, and I'd rather discuss this with him on Monday."

"That will work. They also had a question about staging. Who staged the house?"

"Staged? Oh, I did."

"They really liked your style and wondered if you freelanced your work."

"Freelanced my work? Like, do I decorate other houses?"

"Yes."

"No."

"Could you?"

Um ...

"Maybe?"

"Let me give you their number and you can follow up."

Mary Jo gives me the number, and I write it down.

"Call me Monday?" she asks.

"I will."

"Wonderful."

"Bye, Mary Jo, and thank you."

"That's my job."

It's Saturday, and my mom and I are sitting at Russ Park, having lunch. Something we've never done before.

Since we talked about everything the other night, she's cried more in the past few days than I've ever seen her cry in my entire life.

Mavis Morgan isn't Mavis Morgan anymore.

"The reason I used to try to fix everything in your life, Tess, I suppose, is that you suffered a lot of heartbreak before the age of five. I guess I just never wanted your heart to hurt again, so I meddled." She holds her face to the wintery sun. A rare occurrence in Dillon Creek—and in November at that.

"If it makes you feel any better, I haven't been able to remember much more."

Her eyes meet mine. "From what Ike told us, it was a lot of Elizabeth leaving you at all hours of the night to get her next fix. I slept in your bed with you until you were ten."

"I thought that was you being you." I laugh. "Overprotective mama bear." I give her shoulder a nudge and a smile.

"Yes, on both fronts." She smiles back and takes a bite of her sandwich.

"Thank you," I whisper.

"You don't have to thank me, Tess. That is my job as your mother. That's what Elizabeth should have done for you."

My mom takes my hand. "I also realized that through the grief, I was drinking way too much. I guess it was a side effect of the grief that I still feel over your brother. So, I put the plug in the jug, as they—whoever they are—say." She smiles and pats my hand. Then, "Have you talked to Casey?"

Really, I told her we were taking a break. I didn't tell her that he'd met Austin. In fact, I didn't tell her that the little boy in the video that had gone viral was Austin. She'll realize it someday.

"No."

She shrugs and then sighs. "I've been, um, seeing a counselor, a therapist, a shrink—whatever you call them."

"Yeah?"

"Yeah. A recommendation of Dr. Cain." She toys with a twisted paper towel in her hand. "I've been harboring a lot of resentment for a long time, which has made me a bitter, stiff, old woman." She's quiet for a moment. "I wish I had spent more of my life in forgiveness instead of being so self-righteous, Tess. I wish I had let go of things that didn't make a difference either way. Life has a way of coming full circle when we least expect it to. I wish I had never made you wear frilly pink dresses or made you do ballet. I wish I had let you play in the mud and get your hands dirty and eat more sugar." She laughs. "I wish I had done a lot of things differently." My mom stares down at her paper towel.

I take her cheek in my hand. "You are one hell of a mom, and I wish I had been more grateful for that."

"Can we start over?"

I smile. "Yes."

"Hello, Tess. I'm your adopted mom, and I'm going to let you make decisions for yourself from now on. I'm not going to meddle in your life, and I'm going to remember each moment as best I can."

I pull her in for a hug. "Have I told you that you're the greatest mom there ever was? I know why you did what you did now. And I want to hang on to each of those memories—because you made each of them out of love," I whisper.

My mom's hug tightens around me.

She doesn't ask about Austin because it's her way of not meddling. She knows I'll make the right decision when the time is right and let her know when I do so.

And I suppose she asked about Casey because she also knows my heart. She knows I've been in love with that boy since we met as kids. My mother has always been the interior decorator. And maybe I've picked up on some of that along the way.

"This corporation out of Seattle wants to meet with me about staging business offices for them."

"Meet with you?"

"Apparently, they liked how I staged the Ketchikan house, and they're looking for a freelancer."

My mother smiles. "It's no surprise to me, Tess. You've been good at everything most of your life."

This response from my mom surprises me. She's never said anything like that to me before.

"I guess I never told you that because I always pushed you to be the best—something I have regrets about now, obviously. I just knew you were destined for greatness, but now, you don't need your mom to tell you that."

"It wouldn't hurt to give them a call."

"No. No, it wouldn't." She sips her iced tea.

"The rain is coming," I say.

We stand and begin to pick up our lunch, our mess, our past, and we tuck it away and set forth for new adventures of new promise, new relationships, and a hopeful future.

"Onward," my mother says.

And we leave our past relationship at Russ Park and go toward new beginnings.

I'm over at Anna's with Colt and Calder as the finals play on their gigantic television that hangs from the wall.

The television goes dark, and fireworks explode from the ground—the opening of the finals. AC/DC's "Thunderstruck" plays.

My stomach grows into a fit of nerves, and I'm not sure I can watch this. I also say this every time I watch Casey ride.

The commentator yells, "And now, your top world contenders in the PBR World Finals!"

The crowd erupts over the music.

He says two names and then gets to Casey's.

With a black cowboy hat on, he lifts his head when the spotlight reaches him, and he waves to the crowd. I trace his long, lean legs up to his chest, protected by a vest, up to his jawline, and to his perfectly built smile.

My heart begins to throb at an unusual pace, and my hands begin to sweat.

Anna reaches over and rubs my back, knowing the nerves always get to me. Even when we watched Casey ride as kids, my body would do the same thing, where my eye would twitch and my mouth would go bone dry and my heart would flip and flop as I tried to hold it together on the outside. I wondered, too, when I took that steer when I was young, if Casey was just as nervous.

As the announcer drawls on, Anna whispers, "Have you talked to Casey at all?"

I told her about everything the night Casey left.

I told her about Austin.

That I'm adopted.

That Casey met Austin without my knowledge.

Anna said something to me that's been rolling around in my head the past few days. *Did you ever stop to think that maybe he did it out of love for you? That maybe he was trying to protect you from the future?"*

After the bull riders are announced, the commentator says, "And what is better than one Atwood brother? Two Atwood brothers!"

The camera flashes to Cash, who's sitting on the back fence next to the chutes.

I know Cash well enough that if he wasn't on national television right now, he'd be rolling his eyes, but instead, he waves and flashes his smile. He lives the sport that he gets to do for a living, but he's never cared for the media or the attention.

The television shows the riders on their bulls.

I find Casey's name in the lineup next to Top Ten, and I try to breathe.

Come on, Casey. Let's just get this ride over with.

But what about the next ride?

The next year?

Can you live like this? The constant worry of if he'll make it through another round?

If we figure this thing out, is this something I can live with?

Living and dying from weekend to weekend, is this the price I'd be willing to pay for loving a cowboy? One that's extremely good at what he does? I could never ask him to give it up, not something he's worked so hard for.

Maybe Casey and I are meant for moments, pockets in life where we get time to rest in each other. Maybe we're not meant for the long-term.

I tuck that thought away in my heart when I stand and walk to the bathroom because I'm going to be sick.

"Tess, you all right?" Anna asks.

I nod and continue to the bathroom. I calmly shut the door behind me and expel every last thing from my stomach in the toilet, not sure if it was the thought about Casey and me not being together or the fact that he's up for the ride of his life.

But I know I'm absolutely in love with him.

The truth is, I'm not okay.

The truth is, I want to be with Casey for the rest of our lives.

The truth is, I can't stand the thought of us not walking together in this thing called life.

The truth is, I can't ask him to walk away from what he loves, and yet I can't put myself through this every time he rides.

And the devastating part of all of this is that I need to make a choice that just might break both of us.

My eyes start to fill with tears. *Swallow that shit, Tess, and go watch him ride one last time.*

"Tess?" I hear Anna say on the other side of the door. "Can I get you anything?"

"No." My voice is hoarse with love and sadness. "I'll be out in a minute."

I lean over the sink and splash cold water on my face. Look at the woman staring back at me with uncertainty of the future, full of fear, courage, strength.

The little girl who overcame her biological mother's sadness and addiction and lived.

The little girl who fell for a boy whose heart she was destined to love.

The woman who lost her job.

The woman who left for the great wide open to live in unfamiliar territory.

The woman who sat through years of grief from the loss of her own son, only to find out they are two in the same— they are both loved so much by so many. That she understands him more than most because she's walked in the same shoes.

And the woman who, no matter what, is a good person with a heart full of love to give.

"Tess? Casey is next."

"No matter what," I whisper back to the woman in the mirror, "you will be okay."

I walk back into the living room and take my seat next to Anna as Casey slides on Top Ten.

Breathe, I tell myself, *just breathe.*

And quietly, I say a prayer for Casey, for the bull, and for us.

The commentator starts, "Now, the last time Casey Atwood took to this bull, he rode him to a near perfect finish, Tuff. That's what we're hoping Casey will do tonight, folks."

I want to throw up again, but there's nothing left to give.

When the camera flashes to his hands, I see on his left wrist is a bracelet.

A bracelet with small, colorful rubber bands that I made him when we were maybe eight.

My heart doubles over itself.

I remember when I gave it to him. I told him it was for good luck when he rode sheep—mutton busting is what it's called.

The bracelet has lasted all these years? It's hard to believe. Could it be the same bracelet? Why didn't he tell me he wore it when he rode?

Casey gives the nod.

The chute flies open.

Top Ten fights like hell, but Casey flows, like he's dancing with him. His body like a rubber band, it follows the lead of the bull and yet anticipates the bull's movements with ease and responds instead of reacts.

Twist.

Jump.

Buck.

Flashback: the first time I saw Casey with a ten-gallon cowboy hat. The hat much too big for his head.

Buck.

Jump.

Twist.

Flashback: the first time his hand touched mine in the middle of the mustard field off of Grizzly Bluff Road.

Twist.

Jump.

Buck.

Flashback: the first time his lips touched mine out at the ranch in the middle of summer when the stars in the night sky urged us together.

Buck.

Jump.

Twist.

Flashback: the first time we made love and I felt every inch of him in my heart.

The horn sounds, bringing me back to their dance.

Casey tries to pull the rope, but it's stuck.

I put my hands to my lips.

He gets his hand free and hits the arena dirt hard.

Top Ten flips around and scrapes his hoof against the dirt. Stares Casey down.

The bullfighters are trying to distract the bull, but it's no use.

Cash jumps off the fence and sprints toward Casey.

But it's all too late.

Top Ten charges for Casey, and Cash charges for Top Ten.

The bull's horn flips Casey's body into the air, and he lands hard on the arena dirt once again.

Cash falls before his brother, so if the bull comes back, he'll get Cash first.

The arena falls silent, and I hear my heartbeat in my ears.

"Casey?" I think I say.

Top Ten starts to charge once more, picking up Cash this time and tossing him into the air like a rag doll, leaving Casey's lifeless body untouched, as if he knew what he'd done.

And I fall to pieces on the floor.

43

Casey

Conroy is standing above me. "Cowboy, that was one hell of a ride." He helps me to my feet.

I embrace my brother for all the moments we didn't get together, feeling a lump in my throat.

"Where is everyone?" I look around the empty arena and back to my dead brother. "Am I ... am I dead?"

Conroy sighs, placing his hands on his hips. "He tried to warn you—Top Ten. The next time, he'd come after you."

I look down at my body, which is all in one piece, except for my blood-soaked shirt.

Conroy hands me my rope. "Come on. I want to show you something."

"Conroy, wait." I follow. "I'm not ready to die. Please." And all I can think about is Tess.

"Unfortunately, Case, I don't get to dictate who dies and who lives or what miracles are performed. Come on, cowboy. Hurry up." All of a sudden, we're back in Dillon Creek, at Anna and Colt's house. "Look, we don't have a lot of time."

We're in the living room, and Tess is on the floor while my brothers are on their phones.

It's chaos.

I start to run for Tess, but Conroy stops me.

"You can't do that, Case. Off-limits. Come on. Let's go."

Now, we're at the ranch. My mom is on the phone, pacing, tears falling, and my dad has his head hanging in his lap, unable to move.

I look to Conroy, and he shrugs.

"Sometimes, we got to give up what we love for who we love. Let's go."

Next, we're in an ambulance, but it's not my ambulance; it's Cash's.

"What … what the hell happened?" I look down at our brother, who's got blood everywhere, while the EMTs work on him.

"Cash jumped in. He took the last and final blow for you."

I can't think.

I can't move.

"One, two, three, *clear*!" The pads on his chest bolt his body upward.

Conroy looks back at me. "Cash might be a shithead sometimes, but those are his demons he's fighting, not yours. I suggest you accept him for what he is. You'll miss a lot of great moments together if you don't. Settle the score. Come on. Next stop."

It's to another ambulance.

Except the man who's lying there is me.

The EMTs hang their heads.

My shirt, once clean and starched, is now covered with my own blood and maybe Cash's blood.

Despair fills me. "I should have quit sooner."

Conroy says, "Sometimes, people don't know the devastating impacts their decisions have on others," he sighs. "Just like the night I got into the Jeep. One decision can not only change our lives, but also the lives of the people we love most."

We're back on Waddington, where my brother and Tripp died.

It's daytime though. The yellow mustard plants have filled the empty void of the accident scene eight years ago. The sun is bright, and the sky is blue.

Two wooden crosses are attached to the post of the barbed-wire fence.

"I had a choice, Case. I had a choice, and I chose wrong. Sometimes, we get second chances in life, and sometimes, we don't." Conroy walks over to me and takes my shoulder. "You need to decide."

And with that, he pushes me, and I fall. I continue to fall until my body crashes hard, and it fills with me with the most unbelievable pain I've ever experienced.

When I look up, the EMTs gasp, staring down at me.

"Monroe! We have a heartbeat!" one says to the other. "Welcome back, Casey." The EMT breathes hard. "We're doing all we can, Casey. Just stay with us this time, okay?"

But I can't seem to keep my eyes open. I try to nod to the EMT, but I can't.

My eyes slowly close again.

I hear a machine above me beep, followed by a long-drawn-out tone.

"Fuck!" I barely hear the EMT shout. "Give me the paddles again, Monroe! Quick! We lost him again."

I open my eyes this time, but I'm in the barn just off the front pasture. Tess is lying next to me under a blanket while a fury of rain pours down.

It's a memory.

Her head was on my chest, and I said, "I think I've died and gone to heaven."

Tess laughed and kissed my lips. We'd just made love—or whatever it was two teenagers were capable of. Maybe it was sweltering heat brought in by a storm but when the rain poured and the wind pushed, the heat did too.

"What do we do now?"

"Continue," I said, more of a joke.

"No, I mean, are we a couple now?"

I shrugged. I didn't know what to say. I didn't want to tie her down before she left for college. I didn't want to be the one responsible for holding her to our small town when she had so much talent for everything.

With the way I'd been riding lately, I'd be traveling with the circuit. The PBR had contacted me, and I was ready to sign on the dotted line. I just needed another year until I was eighteen.

I couldn't ask Tess to wait for me. Just wouldn't be fair. She deserved to live her life, and if it meant that I had to break her heart for her to be free, I'd do it.

So, instead of giving her the response I felt in my bones, I said, "Let's not put labels on it. Let's just do our thing, Tess. We're good at that, right, you and me?"

It was quiet for a minute, and then she said, "Yeah, okay."

But the truth was, I was absolutely in love with Tess Morgan. But I wasn't going to be responsible for holding her down when I knew my job was going to take me all over the world.

Now, I'm back in my body at age twenty-seven, standing in the barn, wondering about timing and death and if I made the right decisions in life.

The rain pours down on the roof.

Did I make the right choices?

Am I being given a second chance to make things right?

I'm moving once more. Now, I'm at a birthday party, only as a spectator, not part of the scene. I see me standing with my brothers, my parents. Kids are running around, and parents are standing and talking. Across the way, I see the death stare that Tess gives the other me as she makes her way to the birthday cake, and I give it right back.

We hate each other?

I walk over to the cake, and it reads *Happy 8th birthday, Austin.*

I look up and see a broken little boy—our little boy—watching his parents struggle to like each other, tolerate each other.

The other me walks over to Tess, and I move close to listen.

I notice that neither of them are wearing wedding rings.

Did we just fall apart?

"While you were out working, I managed to throw our son's birthday party. Thanks for the help." Tess glares at the other me.

"You know it's a busy time of year for us, Tess."

She shakes her head. "That's funny because your parents seemed to step up and help, but you couldn't?" She shakes her head. "No. No, you're just resentful with me because you didn't get to live your dream of riding bulls. It was a decision we both made that night, remember? We'd decided to have sex. We decided to have the baby. We decided to keep the baby. Remember?"

"So, now, I'm a bad dad?"

"No, that's not what I'm saying at all," she says in a hushed tone. "You are a good dad—when you can manage to show up." Tess places her hands on her hips. Bites her lip. Glares at the other me.

"Oh, says the woman who's bitter because she didn't get to go to college and do her own thing. And now, we are both raising a child instead."

"I'm not bitter."

"Oh, bullshit, Tess. Bullshit."

Tess holds out her finger and points at the other me. "Listen, Casey, I will always be a mother first. Always. As for us, we ended two years ago when you just stopped showing up for life."

The birthday scene fades … and I'm falling again.

"Clear!" the same EMT shouts. "Come on, Casey!"

I see the worry on the EMT's face, but I'm not the Casey lying there right now. I'm another spectator in the ambulance.

I need to get back in my own body. But how?

The other me on the gurney jolts. The machine above the other me starts to beep consistently again.

The ambulance brakes, and the back doors fly open. I jump out of the way, so they can do what they do.

There's a lot of blood.

The EMT who was working on me is giving facts to the team that's just come out from the hospital doors.

"He's coded three times. I can't get his vitals to stabilize."

That's when Conroy appears next to me again. "You need to decide," he says.

"I want to live, Conroy."

"That's not what I mean, Case. I know you want to live." He pats my back as they wheel the other me, the badly broken me, into the hospital. "I mean, what kind of life do you want to lead? One with love and integrity and honesty? Or one full of ego-driven pride that keeps putting you on that bull for another round? Your destiny is up to you."

With that, Conroy disappears again, and I'm left with myself.

Another ambulance comes in, and another team comes out of the sliding doors of the hospital. They swing open the doors of the ambulance, and it's Cash's body that comes out.

"Barely stable," one EMT who jumps out of the ambulance says.

I bend over and try to catch my breath.

44

Tess

"Casey and Cash Atwood. They were brought in by ambulance," Colt says to the woman sitting behind the desk.

Anna and I walk over to the seating area with Laurel and Daryl. I put my arms around Laurel, not sure what to do or say, my body feeling as though it weighs millions of pounds.

Colt's jet got us to Las Vegas in no time at all.

I see Colt's head drop, and without another thought, I walk to the counter and look him in his eyes.

"What did she say?"

"They're doing everything they can."

I nod, my body numb, my fingers tingling. All I want is Casey back. My chest fills with mud so much so that I can barely breathe.

I look back at the woman behind the desk. "Please, miss, I need to go back and see him."

She frowns, trying to soften the blow I know she's about to deliver. "I'm sorry, ma'am. I can't let you go back there. We will let you know when something changes."

She doesn't say *when he stabilizes* or *when he's ready*. She gives me nothing promising life.

The mud that's in my chest spreads to my arms, my hands, my legs.

"Come on." Colt takes me by the shoulders. "Let's go sit down, Tess, okay?"

Fear freely moves in and out of my heart and my head, pushing my mind to tell me things that aren't true. Playing pictures in my head of what things look like back there.

He's going to die alone on a gurney in the emergency room.

He's going to die, and he'll never know how much I love him.

I look over at Daryl and Laurel. They've been here before. Though it was in a field and their son was already gone.

Now, they have two sons in the emergency room, fighting for their lives.

It comes to my mind that a mother's love never fades. No matter how old a child gets, what choices the child makes, whether you've raised the child or not, whether you're biologically related to the child or not, a mother's love is one of the purest phenomena in the world.

I think back to my mothers, the one who raised me and the one who gave me life.

My biological mother loved me like I love Austin. She did the best she could with the skills that she had.

The mother who raised me put the life back into me. She took the fear away that I'd had as a child—the fear of abandonment, of loss—and showed me love. And by God's grace, she gave me a brother that we got to love until he died.

But isn't that the price we pay for love when someone passes away? Grief and heartache?

It seems like hours have passed before two men in white coats come out to the waiting room, my heart dying inside the seconds it takes the men to reach us.

"Atwoods?" one man says.

The Atwood men stand. Exchange handshakes with the men in coats.

"I'm Dr. Levitt, and this is Dr. Sullivan. Please, come with us."

I grab Anna's hand and Laurel's hand as we follow Dr. Levitt and Dr. Sullivan down the sterile, stark white hallway, behind a locked door, and into a conference room.

"Please, have a seat," Dr. Sullivan says.

We sit in big, luxury leather chairs, ones I assume where teams of doctors design treatment plans and create big ideas.

"First of all, both men will be fine."

Laurel bursts into tears, and Daryl puts his arms around her.

I choke back a sob and keep it there alongside the lump of gratitude that clings to my insides.

"We were able to finally stop the bleeding for Casey, and while the horn did not hit any internal organs, he did lose a lot of blood. We're hoping that the blood loss to the brain did not cause brain damage. Now that he's stable, we will get him in for a CT scan as soon as possible. He has three broken ribs and a broken arm. As for Cash, he, too, lost a lot of blood but not nearly as much as his brother. And the horn did hit the spleen, and the damage was too severe to save it, so we had to remove it."

"Transplant?" Calder asks.

"No. Spleens can be removed, and people live long, happy lives," Dr. Levitt says. "Additionally, he took a hit to the head, which caused a mild contusion on his brain. We do feel the contusion needs surgery, and we will closely monitor him for the next few days, just to be sure."

"When can we see them?" I ask, surprised by my own words.

"Soon," Dr. Sullivan says.

Dr. Levitt asks, "Do you have any questions?"

"What is the recovery time for their injuries?" Colt asks.

Dr. Levitt and Dr. Sullivan exchange glances.

"We highly encourage these young men to find a different line of work. While these injuries are severe, they aren't life-threatening anymore, and it is only a matter of time before this happens again. I would add, however, that they should probably both be well and healed within six months," Dr. Levitt says.

Colt and Calder exchange glances, knowing they'll have a battle on their hands.

The doctors stand, as do Colt, Calder, and Daryl.

"Thank you, Dr. Sullivan and Dr. Levitt, for saving our boys," Daryl says.

They exchange handshakes.

Dr. Levitt looks at his watch. "In a few hours, you can come back and see both of them. In the meantime, please, go get something to eat."

"Is there a Tess Morgan?" a woman wearing scrubs asks.

I'm sitting in the waiting room, staring at the white wall ahead of me, lost in thought.

The mud is still heavy in my bones.

"That's me."

"Casey is asking for you."

I look back to Laurel.

"Go, honey," she whispers and kisses me on the cheek. "You two need each other right now."

I stare back at Laurel as tears come to my eyes. "Are you sure?"

"There are a lot of things I'm unsure of in life these days, Tess, but this isn't one of them." Laurel pats me on the back as I stand.

Anna grabs my hand and kisses it.

Nodding, I follow the woman in scrubs behind the locked door and down a long hallway.

She turns left into a room. My heart begins to pound, and the mud spreads once again, making it hard for me to breathe. I stop just before the room. Look up to the ceiling and hold back the tears.

They're tears of gratitude, but I'm not sure he'll understand that when I walk in there.

I try my best to disguise them and walk around the corner to see the man I love.

Machines beep.

"Hey," he says softly and reaches for me.

I walk to him faster than I've ever walked to anyone, taking his hand in mine, kissing his palm. But the tears fall.

"Hey." He reaches up and lightly pushes the fallen strands of hair from my face, but it's no use; they still continue to fall around my face. "I'm okay. See?" He's weak.

I study his face. A stitched-up laceration across his forehead has created two black eyes. His face is somewhat swollen.

Tears keep falling. "I'm so sorry, Casey. I'm so sorry for being so childish with you and for taking us—you—for granted." My words are rushed and messy and full of worry.

Still unsure of where to sit or move or adjust, I stay still, knowing underneath the hospital gown is where he was ripped open from one side to the other.

As he carefully pulls me, I see a single tear streaming from his eye.

"I thought—" He tries to clear the hoarseness from his tone, winces, stops for a moment, and allows the pain to pass. "I thought I was going to lose you forever. I thought I'd never be able to tell you exactly how I feel about you. How much time I've spent loving you." He's quiet for a moment. "Can ... can I tell you a weird-ass story?" he asks.

"Of course."

And Casey begins to tell me the story what our lives would have looked like had we not given Austin to a mom and dad far more capable of raising a child than we were at that age.

He tells me about ambulance rides and trips to Dillon Creek. Seeing me cry on the living room floor of Colt and Anna's after he got hurt. Seeing us in the barn after we made love. How he told me we'd be better just doing our thing than boyfriend and girlfriend—words that nearly ripped out my heart.

"Today, I know we made the right decision for Austin."

I think about my adoption and Austin's adoption and how things work out the way they're supposed to—even if they're painful. And how life can be absolutely beautiful and heartbreaking, all at the same time.

"Yeah, me too." And for the first time in my life, I believe it.

"I'm sorry. I'm sorry I went and saw him without—"

"No, no, no. I'm sorry. You had to do what you had to do for you. I wasn't ready. I put the blame on you." I turn my head to look at him. "Casey Atwood, I hope you can forgive me one day."

"Baby," he says, his voice hoarse, "forgiveness isn't needed in this situation. However, I would love to live the rest of my days with you, if you'll have me?"

Quiet nerves grow in my stomach.

I hear the words of Dr. Levitt and Dr. Sullivan. *"We highly encourage these young men to find a different line of work. While these injuries are severe, they aren't life-threatening anymore, and it is only a matter of time before this happens again."*

But I realize now that I will go through fire and pain and fear and nerves—life—to be with Casey if it means he gets to do what he loves. So, the small ball of nerves that moves and expands in my stomach sits quietly and waits for the next ride.

"I was hoping you'd ask." I put my mouth to his and kiss him in the softest way possible.

He groans in my mouth. "Oh, Ms. Morgan, the things you do to me."

I pull away, not wanting to go any further on this hospital bed, and giggle.

"When I leave this place," he whispers in my ear, "you'd better believe that we aren't leaving the house for at least a week because I'm going to do things to your body that would make Hugh Hefner blink twice from the grave."

I hold my breath, and an ache starts between my legs. "Don't make promises you can't keep," I whisper.

"I'm not in the business of unkept promises."

Smiling against his chest, I look up at him, but he's fallen fast asleep.

45

Casey

It's been four weeks, and I'm getting around good.

I always wondered why Colt bought that damn private plane, but I was grateful. Beats a fourteen-hour car ride or flying commercial any day.

I kept my promise to Tess and made love to her over and over and over. In the living room of her place. In the shower. In her bed, we made love slowly. Against the bedroom door. Out in the barn at my parents' place.

She comes out in just a towel and kisses me before she takes her coffee from the counter.

"I want to show you something today."

She leans against the counter, taking a sip of coffee. "Where?"

"Jagger Hill." I walk to her and bend down to kiss her neck low and slow.

She softly whimpers in my ear as I remove her towel to expose the beautiful body God gave her.

I undo my belt buckle, my jeans, and marvel at her naked body standing in front of me.

She runs her hands alongside the bandages that are still there to keep the entrance wound and the exit wound from infection. Tess pushes herself up onto the counter, her ass on the edge so that I can get between her legs. I take her mouth hard as she puts her hand around my length.

"Are you always this ready?"

"Only for you," she whispers.

With that, I slip inside her and give us both what we need. This time, it's quick and it's hard and it's so good. We climax together.

Breathlessly, we both come up for air.

"You'd better get some clothes on, Tess Morgan, or we will spend the whole damn day in this kitchen." I shake my head and kiss her mouth one last time before I smack her naked behind as she struts off to the bedroom.

"Hey, did you call Mary Jo?" I ask, rinsing out our coffee mugs.

"I did," she calls from the bedroom. "Told her we aren't selling. That we're keeping it for us." Tess walks back out to the kitchen in a T-shirt and jeans that fit her body so perfectly. "You know what she said?"

"What'd she say?" I ask.

"She said that she couldn't tell me how excited she was to hear that. It was almost like she was relieved."

Tess's cheeks are still pink.

The afterglow, I think to myself as I cup her cheek in my hand. "Did you talk to Jacob?"

"I did. He and Martin will come out to Dillon Creek when he gets his leave in June. I'm not sure where we'll put them." Tess looks around at her small house.

I slide my arm around her waist. "Come on. I've got something to show you."

"Why are you being so sneaky, Mr. Atwood?"

"Sneaky? Me? Never. Come on."

We head up the hill in my truck.

She shoots a look back at me. "I haven't been up here since we were kids."

"They kept the place up. Did a remodel that will blow your mind," I say casually as we exit the truck.

Up on top of Jagger Hill, you can see the entire Eel River Valley from Dillon Creek to Fortuna, to Belle's Hollow, to Rio Dell. You can see the Dillon Creek town steeple from First Christian Church.

Tess has loved this place since we were kids. From the property that it sits on to the plain at the top of the hill, to the view, to the house. She first fell in love with this place when Betsy Jagger invited her and her mom for some tea business. Then, Tess house-sat for the Jaggers as she got older. And then the Jaggers got older and older and eventually died in Southern California near their grown children.

The front of the house has the views while the back of the house opens up to twenty acres of land, complete with a barn, a riding arena, and redwood trees—Tess's favorite.

"This view is just incredible, and it hasn't changed over the years." She carefully takes me around the middle and follows me toward the house.

"I hope you have a key, Casey, because breaking and entering is not on my list of to-dos today." She laughs.

"Turns out"—I pull the keys from my pocket—"I do have a set of keys."

"Who gave you those?"

I unlock the front door. The house has a wide open floor plan with ceiling-to-floor windows on the back of the house as well as the front of the house.

"It's empty." Tess looks around, takes in the scent, and closes her eyes. "I can hear Betsy Jagger's voice in my head right now. 'Tess Morgan, life ain't gonna be beautiful unless you make it that way.' "

The Jaggers moved to Dillon Creek by way of Texas in their mid-thirties. The Jagger house was a vacation home until Gary Jagger retired from the oil company and made Dillon Creek their permanent residence until they got too old.

"She really liked you."

"She liked me because I listened to what she had to say."

"Come on." I take her hand and lead her to the living room—or the great room, whatever they call it.

On the mantel sits a white box.

My stomach begins to tie into knots, and my hands begin to sweat. Tess does a full turn and glances to the left—the wall of windows that overlook Eel River Valley and our future together—and ahead of us to the rock fireplace that trails up to the vaulted ceilings.

"God, I love this house." She turns to the view, and behind her, I grab the white box from the mantel.

Now. Do it now.

"Tess Elizabeth Morgan." I get down on one knee.

She turns and covers her mouth, looking down at me, unable to speak.

"I love you for all the reasons you think you're imperfect. From the day we met as kids, I knew you were the one and that all we needed was time. Who knew that our fate would take as many twists and turns as it has, and yet here we are, standing together where it all started. I'd be the happiest man in the world if you'd be my wife."

Tess's eyes fill with tears. "Yes," she whispers. "*Yes!*"

I slide the ring on her finger, and she doesn't take a second glance. She just throws her arms around me and kisses me in the most meaningful way, making my knees weak and my heart softer.

"How'd … how'd you get the ring back?"

"I have my ways. Besides, you don't hide things very well."

She pulls away too soon. "What about my parents?"

"Tess, I wouldn't have asked you to marry me if I hadn't asked for your dad's permission first."

Tess lets out a slow sigh. "He agreed?"

"Of course he agreed."

I kiss her again and again and again.

"We should go. I don't want to get in trouble for being in a house that doesn't belong to us, Case."

"Why would we get in trouble for being in a home we own?"

That's when her face turns to disbelief.

Her eyes wide, she says, "Wh-what?"

"That is, if you want it." I shrug.

"Ours? This ... this is our house?"

"Yeah."

Tess covers her mouth with her shaking hand and tries to put together words. "I swear to God, Casey, I have not cried this damn much in my whole life." She spins around in the living room, taking in every angle, every aspect, every piece of wood. She faces me again. "I can't believe this is ours, that you're mine, and this is us."

"But I was hoping someone could decorate the place. Do you know anyone?" I walk toward her and take her hands in mine. "I was thinking we could get married in the back."

She pulls me to her and begins to laugh and cry and laugh again. "Yeah, that sounds perfect, Case. That sounds perfect. But the only thing I want in this whole world is you."

"I'm here, baby, forever."

46

The Ladybugs

"Erla Brockmeyer was called home to be with the Lord in her sleep. Some say she died from a broken heart, and others say she died from Alzheimer's, but truth be told, she was just tired, and she missed her husband dearly. But it all doesn't matter because she's at peace now," Pastor Mike starts.

Scarlet wipes fallen tears from her eyes, the ones that not just burn her eyes, but also burn all the way down to her soul. Her regrets are many. Too many to count. She planned to come home for Christmas, but something always seemed to come up.

Mabe squeezes Scarlet's hand, as does Clyda on the other side of her.

Scarlet's mother didn't make it home for her own mother's funeral, which is no surprise. She has a way of cutting others out of her life as easy as flipping burgers.

But it's really nice to be surrounded by Scarlet's grandma's friends, The Ladybugs.

As Pastor Mike goes on, Scarlet thinks about her own life as a businesswoman. She, too, is a bit cutthroat but never with family. Getting married and divorced from a man she settled for was never on her list of things to do in her life, because if she is being honest with herself, her heart has never fully recovered from Cash Atwood.

Not since that summer when they were seventeen.

Not since he broke her heart.

But sometimes, stones are better left unturned. Some stones are better left where they lie. And some stones are better left painted a different color than their natural shade.

Now, Scarlet's job is in Dillon Creek, to clean out her grandmother's home, sell it, and move on.

A new woman, Patty—as Mabe introduced her—sits next to Mabe and cries.

"She's going through a lot right now," Mabe whispers.

Scarlet nods.

The good pastor goes on about righteous love and forgiveness and that Erla expressed both. He talks about being a champion for God's grace.

Patty wails.

Mabe stands and takes Patty outside.

Scarlet wonders if Patty is different in the head or if she's on the brink of an emotional breakdown, and she passes no judgment, as Scarlet herself has been there a time or two. Her divorce hit her harder than she would like to admit.

Maybe it was me, she thinks. Maybe she was too cold sometimes. She knew she wasn't completely in love with her ex-husband. Maybe her heart never grew past the Atwood brother who was destined to do big things in the rodeo arena.

Here Scarlet is, sitting at her grandmother's funeral, thinking about herself.

Clyda squeezes her hand at Pastor Mike's words, which she did not hear.

Perhaps she ought to do more listening and less thinking of herself. Less thinking in general.

She's also angry with her mother for not coming to her own mother's burial. Putting the burden on Scarlet to plan everything. Her mother can be quite self-centered too.

Grief can be sneaky. Sometimes, it lives quietly in others, dormant, not demonstrating its true colors until one day, all the regret, all the missed opportunities of time well spent seeps into the hearts of loved ones, and the grief finally begins.

She thinks about the last time she heard her grandma's voice. The call she forwarded to voice mail because she just didn't want to talk, too busy sulking in her own worries, her own self-pity, her Cadillac problems. If she could only go back and rewind to that moment, answer the call, she could have spoken to her grandma one last time.

Scarlet tries to catch the tears that fall, one by one, but it's no use, so she allows them to fall and allows herself to feel the weight of them. Her grandmother was her soft place to land. She came to Dillon Creek when things got to be too much in the city. A quiet place to get well, get close to her roots again, and find peace. But one day, Dillon Creek stopped being that place for reasons she's not ready to discuss. That old prayer that goes, "Accept the things I cannot change," well, Scarlet can't quite accept those things.

Scarlet built her life based on goals, success, and never once took time to look back and see where the inside job—the one that she'd constructed her heart around—faltered. She always knew that her heart would catch up with her one day; she just didn't know it would be at her grandmother's funeral at First Christian Church. Her tears fall quietly, and her eyes grow blurry.

The two constants in her life—her grandpa Don and grandma Erla—are now gone, and Scarlet is left to pick up the pieces and find a new road. Not knowing where this new road will take her scares the hell out of her.

47

Tess
Six Months Later

Martin and I are still at the table with the meal we just finished. Casey has taken Jacob out to the barn to look at his hunting equipment.

My parents have left after a hug and good-bye for Martin and Jacob. My parents have turned a corner with their grief, with me.

The Atwoods have gone, too, and the exchange between the two families went better than expected.

We had no idea how a big family dinner would go in our new home, but it's like Ike's letter said—*Sometimes, you've got to find the healing in order to mend the bridges.*

Martin's hands are soft, his skin thin, and in some places, there are little purple bruises. Between his fingers is his napkin, twisted and round. Since Esther died, he doesn't wear the same smile I remember. His face is not as full, his heart probably not the same.

"I am so proud of the woman you have become, Tess. I know your life with your biological mother was hard. As your grandfather, I tried and pushed Elizabeth. Then, one day, I pushed too far, and she took you away for several weeks. Your grandmother and I were devastated. We—" His voice becomes broken. "We were not sure what to do, but we did know you would be better off far away from Alaska. Hidden somewhere where he could not find you."

"He?" I ask. "My biological father?"

Martin nods. "He died in prison. Serving a life sentence for a double homicide for killing his wife and his teenage daughter in 2009."

There are no words to fill this moment.

"In our culture, it is the raven that we hold in high esteem. It is the raven that has taught our people many life lessons in forgiveness and love and respect and courage and bravery. Every time he came around you and your mother, the raven would put a dead mouse on our porch to signify his company with Elizabeth and you. That was when we knew he was back. We would start to notice the raven weeks before. He would fly overhead, make his calls, be loud or sometimes quiet." He smiles only a little. "Esther and I decided enough was enough, and that day, when we went to get you for good, we opened our front door, and a pile of dead mice was lying on our porch. We knew something was awfully wrong. We went to Elizabeth's to find her on the couch with the devil stuck in her arm, and you—" He covers his eyes with his hands so that I can't see his tears.

This is a memory I don't have. But sometimes, the memory can play tricks on us, allow us to see only what we want to see to preserve ourselves, our hearts.

"It's all right, Grandfather. I'm okay now. Because of you and Grandmother, I'm okay."

He sucks in a gulp of air.

It's the first time I've called Martin and Esther grandfather and grandmother.

"You were so little, my sweet girl. So little. At four, no child should see that. I am sorry we did not come sooner. That we did not do what we knew to be right in our hearts sooner." Tears silently fall from his eyes.

I put my hand in his. His big, soft hands bury mine.

"You have faith in your children, that they will get right and take on their responsibilities as they should. We raised Elizabeth right, and it was her addiction that turned her into someone she was not. But I know she loved you with all her heart, and I also know that she knew she had to let you go to let you fly. After Elizabeth died trying to deliver Jacob out on the streets and you were safely with the Morgans, your grandmother and I felt relief. One day shortly after Jacob was born, we walked out to our old barn to do some cleanup, and when we opened the door, thousands of butterflies flew out in a swarm. We stood there and cried. In our culture, a butterfly symbolizes transformation." He nods quietly to himself, perhaps remembering that moment. "So, if you see butterflies, know it is your other mother, making sure you are all right."

Tears make their way to the edge of my bottom lids.

"But you see," Martin continues, "nature has a way of taking care of its people because the man who helped create you died in prison. It is an unwritten law in prison—among the inmates, I suppose—that if a child is harmed on the outside by the hands of an inmate, he will not survive prison. And so it was."

Before anyone can interrupt this moment, I lean over and embrace my grandfather. "Thank you for putting me and Jacob first. Thank you for giving up time with me for all these years to do what was best for me."

The door swings open, and Austin comes running at me.

"Tess, look what Casey gave me!" Austin falls into my arms, and in his hands is Casey's 2020 PBR World Finals Champion belt buckle. But all I can think about is this sweet, little boy who smells of the outside and hay barns and sweat, in my arms after all these years.

And absolutely nothing could be more right in the world at this moment.

"Children are full of forgiveness, are they not?" my grandfather whispers.

Danielle and Trent—Austin's mom and dad—follow in behind him. I nod in gratitude for them allowing me time with their son.

They nod back, and Danielle's head falls against Trent's chest. They're incredible parents.

Casey and Jacob follow inside.

"Casey!" Austin squeals. "Can you teach me how to ride a bull?"

Danielle's mouth drops open. Trent laughs.

Casey leans on the kitchen counter and smiles. "Baby steps, kid. Baby steps."

Danielle is relieved.

And I tighten my arms around Austin, knowing he's got the heart and the toughness to ride like Casey, but I hope, for Danielle's and his future wife's sakes, that he finds a different line of work.

Trent turns to Casey. "How's retirement treating you? Do you miss it?"

"Man, I can tell you everything I don't miss. The travel, time away from family and friends. The beating my body took every weekend." He laughs.

Danielle turns to me. "I absolutely love your decorating style, Tess. Your taste is just incredible."

"Thank you. I really enjoy it."

"Have you thought about being an interior designer?"

"Well, actually …" I hand her my new business card that reads *Tess Morgan, Interior Designer*.

"Oh, my friends are going to die over this. Would you consider coming out for a visit to Idaho?"

I smile not only with my mouth, but also with my heart. "In a heartbeat." Because that means Casey and I will get more time with Austin.

I reached out to the adoption agency and asked if they could forward our contact information to Austin's parents, and we were prepared if they didn't want anything to do with us. It was the call I received about two months ago that still sits with my heart on a daily basis.

"We've always been very honest with Austin about where he came from. He knows he has another mom and dad," she said. "We have full faith that God put Austin in our lives at the time we needed him most," she went on.

After we got off the phone, I wept for all the right reasons. All the good ones.

"Come on. Let's go outside and play, Tess." Austin takes my hand.

With that, after Jacob and I help Grandfather up, Jacob kisses my cheek. "I'm so glad I gained a sister."

I lost Tripp, but I gained Jacob, and for that, I'm extremely grateful. Everything happens in its own timing as long as you trust in a power greater than yourself.

As we watch Austin run out into the open field, a big yellow butterfly flutters next to him while an eagle sits on its perch, and we all stand and watch him run.

No matter what, I know Austin will be watched over as he grows into the man he's supposed to be.

Casey takes me by the hand, kisses it, and whispers, "Have you told Austin he's going to be a big brother yet?"

Of course it should be a wedding and then a child, but in true Casey and Tess fashion, we've never done anything by the book, and that's the way I like it.

Ike's letter that drew Casey and me to Ketchikan comes to mind.

I was raised in a community where forgiveness is the cornerstone to happiness.

Sometimes, you've got to find the healing in order to mend the bridges.

I think Ike knew all along what he was doing, and he was absolutely right.

Epilogue

Up on top of Dillon Creek Cemetery, Erla joins her husband, Don, as she looks down to Mabe.

"She'll be all right, Erla," Don says, putting a hand on his wife's shoulder.

"How do you know, Don?"

"Because I watched you. Besides, she'll be here soon enough," Don says as John and Francine join them.

"So, how does this whole heaven thing work?" Erla asks, squeezing her husband's hand.

Don looks at Conroy. "A day at a time, Erla. A day at a time."

Tripp Morgan, Borges Atwood, and Joe Crane come forward and stand with Conroy, Erla, Don, John, and Francine. They stare down at their quiet little town and wait for the next person to arrive.

The End

Acknowledgments

First and foremost, a huge thank you to my editor, Jovana Shirley, who always goes above and beyond for my books and can shine and polish my words like no other. What started as a professional relationship has turned into a friendship, and I'm extremely grateful for you.

Julie Deaton, my proofreader, a huge thank you for her eagle eyes and attention to detail. You are a treasure. It should also be noted that I only send you voice messages so that I can get yours in return. Your Southern accent gets me every time.

Ashley Bolton at Ashley Bolton Photography, for the incredible book-cover photography and your ease and patience behind the camera. You, my friend, have a very special talent.

Hang Le, my cover designer, thank you for taking my thoughts and input and creating the masterpieces you have with the entire Dillon Creek series. It is an absolute joy to work with you.

Merritt Brodt, the owner of At the Bluff (a wedding venue/local ranch), thank you for allowing Ashley and me onto your beautiful property to capture photos of the covers for the Dillon Creek series.

Jessica Estep and Kelly Emery at InkSlinger PR, thank you for all of your help with all things related to book publicity. You both are incredible to work with.

Alex and Kelley Renner, the cover models, thank you for capturing the essence of Casey and Tess. From the first time I saw the two of you together on film, I knew you both were a perfect fit.

Thank you to former bull riders Brian Hunter and Robert Frawley for answering my questions about bull riding.

Chad Denton, former/retired professional bull rider for the PBR, thank you for all your time with all of my incessant questions and my badgering of the smallest details again and again. To my best friend, Jennifer Renner, for putting me in touch with the Dentons.

Brandon, Teyler, and Kate, you are my world, my soft place to land. Thank you for your patience and your grace with each book that I write.

And last but certainly not least, thank you to God. Without you, I'm nothing. Thank you for this life, for filling me with stories and the ability to tell them.

A Note to the Reader

THANK YOU FOR READING *SAVING TESS*.

If you enjoyed the book, please consider leaving an honest review on the website you purchased the book from. By leaving a review, it makes the book more visible to more readers. The more reviews, the better promotional opportunities for the author.

Get the latest information on book releases, sales, and more.

Sign up for J. Lynn Bailey's newsletter at http://bit.ly/2VVmqna to get sneak peeks, early excerpts, and free books.

Have you joined my reading group The Bailey Bunch? Join below for behind-the-scenes book information, giveaways, and top-secret book information. Learn about the inner workings of my writing process, and my crazy ideas.

The Bailey Bunch: http://bit.ly/2EscfjT

CONNECT WITH J. LYNN ONLINE:

www.facebook.com/AuthorJLynnBailey

www.instagram.com/jlynnbaileybooks/

https://twitter.com/authorJLynn

www.jlynnbaileybooks.com

About the Author

J. Lynn Bailey is an award-winning author who has loved to write since she learned to read around the second grade. She earned a bachelor's degree and master's degree from Humboldt State University.

When she isn't running her children to their next sporting event, watching *North Woods Law*, or on the hunt for her next Laffy Taffy joke, you can probably find her holed up in her writing room, feverishly working on her next book. She lives in Northern California with her family.

OTHER BOOKS WRITTEN BY J. LYNN BAILEY

THE GRANITE HARBOR SERIES

Peony Red
Violet Ugly
Magnolia Road
Lilies on Main

THE DILLON CREEK SERIES

Taking Anna
Little White Christmas
Saving Tess

STAND-ALONES

Standing Sideways
The Light We See
Black Five

www.ingramcontent.com/pod-product-compliance
Lightning Source LLC
Chambersburg PA
CBHW051531100726
47898CB00005B/1660